SWEET S

"Come, Silver Dove. Relax before the warmth of the fire and I will brush your hair."

She could only comply, and within seconds her long hair was covering his lap, her back lightly brushing against his chest as her slender thighs were surrounded by his powerful ones. Her eyes closed as she felt his fingers roaming through her hair.

"Did you wish to go to this place called Oregon, Silver Dove?"

"It doesn't matter now."

"What does matter now?"

For a single moment, she was almost tempted to blurt out, *You are the only thing that matters to me, Wind Dancer,* but she caught herself in time. Such a confession would surely give this man too much power over her. Instead she responded, "I am not sure."

Turning her body on his lap, he forced her face to turn to him. "Wakan Tanka whispered to me of you long ago. This night He joined our paths through this life and all eternity." Looking deeply into the turquoise eyes rimmed with gold, he whispered, "You are the beating of my heart, the reason for my walk through this life."

Danielle felt her inner being melting from the heartfelt tenderness of his words. "Wind Dancer . . . I . . ."

"*Shh,* my heart." His finger lightly traced the outline of her lower lip. "What is between us is something deeper than words can say." Slowly, his head lowered and followed the trail of his finger. He drew her lips apart, savoring the honeyed taste of sweet ambrosia. Within seconds, the gentle touch of his lips turned to seeking hunger, and Danielle pressed herself closer to him. She was powerless to resist . . .

SAVAGE HEAVEN

KATHLEEN DRYMON

ZEBRA BOOKS
KENSINGTON PUBLISHING CORP.

ZEBRA BOOKS are published by

Kensington Publishing Corp.
850 Third Avenue
New York, NY 10022

First Printing: February, 1995

Printed in the United States of America

To Charlie and Cathy Powers:
Throughout the years, you have always been there. Your friendship means more than you will ever know.

Prologue

Hannibal, Missouri
Fall, 1839

A light rain drizzled steadily over the mourners who stood on the little hill overlooking the Hansen farmhouse. Solemnly they watched as twin caskets were lowered into the earth. Eight-year-old Charity Danielle Hansen stood next to her aunt and uncle, whom she had met only the day before, and wondered if her tears would ever stop flowing. As it had so often this day, her small hand reached up and wiped moisture from her turquoise eyes, the irises surrounded with delicate flecks of gold. Feeling numb inside and out, she no longer cared if her pale curls were sheltered from the elements by her aunt Beth's umbrella. Her tears mingled with the raindrops, and as the first shovel of dirt was thrown atop her mother's casket, she knew that life as she had known it was over.

If she strained hard she thought she could still hear her mother's lilting voice singing and laughing as she went about her work in the front room of their small farmhouse, which her father had built five years earlier. Overnight, it seemed, both her father and mother had succumbed to cholera, and Danielle had been left alone. Yesterday her father's brother, Tad Hansen, and his wife, Beth, had arrived in Hannibal to take charge of their niece and to take up residence at the farm.

As the small funeral procession slowly made its way back to the farmhouse, Danielle silently trudged along behind her aunt and uncle. Her young heart ached with grief, and she silently wondered if she would ever know happiness again.

Drawing back a ragged sniffle, her shimmering eyes looked up to the heavens, and the pelting rain washed away her tears. *Why, God? Why have You taken away the only people who ever loved me?* her tiny heart silently cried. *Who will ever love me again?*

The Great Plains

The season of the falling leaves, 1839

At the age of fourteen summers, an Oglala Sioux by the name of Two Hawks is instructed by the shaman of his village, Medicine Wolf, that it is time for him to seek out his vision. The youth's father is chief of the Oglala, as his father was before him. It is with great ceremony that the old medicine man prepares the sweat lodge for Two Hawks. Medicine Wolf has gone into the sacred hills and gathered the rocks for the ceremony; those with green moss etched across the surface of the lime, holding secret spirit writing. As the young brave chosen by Medicine Wolf brings the heated rocks, one at a time into the lodge, the shaman gently touches each stone with his pipe bowl, which during the ceremony is resting in the fork of a deer antler. Before the rocks are sprinkled with green cedar and a small amount of cool water, Medicine Wolf reads the secret writing, and in turn, he instructs Two Hawks on the preparations to be made for his vision quest.

For four days, the youth sits in the spot designated by Medicine Wolf. The first day, he builds a small fire made out of cedar in a shallow pit. The cedar smoke becomes the breath of all green, living things to the boy. Fanning the swirling smoke with the sacred eagle feather his father gave him before he set out on his journey to the sacred hills, the youth entreats Wakán Tanka to bless him with a vision. The days and nights grow long as the youth sits there upon Mother Earth before his fire of cedar, without food or drink.

On the fourth afternoon, feeling physically weak, but sensing that his soul is in that place where it is free to commune with the spirits living far beyond the star path, Two Hawks is lifted, his body levitated from Mother Earth. For a moment, he feels the familiarity of the hard earth being taken away. His heart fills with fear, but soon the fear is replaced by calm as he views the encircling presence of the sacred *wakinyan* of his people.

He is carried beyond the clouds, to a spot that shelters the sacred hills. In that moment he can see all things. His vision fills with the people of his father's tribe, and as each face comes before his inner sight, his heart swells with love. He is one with the people. He feels their plight, their joy and sadness, their hunger and fullness. As the ancient spirit songs, known only to those who have gone on to the spirit world, fill his ears, his feet begin to move to the tempo of a primeval dance. The motion of the beating wings of the sacred thunderbirds aids his dance steps, and enshrouds him with a sense of security and knowledge far beyond his young years.

As he dances upon the wind made from their wings, the sacred *wakinyan* speak to him of the days that will come, when he will need the wisdom of his forefathers. They assure him that, from this day forth, they will aid him with their strength and teach him, through their eyes, that which will make him a great leader of the people.

Time seems without meaning as he dances upon the wind; his soul rejoicing at the oneness he feels with all things upon Mother Earth. It is shortly before Wi, the sun, disappears from the sky when he is returned to his fire of cedar. Feeling an exhilarating exhaustion, he lies near his fire with his eyes tightly shut, wanting to hold on to the incredible vision as long as possible.

When at last the youth opens his eyes, the sight that meets his gaze causes him to draw in a gulping breath of air, his heart trembling as it skips several beats. Peering into the swirling smoke made from his fire, a flawless, shimmering, silver dove lightly flutters its wings. As the bird draws close for his inspection, he is regarded by the beautiful features of a girl-woman. For a breathless moment, turquoise eyes rimmed with glittering gold stare at him. From some place deep within the boy's mind, the dove speaks to him without the sound of words as a glistening tear escapes the beautiful eyes. *Who will ever love me again?*

The question goes straight to the heart of the youth. He would have called out to the beautiful girl-woman, but like the rest of his vision, she vanishes into the cloak of smoke, whence she came.

Chapter One

Independence, Missouri.
June 1849.

After two long months, the waiting was finally over! Fifty wagons and over two hundred men, plus their women and children, had assembled themselves in Independence, at the jumping-off place of the Oregon Trail. It was nearly ten in the morning when the first wagon pulled out of Independence, but this first day would be the last for such a late start. The wagon master, Jonathon Beckon, had warned each family that from here on out it would be an eighteen-hour day. The first wagon would start out tomorrow at four in the morning; stragglers would be left behind.

Danielle Hansen had pulled off her gingham sunbonnet an hour ago, and sitting atop the jockey box on the front of her uncle's covered wagon, she swatted at the pesky fly that appeared determined to plague her. The initial excitement—brought on by the signal from the wagon master and hearing her Uncle Tad calling loudly to his oxen and snapping a long, sharp, whip over their backs—had dulled considerably over the last few miles of swallowing dust and being jostled unbearably atop the wagon seat.

Beth Hansen, a slender woman with a ready smile and light auburn hair, noticed her niece's irritation. "Why don't you get down and walk for a while, Danielle?" If Beth had not had the first half-day's duty of driving the team of oxen, she too would be walking, with the hope of catching a cooling breeze. A walk on solid ground would be preferable to the constant rough motion of the wagon.

"Maybe I will, for just a little while, Aunt Beth." Danielle was grateful for her aunt's suggestion; she had not wanted to make it herself, knowing that Beth must also be feeling the heat and discomfort.

"Maybe Samuel will show up soon, and you can ride double for a while with him." Glimpsing her niece's sudden frown as she climbed down from the wagon seat, Beth added, "At least you can ride ahead of the wagon train, and get away from this infernal dust."

Grabbing hold of the bonnet lying on the seat, Danielle did not reply. At the moment, she thought, Samuel Taylor's presence might only irritate her further. She was not sure that she wouldn't prefer the relentless dust to having to sit close to Samuel upon horseback.

For a time, Danielle walked along with the wagon, keeping a steady pace with the grease bucket that was rocking back and forth on the hook secured to the undercarriage connecting rods of the vehicle. As she became lost in thought, her pace began to slow. It wasn't that she didn't have some feelings for Samuel, she told herself. It was just that she wasn't sure what those feelings were, and if they were strong enough for her to spend the rest of her life with him.

"Oh, if it were looks, Samuel was handsome enough. At least he was if she had to gauge a man's looks by the glances he received from other young women. In Independence, she had witnessed several casting sidelong glances in his direction. She knew him to be kindhearted, though at times he showed this in a rough sort of fashion; and there was no denying that he was a hard worker, just like his brothers and his father. But Danielle knew that appreciation for these virtues did not constitute love. More often than not, she regretted her hasty agreement, two months ago, to become his wife. She reflected over that evening when her good senses had been dulled by his wearing her down with constant proposals.

Uncle Tad and Aunt Beth had been pleased with the news. In all the excitement, no one seemed to notice that Danielle stood silently by while the young man supplied them with all the details for the upcoming event. He would continue on to Oregon with his parents who, like the Hansens, had been waiting in Independence for the wagon master to say when they had enough covered wagons to start the long journey. When they arrived in Oregon, he and Danielle would be married, and there in the fertile Willamette Valley, they would build their farmhouse and raise their children.

A farmer's wife! Danielle kicked at a small rock as her mood worsened. Why was it she couldn't be satisfied with her lot in life, as most young women were? Her aunt and uncle had appeared happy enough with their place in life over the years. Why was it that she always seemed to want more? Ten years ago, when her parents had died, a small portion of her heart had closed up and still remained empty. Aunt Beth and Uncle Tad had been good to her, she could not deny that, but the love that she had desired had not been given. Samuel Taylor was no different. He had not touched that emptiness in her heart. She wondered if she would ever know true love again—a love that was unquestionable, given freely without reserve.

At eighteen, Danielle had lived a rather boring life on the Hansen farm until the day they left Hannibal for Independence. Tad Hansen was not the farmer that her father had been. Often, over the past ten years, he had spoken about moving west, to lands undiscovered. When reports had captured his attention about the fertile land available in Oregon, Tad Hansen spoke to several of his neighbors about joining up with a wagon train in Independence. Samuel Taylor's family quickly got caught up in the dream of moving on to Oregon. For over two years, her aunt and uncle had saved every penny, and after selling her father's farm and much of the furnishings in the house, Tad had bought a covered wagon and enough supplies to see them to their journey's end, with a little left over to start anew at the end of the trail. Without children of their own, Beth and Tad had eagerly expressed their hope that the young couple would build their home near the one they intended to build. But even though her kin would be close by, Danielle's thoughts about the upcoming marriage did not lie easily upon her heart.

There was little, for now, that Danielle could do to change things. Perhaps, during the long months it would take to reach Oregon, she would learn to love Samuel. She had known other young women who had married without the benefit of love.

Penny Smith, a young woman on that very wagon train, had confessed to Danielle in Independence that she had married her husband, William, only because she was pregnant; she was not even sure if William was the baby's father!

"Danielle, can I walk with you?" A young girl no older then ten, with long, blond braids swinging freely over her shoulders, caught up with Danielle. In an easy manner, she grabbed Danielle's hand and began to swing it back and forth.

"Why, of course you can walk with me, Molly. I'm glad for the company." Danielle smiled down at the girl, hoping that she had not made a mistake, and this was Sally instead of Molly. The Taylors' twin girls looked so much alike, it was hard even for their father to tell them apart. The girl skipped along, immune to the dust that was being stirred up by the wagons and teams that stretched in an endless line in front of them.

"I know a secret, I know a secret," Molly Taylor chimed as she grinned at Danielle. "Do you want to know what my secret is, Danielle?"

Danielle's gold-rimmed eyes sparkled good-naturedly at the girl's childish excitement. Anything to halt the drawn-out boredom of this first day, she thought. "What is your secret, you little minx?" She grinned and took up the motion of swinging her hand. If nothing else came out of her loveless marriage, Danielle could content herself with thoughts of having children. Being an only child, she anxiously awaited the day when she would have her own children. Samuel's parents had such a large family—nine children in all—she was sure Samuel would want lots of little blond-haired babies.

"Sammy told Momma something this morning,

but she told me I couldn't breathe a word of it. You can't be telling on me if I let you know what he said." The little girl watched Danielle's features intently, waiting for her promise.

If it was something Samuel had told his mother, Danielle wasn't sure she wanted to hear it. Looking down at Molly, though, she didn't have the heart to dash her excitement. With a false show of interest, she eagerly nodded her head. "I won't say a word of it, Molly. I promise."

Eagerly copying a gossiping adult, Molly placed her hand up next to her mouth, as though making sure no one else would be able to hear her. "Sammy told Momma that you are the prettiest girl on the wagon train. Even prettier than Mary Lou Simmons and Viola Lambert!" Drawing a deep breath, she hurriedly went on, "Momma caught me listening and said that children shouldn't be . . . be . . ." Molly couldn't think of the big word her momma had used.

"Eavesdropping," Danielle supplied, not as enthused by the young girl's secret as Molly would have liked.

"That's the word Momma used," Molly cried. "You won't tell on me for telling Sammy's secret, will you? You promised you wouldn't. I wanted to be the one to tell you, before Sally did." A smug look came over the girl's face as her twin approached them and took hold of Danielle's other hand.

For the rest of the morning, Danielle was entertained by the lively company of Molly and Sally Taylor. It was not until long after midday that the wagon master called the wagon train to a halt for a few minutes' rest and Danielle made her way back to her uncle's wagon. There she found her aunt and uncle, like most on the wagon train, relishing every second of inactivity as they sipped tin cups of cool water and ate biscuits left over from breakfast.

Tad Hansen was usually a quiet man, but this day he could not contain his excitement. As Danielle sat down next to her aunt on a quilted blanket spread over the ground, he took in her reddened cheeks, and the flyaway traces of wheat-white hair that had escaped the confines of her sunbonnet. "Well, girl, we're on our way. Our first morning's already behind us. Though there would be endless more like this one, at least the first is past."

Danielle couldn't help smiling at her uncle's happiness to at last be on the trail and heading for Oregon. As her aunt pressed a tin cup of water into her hand, Danielle agreed, "I guess this is the most important day of our trip." It was too bad she couldn't muster up any kind of enthusiasm when she thought about the end of their long journey.

"Your Samuel and I were riding ahead with Mr. Beckon for the better part of the morning. He 'pears to know the trail well enough, and his two scouts are likely enough fellows."

Your Samuel, His words replayed themselves in her mind, and Danielle pressed the cup to her lips to hide her displeasure. She decided to ignore all references to Samuel and instead ask her own questions. "Did Mr. Beckon say anything about having had trouble in the past with Indians or bushwhackers?" She had heard stories, while waiting in Independence, of marauding Indians and renegade buffalo hunters who reportedly attempted to overpower stragglers on a wagon train. They were wont to steal the stragglers blind and murder those who tried to resist or defend themselves. They had been told that Jonathon Beckon had made this trip from Independence at least a half-dozen times, and Danielle was anxious to hear if he had ever had any trouble.

Tad Hansen saw the sparkle of excitement in his niece's azure eyes and worried about her strange lust for adventure. To him, a woman's place was in the home, but from his first meeting with his niece, he had realized that his brother had allowed her to run wild. At the age of eight, she had been able to shoot a rifle better than a lot of men he had known. She was better suited to helping break horses than cooking a meal. He knew that, at first glance, no one would see more than a lovely young woman. It was not until you got to know Danielle better that you learned of her headstrong ways. Well, once they reached Oregon and she married Samuel, that wilder side of her nature would calm down. Just wait until she had a baby or two chasing after her skirts. "Mr. Beckon assures me that a wagon train of this size has little to fear from either Indians or bushwhackers."

His words were like a small droplet of water attempting to extinguish her flare for adventure. Now, revived by her drink and the few moments of rest beneath the shade of the wagon, Danielle replied in a tone that was filled with anticipation, "Well, one never knows what heathens will get a notion to do!" She had no fear of harm coming to anyone in her family. The wagon train was well armed, and though Aunt Beth had refused to learn how to shoot a weapon, Danielle had grown up hunting in the woods behind the Hansen farmhouse, and with her perfect aim, she lacked little courage. Untying her bonnet, she brushed back wayward curls that had escaped the slender double braids encircling the crown of her head. "If you are going to drive the wagon now, Uncle Tad, will it be all right if I ride Old Major?" Though Danielle truly loved her kin, there were many times she had resented her uncle's ruling of her life, as when he had sold her horse before they set out for Independence. He claimed that the animal was too old to make the trip to Oregon, and that once they arrived in Willamette Valley, he would purchase her a new mount. It galled her that she had to beg his favor to ride a horse that had once belonged to her father.

"Old Major's been ridden pretty hard today, but I reckon you can ride him for a little while." Tad saw the instant flare of challenge that came to her eyes, and knew that if he refused her, there would be an argument.

Just then Samuel Taylor rode up to the Hansen wagon. With a polite nod cast in Tad and Beth's direction, he pushed the brim of his hat back on his forehead, and with a wide grin aimed at Danielle, he said, "I'd be right proud to ride along with you, Danielle." He had heard Tad give her permission to ride his big bay stallion, and he dared not miss out on the opportunity to be alone with her. It seemed they were rarely afforded even a few minutes to speak in private.

Danielle would have liked to be able to refuse him, and insist that, whatever direction he was riding, she was going in the opposite. As both her aunt and her uncle gazed expectantly upon her, she knew that such an outburst would only humiliate herself. All she could do was nod her head at the invitation. The young man with gold-streaked pale brown hair watched her rise from the quilt then hurriedly make her way to the back of the wagon, where Old Major was tied.

Danielle did find some measure of enjoyment while riding in Samuel's company. The pair slowly overtook the long line of wagons and rolling dust without a call being issued from Mr. Beckon or his foreman, the bowlegged Tom Carlton. Both men believed the couple safe enough as they glimpsed Samuel's rifle in the scabbard of his saddle. Being only a day's ride from Independence, no one was expecting trouble. The scouts were still out, but since they had reported no sign of Indians at all that morning, danger was not paramount in either man's thoughts.

Beth Hansen had made her niece three gowns to wear on the journey, all fashioned with split skirts to accommodate Danielle's love for riding. Now, with her long, shapely legs thrown over Old Major's saddle and her sunbonnet dangling by its ribbons down her back, she pushed the sturdy stallion to a pace Samuel had difficulty matching.

"Let's stop near the copse of trees on that hill, Danielle," he called out, hoping that she would comply. He had already discovered that Danielle Hansen had a mind of her own. It was a rare occurrence when she would easily bow to anyone's wishes if they did not suit her mood.

Danielle knew that Samuel was no great horseman; she had outraced him several times in the past. Farmers spent little time perfecting their horsemanship, and seeing that he was having a hard time staying up with her and Old Major, she nodded in his direction. Then a small grin split her face, and she hit the stallion's sides with booted heels, sending Old Major in lengthening strides toward the trees. She did not wish to hurt Samuel's feelings, but she had never been one to hold back on a race!

Dismounting and grinning widely as she leaned against the wide trunk of a tree, she watched Samuel pull his horse to a halt and dismount. "The next time we race, we should wager something on the outcome." Danielle had no idea what made her say such a thing. The sheer exhilaration of the ride, after her long morning of dust and heat, must have gone straight to her head.

Samuel's blue eyes ignited with warm lights at her playful words and disheveled appearance. He wished he had pushed harder to get her to wed him before they left Independence. The top button of her gown had come undone, and as full breasts strained against the material of her blouse with each deep breath, the temptation to reach out and caress that tiny portion of pale flesh was almost more than he could bear. "The next time we'll wager a kiss." He stepped closer until he was standing directly in front of her.

Danielle instantly felt her face beginning to flush. "I didn't mean . . ." More likely, she would have wagered upon the prospect of their not getting married. The winner could call off all past promises and obligations!

Before she could explain what she meant, Samuel reached out and pulled her up tightly against his chest. The contact of his body was not altogether unpleasant. Samuel was a powerfully built young man, and Danielle could feel the strength of muscle beneath the plaid shirt which was tucked into his breeches and rolled up at the sleeves. But as his head lowered and his mouth slanted over her own, her hands splayed against his chest and she attempted to push him away.

Samuel had made only a few attempts to kiss her in the past, and she had always reacted in the same fashion. She seemed to respond at first, but then with the contact of his mouth over hers, she always pushed him away. He thought it was her young woman's modesty. And with that thought, the fever in his blood rose to an even higher degree, and he became anxious to claim her as his own.

The first time Samuel has kissed Danielle, she was not so eager to push him away. She had never been kissed before, and she was curious about the whole affair. But as Samuel had pulled her against him and covered her lips with his own, the pleasure she had expected never came. Samuel was as inexperienced as she. Instead of allowing a sensual molding of their mouths, he had used forceful pressure on her. Her lips were pressed against her teeth in a very uncomfortable manner, which left her mouth sore later. Since that first night, she had been adamant in her refusal to share another kiss with him. She enjoyed the contact of hard, male flesh against her softer, womanly curves, but Samuel's other attentions had no appeal for her. "Please, Samuel," she now gasped aloud, and broke free of his grip. "I think we should head back to the wagon train before we are missed." She should never have raced him to the trees. She turned to make her way back to Old Major, but before she could reach her horse, she was halted by his strong grip on her arm.

The blue eyes looking down at her had turned hard; her maidenly shyness this afternoon left Samuel irritated. No one else was around, and what if anyone did see them kissing? After all, they were to wed in a few months. He pulled her back into his arms, and before his mouth lowered again, he said, "What harm is there, Danielle? You are to be my wife shortly."

A touch of panic seized Danielle's heart as she felt the hard strength in his arms. Samuel had never been this daring. Before his lips settled over her own, she turned her head, and with a yank, she broke free of his hold.

Samuel sensed she had been pushed to the limit. His hands fell as he watched her run back to her horse. "I reckon as how the kisses and what more goes on between a married couple can wait for the time being, Danielle. I'm content with my thoughts of what we will share when we reach Oregon."

Danielle shuddered at his words. Once she was Samuel Taylor's wife, there would be no drawing away from him. Such thoughts quickened her steps to her horse, and she did not wait for Samuel before she was turning Old major's head back toward the wagon train.

That evening, Danielle was quiet as the Hansen family sat around their small camp fire. Earlier, Samuel had stopped by, but finding Danielle even more untalkative than usual, he left early to take his position with the first watch.

As she sat on the quilt, resting her back against a wagon wheel and listening to the easy banter between her aunt and uncle, Danielle wondered if her married life with Samuel would be similar. There was a light, loving manner about her aunt and uncle as they joked, and spoke of the future in Oregon. It was plain that, even after twenty years of marriage, the couple still cared deeply for one another. Looking up at the star-brilliant night, Danielle asked herself if she could ever learn to love Samuel as her aunt loved her uncle. In that empty portion of her heart, a small voice replied that love came from the soul; it was not something that could be won by force.

"You're quiet tonight, girl. I hope this first day on the trail didn't wear you out. There are still several days before we reach Fort Kearney." Tad Hansen knew that at fifteen to twenty miles a day, their journey would seem like an endless trudge to a young woman.

"I'm fine, Uncle Tad, just a little restless, I guess. I think I'll take a short walk around camp before going to bed."

Shortly after the sun had set, Jonathon Beckon had signaled for the wagon train to form a square, in which all the animals were kept. The night watch had been set at intervals to ensure that they would not be taken unawares as the majority of the occupants of the wagons got some rest.

Walking around the encampment of wagons, Danielle spent a few minutes visiting with Penny Smith and her young husband, William. Their simple box wagon was fitted with wooden bows stretched in an arch overhead and covered with canvas. William certainly seemed extremely happy with his pregnant wife.

After Danielle left the Smiths' camp fire, Thelma Anderson called out to her, and Thelma's chubby-faced daughter, Bertie, waved enthusiastically from her mother's ample lap. Most of the people on the wagon train were friendly, having gotten to know each other in Independence.

By the time Danielle returned to her own family's wagon, Tad and Beth had already turned in for the night. It was a cool summer evening, and drawing her shawl a bit tighter around her shoulders, she sat near the dwindling firelight and thought gloomily of her first day on the trail. It was one day closer to the day when she would marry Samuel Taylor.

Chapter Two

Fort Kearney was the first glimpse of civilization the Beckon wagon train had in days. As the last wagon pulled through the wooden gates shortly before dusk, Jonathon Beckon announced that the wagon train would be spending the night behind the stout, safe walls of the fort.

With a feeling of ease, and the knowledge that they were safe, the settlers made a circle of wagons behind the fort's walls, and for the first time since they had left Independence, sleep was not the most monumental thing on everyone's mind. After dinner was cleared away, several men built up a large fire inside the circle of wagons, and old Sage Mansfield brought out his fiddle. As the lively adventurers and many of the soldiers stomped and clapped, Sage drew back the bow and plucked a lively tune over the strings.

Having left the Hansen wagon with her aunt and uncle for the evening's entertainment, Danielle visited with Penny Smith, who stood off to the side of the revelers. They watched as couples began to pair off and start dancing. A grin split Danielle's lips as she watched her uncle grab hold of his wife's hand and pull her along with him, his feet already keeping step to the music as he swung her in a circle and full skirts and petticoats flew out around her ankles.

"Your uncle seems to know how to keep a lady happy." Penny smiled as they watched the couple dancing. Neither young woman could avoid glimpsing the wide smile upon Beth Hansen's face, nor did they miss the possessive manner in which Tad's hands held her around the waist.

Before Danielle could reply, Penny nodded her head toward the onlookers on the other side of the brightly burning fire. "Why, there's that good-looking young man of yours, Danielle." Brown eyes sparkled as she took in Samuel Taylor's broad chest and tight-fitting breeches before turning her gaze back to the woman at her side. "I think he's looking for you. There, I told you. He's seen us now." Her smiled widened as Samuel made eye contact and started weaving his way around the crowd and the dancers.

Danielle had tried since that first day on the trail to make certain that she and Samuel were not given the opportunity to be alone. Most days, she rode in the wagon or walked, not attempting to ride her uncle's horse again since she was afraid that Samuel would insist on accompanying her. Looking at him now, boldly making his way to her side, she knew there would be no avoiding him this evening.

"Come on, Danielle, let's show these folks how to dance." Samuel's blue eyes glittered with interest as they swept over Danielle's fresh dress. Her pale locks, which were usually braided and wrapped atop her head, had been left unbound, the silken tresses hanging about her hips. A bright ribbon held the curls away from her face.

"I . . . I don't think so, Samuel. Not tonight. I have a slight headache," she was quick to respond, hoping he would not press her.

Penny was just as quick with her response as she stepped between Samuel and Danielle without a second thought. "I certainly would love to dance, Mr. Taylor. Of course, that is if'n you don't mind turning a married woman about on your arm? The music is wonderful, and I can assure you that my William wouldn't mind in the least."

There was no way Samuel could get out of sharing a dance with the vivacious Penny Smith. Before he could even answer, she was wrapping her hand in his. She fluttered her lashes in a most provocative fashion that was meant to take a man completely off guard. "Well, I guess if Danielle isn't up to it this evening, there isn't any harm." A flush crept up the young man's neck as he felt the slight movement of Penny's little finger caressing his palm. Without another word spoken, or another look cast in Danielle's direction, for fear she would be able to discern the lust that instantly came over him, Samuel led Penny toward the other dancers.

Penny was only three months pregnant, and as Samuel danced with her to the lively music of the fiddle, not the slightest hint of her condition was revealed. For a few minutes, Danielle watched them from the sidelines. Objectively, Danielle realized that there was no burning jealousy snaking its way through her heart at the sight of Penny Smith in her fiancé's arms. She felt only a slight hint of irritation over Penny's conduct toward other men when she had such a loving and devoted husband.

As the music played on, the couple appeared not to be tiring of each other's company. Danielle turned away and slowly walked back to the Hansen wagon.

Not lingering outside the wagon, Danielle stretched out on the small pallet which her aunt spread out for her inside the wagon each evening. She did not wish to be sitting alone outside if Samuel came looking for her. She had all but made up her mind to call off their wedding plans. She was not sure if she should tell Samuel and her aunt and uncle now, or wait until they reached Willamette Valley.

Early the next morning, the wagon train pulled out of Fort Kearney, rolling west along the Platte River. Their next destination was Fort Laramie. As soon as daybreak came, Danielle climbed down from the wagon and walked alongside it as Beth Hansen drove the team of oxen.

A couple of miles outside Fort Kearney, Penny made her way to Danielle's side. "Why did you leave the dancing so early last night, Danielle? When Samuel looked around and found you were gone, I thought I was going to have to hog-tie him to keep him at my side. He remained with me for the rest of the evening only because I pleaded with him for one more dance, and then another and another." Her tinkling laughter exploded with secret undercurrents that Danielle at that moment had no interest in exploring.

"I was tired last night, Penny. I returned to the wagon and went to sleep. I'm glad you and Samuel had a good time. I know he loves to dance, and it was kind of you to keep him company."

Penny Smith was a born flirt, not caring what man she flirted with, nor did it matter if his wife or his fiancée was nearby. She enjoyed glimpsing the interest in a man's eyes when another woman was present. Looking at Danielle, she did not see a stirring of anger or jealousy in the other woman's features, as she would have expected.

"Why, Lord almighty," Penny exclaimed. "After all of this boring walking and bouncing around on a wagon seat, the first bit of excitement we come across and you're tired?" At that moment, Abner Sweeny passed the two women as he rode toward the front of the wagon train. Not one to miss an occasion to flaunt her wares, Penny swayed her hips a bit more lushly, and her lips drew back in a large smile, which exposed dimples in her cheeks. "How you doing this morning, Mr. Sweeny?" she called in an overly friendly manner.

"Just fine, ladies," the man upon horseback replied as he touched the brim of his hat, his green eyes lingering for a few seconds longer than necessary upon Penny Smith.

"That's one fine-looking man," Penny sighed as he rode on without another word.

Danielle absently nodded her head. She had not really thought much about Abner Sweeny in the past. He had a plump little wife, who was always friendly, and three teenage girls.

"I bet old Abner knows how to keep Mrs. Sweeny happy during those long nights in this nowhere land!"

Penny's meaning was not lost on Danielle. Penny was wilder than any other young woman Danielle had ever met before, but there was an easy nature about her that appealed to Danielle.

"Is that why you were at the dancing last night without William, Penny? Doesn't he know how to keep you happy?" Since Penny had spoken very freely about her relationship with her husband, and even other men, Danielle had no doubt that her friend would not mind being questioned on this subject. Perhaps somehow Danielle might even be able to help her if she wanted to talk about it.

"The truth is, Danielle, William and I did have a fight last night before I left our wagon to join the dancing. William stayed behind and, more than likely, was pouting as usual. I've told you that William wasn't my first man, and I'm one for betting he wont' be my last!"

Danielle was taken aback by such a comment. If she had been the type to take on a bet, one thing would have been certain: she would never wager on Penny Smith's virtue!

Noticing how quickly Danielle turned her gaze away, as though wishing to change the subject, Penny laughed. "Well, you tell me, Danielle, what's a woman to do? Lately, William's been quick to finish his business in bed, if you know what I mean."

Danielle felt a blush scorching her cheeks. She could only imagine what Penny was implying, and scolded herself for ever thinking she could help this woman with her marital problems!

"He tells me that he's too tired to last long enough, to pleasure me like I really want. He claims it's the long days of driving the wagon, but that it will get better once we reach Oregon. So he thinks I should suffer through until then! Well, last night I had all I could take, and I downright told him so! Right before he fell back on the mattress and began snoring, I told him that if'n he couldn't take care of business at home, I would find someone else who would be right happy to tend to the matter for him!"

"You didn't say that to him?" With the question, a small part of Danielle's mind wondered if Samuel was the man she had chosen to tend to her needs.

A wide, mischievous grin appeared over her lightly freckled features. "Don't be such a prude, Danielle. You'll be finding out quick enough what I'm talking about, after you're married a little while. But then again, maybe you won't! Samuel seems to have a bit of stamina. I doubt he would leave a lady short! We must have danced to a half-dozen tunes last night before Samuel walked me back to my wagon."

Danielle felt uncomfortable talking about Samuel with the other young woman. It wasn't that she habored any romantic feelings about the man she was supposed to marry; it was the catty looks that Penny cast in her direction, as though trying to read more into her words than she intended.

"It's too bad I didn't catch sight of Samuel Taylor before you did, Danielle. I bet I could've given you a run for your money." Penny knew that, in looks, Danielle Hansen walked away with the prize, but Penny knew other ways to draw and keep a man's attention. Ways she was sure Danielle was too naive about. Given more time alone with Samuel, as she had been last night, she was sure she could have him panting a heated trail behind her skirts, as other men had done in the past.

"Well, I guess marriage puts the reins on such

things. Samuel and his family came from Hannibal with my aunt and uncle, so you wouldn't have had the opportunity to meet Samuel before I did." Perhaps if Penny had met Samuel first, she would not be in the situation she now found herself in, Danielle thought, as once again she wondered how she would be able to cancel her wedding plans.

"Why, you just never know, Danielle. A man, and a strong, handsome one such as your Samuel, will do most anything if'n he's not happy at home," Penny said, and shoved back a handful of shoulder-length brown hair to emphasize this statement. At the moment, Jeffery Johnston walked past, and the young woman stepped up her pace. With a wave thrown over her shoulder in Danielle's direction, she was soon deep in conversation as she flirted outrageously with the nineteen-year-old young man.

Danielle shook her head at the contradiction that Penny Smith portrayed. She claimed that a man would wander away from the marriage vows if not treated right at home, but in her case, it wasn't William who was doing the roaming! If she did indeed marry Samuel, would she ever care enough to make any special effort to keep him from straying away with a woman like Penny Smith?

It was shortly after dinner that evening when Penny arrived at the Hansen wagon. For a few minutes, she sat around their fire and spoke cordially with Tad and Beth. After a while, she invited Danielle to take an evening stroll with her.

As soon as they were out of hearing distance from the wagon, Penny grinned. "I've brought a bar of soap and a towel. Let's go down to the river and bathe."

The temptation of a bath was more than Danielle could resist. It had been days since she had had a real bath, not just a sponge bath in the back of the wagon. "Let met get my things and tell Aunt Beth where we're going."

Grabbing hold of her arm, Penny warned, "No, don't tell her, Danielle. She might insist on coming along or sending someone, like your uncle, to stand guard. It's such a lovely night, and it will be fun to lie around in the water. Just the two of us!"

With some reluctance, Danielle nodded her head. The picture in her mind that Penny had created, of being able to take a leisurely swim in the cool depths of the Platte River, was more than she could bear.

"I knew you would come with me." Penny grinned again and began to lead her friend away from the safety of the encircled wagons and into the dark night.

As they neared the river's edge, the two stood in silence for a minute and listened to the night sounds all around them. It was Penny who broke the quiet with a small giggle. "I just can't wait to get out of this gown!" She hurriedly began to undo the row of buttons down the front of her dress. "You know, I was offered a job in Independence at the Silver Star, but I refused, not wanting to stay undressed much of the time. Now here I am, dying to get out of my clothes!"

Danielle laughed along with her friend, not knowing if she should believe her or not. The Silver Star had been pointed out to her while she had been in Independence; it was a house of ill repute, with women in various styles of dress hanging around the front porch and looking down at the street from opened windows. Putting Penny's comment out of her mind, she quickly undressed. After kicking off her sturdy boots and unbraiding her long, pale hair, she stood for a few seconds on the bank before diving into the cool depths of swirling water. "It's wonderful, Penny, come on it," she called as she swam with the current, then made her way back to where Penny was still standing along the bank.

"I can't swim," the other girl confessed. "I'm just going to sit here at the edge of the water and cool off." Penny already regretted that she had invited Danielle to accompany her. She had seen the girl standing naked beneath the moonlight at the river's edge, and with the glance, hot-burning, jealousy had knifed its way through her belly. Danielle's slender figure and beautiful curling silver-white hair defied competition, even though she appeared unaware of her natural beauty. No wonder Samuel Taylor had not been easily lured into a shadowed corner for a few minutes last night. Penny had attempted to attract him with her knowing charms, and though she had sensed that his resistance was weak, she had been able only to entice him into walking her back to her wagon. After watching Danielle standing naked on the river's edge, she knew what she was up against.

Danielle swam about in the water as Penny remained near the shore. "This was a wonderful idea, Penny. Thanks for inviting me." Turning over on her back, she floated for a while, and gazing up at the star-bright night and the full moon, she forgot about Samuel Taylor and her worries for the future.

Beginning to lather her hair, Penny put aside the silent rivalry she felt with the other woman. "After all the trail dust we've had to endure, I think we deserve treating ourselves to a simple pleasure such as taking a bath. Do you want to use some of this soap?"

A few minutes later, both young women were sitting along the river's edge with their bodies half revealed out of the water as they washed their hair. Then they allowed the stirring night breeze to dry their hair before they began to dress, and return to the wagons.

"Are you anxious to get to Oregon and to be able to wed your Samuel?" Penny had a sly look as she asked the question.

The carefree mood that Danielle had been feeling took a plunge with the question. "I suppose any young woman would be pleased at the prospect of marriage." She could not admit to Penny that she had no intention of ever wedding Samuel Taylor. It would be best for her to talk to her aunt and uncle before announcing her decision to anyone else.

"Well, Danielle, I don't wish to frighten you, but I think I should share a certain piece of information with you. It has to do with a man and woman and the marriage bed, especially on their wedding night."

Danielle turned her head to look more closely at the other young woman. It was not too often that she heard Penny speaking in such a serious tone.

"I'm afraid I might have misled you into thinking that it is a wonderful experience to lie with a man. You have to understand," she quickly added as she glimpsed the frown marring Danielle's brow with confusion, "that much of what I said to you in the past was a means for me to cover up the horrible side of pleasuring a man." Penny smiled as she watched the confusion turn to question. "The truth is, Danielle, more often than not, it is a very painful ordeal that we women are subjected to, in order to keep our men happy." She almost choked getting this little lie out of her mouth.

Danielle lifted one fine, pale brow at this bold statement. She had suspected that Penny did not always tell the truth, but this was going a little too far! From their first meeting, she had been under the impression that there was little else on Penny's mind besides the sexual act that went on between a man and a woman.

Penny realized that she might have overplayed her hand, and quickly tried to explain. "I have tried to appear that I enjoy William's attentions, but the truth is, I don't, nor does any other woman. I am thinking about leaving William as soon as we reach Oregon." Penny had been thinking hard on this idea, and with the passage of each day, it was growing more appealing to her. She could easily move away from William and claim to be a widow with a small child, if she didn't leave the baby with him.

A look of confusion washed over Danielle's features. If Penny didn't like the act, what was all the talk this morning about William not lasting long enough to pleasure her as she wanted? Had the girl made it up, and everything else she had said about sex? Danielle was certainly no authority, however, and could not dispute a word of what Penny was saying. The only information her aunt had given her on the subject was that it was a wife's duty to submit to whatever her husband desired. Now she wondered if all along her aunt, like Penny, had just been covering up a very uncomfortable portion of her life. She remembered vividly the times when Samuel had tried to force his kisses upon her, and how she had felt only revulsion. But surely Uncle Tad would not be so unkind to Aunt Beth? "But what about the baby?" she blurted out as she digested the information Penny had just given her. "If you leave William, how will you take care of yourself and a baby?"

"Oh, don't worry about me or my baby." Penny had not missed that look of wonder upon Danielle's face. Rising to her feet, Penny began to dress. If everything worked out as she wanted, she and her child, if she decided to keep the baby, would not be alone for long. Danielle might be beautiful and have a gorgeous body, but Penny was sure the other girl would not go to her marriage bed willingly after this night. If Danielle kept on resisting Samuel, perhaps Penny would have a chance to sample the bulge she had felt beneath his trousers last night when they had danced. And once that was accomplished, there was no telling how much more she would gain from Samuel Taylor.

The wagon train pushed on with the same routine of hardship, and by a day's end everyone was exhausted. Danielle grew even more resolved not to become Samuel's bride. More and more, she avoided being in his presence. If he rode up to the Hansen wagon, she made any excuse to avoid conversation. She stayed closer to the wagon in the evening, rarely walking around the encampment to visit anyone, except when Penny arrived with one of her invitations to join her at the river for a bath.

With the trail cutting westward along the Platte, bathing was too much of a temptation for Danielle, who found much respite from the warm nights. Several times, the two young women made their way through the dark night to the river's edge without anyone on the wagon train being the wiser.

Most of their conversation centered around Penny complaining about the marriage bed she was forced to share with her husband. Overnight she had found a dislike for sex, and the more she expressed her newfound loathing for the act, the more uncomfortable Danielle became in the other woman's presence. Danielle could not help feeling that Penny's words were only a show for her benefit, but for the life of her, she couldn't understand why.

"Can you believe it, Danielle, even in my condition, William pesters me without letup? Why, only last night he woke me from a sound sleep and had his way with me. When I protest, he claims that it is his right, and I have no say on the matter!"

Sitting naked next to the riverbank, their bodies half in and half out of the cool water after bathing, Danielle was about to say that William didn't seem to be the sort of man who would make a woman do anything she didn't want to do, when she heard a noise not far away. Danielle was sure she had heard the snapping of a branch, and in low tones she asked, "Did you hear that noise, Penny? It came from that direction."

Penny quickly shook her head. "I didn't hear anything." She sat up straighter and, for a minute, listened to the silence that seemed to hang all around them. With a small laugh, she said in a more normal tone, "No one's out there, unless it's that handsome Samuel of yours. He's on guard duty this evening, isn't he?"

For a young woman who had recently claimed to have forsworn men, Danielle thought Penny's interest in Samuel a bit strange. "I don't know if Samuel is on guard duty or not," nor did she really care. Reaching out, she gathered her gown in her hand and climbed to the bank. "I think we should get back to the wagon train, Penny," she whispered hurriedly. The quiet left her feeling ill at ease, and she could not put out of her mind the noise she had heard earlier.

Penny was reluctant to leave the coolness of the water, but as she watched Danielle hurriedly dressing, she pulled herself up the bank. For an added minute she stood unclad, delighting in the night breeze that caressed her flesh. She could have these minutes to remember tomorrow as the afternoon heat beat down on her relentlessly.

Danielle was irritated at the delay, and while Penny took her time dressing, her gaze scanned the area around the river. It was too dark to make out anything other than the outlined shadows of the trees, but this did not lessen Danielle's unease. As they made their way back to the wagons, Danielle could not shed the feeling that they were being watched. At last they returned to the safety of the wagons, and Danielle hurriedly made her way back to her uncle's vehicle. Climbing into the back of the wagon and stretching out on the pallet, she found that sleep eluded her. Each time she shut her eyes, some small noise would pull her back awake, and she would lie with the sound of her heartbeat rushing in her ears. Danielle could not shake the fear that she and Penny had been observed at the riverbank. Perhaps Penny had been right, and it was Samuel who had stepped on the branch, but even this thought did not give her any relief.

Chapter Three

The next morning, the scouts picked up signs of Indian ponies having been in the area. Tad Hansen gave his family the report during the afternoon break, and for the rest of the day, Danielle stayed close to the Hansen wagon. That evening, when she saw Penny, the other woman appeared to have little concern about the event.

"Them Injuns, if that was who was down by the river, are more than likely miles from here by now," she declared. "And anyway, who is to say it weren't one of the men from the wagon train that you heard? William said that the scouts only saw signs of a few ponies and those were close to the wagons."

The other young woman's confident words did little to relieve Danielle of her fear that they had narrowly escaped being taken by surprise by Indians. "I still think we should wait a few days before going back to the river." Penny had suggested they go for a bath that evening, but Danielle had refused. "I think I can be satisfied with a sponge bath like in the past, and like everyone on the wagon train is content to do."

Penny felt the day's dirt crushed on her body,

and if she had been of a braver constitution, she might have dared to go alone to the river. "I guess you're right, and we should stay near the wagon train for a couple of days," she relented, seeing that she could not persuade Danielle to join her.

Two long, hot, miserable days passed before Penny came again to the Hansen wagon shortly after the supper dishes had been washed and put away. Tad and Beth Hansen greeted her warmly, pleased that the young woman had befriended their niece, and that the two young women periodically went about the wagon train visiting with other travelers. They thought little of their niece walking off with Penny Smith this evening, since it was like many evenings in the past.

Danielle was a little more on edge than usual, and the thought of a long swim in the river was too welcome to resist. Earlier that afternoon, Samuel had cornered her not far from the Hansen wagon, and had demanded to know why she had been avoiding him.

"You are going to be my wife, Danielle! Do you think that, after we are wed, you will still be able to avoid me?" he had asked in a rather harsh tone.

It had been on the tip of Danielle's tongue to confess that she had no intention of ever marrying him; but as she looked into his hard, blue eyes, she could not bring herself to say the words. Instead, she made up excuses, of having been busy helping her aunt around the wagon, and of being too worn out to be very good company to anyone lately.

Samuel had been persistent, and grabbing hold of her forearms, he had tried to kiss her.

She had tried to avoid contact with his mouth, by turning her face away. She would have been subjected to an even bolder attempt, but Josh

Peterson had walked by them and had looked, with question, in their direction.

Samuel immediately released her arms as he felt the other man's eyes upon him. Without another word, he had walked away from her, taking long, angry strides.

The tension of having to deal with Samuel was becoming far too much for Danielle to deal with, and as she walked to the river with Penny, she made up her mind that either tonight or in the morning, she would tell her uncle that she would not be marrying Samuel Taylor. She hoped her aunt and uncle would understand and respect her decision, although they would certainly be disappointed. They truly liked Samuel, and saw in the young man much of what they hoped for their niece to find in a husband. Danielle did not view these same qualities—of being hardworking and a farmer—as enough to make her spend her life with a man she did not love.

The cool, refreshing water soothed Danielle's worried mind as she swam along with the current. Penny sat in waist-deep water near the shore. Lying naked atop the water and allowing the cool liquid to soothe her muscle-sore limbs, Danielle gazed up into the vast night sky. There was only a sliver of moonlight in the velvet expanse of heavens, but millions of twinkling stars aided the light that was cast along the riverbank through the canopy of encircling trees.

Danielle was unsure of how much time had passed before she began to swim back to Penny. It was with some surprise, though, that she found the other young woman gone from the edge of the riverbank. She looked around the area, but Penny was nowhere to be seen. Looking up along the bank,

Danielle saw that Penny's clothes were also gone. Unable to imagine why Penny would leave the river without her, but assuming she had returned to the wagon train, Danielle climbed out onto the riverbank and nervously began to dress. Whatever could have possessed Penny to leave her here alone? Had one of the night guards come across her, and had she remained quiet to protect Danielle's modesty? Questions swirled around in her brain as she heard the whistle of birds in the trees around her. The rushing sound of the river seemed to keep a steady beat with her heart as it dashed harshly against her rib cage.

Whatever Penny's reason for leaving, Danielle did not feel comfortable all alone out here in the dark. She did not bother to braid her hair and wrap the twin braids about the crown of her head. As soon as she pulled on her boots, she started off through the trees and headed back in the direction of the wagon train.

A rustle in the underbrush caught her attention; gazing into the darkness, she tried to make out the shape of whatever had caused the noise. Another rustle of leaves behind her and her steps became faster. She heard several calls, which now seemed to be all around her. She saw a camp fire from the wagon train, and some of her pent-up breath expelled. She had only a short distance to go. Then she felt a hand wrap around her forearm as someone stepped up behind her. "Penny?" she gasped aloud before her mouth was covered by a large hand and she was half lifted, half dragged back into the cover of trees.

* * *

Indians! Sweet, merciful Jesus, she and Penny had been captured by Indians! Without any kind of warning, she was dragged between two braves, who were dressed only in breechcloths. One kept his hand over her mouth as they pulled her along through the trees. The other took a piece of red trade cloth from the waist of his breechcloth and tied the strip of material over her mouth. She screamed with the terror that had set her limbs to trembling and her heartbeat racing at a panicked pace, but the noise leaving her throat was only a strangled sound, smothered by the Indian's gag.

The warriors did not loosen their hold upon her arms until they broke through the copse of trees, and were met by a dozen equally terrifying Indians. Penny was with this group of braves. Her mouth was also covered, and her hands had been tied behind her back. A long piece of leather was secured around her throat, and the opposite end of the leather thong was being held by one of the band who, Danielle quickly learned, was the leader of the group.

This fierce-looking warrior ordered the same done to Danielle. Then, with words that neither woman understood, he ordered Penny placed behind one of the braves on his horse. With a motion to the two Indians standing next to Danielle, he indicated that she was to be lifted up behind him.

Coming to her senses at that moment, and knowing that this might be the last time she would ever have another chance to gain her freedom, she began to kick out at the man upon horseback. With her hands tied behind her back, she fought off the man holding on to her and the one reaching down for her.

Ignoring her attempt at freedom and the ineffectual noises coming from her throat, the large Indian on horseback reached down and clutched the front of Danielle's gown. As the material gave way about her bodice, the tearing noise loud in the quiet forest, the warrior pulled Danielle up in front of him instead of behind him, as he'd originally planned.

Though Danielle had heard the noise made by the tearing of the material, she was unaware of the damage done to her gown. All she could think of was that she had to get away from these savages! Somehow, she had to do something to keep them from taking her and Penny away. She had to let someone from the wagon train know what was happening to them.

Kicking his pony's sides, the lead Indian started the small band off in the opposite direction from the wagon train. She had to do something, and she had to do it now. Once again, she made an effort to gain her freedom. With a feigned movement of her body, Danielle acted as though she were going to swoon. As the Indian leaned toward her, she pushed with all the strength she could muster against his chest, her body turning to the side with the hopes that she would fall to the ground. With any kind of luck, she could jump to the ground, and in the confusion maybe she would be able to run and hide in the trees. If she could escape, she could get help from the wagon train to set out a search party for Penny.

The large Indian had little patience for Danielle's attempt to dislodge herself from his horse. With a hard jerk of his hand, which held the leather strap around her neck, he tightened the thong and pulled her backward against his chest. His iron-hewed forearms pressed against her breasts, and for short moments, air was shut out of her lungs.

Within seconds, Danielle was slumping upon the pony in front of him as his arm tightened the pressure. He deliberately waited an added moment before he loosened the leather thong. Danielle gulped in great breaths of the night air. As consciousness swirled in and out of her mind, a small voice told her that this savage held the upper hand. Another attempt to dislodge herself from his horse might mean that he would lose all patience and take her life. As the group rode on, her head began to clear and she glanced over to see how Penny was faring. The other young woman appeared to have lost all will to fight her captors. She rode silently behind her abductor, her brown eyes large with fear.

The frightening ride went on endlessly through the long night. The Indians never slowed or halted their pace over the rough terrain as the hours put distance between them and the Beckon wagon train. With each mile, Danielle's head filled with all the horrible stories she had heard about Indians capturing white women and children. In Independence, there had been much talk on this subject. Occasionally children were adopted and treated as fairly as possible by the savages. But for the most part, the women were abused cruelly at the hands of their vicious captors. It was reported that some of the women were sold off to other tribes, becoming slaves to whoever paid the desired price of a horse or blanket. One woman who had lived with Indians for three years had killed herself with a pistol when rescued, because she could not live down, the shame and the abuse that had been inflicted upon her. Danielle wondered whether she, like the woman, would have the nerve to take her own life—if, in fact, she and Penny were rescued.

After the first morning light had broken over the eastern sky, the leader of the raiding party signaled that the band should stop to give their ponies a rest. Both Danielle and Penny were exhausted and had to be helped to dismount.

With the cloths removed from their mouths and their hands untied, the two women were given dried strips of buffalo meat to eat. For the first time since their abduction, they were allowed to remain together, and as their eyes watched their captors, they spoke in low tones.

"Do you think that anyone from the wagon train will figure out what happened to us?" Danielle questioned as she felt the sharp sting of tears filling her eyes.

Penny silently shook her head, her gaze watching the leader deep in conversation with another brave. Biting off a piece of the dried meat, she gave Danielle little encouragement. "As fast as these Injuns are traveling, we'll be in the next state before Mr. Beckon's scouts pick up any sign of our trail."

Danielle's heart sank with her friend's words, even though she had thought the same thing earlier that morning. "What are we going to do, Penny?" She hoped that Penny would have some kind of plan. In the past the other young woman always seemed to take charge of what was going on around her, and Danielle hoped this would be true now.

Penny's features were pale as she turned her head back in Danielle's direction. "At the moment, I see little that we can do. You know what happened when you tried to get away from that brute."

She nodded toward the leader, and both women regarded the cruel-featured warrior. With the light of morning, he seemed even meaner than he had last night. A savage-looking scar, paler than the rest of his flesh, ran from his right cheekbone to the center of his chin. As his eyes turned in their direction, they lacked any trace of warmth for the women. "That's one man I wouldn't want near me!" Penny shuddered, knowing that no woman would find kindness from his touch.

Well, that's a first! The thought went crazily through Danielle's mind. Penny had at last found a man she didn't want to seduce! And Lord God above, who could blame her? He was the most savage of the group. As he stood near his braves and stared at the two of them, Danielle felt her flesh beginning to crawl with revulsion. Feeling the heat of his gaze roaming over her figure, her hand automatically went upward, as though to shield her bosom from his glance. She noticed, for the first time, the ragged tear over her gown, and looking down, she saw that the upper, swelling, pale flesh of her right bosom was revealed. She tried to draw the material together, and as the Indian's gaze never wavered, she turned her back, trying to secure the ragged edges of the cloth.

"William is going to be out of his mind with worry," Penny said aloud, taking Danielle's mind off her gown.

For the first time, Danielle realize, Penny had spoken in kind tones about her husband. She would have reached out and offered the other young woman some comfort, but she had no comfort to give. She was as frightened as Penny, and could only imagine how her own family was reacting to her disappearance. Before daylight, Aunt

Beth would have awakened to discover that her niece had not slept on her pallet. Her uncle would have made a search throughout the wagon train. Perhaps he would have thought that she was with Samuel, but not finding her at the Taylor wagon, both men would have joined forces to look for her. In their search, they would find that Penny was also missing. They would discover that there was little they could do except wait and see what Mr. Beckon's scouts could turn up. She could only imagine the horror her aunt and uncle would be feeling, when they learned that their niece had been abducted by Indians!

The break in the hard riding was at an end, and once again, Penny was placed in back of one of the braves and Danielle was put in front of the Indian leader. More than once that day, Danielle felt her abductor's attention focusing directly upon her. She felt his fingers run through her long, pale tresses in a harsh sort of caress. Then she felt him trace his hand over her back, assessing her shape beneath the material of her gown. With each attention given, she felt her body shiver in utter revulsion.

Perhaps she was being punished for not being satisfied with Samuel. She felt the Indian shifting his weight, his large thigh pushing up tightly against hers. Her body stiffened. She felt the tired strain of every muscle as she forced herself to keep her back straight, and not to slump wearily against the Indian's chest. She held her legs uncomfortably forward, to avoid further contact with his thighs. *Would God play such a cruel trick on me?* she wondered as exhaustion sapped her of rational thought. If she had been content with Samuel, and the life her aunt and uncle had desired for her, would she be in this situation? Perhaps not, a small portion of her mind reasoned. If she had been content, would she have sought out the danger that going to the river at night, with only Penny for company, had caused? None of the other young women on the wagon train would have taken such daring steps in order to have a bath. She and Penny had been dissatisfied with their everyday routine; now they were going to pay the ultimate price for their actions.

Chapter Four

The Indian raiding party traveled hard for the next three days and nights. They halted their mounts only well into the dark of night, and then only because both riders and animals were exhausted. Each evening Danielle and Penny were tied together, their backs leaning against the trunk of a tree. Though worn out, they spoke in low tones about their fate and their hope that someone was searching for them.

Penny believed that, by now, the scouts had reported the abduction to Fort Kearney. Bolstering this belief, she whispered softly, "It might be anytime now that the soldiers will come against these savages! When this happens, be sure you stay low, and out of harm's way."

Danielle was not as confident that a search party was looking for them, unless her uncle and Samuel and William Smith had set out on their own. She did not reveal her thoughts to Penny, but she could not see Mr. Beckon allowing his scouts to leave to report to the military fort that two women had been abducted. More than likely, they would report the news when they reached Fort Laramie; and there would still be a couple of days before the wagon train arrived there. With the threat of Indians, Mr. Beckon would be more cautious, and not willing to be caught at a disadvantage by letting his scouts return to Fort Kearney, and hence leave the wagon train unprotected.

During these evenings in their upright position against the tree, sleeping was difficult; but exhaustion eventually overcame worries and fears, and forgetfulness was attained in slumber.

For Danielle, the long days were an emotional strain as well. The Indian leader's treatment of her was becoming more personal. His large hands often went around her waist as they rode together. More than once she had pushed at his wandering fingers as they had caressed her thigh or breast.

Danielle did not believe that her futile attempts at keeping her distance from this brave were taken into consideration. He had his own reasons for keeping some restraint on his desires, and for the time being, she was thankful for whatever these reasons were.

Penny did not seem to be having the same problem with the Indian she was riding with. He appeared indifferent to the white woman who rode behind him. After the second day on the trail, Danielle thought she knew why the main group of Indians were leaving the women alone. The leader had claimed both women for himself!

More than once, Danielle had seen the brave looking upon Penny with chillingly cold, black eyes. His glance was that of appraisal and ownership. No, there was no denying the possessive look that crossed his hard features when he looked upon them.

It was on the third day, during a break in the afternoon, that Penny once again received one of these stony looks from the Indian leader. This time, instead of looking away from his cool inspection, the young woman smiled boldly in return. The Indian did not miss the movement of her lips, and silently, his gaze went lower to her swelling bosom. His dark eyes did not leave their frank perusal, and when they did lift to her face, there was still no warmth in the dark gaze.

Danielle had watched the interaction between the two. The first chance she had, she warned, "I would be careful how you act around him, Penny. I don't think he's the type a woman can play flirtation games with." She wondered what had happened to Penny's belief that this was one man she wanted nothing to do with.

"I'm sure you're right, Danielle, But he's a man! I've been doing some thinking over the past couple of days. Whenever we get to where these savages are taking us, I'm going to need a man to take care of me until we're rescued. Old Scarface there"—she nodded in his direction—"will do as well as any other, perhaps even better. Everyone seems to be taking orders from him, and you have to admit his body isn't that bad." He wore only a leather breechcloth, like the rest of his braves, and his muscular limbs appeared lithe and firm.

Danielle could not feel any attraction toward this Indian who had treated her so harshly over the past few days. There was much about the warrior that frightened her. He was a man who was used to taking what he wanted, and not inclined to give a second thought toward affection or warmth. She knew there wasn't any sense in trying to tell Penny to be careful. Penny would do exactly what she wanted to do, no matter what anyone else said.

She, as well as Penny, would soon find out exactly what kind of heartless beast this leader truly was.

Midday of the fourth afternoon, the raiding party coaxed their mounts up a winding forest path, high in the mountains. Allowing their captives to dismount for a short time, the Indians pulled out an assortment of paints from their parfleches. The two women watched as each man began to paint his face and chest. Then they painted decorations of animals or spiritual signs upon their horses' flanks. Some of the warriors combed out and rebraided their long hair, adorning themselves with eagle feathers and beaded headbands. Danielle noticed one warrior placing a necklace of bear claws and brass bells around his neck. Another wore a necklace of dentalium shells and brass studs; another, a closely fitting necklace, of bone beads and quilled fringe. The leader adorned himself in a buckskin shirt, which was handsomely painted and decorated with quillwork and tufts of human hair, then indicated that he was ready to remount.

The raiding party was close to their village, and they had taken time out to decorate themselves for their homecoming. Looking down at her own torn and dirty gown, Danielle could only imagine what reception would be given to two white women who had not been allowed a bath, nor a brush to sweep through their gnarled hair. If their abductors had plans of selling or trading them, they certainly would not get a very good profit. An insane thought struck Danielle before she was placed atop the horse—that if nothing else came out of this, she would have some satisfaction in not earning for Scarface and his band a high bargaining price!

Riding the forest trail, the small band of Indians soon broke through the enclosing forest. The braves sat their mounts upon a rise that overlooked a lush, green valley. Over a thousand conical-shaped dwellings were set up not far from a river that slashed through the valley floor. Danielle caught her breath at the primitive beauty that was spread out before her. Though the actions of these Indian warriors were contemptible and unforgivable, Danielle admitted that the savage pageantry of the Indian village—with its lodges decorated with religious symbols as well as images from the dwellers' visions and dreams—left her utterly breathless.

Danielle's thoughts of beauty soon fled. Throughout the settlement, the call was shouted that the raiding party had returned, and that they had brought back two captives. Danielle watched in wide-eyed fear as the warriors made their way directly through the center of the village.

Danielle glimpsed old men sitting outside their lodges before fires, and women placing strips of meat upon drying racks or stirring blackened pots which rested against the open coals of their outside fires. Villagers came out of their lodges as they heard the commotion of barking dogs and children shouting as they ran behind the returning braves. A long procession began to form behind the party of warriors and their captives, and glimpsing many angry faces, Danielle tried to keep her eyes downcast; but the fear of the unknown would not allow her this simple comfort. She had to see what fate would greet her. Her vision swirled with the many faces of men and women who were dressed in garments of soft hides, decorated with beads and feathers. Some of the women carried sticks in their fists, and shook them threateningly at the captives. Though Danielle was lost to their cries of lust-filled vengeance against the captives, she was not lost to the heat and anger in their tone. As she looked at Penny, their gazes caught in a fear-filled union.

The leader of the braves ignored those encircling them, and kept his pony moving toward the center of the village, not halting until he came to a large lodge that had been painted with images of the Sioux's sacred thunderbirds.

The hide entrance flap of the lodge was pushed aside and a powerfully built warrior stepped out. He wore his long black hair pulled back in braids that lay down his back, his loins were covered with a breechcloth. As he stood to his full height, his muscular arms crossed over his broad chest, his features did not show any warmth of welcome as he gazed over each warrior upon horseback before his dark eyes settled upon their leader. His features were stoic as his gaze passed over Penny, sitting behind the brave known as Spotted Pony; then his regard slowly went over Danielle. Not the slightest flicker of an eyebrow betrayed his impassive stance as ebony eyes swept silently over the woman with the silver hair. His gaze left the woman's fear-filled features and went to the man sitting behind her. "So, you have at last returned to your village, Red Fox. You and those who follow you have been away a long time. The families of these warriors have been worried that you would not return." Since he spoke in the Sioux language, the two women had no idea what he was saying.

The Indian sitting behind Danielle puffed out his

chest as he was addressed by the chief of his village. "What reason would families of our people have to fear for their loved ones, Wind Dancer? These braves and I are stronger than any we have come up against. We prove it by bringing back these captives." Thus saying, he gave Danielle a shove, which completely took her by surprise and sent her sprawling to the dust at his horse's feet.

The warrior-chief's instant reaction was anger as he watched Red Fox's treatment of the woman. But even this emotion he kept well hidden beneath the surface of his stolid features as dark eyes went to the woman, watching her gain her feet and glare hatred upon Red Fox. Assured that she was unharmed, he looked back to the brave. "Where did you get these women?" As he awaited the answer, his gaze again went to Penny, and for an added moment, his regard searched her in an appraising manner.

"We took them from one of the *wasichu's* wagon train, which was heading west." Red Fox did not miss the appraisal in Wind Dancer's eyes as he looked at the young woman on the back of Spotted Pony's horse.

"You know well, Red Fox, that the council decided that there would be no more raids upon the white man's covered wagons until after the great council of the Sioux nations, when we will discuss how best to rid our land of these pale-skinned men." There was anger in the strong voice that the chief directed upon the one known as Red Fox. His feelings of displeasure were lost on no one standing nearby.

"We did not raid the wagon train." Red Fox had known better than to disobey the decisions made by the council of his village. "We followed the covered wagons for a few days and nights, and these two *wasicun winyan* were foolish enough to go to the river alone at night."

"The blue coats from their soldier fort will be called to make a search for the *wasicun winyan,*" Wind Dancer responded, his features still angry with disapproval.

"Then we will kill the blue coats, and drive the *wasichu* from our lands!" Red Fox spat out heatedly. His band of braves called out their agreement to such an action taken against the white men who wore the blue coats.

"You speak as a child, Red Fox. Your actions threaten the women and children of our village." Wind Dancer, unlike many of his tribe, had learned that there was little his people could do to halt the influx of white men, who came in greater numbers each year to cross the Sioux lands.

"These are not the first *wasicun winyan* to come to our village as slaves, Wind Dancer. I did not hear you speak out in defense of the others," Red Fox reminded his chief. Wind Dancer was a powerful Oglala chief, and Red Fox wisely tried to calm the anger he knew the larger man was holding in check. Red Fox had known that he would be confronted by Wind Dancer, and forced to explain his actions. That was why he had come directly to his chief's lodge instead of going to his own. He would make a gift of the brown-haired woman to Wind Dancer and, with this offering, pacify his temper. "Perhaps our chief would take one of these women into his lodge. I give you the choice of the *wasicun winyan.*" Red Fox silently waited for Wind Dancer to refuse the offer, or take the woman with the brown hair, who sat behind Spotted Pony. Wind Dancer had hardly given the silver-haired woman a second glance, and inwardly Red Fox smiled to himself. He had seen the silver-haired woman's rare beauty that night when she had been captured. Now, dirty and weary, with her pale hair tangled and littered with twigs and grass, she appeared hardly worthwhile to anyone. He had been right in giving Wind Dancer his choice. He would choose the brown-haired woman, and he, Red Fox, would have the silver-haired beauty!

To Wind Dancer, there was not a choice to be made; there had never been a choice. He wished only, that the silver-haired woman had come to him in a different way. He was growing hard in his dealings with braves such as Red Fox. They did not carry the welfare of the people on their shoulders, as he now did. They thought only of raiding and warring, leaving it up to him and the other leaders of the tribe to ensure that the people survived. Before speaking, Wind Dancer allowed his glance to touch lightly upon the woman with the brown hair before they went to the young woman standing upon Mother Earth. "I will take the woman with the silver hair, Red Fox." With a movement of his arm, he reached out and pulled Danielle away from Red Fox's pony. "I thank you for this gift, but I also warn you that it is up to you and your braves to set an extra watch around the village to ensure that the blue coats do not locate our summer valley." With the woman standing at his side, Wind Dancer crossed his arms over his chest as he awaited Red Fox's next move. He was not a stupid man and had easily caught sight of the beauty which the pale-haired woman possessed. It was incredible to him that Red Fox had made such an offer, but he had also known that the warrior had expected him to choose the woman sitting behind Spotted Pony. He had bided his time in the past, with the hopes that Red Fox would change his impulsive ways. If he offered a challenge because of his choice of the two women, Wind Dancer would happily oblige him.

The hard glint within the chief's coal-black eyes was not lost upon Red Fox or those watching. He had not expected Wind Dancer to choose the pale-haired woman; he had wanted her for himself! An unreasonable anger filled him as he watched the large warrior pull the woman to his side. For an insane moment, he had visions of pulling his tomahawk free of its sheath and charging the warrior upon horseback! With any luck, the first blow would be deadly; with no luck, Wind Dancer would kill him within moments. Common sense won out as he gazed into the icy stare that was directed toward him. Though his fingers itched for the feel of the wood handle of his tomahawk, Red Fox forced himself to stay his hand. "The white-haired woman is mine, Wind Dancer. You can take the other!"

The crowd instantly grew quiet with Red Fox's words. Danielle stared from the large Indian who had pulled her to his side to the one who had captured her and brought her to this village. She could not help noticing the anger that filled the warrior's features, and the hard tone he had just used.

"If you had wanted the woman, you should not have given me the choice between your captives. I have chosen the one that I will have." Wind Dancer's voice sounded cool and deadly calm; his posture appeared relaxed with his arms crossed over his chest, but those around him knew that, any instant, he could become a deadly opponent.

Red Fox also knew this to be true, and after one more glance at Danielle, he harshly kicked his pony's sides. Pulling his mount up next to Spotted Pony, he reached out and caught hold of Penny around the waist. He dragged her from the warrior's horse and held her precariously across his lap without a thought to the cruelty of his actions.

Penny's cry of fear and alarm flooded over Danielle, and without a thought to her own actions, she made a step in Red Fox's direction. The warrior chief reached out a hand and caught hold of her arm before she could take a second step. With a motion of his head, his dark eyes looking deeply into her face, he warned her not to interfere with what Red Fox was doing to the other woman.

Drawing in deep breaths of air, Danielle knew that she was powerless, that she could do nothing but stand by and watch as Penny fought to right herself in front of her cruel captive. As last she succeeded, with tears streaming down her cheeks as one harsh hand held on to a fistful of her hair and the other hand pressed hard against her breasts.

With Penny frantically trying to keep her seat in front of the brave, Red Fox turned away from his chief and the pale-haired woman. A loud cry erupted from his lips as he swung his pony's head about, and with the rest of the braves upon horseback following, he rode through the village to his own lodge.

Danielle was confused as she watched her captor and Penny riding off, leaving her with the large warrior. He held tightly to her forearm, his gaze silently circling those who stood around them, and shortly, one by one, the villagers made their way back to their own homes, content for the moment that most of the action between Red Fox and their chief was at a finish.

As Danielle watched everyone leaving her to whatever fate this man had in mind for her, she was caught up in desperation. She felt like falling to the ground and crying her heart out. She wished no more than to be allowed to wallow in her fear and terror until she woke up and realized that the whole ordeal had been some terrible dream. With the warrior holding tightly to her arm, however, she was unable to fall to the ground. As he began to lead her toward the entrance flap of his lodge, her panic intensified to a horror-filled degree.

She tried to pull away from him, digging the heels of her boots into the earth and refusing to follow him into his lodge. Once she stepped inside that hide-covered tepee, she would be totally at his mercy! Outside in the open, she might still have some slim chance of escape.

Wind Dancer was not lost to the fear that filled her; in her place, he would feel the same. Once, years ago, he had been captured as a boy by two Crow warriors. He could still taste the fear he had felt in his mouth, when he had been taken to their village. But unlike this woman, he had also known the sweet taste of victory as his father had ridden into the Crow village and had challenged the two warriors. Killing them both, he had earned great honor, even among the enemy. He had taken his son before the entire village up on the back of his pony and had ridden out of the Crow encampment.

His grip never intensified its strength upon her

arm, but he did not break his hold. He drew her along with him, ignoring her attempts to remain outside. Bending his large frame through the entrance flap, he boldly pulled her inside after him.

Chapter Five

Wind Dancer's lodge was made of twenty buffalo skins, cut and sewn together to produce a semicircular cover. The cover had been fastened at the front of the lodge with lacing pins. Smoke flap poles were pushed through the holes in the corner of the flaps, leaving an opening at the top for the smoke from the small, central fire pit to escape. The lower edges of the tepee were secured with heavy hardwood pegs, which had been driven through holes in the hide. The aged buffalo skins had been painted in vermilion and blue to depict Wind Dancer's vision signs of the sacred *wakinyan*—the thunderbirds of his people.

Inside the lodge, not daring even to draw a full breath, Danielle quickly glanced around. She looked over everything without taking the time to fully appreciate what she was seeing. There was a colorfully beaded, willow backrest, and a mound of thick furs that made up a pallet on one side of the pit fire. Along the opposite interior wall, there were ties which secured a beautifully painted war shield, two rawhide parfleches, a quiver full of arrows, a stout wooden bow, and an assortment of beaded bags with fringe lacings. She saw elaborate headdresses and a variety of male clothing along another wall.

As the warrior moved away from the entrance flap, Danielle stood exactly where he had left her, not daring to move lest she draw his attention. She watched him with a wary eye as he bent to the shallow pit fire and, taking up a wooden bowl, scooped out an amount of savory-smelling buffalo stew, flavored with wild onions, from a blackened pot. Straightening to his full, tall height, his eyes settled upon Danielle, and with a look toward the bowl in his hand and a nod in her direction, he indicated that the stew was for her. "*Yúta.*" He pointed to the bowl and then his mouth.

She stood silently where he had left her near the entrance flap, not sure what she should do, fearing that any movement on her part would be the wrong one to make.

"Come, Mázaska Wakínyela, the food is good. You will feel better once you have something inside your body to warm you." Wind Dancer's tone was gentle and coaxing. He viewed her fear, and in the quiet of his lodge, he could feel the tension that filled the air as the pale-haired woman, whom he had named Silver Dove, watched his movements with distrust.

With a soft sigh escaping his lips, he slowly approached her. Her glance turned quickly back toward the entrance flap, and he wondered if she was going to try and flee. But she stood still, and he gently took her by the hand and drew her to his fire. "*Íyotaka.*" He spoke the Indian word softly, but there was no misunderstanding this time as he pulled her gently down to the fur near the edge of the fire. "*Yúta.*" He handed her the bowl of stew and once again pointed to the bowl and his own mouth, indicating that she should eat.

Looking at him, Danielle felt a tear fill her eye and slowly roll down her cheek. He would make her eat to ensure that she not fall faint when he assaulted her! The terror-striking thought filled her head, and she could not control the trembling that shook her limbs.

Wind Dancer reached out a hand and brushed away the liquid from her cheek; he could not help feeling the softness of her pale flesh. His dark eyes were truly able, for the first time, to feast upon her beauty. Without will, his hand traveled from her cheek to the soft curls framing her heart-shaped face—the same face he had looked upon so often in his dreams, whether they be at night upon his sleeping pallet, or during the day. Her soft hair felt like thistledown, or the delicate tufts of white hair that decorate the dandelion. He did not see her ragged, ill-kempt appearance. To his eyes, she was the most beautiful woman upon Mother Earth, and by an incredible miracle, she had been delivered into his keeping.

Danielle jerked away from his gentle touch. Her entire body was shaking visibly. Though she tried to lift her chin and appear brave, she could not help the trembling that shook her bottom lip.

Wind Dancer halted his exploration of the woman. With a warm smile upon is bronzed, handsome face, he indicated once again for her to eat the food in the bowl.

Danielle wished herself far from this Indian village and the large Indian sitting next to her. She wished herself back at the wagon train, back in Hannibal, or even in Oregon and married to Samuel Taylor. But she could wish all she wanted to—

she knew that nothing could change her fate! Lowering her eyes to the bowl in her lap, with purely survival instincts, she plucked a moist, juicy piece of meat out of the bowl and put it in her mouth. She had had no appetite since her abduction from the wagon train, and she feared she would not be able to keep the meat down, but with the first morsel of food reaching her belly, her body rebelled with pent-up hunger.

Wind Dancer appeared pleased when at last she tilted the bowl up to her lips and drank the savory juice within. Taking the bowl from her hands and setting it aside, he spoke softly in the Sioux tongue. First, he pointed to himself and pronounced the words that would tell her that his name was Wind Dancer, "Taté Wacípi." Pointing to her, he repeated the Sioux words for Silver Dove over and over: "Mázaska Wakínyela, Mázaska Wakínyela."

With eyes wide, Danielle watched his every movement, not sure exactly what he was saying but too afraid not to pay close attention. She soon realized he was telling her his name. As he pointed to her and several times said, "Mázaska Wakínyela," she realized that he had given her an Indian name. *Well, she would just keep the name she had always had, thank you very much!*

Wind Dancer did not miss any slight movement of her features. When the realization came to her that he was teaching her his name, and the name he had chosen for her, a warm smile came over his lips. Wakán Tanka had surely blessed him this day! The blessing had come as such a surprise, though, he was unsure what he should do with her. She was his vision gift, and in no fashion would he dishonor what the Great Spirit had bestowed upon him. As he sat there pondering while he feasted his eyes on her beauty, the image of the old woman called Ptanyétu Winúhcala—Autumn Woman—came to mind. Having lived alone for the past two winters, Autumn Woman might be pleased to have the company of a young woman in her lodge. She would welcome the meat and furs he would bring to her lodge in payment for taking care of Silver Dove. Glimpsing the fear within the turquoise eyes rimmed with delicate flecks of gold, he tenderly reached out and brushed away a smudge of dirt upon her chin. "You have no reason to fear any longer, Mázaska Wakínyela. I will watch over you and see that no harm befalls you. I have waited a long time for this day to arrive," he said softly in his own tongue.

Danielle had no idea what this warrior was saying, but looking into his warm dark gaze, she knew that he was offering her comfort. Still, her fear of the unknown was too overpowering for her to accept any consolation from him. She wanted to be released; allowed to return to the safety of her family! "Please let me go." The words were forced out of her dry throat, and touched his ears in a soft whisper.

These were the first words that Wind Dancer had heard her speak, and the lilting tone touched him deeply in his spirit. Autumn Woman would teach her the way of the people, and one day he would see the fear and distrust in her eyes turn to joy. With these thoughts, he rose to his feet, and reaching down, he took her hand into his own.

Danielle had no idea where the warrior was taking her as he drew her to her feet and out of his lodge. Once outside, he led her through the village. She felt more than one pair of eyes following their steps. Looking around the village, Danielle wondered what had happened to Penny. Was the other girl in a similar situation? Confused and unsure, she had no choice except to follow where the large man led.

On the outer border of the village, near the river, Wind Dancer halted before a small lodge. Standing outside the entrance flap, he called for permission to enter before pushing aside the hide covering. As he drew Danielle along with him, the couple had to squint their eyes within the smoky interior of the lodge. As Danielle slowly became used to the sharp sting of the smoke caused by the shallow pit fire, she saw an elderly gray-haired woman leaning against a beaded backrest not far from her fire. The old woman's snapping black eyes went from the white woman standing next to her chief then back to Wind Dancer himself.

As she struggled to pull herself to her feet, the sound of her clicking tongue against her bottom teeth filled the lodge. As she approached the couple, her gray head turned at an angle as she looked directly at Danielle. "Why have you brought this *wasicun winyan* to my lodge, Wind Dancer?" Like the rest of the villagers, she had been told about the two white captives whom Red Fox had brought back from his raiding. She had heard about the confrontation between Red Fox and Wind Dancer, and how foolish the brave had been in giving their chief his choice of the two women. A sparkle came into her eyes when she thought about Wind Dancer choosing the very woman that Red Fox had wished for himself. She had never liked the overly bold and often rude brave called Red Fox, and had derived some enjoyment when she had been informed that Wind Dancer had bested him.

"She is to be called Silver Dove. I have brought her to your lodge with the hope that you will allow her to stay with you and learn the ways of the people."

"Buy why would you wish this *wasicun winyan* to learn all these things, my chief?" Her tongue clicked loudly as the sharp eyes searched out Wind Dancer's face.

"Wakán Tanka brought this woman to our village, and to me." When Autumn Woman had said the words "white woman," Wind Dancer felt his irritation grow. To him, Silver Dove was the center of his universe. He saw her not as white or Indian, but as the woman who was destined to travel his life path with him.

"I thought Red Fox brought the woman to our village."

Wind Dancer's lips drew back in a smile at the old woman's craftiness. "You are right, Autumn Woman. Red Fox did bring her here, but he was directed by the mighty hand of Wakán Tanka. I have known since my youth that she would one day come to me. Silver Dove is my vision gift. She is the one who shall complete my life cycle."

Autumn Woman knew that Wind Dancer had been gifted with powerful medicine from the Great Spirit. She would not think of questioning what he claimed the woman meant to him. "Silver Dove." She lightly repeated the name, and turning her aged head at one angle and then another, she studied the woman that Wind Dancer had brought to her lodge. Her hand, as the warrior's had in his lodge, reached out, and with awe written clearly on her wrinkled features, she trailed her fingers through the long, pale curls. "You are certain that you wish her to stay in my lodge, Wind Dancer?

You could teach her—in your own lodge—all she needs to know to live among the people." Autumn Woman wondered at Wind Dancer's reasons. There was no denying that the white woman was beautiful. Any man would desire such a woman for his own. Wind Dancer was a young man, in his prime, and from all the accounts that circulated through the village, she knew he had a liking for a pretty maiden. This young warrior could use the white woman for a time before making a decision about having her join him upon his life path.

Since a young age, Wind Dancer had fought with his inner self to control his emotions, but he was finding this task difficult at the moment. He felt a sharp pang of jealousy tighten his gut as he watched the old woman's hand lightly roam over Silver Dove's pale curls. It would be an easy thing to agree with the old woman, and take Silver Dove back to his lodge with him. He could teach her what she had to learn of his people's ways, and much, much more! But looking at Silver Dove, and seeing the fear and confusion on her delicate features, he knew it would be better for her to stay with Autumn Woman. "I will bring meat for your lodge, and hides and furs to keep you both warm and clothed." This was the only answer that Wind Dancer could give. He needed time to consider what future steps to take as far as this woman was concerned. She was like no other woman. She was his spirit gift.

Autumn Woman's eyes showed concern as she watched the young chief leave her lodge. She was glad she was an old lady, and did not have the troubled heart of one who was younger. Wind Dancer was wise, as his father had been before him, but this young woman with the silver hair was something entirely different. She was a *wasicun winyan,* and that could mean much trouble for the Oglala chief!

A movement from Danielle brought the old woman's attention back to her. She grinned widely, revealing two missing bottom teeth. Using her hands to sign to the young woman, then repeating everything twice in her native tongue, the old woman asked Danielle if she was hungry. As the young woman shook her head, indicating that she was not hungry, the older woman silently took her hand and drew her close to the fire.

Pulling her down to a sitting position at the edge of the shallow pit fire Autumn Woman began Danielle's first lesson by stating her name over and over and thumping her aged chest. She did not relent until at last Danielle repeated the words then repeated them again to her satisfaction. There was to be no break, for she quickly began to say the words that meant Silver Dove, and as she had done to herself, she now lightly thumped Danielle's chest.

Danielle balked at repeating the words the old woman was badgering her to say. They were the same ones the warrior had spoken to her in his lodge, and she knew they were the name he had given her. The old Indian woman was persistent and would not give her a moment's reprieve. She soon repeated the name "Silver Dove" and pointed to herself.

It was shortly before dusk when the old woman appeared content with her charge's first lesson. Taking hold of her hand, she drew her away from the fire. Before leaving through the entrance flap, she retrieved a leather water bag. She led Danielle to the river, and walking down the bank a short way, away from prying eyes, she indicated that Danielle was to disrobe and bathe.

Too fearful not to comply with the orders, Danielle silently slipped her torn and dirty dress off her body. Keeping her underclothing on, she waded out into the cool water.

Autumn Woman loudly clicked her tongue and, smiling to herself, knew that this white woman had much to learn of the Sioux ways. It was a good thing that Wind Dancer had brought her for training and instruction. The young woman would soon learn that it was proper for the people to bathe naked. Grandmother River delighted in touching the flesh of her children. The water of the river could soothe and heal as well as clean the skin. Without a word, the old woman unlaced the ties of her own doe-hide dress and dove into the cool depths not far from Danielle, making a big splash. She had not felt like swimming lately; she had not felt like doing anything since she was old and all alone. With this young woman staying in her lodge and depending on her wisdom, some of the feelings of her youth returned.

When Danielle and Autumn Woman went back to their lodge, they found that Wind Dancer had already come and gone. True to his word, he had left a haunch of elk meat and several soft hides, which could be used for sewing dresses and moccasins. He had also left a pile of lush furs for Danielle to fashion into a sleeping pallet. Lying stop the furs was a small beaded bag with quilled fringe. Inside Danielle found a quill comb, which had a carved handle boasting the scene of a buffalo hunt.

Autumn Woman smiled widely at the generous gifts, and pointing to each in turn, she told Danielle the Sioux name. Danielle did not respond as she stared at the beautiful comb in her hand. She was confused by everything that had taken place since she had arrived in this village. She had expected that she would be set upon and mistreated by those in this village. Instead, she had been brought to this old lady and given lavish gifts. After Autumn Woman nudged her with a frown of irritation, Danielle repeated the name for the comb in her hand.

The old woman's dark eyes gleamed with delight as she took the comb out of Danielle's hand and turned it about on her palm. "Wind Dancer must like the *wasicun winyan* very much to give her such a fine gift," she said aloud, knowing that the young woman called Silver Dove didn't know what she was talking about.

After the elk meat and furs had been put in their place, Autumn Woman drew Danielle back to the fire. As the young woman sat upon a soft fur that Wind Dancer had brought to the lodge, the aged Indian woman combed out her long, pale tresses with the quill comb. To Autumn Woman, the fine strands of wheat-colored hair, now that they were clean from her washing, were as soft to the touch as the finest piece of fur. She ran her aged fingers through the length, and every now and then, a grunt of praise left her lips and her tongue clicked in approval.

Before retiring for the night to their sleeping pallets of soft furs, Autumn Woman handed Danielle some pemmican, and as the young woman nibbled at the food, she pointed out everything in the lodge and waited for Danielle to repeat the words to her. Autumn Woman finished the lesson by repeating her name, then that of Silver Dove. Before allowing the girl to lie down, she held up the quill comb and said the Sioux word for it once again, then said Wind Dancer's name and pointed toward the entrance flap of her lodge. Having no other choice in the matter as the dark eyes watched her every movement, Danielle repeated everything she heard.

Long into the night, Danielle lay upon the mound of soft furs and marveled at her fate in the Indian village. Autumn Woman's loud snores sounded throughout the tepee, and Danielle wondered if she would have a chance to sneak out of the lodge and escape. The thought was given up for this evening as she realized the futility of trying to make her way out of the Indian village in the dark all by herself. Perhaps in a day or two, she would be able to talk to Penny, and she and the other young woman could make some sort of plan for an escape. Thus far, she had been unharmed. She would pray that things would stay the same for the next few days. She believed herself only lucky thus far, and expected that some new horror would befall her; after all, she was in an Indian village and surrounded by deadly savages!

She thought of her Uncle Tad and Aunt Beth, and tears filled her eyes with their images. They would be worried to death about her, and would surely be expecting the worst. The truth was that Danielle herself was unsure of her fate. She had no idea why that large warrior had brought her to the old woman's lodge. Perhaps it was their custom, she thought wearily. This could be the way they trained their captives to be able to serve their owner.

Confused and lonely, Danielle at last shut her eyes, but the image of the handsome warrior known as Wind Dancer would not leave her mind. At first he had frightened her, but there had been something about this man—when his ebony eyes gazed upon her—that had left her feeling strangely warm inside.

Chapter Six

The long summer days slowly passed, and with each one's passing, Danielle became more accustomed to the Sioux way of life. Each morning after rising, Autumn Woman would take Danielle to the river's edge, and the two women would bathe, gather wood for their lodge fire, and fill the leather water pouch. Danielle no longer wore her underclothes when she bathed in the river. In the presence of Autumn Woman, and only a few of the Indian women who ventured out of their lodge at this early hour, much of her shyness had disappeared.

Once the two women returned to their lodge, it seemed that not a moment passed when Autumn Woman was not pointing out something in the lodge to Danielle and repeating its name. It was not long before Danielle began to recognize words, then whole sentences, as the woman spoke while sitting next to her fire and doing her beadwork. Autumn Woman was the type of person who talked continuously.

From the second day of her captivity, Danielle had worn a doe-hide dress, and though it was a bit large on her, she had willingly given up her torn and dirty gown for the clean article of clothing. As the days passed, she watched for any sign of Penny, hoping that she and the other young woman would be able to form some plan for escaping the Indian village.

Two weeks passed after Danielle's arrival at the Sioux village before Wind Dancer came once again to Autumn Woman's lodge. It was early in the evening when he arrived with a parfleche of deer meat, a red trade blanket for Autumn Woman's use, and a small otter pouch containing an assortment of pony beads.

Danielle's turquoise eyes glanced at their visitor before she hurriedly lowered them back to the piece of rabbit fur that she was making into a moccasin according to Autumn Woman's instructions. Not a day had passed when Danielle had not thought about the large warrior. During the first few days of living with Autumn Woman, she worried that Wind Dancer would return for her and demand that she now live in his lodge; but with the passage of time, this fear lessened. Autumn Woman spoke in praising terms whenever she said Wind Dancer's name. Danielle had learned that he was the chief of the village. She was not sure why Red Fox had given her to the other warrior, but she was being treated well in Autumn Woman's lodge, so she didn't care about his reasons. Nervously, she plucked at the sinew thread where she had made a mistake in her sewing. Listening to the conversation between Wind Dancer and Autumn Woman, she tried to make out familiar words.

"Have you done as I instructed, Autumn Woman? Have you been teaching Silver Dove the ways of the people?" As when he had first entered the lodge, Wind Dancer's dark gaze was drawn toward the woman sitting upon the fur at the edge of Autumn Woman's fire. He watched as the firelight played within the strands of hair lying freely down her back; again he was blessed with the thought that he had never seen such beauty before. For the past days, he had deliberately stayed away from Autumn Woman's lodge. He had wanted time to consider this woman who had been brought among his people, time in which to consider this gift that the Great Spirit had delivered to him. He had heard much talk about the people of the silver-haired woman during these days. Some of the women claimed that each morning when she went to bathe at the river with Autumn Woman, Wi sent his blessings from the sky down upon her, and that his warm rays of life caressed her and enhanced her pale beauty. Looking at her now, Wind Dancer had no doubt why these stories were circulating through the village.

Eagerly Autumn Woman nodded her head, her thick gray braids jumping up and down upon her sagging breasts. "Silver Dove is very smart, Wind Dancer. She learns fast. She is much like my second daughter, the one who went to the sky people shortly after she joined with Boy Panther. This one takes much in with her strange-colored eyes, and keeps much to herself."

"That is good, Autumn Woman. You are a good teacher. I would see that you bring her to the buffalo dance. Perhaps you and Silver Dove would join in on the buffalo hunt." Until this moment, Wind Dancer had not considered asking the old woman to join in on the hunt, but looking upon Silver Dove, he knew that he would not enjoy thoughts of leaving her behind. In the back of his mind was the threat that Red Fox might try to reclaim the woman as his own, or perhaps she would find some means to escape.

Autumn Woman eagerly nodded her head at the invitation to join in on the buffalo hunt. It had been some time since she had participated in such an event. With her husband and both daughters having joined the sky people, she had never thought that she would have the opportunity to feel needed again. But now, with another daughter to care for, and one which her chief was obviously interested in, she felt the blood rushing through her veins as she had many winters past. "My daughter and I will go on this buffalo hunt, Wind Dancer." For the first time, she publicly acknowledged Danielle as her adopted daughter.

Wind Dancer gave the old woman a large grin. Danielle looked in their direction and caught sight of his handsome features, and his dark gaze sparkling with good humor.

"May I speak with your daughter for a few minutes, Autumn Woman?" Wind Dancer had always been respectful of the elders of the village, and to him, Autumn Woman deserved much respect. She had willingly given Silver Dove a home and was teaching her the ways of the people. She deserved the respect of a mother, which surprisingly she had claimed to be to the pale-haired woman. If she did not wish him to speak with Silver Dove, he would wait for a better evening to approach her.

Autumn Woman had no intention of refusing Wind Dancer. She had claimed the young woman as her daughter and had offered her the protection of her lodge. She would not allow any warrior to dishonor Silver Dove, and Wind Dancer knew this well. By asking permission to speak to her daughter, he had signified respect not only to her but also to Silver Dove. It would be a high honor in this Oglala village to be mother-in-law to Chief Wind Dancer! "You may sit by my fire and speak with my daughter, Wind Dancer."

Wind Dancer had gone over in his mind what he would say to Silver Dove when he came to Autumn Woman's lodge this evening. Leaving the Indian woman's side as she pretended to be busy sorting through the pony beads, he slowly made his way to the center fire. As Silver Dove's head rose once again from the work in her lap, he was at a loss to say the words that he had prepared. Her fair beauty held him spellbound. His dark gaze traveled over the wide, azure-colored, gold-rimmed eyes, and noticed the shapely, wing-tipped brows. Her nose was narrow, with a slight tilt at the end that lent an appeal as his glance lowered over the creamy-smooth cheeks and settled upon the berry-red, softly pouting lips. He had to restrain the impulse to reach out and run a long finger over those tempting morsels. Her hair, which had been unbraided earlier, fell over her shoulders and down her back below her waist, and now it shimmered with a softly spiraling texture. Drawing in a deep, ragged breath, Wind Dancer lowered himself to sit a small distance from her. Silently he picked up the small beaded bag that hung from a leather tie at his waist. As Danielle watched, he pulled out a pair of silver bracelets that had been fashioned in the design of twin thunderbirds, their eyes sparkling with gold nuggets.

Looking at Wind Dancer, and the gift he was holding out to her, Danielle was not sure what was expected of her.

With a soft smile upon his sensual lips, Wind Dancer stretched out a hand and pulled Danielle's into his own. With a simple movement, he slipped the bracelets over her wrists. "These nuggets sparkle as Wi does in the sky, and who feeds your beauty," he softly stated. Danielle understood only half of what he'd said to her, but she felt a blush staining her cheeks from his close perusal.

"Taté Wacípi." The warrior stated his name and pointed to his broad chest. Anxiously he waited for the young woman's response.

Danielle knew that she had nothing to fear from this powerful-looking man. Softly her lips tilted back as she repeated the name "Wind Dancer," her eyes sparkling as she looked across the fire and into his handsome face.

Wind Dancer felt the air leave his lungs with the sound of her voice filling his ears. His name fell upon him as though a lilting caress. "You will accompany Autumn Woman to the buffalo dance." With this, he rose to his feet and turned away from Autumn Woman's fire. He did not say another word as he pushed aside the entrance flap of the lodge and stepped through. The vision of Silver Dove sitting by the fire lingered in his mind as he made his way back to his own tepee.

Autumn Woman chuckled to herself as she watched the chief leave her lodge, and turning to her daughter, she saw a look that bespoke her lack of understanding of the ways of men and the ways of her people. Silver Dove would learn all in due time, the old woman told herself with some humor.

The following day, the entire village began to make preparations for the buffalo dance, which would be held that evening. The ceremony would be held with the hopes of seeking the blessing of the Great spirit for those who would participate in the buffalo hunt. That afternoon Autumn Woman presented Danielle with a soft, doe-hide gown that she had been painstakingly beading and quilling during the previous week. Since the night Wind Dancer had come to Autumn Woman's lodge and the old woman had declared Silver Dove to be her adopted daughter, she had insisted Danielle call her the Sioux word for mother.

Looking down at the beaded gown and moccasins that Autumn Woman had presented her, Danielle shyly responded, *"Pilamaya, Iná."*

Autumn Woman clicked her tongue loudly and grinned, showing her missing front teeth. "You are an old woman's good daughter, Silver Dove." She nodded her gray head, and when Danielle took off the hide dress that was a little big on her and pulled on the beautiful gown that Autumn Woman had worked so hard on, the old woman anxiously fussed over her.

The dress was a much better fit than the other. Autumn Woman was known among her people to be a fine dressmaker. She had fashioned the dress to enhance the young woman's slender figure. There was heavy beadwork down the arms and along the fringed edges of the bottom. Across the breasts she had sewn red-dyed porcupine quills and had left fringed ties of beads dangling from each end. Most of the beadwork was done in different shades of blue and turquoise because of Silver Dove's eyes, as was the beadwork on the soft, rabbit-hide moccasins.

For the buffalo dance, Autumn Woman had made Silver Dove a headband with beadwork done in white glass beads, except for the turquoise design of a thunderbird in the center. Danielle's hair was left unbound, and having been washed at the river that morning, it curled softly down her back in a shimmering, white-silver cloud.

Danielle had no idea what to expect from the evening, and when the hour came to join the rest of the villagers, she stayed close to Autumn Woman. She had not been abused by any of these people, but she had not had very much contact with anyone other than Autumn Woman thus far. Each day they passed women going to and from the river, but at these times, the older woman was always at her side. She remembered her arrival in the village and the threatening way some of the women had shaken sticks at her and Penny. She would not take any chances this night. She walked along with Autumn Woman toward the large, central fire that some of the braves had built for the ceremony.

Most of the villagers were already standing around the large fire. The scouts had brought the news back to the village the afternoon before that a large herd of buffalo was traveling southwest, and the excitement throughout the entire village was high with the prospect of fresh meat and plenty of hides. Before the ceremony began, an elder, respected man of the tribe, who had dressed for the occasion in all of his finery, mounted his horse and circled the outer edge of the village, singing the buffalo ceremony dance song:

"Many buffalo, I hear,
Many buffalo, I hear,
They are coming now,
They are coming now,
Sharpen your arrows,
Sharpen your knives!"

Looking around at the colorful participants of the ceremony, Danielle saw that many of the young braves wore costumes signifying the buffalo. They wore head pieces of buffalo hide that drew over their faces, sported buffalo horns and a long buffalo tail that descended from the head piece to the ground. Their ankles and wrists were decorated with buffalo hide which had been adorned with tinkling brass bells. Each man held a weapon, and before the shaman began the blessing ceremony, they grouped together and danced in praise of the mighty *tatanka.*

With the finish of the dance, Wicasa Wakán, the holy man of the village, began to call for the blessings of Wakán Tanka upon the ceremony. The aged shaman sat crosslegged upon Maka—the earth, and mother of all things. A small fire had been built before him, and he periodically threw sweetgrass and cedar into the flames. Fanning the incense upon himself and then to the four directions, he lovingly unwrapped the tribe's sacred medicine bundle. Fanning a branch of sweetgrass over the bundle with great respect and reverence, he drew forth an ancient pipe. The power that it held caused the old man to tremble, and those standing around Medicine Wolf had no doubt of the strong spirits at work throughout the village that night.

The handle of the pipe was made from the leg bone of a buffalo, the bowl from red pipestone. With great devotion, Wicasa Wakán filled the pipe bowl with kinnikinnick—Indian tobacco, made from willow bark. Lighting it with a branch of sweetgrass, he drew deeply. Slowly he exhaled and held the pipe above his head, calling on Wi—the sun, which ruled the world. Again he drew upon the pipe and exhaled, this time calling to Skan—the sky, the source of power. Next to Maka—the earth—and finally to Inyan—the rock, the protector of households. All these powers were evoked to bestow their blessings on the ceremony, and to touch the hunters who would leave the village the following morning to seek the *tatanka.*

With the finish of Medicine Wolf's prayers, the villagers began to dance and rejoice in thanksgiving over the upcoming buffalo hunt. A group of women formed a circle around the large fire and began to sway and shuffle their feet to the tempo of a drumbeat that sounded throughout the village. Watching the women dance, Danielle noticed Penny standing alone at the edge of the crowd of onlookers.

Leaving Autumn Woman's side, Danielle hurriedly made her way to the other young woman. This was the first time she had seen Penny since they'd arrived in the village. "Penny," she called aloud as she neared her. As the young woman turned her head, Danielle thought she saw fear in her eyes.

Penny looked her friend over from the top of her head with the beautiful beaded headband holding her long, pale curls back, to her moccasined feet. "Danielle, my God, you look just like one of them, except for that hair of yours!"

There was both anger and jealousy in Penny's tone, and for the time being Danielle ignored her comment. "Have you been treated well, Penny? I've been worried about you. I thought that, perhaps, we could plan some kind of escape together." These last words were spoken in a low whisper.

"Escape!" Penny pronounced the word as though it were totally alien to her.

"Are you all right, Penny?" For the first time, Danielle gave the other young woman a long, hard look. She appeared far thinner than last she had seen her, and she was still wearing the same tattered gown she had arrived in. It was plain that Penny was not faring well in the Indian village.

"Am I all right?" Penny repeated the question, her brown eyes hard as flint as they locked with Danielle's. "I guess you could say that life is better for me now. Instead of having to give my body to every brave in Red Fox's band, like the first night we arrived in this savage village, I only had to service two of his braves, and the bastard himself, this evening before being allowed to leave his lodge!" She spat out the words as though they were vile within her mouth.

Danielle gasped aloud at her bitter confession. "The baby?" was all she could get out. Never had she imagined that life would be so hard for Penny in this village.

"I lost the baby that first night. I was then sent to a small lodge near the river, with hardly any food, until my bleeding stopped. These heathens believe that a woman has great medicine, or power, when she bleeds. Can you imagine that? I can't imagine any woman having any power where these savages are concerned!"

Danielle's heart ached for the woman and her loss. She could not imagine what Penny was going through each day. Her own life, by comparison, was worry-free. Though she felt guilty with the thought, after all Penny had been forced to suffer, she could not help thanking God that Wind Dancer had taken her away from Red Fox! "We must get together and plan an escape from here!" she anxiously entreated.

Before either young woman could speak more about escaping, Autumn Woman glimpsed Danielle across from the fire and hurried to her side. "No talk now! No talk! Time to dance!" She pulled her away from Penny's side and toward the dancers. Autumn Woman did not want her adopted daughter around the white woman who belonged to Red Fox. It was better for Silver Dove that she stay away from the other *wasicun winyan,* and spend her time learning the Sioux ways.

"Who is that old hag, your mother or something?" Penny called aloud as the old woman began to drag Danielle from her side.

"She seems to think she is! I think she has adopted me," Danielle called back, but was soon standing next to Autumn Woman as the circle of women danced around the fire.

Danielle had done little dancing in her past, and the dance of these Sioux women was far different from any thing she had ever seen before. But soon, with Autumn Woman clicking her tongue and grinning at her side, she joined in with the lighthearted movements by swaying her body and taking small steps to the right.

It was not until the finish of the next dance that Danielle caught sight of Wind Dancer. He was standing with a group of braves, and when she looked in his direction, his ebony gaze locked upon her face. Instantly, Danielle felt her features flushing. She turned her head back toward Autumn Woman and the pair of elderly Indian women they had been talking to. After a few minutes, she dared another look in the handsome warrior's direction. She saw a young Indian woman with long, inky-black hair standing next to Wind Dancer. Her slender hand lay against his forearm in a possessive, familiar manner as she spoke to him in low tones.

"That one called Spring Lilly," Autumn Woman grunted as she noticed where her daughter's attention had been diverted. "Chief Wind Dancer does not like her. Spring Lilly is too proud to make a good wife!" She had noticed how the Indian maiden was hanging on to Wind Dancer, and made an effort to reassure Danielle that another woman did not hold their chief's attention in matters of the heart.

Feeling Wind Dancer's dark regard, Danielle quickly turned her head away from the couple. It did not matter to her if the man spoke to another woman, and allowed that woman to drape herself all over him in public.

The two older women who were talking to Autumn Woman gave their admiring attention over to Danielle's dress. Danielle tried to concentrate on the Indian words as they hurriedly spoke in praise of Autumn Woman's beadwork. Danielle had always been a quick learner. She had learned how to read and write at an early age. Since living in Autumn Woman's lodge, she had made a real effort to learn the Sioux tongue. Though she did not plan to be in the village for long, she was not one to waste the time she had, so she paid close attention to everything that Autumn Woman taught her. Who knew? Perhaps what she learned in the Sioux village would aid her in the future.

Danielle felt a presence behind her, and as the three women halted their conversation, she slowly turned to find Wind Dancer standing behind her and smiling warmly at the women next to her.

"I am indeed honored to be standing before such a group of beautiful women." He grinned at Autumn Woman and the older women, his eyes coming back to rest upon Silver Dove. His dark regard swept over her in a single glance as the beating of his heart intensified. This was the most beautiful woman he had ever gazed upon! In her Sioux clothing, and with her glorious hair held back with a beaded headband, in his eyes, she was of the people; in truth, a daughter of his tribe.

Danielle understood some of his words, and as his dark eyes stilled upon her, she felt the heat of a blush staining her cheeks. Autumn Woman clicked her tongue loudly, and grinned knowingly at the two women at her side. "You flatter these old women with words best kept for younger maidens, Wind Dancer."

"Age is a matter of the heart. In my youth, I remember each of you as young and beautiful. That image has not been swept from my heart." Wind Dancer's glance held the three older women and his smile widened as he viewed the blushes that stained their cheeks.

"It is too bad that all young warriors are not as respectful as our chief." One of the women at Autumn Woman's side grinned. It had been some time since she had been reminded of her beauty as a young woman.

Wind Dancer thanked the woman for her kind words before his regard returned to Autumn Woman. "If it pleases you, Autumn Woman, I would ask Silver Dove to walk with me." He did not turn his gaze back to the young woman with the pale hair, but instead, his gaze held upon Autumn Woman as he awaited her answer.

"My daughter would be pleased to walk with

you, Chief Wind Dancer." Autumn Woman felt her pride grow with the request that was asked in front of her friends. Turning toward Danielle, she nodded her gray head as though her word was final.

Understanding his words, and also Autumn Woman's answer, Danielle felt her backbone stiffen. Why should she walk with this man? She was perfectly content to remain with the women!

"Would you like to walk with me this night, Silver Dove?" Wind Dancer must have sensed her feelings, for he now ignored the women, his dark gaze awaiting her answer.

Everyone seemed to be standing and waiting expectantly for her answer—everyone except the young maiden called Spring Lilly, whom Danielle caught sight of from the corner of her eye. She was standing a small distance away, and her lovely features were marred with a dark frown as she stared at Wind Dancer's back. Maybe it was the challenge which she viewed in the other woman's eyes that made her agree to walk with Wind Dancer. Slowly, she nodded her head. As she stepped away from the group with Wind Dancer at her side, the maiden's stony stare conveyed a warning.

The angry glare in Spring Lilly's dark eyes followed the couple as they walked away from the bright light of the central fire. As raw, burning jealousy leaped in her heart, the young woman considered following Wind Dancer and the *wasicun winyan.* Good sense finally won out, and knowing that Wind Dancer would not be pleased at such interference in his personal life, Spring Lilly could only grit her teeth as she clenched her fists at her sides. Seeing Red Fox near the fire, Spring Lilly slowly made her way to his side. An inviting smile curved her lips, even though jealous tension filled her every fiber. Wind Dancer would one day be hers! The *wasicun winyan* would learn to stay away from the man Spring Lilly claimed as her own!

Wind Dancer silently led Silver Dove away from the noise and the crowd around the central fire. He led her to the portion of the village that was opposite the river. He halted his steps at the foot of a small hill, which overlooked the entire valley floor. Taking her hand into his own, he silently began the short climb up the trail that would take them to the top of the hill.

It was a breathtakingly beautiful night, with a multitude of stars overhead and a full moon to enhance the picturesque setting of the Indian village spread out across the valley. A soft sigh escaped Danielle's lips at the sight.

Expanding his arms in a wide arch, Wind Dancer spoke softly, his voice filled with love and pride for all that they were now surveying. "Behold, *wicoti mitawa*—my village."

"You are indeed a very lucky man, Wind Dancer," Danielle said just as softly. She was unable to remember a time in her own life when she had ever known such pride in anything. The short time she had spent in this village, she had come to realize that these Indian people had a simple lifestyle, and seemed to be very content with it. They did not seem to have the confusion of everyday decisions that had filled her own life while she'd lived with her aunt and uncle.

Wind Dancer was not lost to the touch of sadness in her voice, and looking down at her now, he wondered at her thoughts. "Are you happy here in my village, Silver Dove?" His words were spoken in English.

Danielle's head instantly swung around as she stared at him in total disbelief. "You speak English!" Her words were accusatory.

Wind Dancer smiled, showing straight white teeth. "When I was a boy, my father sent me to his sister's tribe to the north. There, I met a white man who ran a trading post. His name was Josh Kingsman. He taught me the *wasichu's* ways, and language."

"But why on earth didn't you tell me this from the beginning? Why have you forced me to learn the language of the Sioux when you can speak English?" This came to her as a stunning surprise. Her first thought was that she could ask him to release her and return her to her aunt and uncle without fear that he wouldn't know what she was saying!

"I wished for you to learn something of my people's ways, as I learned of the *wasichu.*"

"But why would you want that? I don't wish to stay in your village. I want to be returned to the wagon train!"

"Have you been treated unkindly among my people?" He studied her thoughtfully, understanding her desire to return to her own people but having his own desire to keep her at his side. He reminded himself that it would take time for her to adjust to the ways of the Sioux.

Looking into his handsome features, she felt a silent tear slip from her turquoise eye. "Autumn Woman has been kind," she stated truthfully, but thinking about Penny and remembering the terrible abuse the girl had revealed, she could not help wondering when it would be her turn to receive the same brutal treatment. "You have to release me and Penny! If you don't wish to return us to the wagon train because you fear the consequences of such an action, you need only give us a horse to share between us. We will find our own way!" Her words were a desperate plea.

Reaching out a long, tanned finger, Wind Dancer gently wiped away the moisture from her cheek. "Come and sit with me, Silver Dove, and we will talk." As he took her hand into his own, he felt her resistance to be drawn away with him to the tall pine that grew not far from where they now stood. He softly entreated, "You have nothing to fear from me, Silver Dove."

Sit and talk with him! I have nothing to fear! This man was the leader of a tribe of Indians! The leader of those who had so cruelly used Penny! Danielle had been unaware, until this very moment, how much Penny's revelation had affected her. Even as he drew her along with him, she reaffirmed the thought that she and the other girl had to get away from this Indian village!

Approaching the pine tree, Wind Dancer sat upon the ground crosslegged, and still holding Danielle's hand, he gently pulled her to the ground next to him. A few silent minutes passed before he spoke again. "I will tell you of the vision that Wakán Tanka gifted me with when I was no more than a boy of fourteen summers. I have told few of this vision and this day in my life. My father, who lives now with the sky people, and Medicine Wolf, listened to all that I saw and heard that day, and they helped me to determine the power of my vision and its meaning."

Danielle listened silently, and wondered why he would wish to share the event of his vision day with her. As he spoke she prepared in her mind what pleas she could make for her own release.

"Medicine Wolf instructed me to go to the same *hanbelachia*—vision hill—that my grandfather had gone to years before when he was chief of the people and had been blessed with a mighty vision. Upon this *hanbelachia,* I sat for four days and four nights, without food or drink. My inner spirit was purified for the vision that was to come. That first night, I burned sage grass, and with the sage smoke, I drove away all evil forces. Scattering kinnikinnick to the four directions, I began to sing the song of welcome to the Great Spirit, *Hee-ay-hee-ee, hee-ay-hee-ee.*

"It was on the fourth day that I felt my spirit lifted toward the star path, and there among the beauty of the heavens, I was surrounded by wakinyan—the sacred thunderbirds of my people. I danced upon the wind made by their great wings, and I was blessed as they, each in turn, told me of the great wisdom of the mighty chiefs of the Oglala in days long past. They told me the secrets of creation, and about the first man and first woman. They spoke of the discovery of the mighty beast on four legs—the horse—by chief Pale Quiver. They shared with me the strength of my ancestors, and the wisdom that helped them to protect the people, and to lead them through the harsh winters. They told me all of this to prepare me for the day when my father would one day travel up the star path and join the ancestors, and I would become chief of my people."

As he paused, Danielle silently nodded her head, not knowing if she believed a single word of what he was telling her but not daring to object. To herself, though, she thought, *Dancing upon the wind made by the sacred thunderbirds wings, indeed!*

As Wind Dancer turned the bracelets on her wrists, his dark eyes looked deeply into hers as he continued, "With the finish of these blessings, I was once again lowered to my fire by the wakinyan. I kept my eyes shut, rejoicing in such a mighty vision. When I opened my eyes, I found that my vision was not at an end. Through the smoke of my fire, a silver dove came to me. This dove had the image of a girl-woman. The words she spoke to my heart marked my future."

He did not have to finish. Danielle felt her heartbeat still, her breath catch in her throat. She knew what he would say next. It was her image that he'd viewed in the face of the dove. He had named her Silver Dove because of his vision of the girl-woman.

"The image that I looked upon that day, in the form of a dove, had the same turquoise eyes rimmed with gold as your own, Silver Dove. Medicine Wolf had been unsure of the meaning of the dove's image in my vision, but he knew that the girl-woman would one day come into my future. The moment Red Fox brought you before me, I knew the Great Spirit had blessed me. You are the completion of my life circle, Silver Dove."

Danielle looked at him as though not understanding what he was talking about. *The completion of his life circle?*

Wind Dancer knew that all this was strange to her and she was confused, but he continued, "This is the reason why I took you to Autumn Woman's lodge that first day. I wanted you to learn the language and customs of my people."

"You can't mean that you are going to force me

to stay here?" Danielle feared the worst with his words, and as her wide eyes looked into his handsome features, the crucial question passed through her mind: Would she ever see her aunt and uncle again?

"Wakán Tanka brought you to my village, Silver Dove. It is meant that we should share our life paths together." Wind Dancer read the desperation in her beautiful eyes, and tried to say something that would make her understanding easier.

Danielle jerked her hands free from his, and quickly jumped to her feet. "It was Red Fox who brought me here to your village, not your god! He stole me away from my loved ones; from the life I wanted! My entire life has been ruined because of him, and now you!" The outburst broke from her lips upon a sob, and turning from him, she thought of only running away, escaping this Indian chief and this nightmare that had been thrust upon her.

Wind Dancer rose to his full height, and being much quicker than she, within seconds he was holding her by her forearms. As she struggled against his hold, he turned her around to face him. Something she had said had caught his attention, and as he felt an instant stab of fear lance through his heart, he softly questioned, "Did you leave behind on this wagon train the one you would share your heart with?"

Danielle pulled away from him, and brushed aside the tears that were falling without letup. Looking into his intense dark gaze, she was forced to answer him. "The man I was going to marry was on the wagon train, if that is what you want to know." It was rather strange to Danielle, but at the moment, she could hardly draw forth Samuel's image.

Wind Dancer looked deeply into the turquoise eyes, as though delving deeply into her mind to reveal all that he wished to know. "You do not answer the question that I ask of you, Silver Dove. Is this one that you were to join with, the one that you would share your heart with throughout this life path and beyond?"

"Where lies the difference? I was supposed to wed Samuel, and now my life has been utterly ruined!"

"The difference is here inside your breast." Wind Dancer placed his large hand lightly against the swell of her breasts. "At times, we men and women can be strange creatures, who play foolish games with our lives if we are not directed by the hand of the Great Spirit. There is a difference if your heart is not filled with love for this one that you were to join with; this one you call Samuel."

Danielle desired only to break away from his touch. It was as if he could see and feel into her very soul. "I don't know!" she at last cried out. "I am not sure what I feel for Samuel!" She remembered how she had berated herself for not fully appreciating her life and her plans for the future when she had first been captured by Red Fox and his braves. She tried to tell herself that, if given the opportunity again, she would be content to wed Samuel and become a farmer's wife, with her joy in life being the children that she and her husband would have together. Was this enough to say that she loved Samuel Taylor?

Wind Dancer saw the turmoil she was in. Tenderly, he reached up and trailed his fingers through the gossamer tresses that curled around her face.

"Then you should learn your heart, Silver Dove. It is an easy thing. You must speak with your inner spirit, and discover for yourself what your heart feels." With this, he gently pulled her up against his broad chest. His one hand lightly rested upon the small of her back as he held her tenderly against him. His other hand gently drew her chin upward to be met with his face lowering toward her.

Realizing what he was about to do, Danielle had an impulse to bolt away from him. She had been kissed in the past and had found no great pleasure in the act. She did not relish the thought of this Indian chief kissing her now! Her hands rose up from her sides, and placing them against his chest, she tried to push away from him.

Wind Dancer was not to be pushed aside; he would have his way. As though her movements were ineffectual caresses, he slanted his lips over hers. Within seconds all fear fled her, and her own hands eased. Instead of pushing against his chest, she clutched the heavily fringed material of his buckskin shirt. His mouth moving over hers was a tender assault as he seductively traced his tongue over the delicate contours of her lips and caressed the heated tip of her tongue.

Deep within the very foundation of her being, Danielle felt a swirling sensation igniting. She clung to him, feeling his great strength encircling her, the pressure of his mouth intoxicating her. When she felt the branding flame of his tongue probing the softness of her lips and caressing her tongue, a soft moan escaped the back of her throat.

Wind Dancer desired nothing more than to lower her to the ground and sate the burning passion that was racing feverishly through his loins.

With a will that had been curbed with discipline throughout his life, he slowly drew his mouth away. He did not want to take this woman for only one night. He wanted her to stand at his side throughout this life path. She was that part of his soul that he had waited for since he first became a man. He would not take her here upon this hill, then afterward be witness to the disappointment and hurt upon her lovely features.

"Why did you stop?" Danielle questioned upon a soft sigh, her hands still clutching his shirt as though she needed his support in order not to fall to the earth in a trembling pool at his feet.

"Why did you first resist my kiss?" Wind Dancer asked instead of answering, with the hopes that he would be able to cool down his own ardor.

"I didn't know a kiss could be like that," she confessed.

A wide smile pulled his lips back. "Did your Samuel not give you such pleasure?"

Without a second thought about lying, Danielle shook her head. "I never imagined a kiss could feel like that." Samuel's kisses had left her feeling mauled and upset. They had been nothing like the tender assault she had just experienced.

"You did not know that the joining of lips could feel so pleasurable, because you did not join yours with Wind Dancer before," Wind Dancer said, and grinned. He knew that the one she called Samuel had not touched her heart. There was still a chance for him to teach her that she belonged at his side. "We should return to the dancing before Autumn Woman comes to look for you, Silver Dove," Wind Dancer stated instead of obliging her with another kiss. Though he would have liked nothing more than to hold her in his arms, he knew that there would be time for that in the future. For now, he wished to win her trust and her friendship; more would come later.

Chapter Seven

The taste of Wind Dancer's lips beneath her own was a powerful elixir. Sighing softly, Danielle wrapped her slender arms around his neck and drew him closer. She was the one who had initiated this kiss, and sighing, she ran her moist, heated tongue between his parted lips.

"Silver Dove, wake up!" The sound of Autumn Woman's voice intruded upon her sleep.

Danielle moaned softly, lost within the warm folds of her dream images. Hearing her name called, she pressed closer toward the large warrior, still able to feel his strength as he held her tenderly against his chest.

"Wake up, daughter, and eat! Today we leave on the buffalo hunt. No time for Silver Dove to lie on her sleeping pallet and dream the day away!"

Danielle jerked herself fully awake as Autumn Woman's words intruded into her sleep. Feeling the warmth of a blush staining her cheeks, she pretended to be still sleeping, in order to regain her composure, but the old woman would give her no peace.

"The whole tribe is already awake, but Autumn Woman's daughter sleeps on! Families are getting ready to go on the hunt, but Autumn Woman's daughter still sleeps!"

"All right, enough!" Danielle began to pull herself from beneath the bundle of furs that she had snuggled into last night.

"Speak Sioux, daughter. Autumn Woman does not understand the words of the *wasichu.*"

Watching the old woman bundling up her belongings, Danielle softly apologized to her in the Sioux tongue. This woman had been kind to her by taking her into her lodge and offering her protection. Danielle had no intention of being disrespectful toward her.

Autumn Woman smiled widely at the apology. "My new daughter is good to this old mother." Walking away from Danielle, she began to tie her furs and sleeping couch together. "Time for Silver Dove to eat and then help pack up the lodge."

"Pack up the lodge?" These words caught Danielle's full attention.

Clicking her tongue loudly and nodding her gray head, Autumn Woman excitedly explained, "Many suns will pass before the hunters find buffalo. We will need a lodge to sleep in and keep warm."

Danielle would soon learn that an entire Indian village could be packed up and ready to move in a few hours. For the moment, she was confused by the novel idea of packing up one's home and going off on a buffalo hunt. "But how will we carry the lodge, *Iná?*"

Once again the loud clicking noise made by Autumn Woman's tongue touched Danielle's ears. "Wind Dancer brought two fine horses for the buffalo hunt. They are outside the lodge, waiting for my daughter to eat and help pack up the lodge on their backs."

With the mention of Wind Dancer's name, Danielle felt instant heat return to her cheeks. Quickly turning her head, she hoped that the old woman's sharp eyes had not noticed. Pulling on her dress, she made her way to the hot coals of the pit fire and took up the bowl of food Autumn Woman had set aside for her breakfast.

Autumn Woman's eyes were quick to notice the shade of pink that graced Danielle's cheeks after her comment about their chief. Her grin widened. She remembered the look upon her daughter's face when Wind Dancer had brought her back to the dancing the night before. Wind Dancer had told her that first night he had brought the young woman to her lodge that this was the woman who would become his life mate. She had little doubt that eventually this would be the way of things. Given time, their handsome chief would win the girl over.

Autumn Woman hurriedly bustled about the inside of the lodge, stuffing her belongings into parfleche bags and directing Danielle on how to help her dismantle the lodge poles and hide covering so that everything, including the lodge, could be tied atop the travois that Autumn Woman's pony would pull. Autumn Woman mounted the pony, assuring Silver Dove that she was not too ancient to travel on horseback. After she saw the frown on Danielle's features, she added that, if she grew tired, she would ride on the travois while Silver Dove led the pony.

The horse which Wind Dancer had brought for Danielle to ride was a beautiful Appaloosa mare, the animal traditionally associated with the Nez

Percé Indians. Wind Dancer had acquired her when he and his band of warriors had attacked a Crow war party. The Indian saddle had a wooden frame covered with rawhide, and a high pommel and cantle, both of which were covered with soft buckskin. It also had hide and cloth pendants beaded in the Oglala fashion, with Wind Dancer's vision signs. The bridle had a Spanish bit and a rawhide headstall, which also were beaded and painted. There was a beaded pendant in the design of a silver dove, which had been sewn to the bridal and rested upon the mare's forehead, below her ears. There was also a Sioux horse collar, of buckskin and red trade cloth, which was embellished with blue and silver beads. The overall effect was breathtaking, and as Danielle placed her foot in the beaded rawhide stirrup, then settled into the comfortable saddle, she could not remember a time in her life when she had ridden such a beautiful horse.

There had been a flurry of frenzied activity since daybreak for the fifty or so families that were going on the buffalo hunt. At last, everyone was ready, and the long procession began to slowly move out of their summer valley. The scouts went ahead of the main body of travelers, the flanks of the people guarded by the warriors in case of an enemy attack. In this day and time, an attack would be more apt to come from the *wasichu* blue coats than an enemy tribe.

The lively procession was a colorful mixture of warriors, women, and children, as well as a multitude of infants and elderly grandparents. There were many horse-drawn travois such as the one Autumn Woman pulled along behind her pony, and upon most rode women, old and young alike, and their small children. Many of the young women rode astride like Danielle, but as she gazed around, she did not see any of the women's saddles and mounts as beautifully decorated as her own. There were small boys, two and three at a time, riding a single pony, and as one such pony threw its riders to the ground, lighthearted chuckles from the adults greeted their mishap. Cradleboards were slung over pommels; the infants bobbed up and down to the gentle sway of their mother's mounts until they slept without a care in the world.

As the first day progressed, many of the young boys scampered around excitedly, shooting arrows and beating the bushes for rabbits or other small game. With the sighting of a desired animal, whoops and yells were called out as the boys overtook the game in good-natured camaraderie.

The buffalo had been sighted by the scouts miles away from the valley, and it would take several days for the large band of Indians to reach their destination. As Danielle lay on her sleeping pallet, safe within the walls of Autumn Woman's lodge that night, she reflected over the excitement of the day and the beauty she had viewed as she had watched the long line of Sioux people moving over the grasses of the prairie.

On the fourth afternoon, when the scouts excitedly reported back to the travelers that the large herd of buffalo had been sighted, the enthusiastic group quickly began to pitch their tepees and set up an encampment. That night, warriors told of buffalo hunts from days long past, and about daring feats made by warriors. As everyone sat around the open fires, the boasting and story telling continued long into the night.

It was also on this night that, for the first time since the start of the traveling, Wind Dancer sought Danielle out. He found her sitting with Autumn Woman and several other women before a low-burning fire in front of Clear Water's lodge.

Wind Dancer smiled at each woman in turn before he nodded his head in Danielle's direction. "Silver Dove, would you walk with me to the lodge of Black Bull?" His dark gaze focused upon her warmly as he added, "That is, if your mother does not mind."

Black Bull's lodge was only a few feet away from Clear Water's, and clicking her tongue softly, Autumn Woman appeared to be thinking the matter over. At last, she slowly nodded her head as she looked from their chief to her daughter.

Danielle felt her face flush as she glimpsed the wide, knowing smiles given to her by the other women. Silently, she set her sewing aside as she rose to her feet. She did have to thank him for the loan of his beautiful horse, she told herself, even though she was embarrassed at his singling her out.

Expecting her to follow him, Wind Dancer stepped away from the group of women and started toward Black Bull's lodge.

For a single minute longer, Danielle just stood there until, with a loud click of her tongue hitting the back of her teeth, Autumn Woman admonished, "Go with our chief, Silver Dove. I will be watching for your return."

Danielle had no choice but to do as she was told. Wind Dancer turned around and, witnessing her indecision, slowed his pace. Within seconds she was at his side.

Nearing Black Bull's lodge, he said, "Have you enjoyed the Spotted One, Silver Dove?"

At first Danielle was unsure what he was asking her, but she soon realized that he wanted to know how she was enjoying the mare. "She is wonderful, Wind Dancer. Thank you very much for letting me ride her." She had not known the horse's name until now, and realized that she had grown very fond of the animal in a short time. The mare was smart and had been taught to be sensitive to her rider's every wish, with just a slight pressure of her thighs.

"The Spotted One is for you to keep, Silver Dove," Wind Dancer generously offered, his ebony eyes regarding her intently as they neared their destination.

The first thought to come with his generous offer was that of escape! With a horse of her own, it should not be so complicated for her and Penny to plan their escape from the Indian village. Keeping such thoughts to herself, Danielle replied in a tone that she knew was warm and inviting, "Thank you, Chief Wind Dancer. You are very kind to me and Autumn Woman with your gifts."

Wind Dancer's smile widened when her lilting words touched his ears. "The buffalo hunt will begin at daybreak. Will you be watching from the hilltop with the other women?" He wanted this woman to watch the warriors who would swoop down from the hilltop and conquer the mighty *tatanka.* He wanted to know that she would be watching him the moment he rode down among the great herd and made his first kill.

Danielle was not sure how a hunt such as this went, or if the women were allowed to witness the assault on the large animals. She had been told by Autumn Woman that after the warriors had killed the game, the women went to the spot and skinned the hides from the large beasts; then they cut and packed the meat. "If Autumn Woman joins the women on the hilltop, then I will also."

This was good enough for Wind Dancer. Autumn Woman would not miss out on the buffalo kill. "I have thought much upon the night of the buffalo dance, Silver Dove." Wind Dancer's words were spoken in low, husky tones that went straight to claim Danielle's breath, and with instant understanding, she felt her face beginning to heat.

He was referring to the kiss they had shared the night of the buffalo dance. Before Danielle could respond to his statement, Black Bull called out a greeting from where he stood outside his lodge. Danielle sighed with relief, thankful she would not be forced to confess that she also had thought much about that night. Since that night, she had thought of little else besides Wind Dancer's lips upon her own!

Arriving at Black Bull's lodge, Danielle was treated as one of the people and warmly welcomed as Autumn Woman's adopted daughter. Pretty Quill, Black Bull's wife, welcomed Danielle with a warm smile and motioned for the other woman to join her on her furs across the lodge. Wind Dancer joined Black Bull near the fire, where the two men sat smoking Black Bull's pipe and speaking in low tones.

Pretty Quill had just finished sewing a little beaded fur hat for her two-month-old son, and having settled the hat atop his round head, she handed the baby over to Danielle while she turned to her four-year-old, Little Bent Feather, and began to tickle him. With much squealing and giggling, the little boy with warm, dark eyes and little braids down his back rolled around on the mound of furs as his mother lavished her attention upon him.

The noise from the playful antics of mother and son across the small space of the tepee drew Wind Dancer's attention, and as he watched Danielle smiling softly down at the baby in her arms, his chest swelled with an unbearable longing. To his eyes, in that moment, no other woman had ever looked so perfect with a child in her arms. In his heart, he longed for the day when she would cuddle his own child to her breasts.

The heated contact of his dark, feasting gaze drew Danielle's attention over the top of the baby's head, and as her eyes locked with his, it was as though she could read his thoughts. In her mind, she heard the words he had earlier spoken in low, husky tones: *"I have thought much upon the night of the buffalo dance, Silver Dove."* Quickly she turned her head away from his direction, but it was too late. She had felt his gaze traveling over her like a physical caress, and at that moment she felt suffocated in the lodge. What did this man want from her? Why was he making her feel these strange emotions deep inside herself! All she wanted was to be able to return to her old life.

"I really must be getting back to Autumn Woman before she misses me, Pretty Quill." She hurriedly handed the baby back to his mother and rose to her feet. As she started out of the lodge, she could feel Wind Dancer's dark gaze upon her, but she dared not look back. He was affecting her enough already—she didn't need to see the warmth she knew was there in his eyes for her.

Wind Dancer's gaze never wavered as he watched her every step. When finally she had bent her head and left through the entrance flap and Wind Dancer turned back to his friend, Black Bull was grinning widely.

"Has my friend, at last, found the one he would choose as his life mate?" Black Bull was pleased, even though the woman was a *wasicun winyan.* If his friend saw her only as Autumn Woman's adopted daughter, he also would see no more than this. He had been encouraging Wind Dancer to take a mate, and had thought that his choice would be Spring Lilly. He knew, as most in the village did, how much the Indian maiden cared for Wind Dancer. He could see that he had been mistaken. Silver Dove was very beautiful, and she had already proven to the people that she was willing to learn their ways; she had been very apt in learning the language of the people.

"I have not spoken to her about our joining together as one. I do not wish to rush her too soon. I did tell her, though, about my vision." He remembered how she had resisted his conviction that their life paths were to be joined. She had resisted his words until he had taken her into his arms and kissed her. He would not tell this close friend that part of their relationship, though, he decided.

"This woman is the silver dove from your vision?" With Wind Dancer's nodding, Black Bull now understood clearly. "I would give this advice then, my friend." He reached down and relit the pipe the two men had been sharing. "Before going to Pretty Quill's father to ask his permission for the two of us to join, I made sure that I alone held her heart. What warrior wants a woman that does not desire him as much as he does her?"

Black Bull was right; that was why Wind Dancer had tried to stay away from Silver Dove these past days. He had given her time since the buffalo dance to think about him and what they had shared that night. He had known that she had enjoyed his lips pressed against hers. He had hoped that each night, when she shut her eyes, she had seen his image in her dreams, had felt the strength in his arms, and had been awakened to the joy that the blending of their mouths had created. Listening to his friend now, he wondered if he should do more. Black Bull and Pretty Quill were happy. They also had two fine boys to show for the nights they shared together on their sleeping couch. He would listen to Black Bull's wisdom and learn the courting tricks he had used on his own wife.

Pretty Quill busied herself with her sewing as she left the two men to their conversation, but every now and then, she could not prevent the smile that crossed her lips as her husband's words reached her ears.

Chapter Eight

Long before daybreak, Medicine Wolf intoned the prayers to Wakán Tanka, ending by thanking the Great Spirit for the gift of the bountiful *tatanka* and his mate, *pte.* After the prayers, he reminded the braves, young and old alike, to remember the helpless and the old people of the tribe who had no sons to hunt for them. "Do not forget the little ones and their mothers, whose husbands have been killed in battle or while out hunting." Medicine Wolf entreated each brave to be generous of heart, and each brave, in turn, pledged a large portion of his kill to those less fortunate than themselves.

The buffalo hunt then began in earnest. The women sat on horseback or stood with the young children, waiting for the moment when they would be called to rush down the hill and help the men skin the hides and butcher the meat.

Danielle sat atop the Spotted One, nervously holding the reins and only half listening to Autumn Woman's excited chatter. Her eyes gazed upon Wind Dancer who, dressed only in a breechcloth, seemed to stand out among the braves around him as they waited to hear the cry *"Hoka hey,"* which meant to charge.

The buffalo appeared not to notice the line of warriors halfway down the hill and advancing to attack. They peacefully grazed with their backs to the Indians. When *"Hoka hey"* sounded throughout the valley, the hunters riding atop their specially trained buffalo ponies surged forward. The slightest pressure of the rider's knees directed his horse to anticipate every move of an enraged buffalo bull.

Danielle kept her eyes glued to Wind Dancer, who was at the front of the line of hunters. With an indrawn breath, she watched as he approached a huge bull buffalo from the rear. His horse was swift and had been on many buffalo hunts with his master. Circling to the side of the large, shaggy beast, Wind Dancer's mount surged forward, keeping out of range of the buffalo's horns. As he heard the twang of the bowstring, the horse swerved and turned, knowing the bull would be enraged and dangerous after being hit if the arrow did not pierce a vital spot. To Danielle's surprise, the large beast buckled to his knees and fell to his side. Wind Dancer wasted no time on the dying animal, but went on to the next.

Again and again, she saw him hit his target. In disbelief, she watched his arrow go clear through one animal then hit another, sending them both to their death. Many of the women around Danielle gave out a shrill, trilling sound of excitement after watching this miraculous feat performed by their chief.

Several young boys, about thirteen and fourteen years old, shouted out war cries as they saw the two mighty bulls falling in the dust. Throughout the rest of the hunt, they were not far from their chief as they watched and tried to imitate his every movement.

Not many of the young boys hit their mark and killed a buffalo on their first hunt. But a few did, and as the women were allowed to join in, to help butcher the beasts, the proud mothers eagerly helped their sons.

Each of the hunters had his own design and color pattern on his arrow, so it was easy to tell which hunter had killed each animal. Autumn Woman did not have a husband or a son of her own, but because Wind Dancer had been bringing meat to her lodge, she eagerly made her way to her chief's side. Dismounting, she began to help him butcher one of the bulls he had killed.

Danielle was not sure of her own role in this buffalo hunt, but dismounting near Autumn Woman's horse, she made her way to her adopted mother's side. Without instructions, Autumn Woman handed her a sharp knife. As Wind Dancer's hands stilled in his butchering and he looked at Silver Dove, she quickly bent to work alongside Autumn Woman.

"I will start on another, while you and your daughter butcher this bull." Wind Dancer straightened from his labor, his dark eyes gazing upon the crown of Danielle's glorious pale curls.

"*Han,* you were a fierce warrior this day, Wind Dancer. My daughter and I watched you from the hilltop with the other women. I am sure my daughter saw each animal you brought down," Autumn Woman boasted, and Danielle gasped aloud with embarrassment.

Wind Dancer heard the small sound coming from Silver Dove and his lips drew back in a proud smile. He had showed her that he was a mighty hunter this day. He hoped that she had seen him kill the two bulls with one arrow. Wakán Tanka was surely blessing him this day! "Without a wife and children in my lodge, much of my kill will go to the needy of the village." He wanted Silver Dove to know also of his generosity, and it couldn't hurt to mention the fact that he was in need of a mate.

"All the people of the mighty Sioux nation know of the generous heart of our chief. You will make a fine mate for the one you choose to join your side." Autumn Woman was also grinning as she looked at her daughter's bent head, while Danielle tried to appear busy, cutting away strips of raw meat.

Wind Dancer welcomed any praise the old woman was willing to offer in front of Silver Dove. Though the young woman appeared to be ignoring them, he knew she had heard everything they'd said. Tonight after a filling supper of roasted buffalo meat, he had every intention of carrying out the first part of Black Bull's instructions in courting a maiden!

"Do you have to carry on so every time you are in front of him?" Danielle threw the old lady a dark look the moment Wind Dancer had left their side.

"What is wrong with my daughter now? Chief Wind Dancer is a great hunter! Why should Autumn Woman not say words of truth?"

Danielle knew exactly what the old woman was doing, and amazingly, she believed that Wind Dancer was encouraging her. "Oh, never mind!" It would do little good for her to argue with Autumn

Woman. If she had learned nothing else during the time she had spent in the Indian woman's company, she had learned that no one could get the best of her in an argument! "Let's get this job over as soon as possible!" When they returned to the village, she would find Penny, and they would plan their escape. Now that she had a horse, they should be able to sneak out of the village in the middle of the night and ride in the direction of Fort Kearney.

"My daughter is not in a good mood. After some buffalo tongue tonight, Silver Dove will feel better toward her old mother, and Chief Wind Dancer!"

Danielle said no more, but bent her back to the work at hand. The meat was cut into strips and hunks and stacked upon the travois on the backs of the horses. Once back in camp, the women would cut long poles and forked sticks to make drying racks for the meat. The hides would be stretched over wood frames for scraping and tanning.

By midafternoon, most of the fun of the day had disappeared for the women, who worked without respite over the meat. There was not a portion of the buffalo that went to waste, meat being the main part of the Indians' diet. The contents of the stomach and intestines were roasted the first day and eaten, as they were full of vegetable matter and a rich source of much-needed vitamins. The meat was dried and smoked, and the fat and marrow were pounded into a paste and mixed with berries for pemmican. The hides of the buffalo were used for tepees, clothing and covers. The thick skin from the neck was dried and hardened for war shields, the neck being strong enough to turn aside an arrow or a musket ball. The sinews of the beast were used as thread for sewing, the small bones for needles. The brains were made into a paste and used as a tanning acid for hides, the hooves boiled down into glue.

Like the rest of the women, Danielle soon had clothes and arms that were thoroughly blood-stained, and as the afternoon sun beat down relentlessly and she wiped away the sweat from her brow, her forehead was smeared red. Looking at her daughter, Autumn Woman took pity upon her, though she was also filled with pride. The young woman had not uttered a word of complaint as she worked side by side with the other women. "You have done enough, Silver Dove. Why do you not go back to camp and bathe in the stream that runs through the forest?"

It was almost dusk, and as Danielle looked around, she saw that most of the men, women, and children were still hard at work. She silently shook her head at the inviting suggestion that Autumn Woman had offered.

"Do as I tell you, daughter," Autumn Woman insisted. "We are almost finished and will all be going back to camp shortly. You have given much this day. You deserve a cool bath in the stream."

"Are you sure, *Iná?* I can stay until you return to camp with the rest of the women." Danielle had never been one to turn away from a job. She did not like the idea of leaving Autumn Woman alone to finish packing the meat on the travois.

The elder woman smiled kindly upon the younger woman. It was true, Silver Dove did remind her at times of her own daughter. She was kind-hearted, even for a *wasicun winyan.* With the passage of time, Autumn Woman hoped that those of their tribe would overlook Silver Dove's pale looks and see only the goodness in her heart. "Hurry now, daughter, before you have to fight for a place in the stream after the women return to the camp." She clicked her tongue twice and grinned good-naturedly.

Nothing else needed to be said. Danielle was more than ready to leave the bloody task of cutting and packing buffalo meat. She was tired, her back ached, and she felt as though the sun had baked her right through the hide dress. The thought of the cool stream not far from camp was too much for her to resist. Wiping her hands on her skirt, she mounted the Spotted One and headed back to camp to get clean clothing from Autumn Woman's lodge.

A short time later, Danielle was walking down to the stream, and following the stream bank, she found a spot that was deep enough for her to swim in. Stripping off the bloodstained doe-hide dress and moccasins, she quickly unbraided her hair. Then taking up a handful of the yellowish stuff Autumn Woman claimed was soap, she waded out into the cool depths of the swirling stream.

After washing away the filth and grim from her hair and body, Danielle lounged around in the relaxing depths of the crystal-clear water. The thought had filtered through her mind to take this opportunity to flee while the people were all busy with the buffalo meat. But the truth was, she was just too tired to try and escape this evening. And now that she was clean, she felt the full force of her hunger. She doubted she would have the energy to ride the mare far before being forced to rest. Wind Dancer and his braves would not have such a hindrance as sleepiness if they were tracking her. Rolling over on her back for a few minutes, she floated and looked up into the canopy of trees overhead. It had been this enjoyment that had taken her away from the wagon train and caused her capture by Red Fox in the first place. She wondered how her aunt and uncle were doing without her. Did they believe she was dead after these many weeks had passed? Had they given up on ever seeing her again? Had they gone on to Oregon believing she had perished at the hands of savages?

A large splash a short ways upstream drew her instant attention. Danielle quickly lowered her body below the water's surface. With her head the only thing showing, she looked around with some alarm. Had the rest of the band already returned to camp? If so, she hoped it was a woman and not one of the braves who had come this far downstream to bathe. To her utter surprise, she caught sight of Wind Dancer swimming toward her. "Don't come any closer!" she shouted out in English, so flustered at his appearance that she totally forgot to use the Sioux tongue.

Wind Dancer softly chuckled as he heard the desperate demand in her voice. "Why would I not wish to come closer, Silver Dove? Cannot two people share the cool depths of the stream's water?"

"Not when one of the people is a man and the other a woman!" Danielle crossed her arms over her breasts, even though that portion of her body was hidden beneath the water.

Wind Dancer was several feet away from her, and glimpsing the silvery strands of her pale hair floating atop the surface of the water, he had to exert all the force of his will not to go closer so he could reach out and feel its soft texture. Instead of falling victim to his raging desires and frighten her more, he looked into her wide turquoise eyes, then forced his words to remain light. "Is it not a natural thing among the *wasichu* for two friends to bathe together?"

"Certainly not if they are a man and a woman!" Was he implying that such things were common among his own people? If so, she had not been told of such a custom!

Wind Dancer lifted his head then tossed it backward, his long, glistening hair showering droplets of water in every direction. He was standing in waist-deep water, and his powerful chest gleamed with diamond droplets. The muscles in his arms bulged as he lightly rested hands on hips. "I thought that the white man believed the Indians to be backward in their beliefs." He spoke in English for her benefit.

"It is definitely not decent for a man and woman to bathe together, friends or not!"

"And who made up such a law as this?"

"Why . . . why . . . how do I know who makes up such laws? I only know that it is not right!"

"I am chief here, and I say it is right."

"But . . . you . . . you can't just make up any law as you go along!"

"And who is to say that I cannot?" Wind Dancer smiled warmly upon her, and for the first time that day, he won a small smile from the woman of his heart.

"Who is here to say anything against what you say, indeed!" Danielle murmured under her breath as a small smile stole over her lips. If these people believed that it was all right to bathe together, who was she to tell them what was decent or not? She did not fully know their ways, but she did know that they were a people who were touched with all that was around them, from the earth they walked on to the sky overhead that gave them light and life. Perhaps she was the one who was out of place, but if so, it was their fault that she was here! "I was ready to go back to camp anyway. You can have the stream all to yourself, unless some other unsuspecting female comes along and agrees to bathe with you, as your friend." She could not help it, but her smile enlarged.

"There is no other female I would wish to bathe with, Silver Dove." Wind Dancer's words barely reached Danielle's ears, so low did he speak them. In an instant, though, his voice returned in challenge. "I guess, then, that it is true that the *wasicun winyan* cannot swim."

"And who told you that white women can't swim? That Josh Kingsman at that trading post, who taught you how to speak English? For if he did, he didn't know what he was talking about! There are plenty of white women who can swim, and I happen to be one of them!" She remembered, then, that Penny and her aunt were unable to swim, and she wondered if Wind Dancer had been told a partial truth. White girls did not seem to take to rivers and streams the way boys did, but Danielle had learned to swim at an early age, on her father's farm. She loved the outdoors, and had swum almost daily when the weather permitted.

"I do not believe you, Silver Dove."

"You what?" Danielle sputtered. Was he calling her a liar?

"The *wasicun winyan* do not wish to take off their layers of clothing and let Wi kiss their flesh. They are afraid of . . . what is that word?" Wind Dancer appeared to search his mind for the right

English word. "Freckles!" He grinned widely with the word.

"Freckles? You think I wouldn't learn to swim because of freckles?" Danielle pretended outrage, but she admitted that a white man could have said something like that. It was entirely possible that Wind Dancer had been given this bit of information by someone else. "I have never had any freckles, nor would I ever worry about them, or let them stop me from swimming!"

"You have a very brave heart, Silver Dove."

"Thank you," Danielle replied. She was thoroughly enjoying the light banter with this Indian in the middle of a stream, and she was entirely naked to boot!

"There is only a short time longer until dark, Silver Dove, and we will have to join the rest of the people back at camp. Why do we not swim together for this time left us, since you are so brave?" Wind Dancer's ebony eyes glowed warmly as he studied each delicate feature of her face and slender throat.

Danielle knew that the proper thing for her to do was to demand that he turn away while she left the stream, dressed, and returned to camp. But her inner voice spoke softly to her, entreating her to relax and enjoy the moment. *Why not swim for a while with him, Danielle? You have to admit that he is quite handsome standing there so boldly in the water. Remember that kiss he gave you? Perhaps he might be willing to do so again if you swim with him!* How utterly outrageous her inner mind's workings could be, she scolded, for daring such ridiculous thoughts as these! With a will, she forced herself to try and think about Samuel, the man that she was supposed to be in love with—the man she was to marry!

She had no more time to think over the matter, for in the next instant, Wind Dancer dove under water and, reaching out, grabbed hold of her slender ankle. With a slight tug, he pulled her under the surface with him.

She came out sputtering water. Wind Dancer followed, and his husky laughter filled the area around the stream. "You . . . you . . .!"

Before she could say anything more, he reached out a hand and dunked her head below the water again. This time, she shoved his chest with her two feet as hard as possible and sent him backward with a large splash. In the next instant, she was swimming away from him, light laughter escaping her lips.

The minute that Wind Dancer righted himself, he caught a glimpse of a shapely hip and buttock. He felt the instant tightening in his groin. Perhaps, this hope of his, to befriend this young woman, would prove a more dangerous task than he had anticipated. He had no wish to take advantage of her; he desired only that she get to know him and relax in his company. But if the slightest glimpse of her nakedness was able to set hot blood coursing throughout his veins, he was not so sure he should have set this late afternoon swim into motion. As she reached the other side of the stream and turned to look back in his direction, he cautioned himself firmly to keep tight control over his body. He was no impulsive youth, but a man with a mission, which was to gain this woman as his own! Diving back into the water and swimming in her direction, he realized that much of his earlier carefree exuberance was now gone, but it was replaced by heated determination.

Danielle was still laughing over the setback she had caused him. It had been years since she had felt so utterly carefree. Though her aunt and uncle had meant well in raising her, they had unwittingly discouraged that part of her spirit that desired to reach out and grasp hold of life and excitement. She saw a chance to recapture a portion of the sun without being fully exposed, and she took it. As Wind Dancer drew closer, with a squeal of delight she dove back into the water's cool depths. Coming back up a few feet away in the opposite direction, she called with laughter tinging her voice, "And do you still believe that white women can't swim?"

"I will not think this again, Silver Dove. You swim like the friendly otter." He did not add that her body was far suppler and sleaker than an otter's.

For what remained of the late afternoon, the couple frolicked and played in the cool depths of the stream. Wind Dancer purposely kept his distance from her, delighting in her belief that she could outswim him. He knew that if he were close enough for his hands to touch her silken flesh, he would not be able to hold back the raging force of his desires.

Danielle had almost forgotten that she was completely naked, until Wind Dancer called their swimming to a halt. Quickly enough, she realized her predicament, wondered how she was going to get to the bank without becoming a bold display for his dark regard.

Glimpsing the worry in her turquoise eyes, Wind Dancer volunteered, "I will leave the stream first, and make sure that everyone has returned to camp. Then you will be able to take your time to dress."

He saw the relief on her features, and a small smile settled over his sensual lips. He would have given anything to reach out to her and draw her into his embrace, to let her know how much he desired her; but he refrained as the warning bell sounded again in his head. He did not want this woman for only one time, to slack his passions upon. He wanted her to stand at his side, as his woman. He could not take her before the joining ceremony. Instead of giving in to his baser needs, he turned away from her and started toward the opposite bank.

Believing that she had given him enough time to climb the bank and leave her to her privacy, Danielle threw a glance over her shoulder to make sure that she could leave the stream and regain her clothes. With the movement, her breath caught in her chest. The gold flecks that circled the turquoise of her eyes shimmered brightly, and for a few breathless seconds, Danielle looked upon the most magnificent male body she had ever seen—actually the only male body she had ever seen! He was total perfection! A fearless, godlike warrior come to life, and in those passing seconds, his fathomless dark eyes looked straight into her own as she feasted on the imprint of his body—an imprint that would stay in her mind forever! He stood, straight and proud, not an ounce of wasted flesh covering the muscular contours of his shimmering bronze torso. The first traces of moonlight stole across the damp, midnight strands of his hair, which unbound, reached to the center of his broad back. His upper arms and chest were sculpted with powerful, restrained strength, his midriff, a washboard of rippling muscles, hips and buttocks firm and tight. His hard, power-filled thighs and legs were braced apart on Mother Earth. But what drew Danielle's gleaming regard longer than the rest was the turgid length of his mighty shaft, which jutted upward from the junction of his legs. For a blinding second, she felt faint, and dropped her glance to the water swirling around her.

Flushed faced, and hardly daring to draw a breath, Danielle looked up to see if he was still standing there. But he was gone, and upon trembling legs, she made her way out of the water then quickly dressed.

Chapter Nine

Far off in the mountains the night sounds of a lone wolf could be faintly heard. Closer to the Sioux encampment, the sounds of a flute floated softly on the night breeze and circled the silent lodges. This type of flute had the power of the elk charm, and was believed to have the ability to bring a maiden to a warrior's blanket.

Wind Dancer sat with his back braced against a cottonwood, his dark eyes staring at Autumn Woman's tepee. As he blew upon the mouthpiece of the flute, which was carved into the likeness of a bird on the end where the music escaped, he envisioned Silver Dove, lying upon her sleeping pallet and hearing the message from his love song.

Autumn Woman sharply clicked her tongue at her daughter's restlessness as Silver Dove moved about on her sleeping pallet. The old woman was wise enough to know who it was outside their lodge, playing the flute. Though she kept silent, she was tired after the long day of butchering buffalo, and wished that these two young people would come to terms with the feelings they harbored for one another.

Danielle had been unusually quiet since arriving

back at camp after her bath at the stream She had not been able to chase away the sight of Wind Dancer standing so bold and masculine on the stream bank. Nor could she forget the ease with which the two of them had shared the late afternoon hour, swimming and talking. She had never felt as close to Samuel Taylor as she had to the Indian chief that day. Not only was she tormented by her thoughts of Wind Dancer, but she was plagued with guilt over her feelings of disloyalty to Samuel. The haunting music that traveled throughout the camp did nothing to ease her troubled mind. There was a passionate quality to the melody that seemed to call out to her inner spirit. She did not understand this strange effect the music had over her, and once again, she rolled from her stomach to her back trying to find some comfort. Unable to bear the noise any longer, and hearing the clicking of Autumn Woman's tongue, she sat up on her sleeping pallet. "Who is playing that flute?" she softly questioned, hoping that, with the answer, she would be able to lie back down and find sleep.

"Why does my daughter not go and see for herself who is playing the flute?" Autumn Woman snorted. "Silver Dove is moving around on her pallet, and keeping an old lady awake. Go chase the sound of the music; maybe then sleep will come!" Autumn Woman knew that Silver Dove would be safe outside her lodge. Wind Dancer wasn't far, by the sound of the music, and she certainly trusted him well enough. He had told her what his plans were for her adopted daughter, so what harm was there in the girl seeking out the one who was playing the flute? She could find out her answer for herself!

Hearing the irritation in Autumn Woman's

voice, and unable to fall asleep, Danielle did leave the lodge. Maybe a breath of fresh air would clear her mind, and enable her to put to rest her disturbing thoughts of Wind Dancer, she told herself, as she made her way through the entrance flap of the lodge.

From where he sat against the cottonwood tree, Wind Dancer was unable to mistake Silver Dove's glistening pale hair beneath the moonlight as she exited Autumn Woman's lodge. A lazy smile parted his lips as he played the flute. Indeed the flute had power. He watched as the young woman stood before the lodge in indecision. Slowly, her bare feet started to turn in his direction as she followed the sound of the music.

As Danielle drew closer to the small strand of cottonwoods, which were only a few yards away from the encampment, she could make out the figure of a lone man holding a long instrument up to his mouth. Perhaps she had made a mistake by leaving the lodge, she thought, a little belatedly. After all, no one else in the camp seemed to be bothered by the music the warrior was making; why should she be so affected? Feeling guilty about intruding upon the man's privacy, she stopped, and was about to turn around when she heard the music stop and her name being softly called.

"Silver Dove, come and join me." Wind Dancer remembered the warmth of her beautiful eyes that afternoon as they had caressed his body, and a tremor of undisciplined passion stole over his length.

"You?" Danielle instantly recognized his voice, and wondered if he were deliberately trying to torment her.

Wind Dancer smiled and set the flute down by his side. "Did you enjoy the music I was playing for you?" He did not tell her that it was a love song, whose sole purpose was to capture her heart.

"Don't you think it's a bit late for you to be out here playing your flute?" She ignored the reference that he was playing the flute for her.

Wind Dancer noticed that she stood her distance a few feet away from him. In gentle tones, he set out to lure her to his side. "Come, sit next to me, Silver Dove. I will tell you the story of the flute," he invited warmly.

The husky, masculine allure of his voice had the power to encircle her and pull her toward him, but Danielle made a valiant effort to stand her ground.

"I would never harm you in any way, Silver Dove. I but wish to tell you a story of my people." His warm tone entreated her as he saw her standing in indecision.

Her inner self reminded her, *The night of the buffalo dance he spoke similar words when he shared his vision with you. That night he shared more than his vision with you; he showed you what a real kiss was!* That wilder side of her nature tried to confuse her, and seeming to have little power to resist, she soon took the steps that brought her closer to his side. *What can a little story hurt, anyway? You certainly don't have to stay here and suffer his attentions! That is, if he tries to kiss you again!*

She was standing close enough for Wind Dancer to reach out and draw her to a sitting position at his side. For a moment, which seemed to hang on endlessly, the couple stared at one another. The warm depths of his ebony eyes searched her face and lingered upon her azure gaze.

It was Wind Dancer who at last broke the silence. "Your beauty truly astounds me, Silver Dove. The earth signs resound in your eyes, the pureness of Wi and Skan shimmer softly about you in the silver cover of your hair."

Danielle felt herself dissolving from within. "The flute!" she gasped out, grasping on to anything that could bring some order to her disheveled senses.

Wind Dancer bestowed a warm, knowing smile, understanding that these feelings she was discovering were as totally new to her as they were to him. Oh, he had had his share of willing maidens in the past; there were those who were still more than willing to lie upon his pallet. The image of Spring Lilly came to mind, but as quickly, the maiden's features fled. Unlike those he had sampled throughout his adulthood, he had never felt such an aching need each time he was in this woman's presence. It was something deeper than the need for satisfaction of the body; it was the desire for a oneness of the heart. "*Han,*" he breathed softly. "The *siyotanka.*" Picking up the instrument, he held it up where the moonlight could touch it. It was two feet long and made from the slender branch of a cedar tree. The limb had been hollowed out with a bow-string drill. The branch had been whittled into the shape of a bird with a long neck and an open beak. The bird's head had been painted the sacred vermillion color of the Sioux.

"It's very beautiful," Danielle whispered, barely able to say the words while she sat so close to Wind Dancer.

Not as beautiful as you, Silver Dove. Nothing was as beautiful as she, Wind Dancer thought to himself, but fearing that he would frighten her, he kept this thought to himself. "I will tell you the story of the first *siyotanka.*" He settled the flute across his lap, and turning his gaze upon her, he began, "There was a time in my people's past when a young man went hunting alone in the forest. He took his bow and his quiver of arrows in search of an elk. This was a time long ago before the *wasichu* came to our lands with their fire sticks.

"The young man was considered a worthy hunter by his tribe, and finding the trail of a large elk, he followed his sign deeper and deeper into the forest."

Danielle settled back against the cottonwood tree as she allowed Wind Dancer's masculine voice to wrap around her senses.

"The young man did not find his elk, but as darkness enclosed the forest, he found that he had become lost. Settling down for the night in his blanket, he awaited Wi to break the sky the following morning so he could find his tracks and return to his village." Wind Dancer drew in a deep breath before continuing. "During the night, the young man had a strange dream, in which a woodpecker called out to him, *Follow me, young man, follow me!* The dream was filled with the beautiful, haunting sounds of an instrument that the young man had never heard before.

"At daybreak, when the young man awoke, the first thing he saw on a branch of the tree that he had been resting against was a woodpecker. The young man remembered his dream and the beautiful music. As the woodpecker flew through the forest, the young man rose from his resting place and followed him.

"After a time, the woodpecker alighted on the

branch of a cedar tree and began to tap out holes in the branch. The wind suddenly blew, and the young man heard the sound of the beautiful music, the same music from his dream the night before.

"Thanking the woodpecker for his gift, the young man took the cedar branch back to his village. In his lodge, he carved the branch into a *siyotanka,* a flute. The end of the flute he shaped into the image of the woodpecker's head, which he then painted red.

"In those days, there was a beautiful young maiden in the village, who was the daughter of the chief. She was a haughty young woman who knew well her beauty, and delighted in teasing the many warriors that came to her father's lodge to court her.

"One evening, after the young man had finished working on his flute, he sat against a tree and played the beautiful, haunting music. The young maiden heard the sound from her father's lodge, and unable to resist the alluring sound, she sought out the one who was playing the *siyotanka.* The moment she saw the young man, she fell madly in love, and told him that he was the one she would join with. Her father had received many generous offers for the maiden's hand, but she had refused all until now. That evening she told the young man to bring to her father's lodge anything that he wished for a bride-price. His gift would be accepted, and she would become his bride."

With the finish of Wind Dancer's story, Danielle softly ventured, "And you think this maiden fell in love with the young man because of the flute?"

"Our legend says it is so." His dark eyes studied her further.

"Don't you think that the young man could have

had something to do with it?" In the back of her mind, she remembered how Wind Dancer's music had disturbed her while she was trying to sleep. Though she tried to explain away the flute and its meaning to these people, she was having a hard time convincing herself. One thing was certain, however: she had not come out here in the middle of the night to tell Wind Dancer that she would join with him! She was going to wed Samuel, as soon as she and Penny could plan an escape and she could get back to her aunt and uncle!

"I believe that the young man desired the maiden more than life itself. The music drew her to him, and led her to open her heart." These words were a husky mixture of his own desire and a legend from days long past. "When will you allow yourself to open your heart to me, Silver Dove?"

Looking into his handsome features, Danielle was lost within the tenderness and warmth she saw there, but she stubbornly refused to allow herself to give in to the strong emotions that played havoc within her every time she was in his presence. "When will you release me, Wind Dancer, and let me return to my own people?"

She needed more time, Wind Dancer realized, with an indrawn sigh. He could have told her that he would never be able to release her; that she was his destiny. His life would be empty if he allowed her to return to her family, and she did not know that, without him, she would be living within an empty shell. The Great Spirit had ordained their joining! But he kept these words unspoken within his heart, not wishing to press her too hard, too fast. She would learn, in time, what her heart already knew—she was to be his, she had always been his! "There is something I have thought much upon lately." Instead of answering her question, he made this statement in an easy manner.

"And what is that?" Danielle was almost afraid to ask him what was on his mind. Nervously, she played with the twin bracelets on her wrists.

"The kiss we shared the night of the buffalo dance."

A small groan escaped her throat. She should had known he would say this! Her first reaction was to get to her feet and return to Autumn Woman's lodge, but again that wayward side of her nature prodded her: *He thinks about that kiss as much as you do, Danielle! Each night your dreams are plagued by the sensual assault of his mouth covering your own. Why not allow him to kiss you again, and see if that night was more than an illusion? By doing so, you will be able, once and for all, to chase all thoughts of that kiss from your mind!* She did not reason that if the kiss proved to be as irresistibly wonderful as on the night of the buffalo dance, she would be drawn in, even deeper, into the spell that he was weaving around her. Instead, she turned her lips up to him, and in a throaty whisper confessed, "I, too, have thought much about that night, Wind Dancer."

Looking down at her, he marveled at her pure innocence. Her lips were parted, and he knew from past experience that they were sweeter than any ripe berry. Ever so slowly, his dark head descended, his mouth at first gently settling over hers, then the pressure increased as he wrapped his arms around her and drew her up against his chest. She felt like paradise in his arms, soft and sweet, her scent of wildflowers and woman filling his nostrils as her honey taste drew his heated tongue between her teeth. He tasted fully the sweet nectar of her. His tongue sought out each hidden crevice of her mouth, its heated moistness swirling around hers in an erotic play of seeking and caressing. Feeling her hands tighten around his neck, he increased the tempo of his ardor.

Danielle clung to him, as though she were lost upon the rapture of a crashing storm. The touch of his mouth upon hers, the feel of his heated tongue plunging into her moist depths, and the strength that he enfolded her with combined to bring about an aching need of hot desire igniting deep within the foundation of her being. As he drew her tongue into his mouth and gently suckled, a soft moan escaped from the back of her throat. She had never experienced anything so overwhelming. She was aflame one minute, then shivering the next. This thing that he was doing to her mouth was so erotic, she wanted it to go on forever, only she wanted more . . . much . . . much . . . more!

Drawing her closer into his lap, Wind Dancer lightly caressed the slender curve of her throat and the rising fullness of her breasts. As his mouth plied her with feverish, irresistible kisses, his fingers gently eased apart the lacings at the top of her dress. As the top portion of the gown parted, his long-bronzed fingers splayed over the upper fullness of her straining flesh. He was blessed with the glorious feeling of her tender flesh, the same flesh that he could only imagine the feel of that afternoon while swimming with her in the stream.

As his mouth drew away from her honey-sweet lips, and slowly followed the same path of his hand, he easily felt the wild pulse beat along her throat. He feathered kisses over the corners of her mouth, across her fragile jawline, and down her throat to settle in heated delight on the swollen curve of one breast which, revealed beneath the moonlight, was a pale temptation with a rosebud crest.

Like a moth drawn to flickering flame, Wind Dancer's dark head lowered, his mouth parting as he drew in the succulent morsel, and ever so seductively, his moist tongue lathed the ripened peak, eliciting a passionate response from the woman sprawled across his lap.

No man had ever dared be so bold! No man had ever kissed her so, touched her breasts, or done the wicked things that this Indian chief was daring at this moment! Danielle's every nerve was attuned to the attention being lavished upon her breast. The feel of his branding tongue caressing the russet point sent electric currents of searing heat exploding in the depths of her womanhood. As he drew the bud in and lightly suckled, she gave over to the carnal wantonness. She twined her fingers within the long strands of midnight hair lying over his shoulders and, unwittingly, caused her lower body to move against him, as though she were seeking a means to stem the flood of desire that was racing throughout her veins and centering within her woman's depths.

As her buttocks squirmed against his lap and rubbed, back and forth, against the swollen length of his manhood, Wind Dancer's breath caught sharply in his chest. *It would be so easy at this moment to take her for my own, and have a finish to these feelings of aching desire that run rampant through me every time I am near her,* a small, wayward part of his mind whispered softly. But the more sensible side, that portion of his brain that had early in his past learned to be patient and use control no matter the circumstances, silently warned, *Have a care, Wind Dancer. You do not want to destroy the small trust that has slowly begun to grow between you two. You do not desire this woman for one night, no matter what havoc is being played within your body! She is the one who will be your life mate!* As Wind Dancer drew his mouth away from her breasts and looked into her passion-laced features, he glimpsed the willingness within the turquoise eyes, but his strong self-control won out. Tenderly, he placed a kiss upon the fullness of her breast, and as he saw her close her eyes, as though in ecstasy, a soft smile came over his lips. She was hot for his touch, as he was for the feel of her soft flesh beneath his hand. Tomorrow, she would have much more to think about besides the kiss shared at the buffalo dance. Slowly, he would win her consent to become his mate. He had not thought that courting a maiden could be so pleasurable! With her eyes still closed, his lips slanted over hers in a tender kiss before he gathered her up into his arms and started walking toward Autumn Woman's lodge.

If left up to Danielle, she would have stayed in his arms forever. The feelings he evoked in her body were so seductively wonderful, she never wanted them to stop. If she had had more nerve, she might have told him so, but all she could do was submit to his carrying her to the lodge. With the steady pounding of his heartbeat filling her ear, she was not sure if she had the strength to walk the distance to her adopted mother's lodge.

"There is much that I will teach you, Silver Dove. Things that take place between a man and a woman, but it is not yet the time." At Autumn Woman's lodge, he gently let her feet slip to the earth, but still holding her in his arms, he kissed her once again, before softly adding, "Soon, my heart, soon, I will show you all that my body longs to share with you."

Danielle could not speak. There was nothing she could say to his words of promise. Upon wobbly legs she made her way through the entrance flap of Autumn Woman's lodge, and to her sleeping couch. Clutching her eyes tightly shut as the fierce racing of her heart threatened to overwhelm her, she tried to bring some order over her trembling emotions. Her flesh tingled as though she could still feel Wind Dancer's hands upon her. Her naked nipples were now sensitive points as they pressed against the fur covers, and imagining Wind Dancer's mouth plying them so expertly caused waves of heated desire to course over her limbs. Having to bite upon the back of her hand to stifle the moan that was threatening to escape, she scolded herself for having left the tepee in the first place.

Long into the night, Danielle tried to chase the alluring sound of the *siyotanka* from her mind, as his words kept repeating themselves, over and over in her mind, *There is much that I will teach you, Silver Dove. Things that take place between a man and a woman. . . . Soon, my heart, soon, I will show you all that my body longs to share with you."*

Chapter Ten

The small Sioux encampment spent one more day resting and preparing the buffalo meat and hides before packing up their households and starting the long trek that would lead them back to their summer valley.

Each night, Danielle restlessly willed herself to sleep as Wind Dancer's flute music traveled throughout the encampment. Each morning when they broke camp, she would watch him riding to the head of the formation, and her eyes would greedily devour the sight of his large, bronzed body sitting atop his pony. In those moments, she would relive the time she had spent in his arms, the first evening he had played his flute for her. Feeling the heat of his ebony gaze returning her glance, she would quickly turn away, afraid that he might read her thoughts and know that she was thinking of that night and remembering each kiss, each touch he had given her body!

Before falling asleep each evening with Wind Dancer's music filling her ears, she contented her confused thoughts with the promise that, as soon as they arrived in the valley, she would find Penny and the two women would make their escape.

Once she got away from these Indians and returned to her family, everything would be all right again! The feelings she harbored for the Indian warrior would vanish once she saw Samuel Taylor again. But with thoughts of Samuel, the fleeting images in her mind of the man she was supposed to marry did not give her any solace. Always, thoughts of Samuel's ineffectual kisses and clumsy hands were replaced by Wind Dancer's more knowledgeable attentions!

The arrival of the hunters back in the valley was a cause for celebration. There was much buffalo meat, and the tribe was assured that they would not go hungry or cold during the coming winter. As the sun lowered, feasting and dancing began around the large, central fire. Danielle excitedly donned the dress Autumn Woman had made her for the buffalo dance. As soon as Autumn Woman had told her there would be a celebration, Danielle decided to seek Penny out. She would find the other young woman, and perhaps later this evening, after the camp slept in exhaustion from their merrymaking, she and Penny would mount the Spotted One and they would be able to get a good distance away from the village before daybreak.

Her heart beat excitedly in her chest as she made her way to the central fire with Autumn Woman. Her turquoise eyes glanced around for any sign of the other white woman. As the evening progressed, she did not see Penny, but several times she caught Red Fox staring in her direction. Once she glanced up to find him and Spring Lilly deep in conversation, the warrior's dark eyes gazing on Danielle even as he was speaking to the Indian maiden.

Wind Dancer also watched her intently throughout the evening, but she did not feel threatened by his glances as she did by Red Fox's. She did little, though, to acknowledge that she even noticed the Oglala chief's presence. She sat throughout the evening with a small group of women, not participating in the dancing as many of the young Indian maidens were, but enjoying the company of the chattering women around her.

As the evening grew late and still there was no sign of Penny, Danielle forced herself to gather her courage and approach Red Fox. Only he could tell her where Penny was, and perhaps he would allow her a moment or two to speak alone with her friend.

She felt the dark, appraising eyes roaming over her as she approached him, and for a few seconds, she thought to turn away and return to the women. She felt ill at ease as a leering smile slanted over his thin lips. His look told her that he had known all along that she would eventually seek him out.

Swallowing, she tried to quell her fear of the warrior, but as hard as she tried, she could not forget his harshness on the trail, nor could she put from her mind the cruelty that Penny claimed Red Fox had forced upon her. The cast of firelight thrown out by the central fire enhanced the scar on his cheek and made him appear even crueler than she remembered.

"So, at last the dove comes to the fox." His words were spoken in low tones so that no one standing nearby could hear them.

Danielle tried to ignore the implication of the words, and keeping her hands tightly clasped together, she tried to ignore direct contact with his seeking eyes. Forcing her voice to sound strong, she managed the question, "Is Penny coming to the celebration this evening, Red Fox?"

Red Fox appeared to consider Danielle's question before he gave an answer. "Why do you wish to waste your time with such a one as the *wasicun winyan?*"

"She is my friend," Danielle quickly replied, feeling her anger beginning to spark from his harsh words. "I had hoped that I could speak with her for a few minutes this evening." Danielle's voice softened; she would have no other way to make contact with Penny except through this man, so she knew that the wisest course of action, for the time being, was to try to remain calm in his presence.

Red Fox was struck by the pale woman's incredible beauty, and once again, red-hot anger coursed through his blood as he thought back to the day he had allowed Wind Dancer to have his pick of the women captives. This woman should have been his, to use as he had wished, not the filthy, whining creature he had been left with! A hard glint filled his ebony eyes. "Have you decided yet when you will come to my blanket, Silver Dove?" His softly spoken question belied the anger that burned in his heart. "I would willingly make room for you in my lodge." If she agreed, he would kick out the wife he had now so he could have total privacy with Silver Dove. He would devote every moment, day and night, to slacking his lust upon her shapely body!

"Never!" Danielle cried out in alarm, and took a step backward.

The smile upon his lips instantly disappeared,

and his features turned hard. Red Fox would have reached out and taken hold of her, and showed her that he could easily force her to do whatever he desired, if they had not been encircled by the villagers. Instead, his lips snarled back and his words were no longer soft, but forceful. "One day, you will belong to Red Fox, have no doubt! I should have kept you that day I brought you to the village, instead of giving Wind Dancer his choice of the women I had captured." Thumping his puffed-out chest with one fist, he swore aloud, "You will belong to no other besides me!"

It was at that moment that Wind Dancer approached the couple. He had been unable to hear their words, but glancing at Silver Dove's pale features and the hard cast upon Red Fox's face, he stepped between them to offer protection to the woman of his heart. His glance was deadly, his large hand resting easily upon the hilt of his hunting knife as he looked at Red Fox. Silence cloaked the villagers standing nearby as they watched the drama unfolding before them.

"Do not be foolhardy, Red Fox, where Silver Dove is concerned." Wind Dancer saw the challenge and glittering anger in Red Fox's eyes. "I do not know what has been said between the two of you, but I do not need to remind any in this village that this woman is a daughter of the people now." He did not mention that she was also a gift that Red Fox had given to him. He didn't have to say this; the other brave was well aware of the fact. Red Fox knew that what was Wind Dancer's he kept, and did not easily part with.

"She was asking me about the *wasicun winyan,* who was captured with her," Red Fox stated, not lost to the fact that Wind Dancer was willing to fight him over this woman, nor was he unaware that he would not last long in a contest of strength with the other warrior. Wind Dancer was well known for his cunning and power against the enemy, or anyone who came up against him. Though Red Fox was a worthy warrior, he would not come out the victor in a fight with Wind Dancer!

Turning away from Red Fox and facing Silver Dove, who was standing behind him, grateful for his protection, he questioned the other warrior, "And did you tell her that you traded the *wasicun winyan* to another tribe?" He saw Silver Dove's features instantly pale, and the gasp that left her lips was not lost upon his ears.

"I did not have the time to tell her this yet," Red Fox admitted. He was not going to tell Silver Dove until the information suited his own purpose, but now that Wind Dancer had revealed that the *wasicun winyan* was gone from their village, he would not have the opportunity to lure the pale beauty to his lodge under the pretext of visiting his captive.

"There is little more, then, that you need to speak with Silver Dove about. She has learned the information that she sought." Wind Dancer faced Red Fox and held his ground until the other warrior silently nodded his dark head and pushed his way out of the small group that had formed around them.

Danielle's turquoise eyes were wide with disbelief as she looked up at Wind Dancer. "Penny was traded away?" She felt tears coming to her eyes.

Wind Dancer lightly placed his hand upon her forearm as he led her away from the villagers. "I learned of the *wasicun winyan's* fate this afternoon after we returned to the village." He spoke softly.

He was not certain how close the two women had been, but knowing that they had been captured together, he was sure that Silver Dove would be upset by the news.

"She was traded away as though she had no more value than a horse!" Danielle shouted, and wiped away the tears that were dampening her cheeks. These Indians were no better than savages! After all the abuse that Penny had been forced to endure at Red Fox's hands, she now had been traded to another village, and the people there would likely treat her just as harshly!

"If I had been here, perhaps I could have stopped Red Fox from taking the woman from my village. I would have traded him for the *wasicun winyan* myself." Wind Dancer hated to see the pain that was revealed on her beautiful face, and indeed, had he been in the village, he would have done exactly what he claimed. He would have done anything to avoid this woman knowing such sorrow of heart!

"And what then, Wind Dancer? Would you, too, have used her, like Red Fox and his braves? On the night of the buffalo dance, she told me how horribly she was being treated. She told me then, but I couldn't help her! Yet I had hoped that somehow . . . somehow, I could do something!" She was enraged at the terror and abuse the other young woman was now suffering, and so she said the first thing that came to her mind. Wind Dancer seemed no different at that moment, than Red Fox or any other Indian!

Wind Dancer felt the pain of her sharp words as they touched his heart, but he understood them. "I would not have used the *wasicun winyan* in such a manner, Silver Dove. She is your friend. I would have traded for her only for that reason." Wind Dancer doubted she would understand him, but with time, he hoped that she would fully learn the depth of his feelings for her.

All Danielle realized was that Penny was gone, and she was left here in this village, all alone! Gone also with the other woman was Danielle's hopes of escaping these savages! She doubted she would have the courage to run away on her own. What was she to do now—remain in this village forever and, perhaps one day, see Red Fox's promises come true? With these thoughts, her tears intensified.

Autumn Woman had witnessed the confrontation between Red Fox and Wind Dancer, and she had followed Silver Dove and her chief to this secluded spot. Standing her distance, she had given them a few minutes to talk, but seeing that her adopted daughter was still upset over the news of the white woman's removal from the village, she made her way to the couple. Clicking her tongue, as she often did with her emotions, she kindly took hold of Silver Dove's arm. "Come with me, daughter. It has been a long day, and we should return to our lodge. When Wi rises in the morning, things will not look the same as they do now."

Once again, Wind Dancer was made aware of how wise Autumn Woman was. His dark eyes watched the two women as they slowly made their way through the village to Autumn Woman's lodge.

After the night of celebrating, Wind Dancer intensified his courtship of the silver-haired beauty he wished to claim for his own. Each evening, shortly after dusk, he arrived at Autumn woman's lodge with a small gift for the older woman and one a little more splendidly chosen for Silver Dove. The first evening he brought her an intricately beaded collar, which had been designed to fasten behind the neck and settle over the upper portion of her breasts. In the center of the collar the workmanship detailed a beautifully beaded red thunderbird with gleaming turquoise and gold-rimmed eyes. Autumn Woman marveled at great length over the attention given to the work.

After he left their lodge that evening, the sound of flute music could be heard as Wind Dancer played the love song he had created for Silver Dove.

The next evening when he arrived at Autumn Woman's lodge, he brought a doe hide which had been softly tanned and bleached white. Autumn Woman clicked her tongue loudly as she ran her hand over the beautiful hide. That evening after he left the women, his flute music once again floated upon the night breeze and circled the lodges in the village.

Upon the third evening, he brought three small willow baskets. One contained a variety of silver, blue, and red beads, while the other baskets held small tinkling bells and little circular mirrors. By the fourth evening, Danielle had had time to get over much of her hurt at discovering Penny's fate, and with the finish of dinner, she anxiously awaited Wind Dancer's arrival.

Shortly after the evening meal, the two women heard his husky voice calling from outside the lodge for permission to enter. Autumn Woman loudly welcomed their chief into the warmth of her tepee, and in a friendly tone, she invited him to sit near her fire.

Wind Dancer's dark regard quickly sought Silver Dove out where she sat on a pile of soft furs, sewing and trying to bead a piece of rabbit fur into a small bag to tie at her waist. His features softened as he viewed her with her silver hair unbound, the edges delicately lying over the dark furs. As her beautiful eyes rose from her work and looked across the lodge at him, he glimpsed the warmth in their depths. Before she lowered them once more, he also witnessed the smile that curved her lips. His heart raced wildly in his chest as he sat down at the old woman's fire. As he looked toward Silver Dove, she appeared not to notice him. He wondered if he had only imagined the warm lights in her green-blue eyes.

"How is our chief this evening?" Autumn Woman pulled him out of his thoughts, which centered wholly upon Silver Dove, and if given the opportunity, he would have been content to sit near the old woman's fire and look upon the pale-haired beauty for the rest of the evening without saying another word.

Nodding his head slowly, he replied, "I am well this evening, Autumn Woman."

The old woman had noticed the parfleche he had brought into her lodge this evening, and greedily she kept eyeing it where it rested at his side. "Would Wind Dancer like a bowl of stew this evening? The elk meat you brought to this old lady's lodge last evening is very tasty."

"I have already eaten," Wind Dancer replied kindly.

He seemed bent upon taking his time to show her what he had in his hide bag, the old lady thought. Wisely, she tried to bring the subject of gifts out into the open. "My daughter was well pleased with your gifts last evening, Wind Dancer. You see her now, sewing the colorful beads on the small bag she is making to hold her needles and threads." She looked toward Silver Dove, knowing that her chief would be powerless to resist following her gaze.

"Besides being very beautiful, your daughter is clever and talented to be able to create such a fine bag, Autumn Woman." Wind Dancer's eyes greedily devoured Silver Dove as he watched her slender fingers working on the soft rabbit fur.

Looking at the little bag in Silver Dove's lap, the old woman didn't see anything so clever about her attempts at sewing and beading. But if the young chief believed her clever and talented, she certainly wouldn't argue with him. Instead, she silently nodded her head at his remark.

"Your daughter will one day make a warrior very proud to be able to stand at her side before his people."

Danielle felt the blush that stained her cheeks from his words. As on previous evenings, when Wind Dancer came to Autumn Woman's lodge and presented his gifts near her fire, he boldly complimented Silver Dove. She heard every word spoken, and now, as on those other nights, she blushed deeply.

"*Han,* my daughter is valued very highly by her mother." Autumn Woman knew how to play her cards, and get all she could from this courtship of her adopted daughter.

"I have brought you a gift, Autumn Woman." Wind Dancer, at last, acknowledged the parfleche at his side, and pushing aside the leather flap, he stuck his hand inside and drew out a fine porcupine comb. It was similar to the one he had given Silver Dove when she first arrived in the village, except the carvings depicted the creatures that had given up their quills in order for the comb to be made.

Autumn Woman nodded her head thankfully. The comb was much finer than the one she had. She would show this one to the women of the village tomorrow as she boasted of their chief coming once again to her lodge to court her daughter.

Usually out of respect, Wind Dancer presented Silver Dove's gifts to her adopted mother, and allowed the old woman to deem if it was proper for the young woman to accept each one or not. After visiting with the old woman, he would leave the lodge without having any conversation with Silver Dove. This evening was different. He did not pull out his gift for her daughter; instead, he softly said, "With your permission, Autumn Woman, I would give Silver Dove this gift myself."

The old woman's eyes looked at the parfleche as she wondered what treasure he had brought to her lodge. But as he sat there and awaited her answer, she knew that she would not find out what was in the parfleche unless she agreed to his wishes. "*Han,* you are respectful of an old woman, Wind Dancer. You may speak to my daughter and show her what is in your pouch." She was about to call Silver Dove over to the fire, but before she could, Wind Dancer rose to his feet, the strap of the parfleche in his hand as he made his way to Silver Dove's side.

As Wind Dancer approached, Silver Dove was trying to spear one of the delicate beads with a tiny needle, which had been an animal bone at one time. She had heard the conversation between him and Autumn Woman, and her heart beat harshly against her chest with his approach. She was all thumbs, and finally gave up her sewing and set the bowl of beads aside. Still she was reluctant to raise her face to look up at him. She had wanted only to escape him and his people, and if she had found Penny, she would have attempted to do so by now. But she found that after each visit Wind Dancer made to Autumn Woman's tepee, she was more confused about what she felt for him. She did not think of him as the chief of the Indian village, or as her captor. She did not fear him, for he was tender when he spoke to her, or about her to Autumn Woman. And the glances he directed toward her each evening were always warm and gentle. Perhaps she was not sure how she was *supposed* to feel about him; after all, he was an Indian, and she a white woman.

Wind Dancer drew in a ragged breath to steady his pulse as he bent to his knees at her side and closely viewed her delicate beauty. Each time he looked on her, it was as if for the first time, when he had seen her in the image of his vision dove. And as her incredible eyes, encased in sparkling gold flecks, slowly rose up and looked directly into his face, he felt his mouth go dry; his entire body began to tremble. He felt blessed to look upon her, for she was his gift from Wakán Tanka.

A few silent seconds passed before Wind Dancer finally spoke. "I have brought you a gift, Silver Dove."

She sighed out a soft breath as he laid the parfleche next to her furs and opened the flap. Slowly he drew out a bundle wrapped in a soft hide cover.

"The time I spent at the trading post, I often

watched the *wasichu,* in order to try and understand his strange ways. My own people are nourished and comforted by things of earth and nature. We love the feel of Mother Earth warm and alive beneath our feet, and our blessings are received from Wakán Tanka. We warriors like best our horses and our buffalo meat, but I think our maidens, like the *wasicun winyan,* wish for pretty things." With this, he smiled warmly as he unwrapped the bundle. "One of my warriors got this, and I traded him something that he had wanted for a long time." He did not mention that the brave had obtained the items on a raid against the white man, nor did he reveal that he had traded the brave one of his finest ponies.

A soft gasp expelled Danielle's lips as she looked down upon the gift. Upon the soft fur lay a hand mirror, a brush, and a comb. The handles of each were made from ivory and the edging trimmed in rich gilt. Danielle's hand reached out and lifted the mirror, and glancing upon the glass, she viewed her own reflection. It had been some time since she had looked into a mirror, but she saw that little had changed, except her face was colored a healthy tan and bright spots of color were visible on her cheeks. It was strange, but she thought there should have been some evidence of everything she had gone through during the past few months, but there was nothing. If anything, she looked healthier and happier.

"Are you pleased with my gift, Silver Dove?" Wind Dancer saw the thoughtful glance she had given the mirror, and wondered at her reaction.

As though his softly spoken question had broken a spell, Danielle gently set the hand mirror back down upon the piece of fur. Without looking upward, she softly murmured, "Thank you, Wind Dancer. Your gift is very beautiful." She would have said more. She would have thanked him for everything he had given her, but she simply could not get the words out of her mouth. Every time she was in his presence, she felt herself tongue-tied and more than a little flushed.

Wind Dancer yearned to reach out and pull her into his arms, but remembering where he was and feeling Autumn Woman's eyes resting upon his back, he restrained the impulse. Instead, he stated honestly, "My gift holds little beauty compared to you, Silver Dove. Wakán Tanka blessed you above all women; in my eyes you are without equal."

The husky tremor in his voice settled over her with the power to melt her bones. As she looked up into his gaze, she was mesmerized by the tender warmth in his sable eyes. She knew that he had meant every word he said to her. She wondered if any other woman had ever felt so cherished in the eyes of a man. Had any other woman ever known such a man as Wind Dancer? In this man was everything a woman could ever desire. Strength, tenderness, wisdom, and oh, to be held in his arms and seduced by those sensual lips! The fleeting image of him standing naked on the stream bank came back to her, and the heat from her flushed face traveled downward over her throat to the very tips of her breasts.

As though able to read all the thoughts within her turquoise eyes, Wind Dancer lightly reached out a hand and a long, bronzed finger caressed the softness of her cheek down to her chin. "Soon, my heart, soon." The husky whisper settled over her and filled her with expectation.

After saying these words of promise, he rose to

his feet and turned away from Danielle. Going back to Autumn Woman's fire, he spoke respectfully to the elder woman. "Thank you, Autumn Woman, for letting me speak with your daughter."

"My daughter and I are pleased that you visit our lodge, Wind Dancer," she returned before he left her lodge. Rising from her fire, the old woman made her way to her adopted daughter's side to inspect the gifts he had given her. Clicking her tongue loudly, she displayed how impressed she was with them. "Wind Dancer is a generous man, daughter. He will make a woman a fine mate one day."

Taking up her sewing once again, Danielle silently reviewed the old woman's words in her mind. With much effort, she tried to bring Samuel's image to the forefront of her thoughts, but reluctantly she gave up the effort. It was useless to try to force thoughts of Samuel Taylor; Wind Dancer's image was too powerful to be competed with.

Chapter Eleven

Shortly before dusk the next day, a large commotion in the village drew Autumn Woman and Silver Dove away from their comfortable fire. The sounds of shouting and laughter, along with the heavy pounding of horses' hooves upon the earth, caused the two women to part the entrance flap of their tepee and step outside. The sight that met their eyes was that of Wind Dancer, chief of the Oglala Sioux, riding atop his best war horse and dressed in his most regal costume. In defference to Silver Dove, he had not worn his scalp shirt that day, but instead wore a beautifully beaded vest which boasted upon each breast the design of a silver dove. Below this were beaded representations of the sacred thunderbirds of his vision. His powerful legs were encased in beaded and fringed leggings, and upon his feet, he wore moccasins with the same beaded design as his vest.

He sat atop his large white stallion, straight and proud, and as Danielle's azure eyes traveled over him from foot to head, her glance was drawn to his magnificent headdress. It had over eighty eagle feathers, tipped with yellow horsehair and white gypsum, each feather Wind Dancer had won *in coup,* through brave deeds. The carefully prepared feathers had been laced into a red trade cloth base and attached around a skull cap. Across his brow was a beaded band bearing the sign of the thunderbird, and at the sides of each temple dangled strips of dyed red leather and ermine fringes. Red trade cloth formed the base for a single extension of feathers which flowed down Wind Dancer's bronzed back and lay upon the rump of his horse. When he stood, the lower portion of the headdress would reach the ground. Where the eagle feathers were secured, their tips were decorated and held in place with ermine fringe and porcupine quill–wrapped buckskin thongs.

He was absolutely breathtaking. As his eyes locked with Silver Dove's, she felt her heart beating at a tremendous rate, and at the same time, her lips drew back into a wide smile.

Many of the villagers had followed Wind Dancer excitedly as, behind him, he lead a string of his ten finest mares. Shouts and calls from the braves encircled them, and tittering laughter from the women made the entire affair fun and exciting.

Watching Silver Dove's expression change to one of joy, Wind Dancer felt his own heart grow as light as the airy clouds overhead. He wanted to shout aloud that he had never seen a more beautiful smile upon the face of any maiden. He wanted to ride his war pony throughout the village, telling all who would listen that he wanted nothing more in all the world than to join with this pale-haired woman! But instead, the patience and endurance he had learned as a young boy held him fast. Only the parting of his lips and the bright sparkle in the depths of his ebony eyes gave way to his feelings. Bending low from the back of his pony, he handed

Autumn Woman the horse-hair rope that he had led the mares with. "I give you these fine animals, Autumn Woman, to show you the high respect I hold for your daughter, Silver Dove." Wind Dancer spoke loudly, so that those standing nearby did not mistake his words. As his glance turned back to Silver Dove once again, he saw that her cheeks were flushed bright, but her smile was still upon her soft lips.

Autumn Woman wondered why Wind Dancer did not come right out and ask for her adopted daughter. The horses were a fine bride-price, much more than she had gained from her true daughter's husband when she had joined. But Wind Dancer did not ask, clicking her tongue loudly as she held the lead rope, she watched the young chief and her daughter smiling upon one another.

"When a Sioux maiden likes a young brave, she wraps a blanket around her shoulders, and when the brave comes to her lodge, she steps outside to meet him. The maiden places the blanket over both their heads, and they speak of secret things as they stand there before her parents' lodge. The people see the young couple, but turn their heads as though they do not know they are there." Autumn Woman instructed her adopted daughter as the two women went to the river to fill their leather bags with water, and gathered the daily wood for their lodge fire.

Danielle had not asked for this lesson in Indian maidenly behavior, but she silently listened to everything the older woman had to say. During the past few days, her feelings for Wind Dancer had intensified. She could not sleep at night as the delicate sound of the *siyotanka* made her restless upon her sleeping couch. She forced herself not to rise and go to Wind Dancer, but instead she tossed and turned, her dreams filled with his handsome image and what they had shared that first evening when he had played his flute for her. Last evening when he had ridden in all his splendor up to Autumn Woman's lodge and had proclaimed his feelings for her before the entire village, she had wanted to tell him how she felt about him. But she dared not, because she was still not sure what those feelings meant. Later that evening, when the alluring music of his flute again floated upon the night air, it had been all she could do to control the wilder side of her nature, which tempted her to throw caution to the wind and claim the prize that awaited her out there in the darkness.

During the next long day, Danielle waged an inner war with her emotions. On the one hand, it was more than likely that she would never see her family or Samual Taylor again. She was a young woman, and Wind Dancer had already shown her that she had a burning passion in her body which craved to be released. Did she think she could remain a spinster, alone for the rest of her life? Would she live out her life in this village with these people, and deny herself the happiness of love and one day having children? But the side of her nature that was ever the fighter, argued, *You could try to run away from this village by yourself. You have a horse—surely you could reach some help before you're recaptured! Don't you miss your aunt and uncle, and what about Samuel, the man you're supposed to marry?*

By the end of the afternoon, Danielle was emotionally exhausted. She did miss her family.

Maybe not as much as she had at first after her capture. She would like nothing more than to see her family again, and assure them that she was unharmed. Samuel Taylor, though, was another matter entirely. She could truthfully admit that she did not miss the young man at all. Once during the day she realized, that if Samuel Taylor had had any of Wild Dancer's strength of character and gentleness, she might have fonder memories of him. But the only memories she had were of a bumbling young man who had been forever trying to force his unwanted attentions upon her!

Perhaps it was these thoughts of Samuel that made Danielle's decision for her that evening after dinner. As she sat on her pallet of furs, her fingers had toyed with the edge of the blanket that Autumn Woman had thrown upon her sleeping couch. When Wind Dancer's husky voice called from outside the lodge, the two women in the tepee looked at one another, neither venturing to call aloud for him to enter. Slowly, Danielle rose to her feet, the blanket trailing in her hand. When she neared the entrance flap, she donned the blanket over her shoulders.

Wind Dancer was surprised to glimpse Silver Dove stepping from the lodge. As her turquoise eyes nervously went over his features and her fingers played with the blanket in indecision, his breath caught in his chest. Without a word spoken, he patiently waited for her to make the first move.

Unsure of herself, and why she had been possessed to come out and bring the blanket with her, Danielle felt her heart pounding as her eyes moved over his perfect male body. He wore a red headband around his forehead with an eagle feather hanging in front of his left ear, his midnight hair hanging over his shoulders and down his back in thick, silken strands. Around his neck he wore a thin beaded necklace; his upper torso was bare. His strength was displayed in the powerful muscles that contoured his chest and tapered down to the waist of his loincloth. His jet-colored eyes searched her features, and she knew that he was waiting to see what she would do. For a crazy second, she thought to fling the blanket to the ground and flee back into the safety of Autumn Woman's lodge, but instead she lifted the blanket silently from her shoulders, and as he stood there before her, she brought the blanket over his head and her own.

Low, husky laughter filled her ears as Wind Dancer's heart sang with joy. Reaching up to help settle the blanket more comfortably about them, he spoke in low tones. "I was not sure for a moment if you would cover us or flee, Silver Dove."

Not certain what was expected of her, and still not sure if she had done the right thing, Danielle could only look up at him with wide, innocent eyes.

Beneath the blanket, his hand rose and he tenderly traced her jawline with his strong fingers. "I am pleased that you did not run, Silver Dove. I admit that if you had, I would have returned again and again to Autumn Woman's lodge until you were willing to give me a sign that you welcome my attentions. I am happy that it is today that you covered us with the blanket."

There was a trace of humor in his tone, and it lightened the moment for Danielle as he smiled tenderly down at her. "You have been waiting for me to do this thing with the blanket?"

"*Han,* Silver Dove. I have waited, it seems to

me forever, for you to show me some sign of welcome."

Once again, Danielle felt her face blush. This seemed to be inevitable when she was in his presence.

"Now tell me, Silver Dove, what gift made your heart open to me?"

Feeling strange beneath the blanket, and standing so close to him, she tried to calm her racing pulse. It was not any of the gifts that had brought her out of the lodge with the blanket, and at that moment, she was not sure what had made her do such a thing. She was confused by these new feelings which seemed to be tearing her apart inside!

"Perhaps, it is the *siyotanka,* then, that has drawn you to me?" She did not speak, and Wind Dancer did not truly expect her to. Like the innocent dove, she was shy to the ways of a man and a woman. Slowly his smile widened as though he had been teasing her. "If not the gifts or my *siyotanka,* then perhaps it is Wind Dancer himself who has caused this moment to come about?"

How near the truth he was, Danielle thought to herself. This man was certainly hard to resist, and with his nearness and handsome good looks, she could barely catch her breath, let alone respond to his jesting words. Forcing herself to say something, she asked the first thing that came to her mind. "Why me, Wind Dancer? Why have you brought all those gifts? Why are you playing the flute each evening? Why do you not approach one of the maidens from your village?" With these questions, she remembered Spring Lilly, the beautiful Indian maiden whom she had seen several times looking upon Wind Dancer with a hungry gaze. Danielle wondered why the handsome warrior did not approach her.

"This is an easy question for me to answer, Silver Dove. I have known its answer since my first breath of this life; I have known since the moment of creation. You and I were created by the Great One for each other. You are the reason I was born to this life, the reason my blood pumps in my heart, the beginning and the ending of my life circle. Before you, there was no reason for my existence. You are the portion of me that Wakán Tanka created into separate beings, only to bring together and join as one."

A few weeks ago, she would not have believed a single word that he spoke. A few days ago, she might have had some doubt, but at this moment she did not shun his answer to her question; instead, she asked another. "How can you be so sure of all this, Wind Dancer?"

This was even an easier question to answer for the warrior chief. "I know this, because my heart is open to the feelings that are stirred within my soul each time I look upon you. I have looked into the very depths of my being, Silver Dove, and I have discovered your image."

His words affected her in so many ways that Danielle didn't know whether to throw herself against his broad chest and cry out her need to be held in his comforting arms; or to get away from him as quickly as possible, mount the Spotted One, and flee the village before she was too caught up in the spell he was casting around her to ever be able to break its hold. Good sense won out. Instead of doing anything hasty, she forced herself to speak. "I must go back into the lodge now, Wind Dancer. Autumn Woman will wonder what I am doing, and I don't wish to worry her. She has been very good to me."

This was not exactly the reception to his words that Wind Dancer had wanted, but wisdom told him not to rush her. *She will return to her place near Autumn Woman's fire, and in her mind, she will hear your words, over and over again,* he told himself. He did not speak, but silently nodded his head and waited for her to withdraw the blanket from over their heads.

Returning to the lodge, Danielle was unable to think of anything except the words that Wind Dancer had told her. A short time later, she disrobed and lay down upon her sleeping couch. It was not long before the music of the *siyotanka* filled the night air, and with the sound, his words filled Danielle's mind: "*. . . my heart is open to the feelings that are stirred within my soul each time I look upon you. I have looked into the very depths of my being, Silver Dove, and I have discovered your image.*"

The sounds made by his flute had the power to gently lure Danielle into thinking only of him—forcing her to forget the differences between them, shutting out the reason that she was in his village and the fact that she had been stolen away from those she loved. There was only room in her thoughts for the handsome warrior who was sitting out there in the dark, playing his flute for her alone.

Glancing across the lodge, Danielle saw that Autumn Woman had already fallen asleep. Her mouth lay partially open as soft snores filled the inner space of the lodge. Silently, Danielle rose from her sleeping couch and dressed. Leaving the lodge, she followed the sound of the music as though she had no will of her own to refuse the notes that carried the haunting tune of love.

Wind Dancer did not lay the flute aside until she stood directly in front of him. "You have at last come to me, Silver Dove. You agree that we shall be joined as one?" His words were softly spoken as he leaned his back against a tree and looked into her face. With the moon full in the night sky, he watched her facial movements.

Can I so easily agree to become this man's wife? Danielle asked herself. Inwardly she knew how ridiculous the question was. How on earth could she agree to such a thing? But as she looked at him patiently awaiting her answer, she could not tell him no. She wanted him as much as he wanted her, and the words he had spoken to her while they had been covered with the blanket had made her realize this much sooner. Slowly her head nodded in agreement, and with that movement, she subconsciously was taking the first steps toward severing her ties with the past. She would be casting away all hopes of ever regaining her old life and being reunited with Samuel Taylor.

Wind Dancer felt his heart skip a beat with the slight movement of her pale head. His heart sang a joyful song, for at last she had agreed to join her life path with his. He did not show his strong reactions at this time, for he feared he might frighten her. He contented himself with the thought that soon . . . soon she would belong to him. What had been destined from his youth, when he had sat upon the vision hill and looked into the eyes of a beautiful silver dove, would at last come to be.

Chapter Twelve

The north winds whispered lightly among the tall pines, shaking the high needles and calling a gentle greeting down into the Sioux's peaceful valley. The black velvet night was alive with the brilliance of a thousand stars, and a full orange moon cast its light upon the evening as Danielle prepared herself for her coming marriage.

Autumn Woman's lodge was filled with other women, who had come to help the bride of Wind Dancer prepare herself for the joining ceremony. Young and old alike came, each woman seeming to have a special idea or talent to contribute. It was the younger women, those newly married and those still maidens, who laughingly led Danielle to the river to help bathe her body and wash her long hair. None allowed her to help in this bathing ritual, for they, too, had gone or would go through this same process before their own joining ceremony.

Many of the younger maidens hung back, not helping with the bathing of a pale woman but taking part by being there. Some looked upon Danielle with envy in their eyes, since she had captured the heart of such a strong, handsome warrior as Wind Dancer, and still others watched the silver-haired woman with a touch of awe. Her long, wheat-white hair curled about her body as she was washed, and her pale, creamy smooth skin shimmered in the moonlight, leaving them speechless.

One of the maidens looked darkly on the white woman who had stolen the heart of the man she had loved for as long as she could remember. Spring Lilly stood with the other young women, but there was no smile upon her lovely face. There was no sparkle in her large, dark eyes, which stared with an icy foreboding.

She had waited these past days—ever since Wind Dancer had told Medicine Wolf of his plans to join with the *wasicun winyan*—for him to come to his senses and forget such a foolish thought. A flush stained her cheeks as she remembered the night she had stolen into Wind Dancer's lodge and slipped into his sleeping couch with him. He had awakened instantly, and though she had pressed her naked body tightly against his and offered him what in the past he had willingly taken, he had pushed her away.

"It is the *wasicun winyan!*" she had accused as tears rolled down her cheeks. "You keep her here in our village and favor her above your own people! Send her away like Red Fox did the other slave!"

Wind Dancer had been shocked to find Spring Lilly climbing between his furs, and had quickly stood and pulled on his breechcloth. Stoking the embers of his fire, he brightened the lodge in order that he could set the maiden's thoughts straight where Silver Dove was concerned. "Silver Dove will not be sent from our village. She is the daughter of Autumn Woman." She had not bothered to rise from his sleeping couch, nor did she attempt to cover her bountiful curves.

"The old crone only claims her because of the gifts you bring to her lodge! The whole village knows of your nightly visits!" Spring Lilly spat out, the tears halting as her eyes sparkled with her anger.

"I am chief of this village, and I will do as I please. Silver Dove will not be sent away. This night, she has agreed to join her life path with mine." Though his words were harshly spoken, Wind Dancer felt some sympathy for Spring Lilly. He had never promised her anything in the past, and he knew of more than one other warrior she had freely shared her charms with, but he recognized that she must be feeling pain. As he saw her features pale at his words, he softened his voice. "Any warrior in this tribe would be more than pleased to take you as his mate, Spring Lilly. You waste your time by coming to my lodge. I told you long ago that there could never be anything between us. Perhaps I should speak to your father, and he can arrange a joining between you and a worthy brave."

"Do not volunteer to help find another for me, Wind Dancer! No other will do—you are the one who fills my heart! My father knows my feeling and would not be pleased that you wish to cast his daughter aside for the *wasicun winyan!*"

It was strange that Wind Dancer had never noticed before the viciousness of tongue that this young woman had. He knew her father, Brave-Bull, well, and was sure that the older warrior would listen with wisdom if he approached him about his daughter. "You have misled yourself, and your heart, Spring Lilly. You will get over these feelings you think you have for me, for there can never be anything more between us."

"But there can be, Wind Dancer." Her voice turned seductively soft as her back arched on the lush furs. With her long, black hair invitingly spread out, her naked form undulated in invitation.

Wind Dancer had no thought of accepting what she was plainly offering. Turning away from the lodge fire, he walked to the entrance flap, and before stepping through, he stated, "I am in need of some fresh air, Spring Lilly. Do not be in my lodge when I return. I do not think Brave-Bull would take too kindly to having to come and take his daughter from a warrior's pallet." With that, he stepped out into the night air.

Spring Lilly viciously pounded the furs on his sleeping pallet. She knew she had lost in this attempt to regain Wind Dancer for her own. Her father would be furious if he knew what she was about, for he admired Wind Dancer greatly.

Spring Lilly was certain that Wind Dancer had been swept up in a spell the *wasicun winyan* had cast upon him. As she stood along the riverbank and watched as the moon shimmered golden light upon the pale woman, she knew she was right! A spell of evil had been cast about her beloved, and no one seemed to know this fact except her. With one last glance thrown in the woman's direction, Spring Lilly started back toward the village, her mind working on a plan that could win Wind Dancer's favor.

With the finish of the bath, the women wrapped Danielle in a large buffalo robe and hurried her back to Autumn Woman's lodge. Once there, they all helped dry her body and hair. Then they rubbed every inch of her body with a smooth lotion that had a sweet, flowery scent.

At first, Danielle tried to push away the hands that reached out to rub the lotion into her flesh, but Autumn Woman stilled her protests. "We will make my daughter beautiful for Wind Dancer. She will smell like pretty flowers, and make the warrior's head swim with happy thoughts!" Pushing Danielle's hands aside, the old woman nodded to her companions, and they had their way.

With this accomplished, two women began to work on her hair. Standing her near the lodge fire, they combed the long pale strands until they dried in shimmering waves. Entwining slender braids above each temple, they bound the lengths of hair with beaded strips of ermine, and allowed the braids to fall over her shoulders as they swept back the rest of the cloud of pale curls to flow over her shoulders and down her back. Over her brow, they placed the headband that Wind Dancer had given her, the thunderbird design of blue beads plainly displayed upon her forehead.

Next followed the dress Autumn Woman had made from the bleached doe-hide that Wind Dancer had brought as a gift. The dress had been fringed at the bottom, along the sleeves, and across the breasts. A heavily beaded belt of blue and silver was wrapped around her waist The same beaded design was on the bleached hide leggings that were pulled over her calves. Finally the women placed the collar of silver and blue beads, with the thunderbird design, over her neck, and settled it over Danielle's shoulders. It lay delicately across her collarbone, covering the upper fullness of her breasts.

With their preparations complete, the women

stood back and murmured among themselves as they admired Silver Dove's rare beauty. None could remember ever seeing a more dazzling maiden before her joining ceremony. Before being pulled out of the lodge, Danielle slipped the twin bracelets over her wrist. Then, with her head swimming, she was escorted by the circle of women to the center of the village, where the large central fire had been erected for the occasion of the joining ceremony.

The bride-to-be's eyes quickly looked around the area for Wind Dancer, but she did not see him right away as the faces of the villagers swam before her. Trembling fingers of fear climbed up her back. As she stood there alone before the fire, she could not help wondering why she was here, waiting for a war chief to become her husband. She should have been home with her aunt and uncle, safe under their roof and looking forward to the day she would wed in a church with their friends in attendance! She should have been marrying Samuel, not standing there and waiting for Wind Dancer and a shaman to come and say some strange words over them that would join them forever!

These thoughts froze in her mind, and she wondered how she had ever gotten this far with Wind Dancer. It seemed now, as she thought about it, that she had had no control over anything since arriving in this village—even her feelings for the warrior chief. One minute she had nodded her head in agreement that she would join with him, and overnight, the evening had come for the joining ceremony. But why had she ever agreed to marry him in the first place?

As though in answer to her desperate thoughts,

Wind Dancer appeared out of the crowd and began to make his way to her side. Danielle's fear-laced gaze told him immediately of her desperation.

For an insane second, Danielle told herself that she should turn away from him and flee! But as his sable glance caught her gaze, her fear was replaced by the wild pounding of her heart. He exuded raw, masculine power as he slowly approached her. He wore the same feathered headdress he had worn the day he had brought Autumn Woman the mares, his hide shirt and leggings similar in color and beadwork to her own. For a second, she wondered if Autumn Woman had also made his joining outfit. But what captured Danielle's full attention was the look on his face as he lowered his gaze away from the touch of her eyes and his heated glance took in her entire form. There was tenderness there within his look that she had never seen on another man's face. Danielle recognized the look for what it was. It was the look a man gives to the woman he truly loves! *He loves you, Danielle. You can see it in his eyes; it is total and complete love that you are witnessing within the depths of his features!* her inner voice whispered, and with the announcement, she asked herself, *How often can a woman see in a man's face the love he feels for her?* She thought of Penny and her William. The young couple had been wed, but had they truly loved? She thought of her aunt and uncle and could not recall ever seeing this look of complete love on their faces.

With these thoughts, the fear and desperation in her glance lessened, and as Wind Dancer stood next to her, he tenderly drew her hand into his own. "Do not fear, Silver Dove," he said in low, husky tones. "It is the will of the Great Spirit that we are to be joined throughout this life as one. You shall be treasured above all things in my heart, from this night forth."

As ever when in his presence, Danielle felt herself trembling, and as her heart fluttered then skipped a beat, she knew that he was speaking the words he felt in his heart. Perhaps this man was an Indian, and by the white man's term, he was wild and savage, but Danielle knew that white skin or bronze, there was no man his equal. He was the type of man that every young woman dreams of finding one day—handsome, tender, strong, and protective. Wind Dancer was a man who feared nothing, not even speaking the words from his heart. As a small, nervous smile trembled about her lips, she knew that for the first time in her life she was reaching for something she truly wanted—love!

Medicine Wolf approached the couple, and after looking at them with probing black eyes, as though he had the power to look into their very minds, he bent down to the small fire that he had readied earlier for the ceremony. As on the evening of the buffalo dance, he pulled from his parfleche sweet grass to burn in the flames. He drew an eagle feather back and forth, fanning the smoke over his body. Believing the smoke possessed the power to purify him, he then drew forth the medicine bundle, which held the tribe's sacred pipe. He filled the bowl with kinnikinnick, lit it, and inhaling deeply, he expelled the smoke to the four directions. His prayers to Wakán Tanka were that he bring forth His mighty blessings upon the ceremony.

After smoking the pipe, he pulled a red blanket from his leather bag; with the pipe in one hand and the blanket in the other, he silently stood before the couple. He brought the blanket over their shoulders, the cover drawing them close together. Holding out the ancient pipe, he instructed them to each lay a hand upon the stem.

Wind Dander did as instructed, and Danielle tentatively settled her left hand next to his on the pipe. Murmuring a prayer, Medicine Wolf tied a piece of red trade cloth over their hands and bound them as one with the pipe.

Taking the eagle feather, Medicine Wolf lightly ran it over their hands and over the length of the pipe. Strangely, Danielle felt some tingling power run up the entire length of her arm. Wind Dancer must have felt it too, for he looked at her at the same instant as her eyes rose to his face in question.

"The Great Spirit is pleased at this joining," Medicine Wolf stated loudly for all to hear. "He blesses this joining of two lives down the same path by his presence here among us this evening. The spirits of our ancestors look down with much joy upon their son, who takes this silver woman to his heart, for it was ordained that this moment should come to pass."

As Medicine Wolf untied the pipe and replaced it in the sacred bundle, Wind Dancer held Danielle's hand tightly. In low tones that only she could hear, he stated, "You are mine, Silver Dove. For now and forever; even throughout eternity, our love will be binding."

Danielle felt tears stinging the backs of her eyes because of the tenderness of his words. She was touched to her heart by the love in his tone. But before she could say any words that might impart some of her own feelings, Autumn Woman approached her and hugged her tightly against her ancient bosom, weeping. "You have been a good daughter to this old woman, Silver Dove. Do not forget your mother now that you have a husband of your own."

Danielle kissed her leathered cheek. "How could I ever forget you, *Iná?* Without you, I don't know where I would be."

"These words are good, daughter, for the winter months are long and lonely for an old woman. I yearn to hold grandchildren on my lap and teach them of past days."

As the villagers circled around and congratulated them, Danielle's eyes lingered upon the tall frame of her husband. She had not thought about having children with Wind Dancer, but Autumn Woman's words gave her a moment's pause. His would surely be the most beautiful children ever created, and Wind Dancer would be a patient and wise father. A blush stole over her cheeks as she imagined that day in the future when she might tell him the news that he would be a father. Her blush intensified as his gaze caught her own; she was reminded that before a babe could be conceived, there had to be a wedding night!

The dancing and feasting went on for hours after the joining ceremony. Life for the plains Indians was a daily trial, and a celebration was prolonged to its fullest. After an appropriate time, Wind Dancer drew his bride away from the group of women whom she had been talking to. "It is time that we retire to my lodge, Silver Dove."

Gazing into his warm dark eyes, Danielle was powerless to resist him. Slowly she nodded her head as excitement and fear intermingled and raced headlong throughout her bloodstream. She knew what would await her once she entered Wind Dancer's lodge and the rest of the world was shut out. The anticipation of being held within the strong arms almost caused her knees to buckle.

Wind Dancer had waited his entire life for this evening to arrive. Since the moment when Medicine Wolf had joined them as one with the pipe, he had savored every movement she made, each changing feature on her beautiful face, the alluring singsong softness that filled his ears each time she spoke. He knew of her nervousness regarding the unknown moments that this night would bring, it was normal apprehension. She was like a wild rose, whose bud has felt only the first caress of morning sunlight. Having received her first taste of loving warmth, she had gently opened. But it would take a full dose of passion to change her from a youthful bud into a lush, mature flower.

Drawing her hand into his own, he led her away from the group of women, and amid the good wishes of the villagers, they silently made their way through the camp to Wind Dancer's large tepee.

Once inside the lodge, Danielle stood nervously a few feet away from the entrance as Wind Dancer went to the center fire pit. Bending to his knees, he fed the embers with wood and stoked the flames into a warm fire. As the light grew within the interior of the lodge, Danielle looked around and found that little had changed since the first day she had been brought to Wind Dancer's lodge.

Straightening to his full height, Wind Dancer gazed over the figure of his bride. She stood not far from the lodge entrance, as though poised for flight. "Are you hungry, Silver Dove?" he softly questioned, hoping that, by speaking, he could help ease her tension now that they were alone.

Danielle had been unable to eat anything throughout the day, and she felt no different now. Silently she shook her head, still not daring to step farther into the lodge—the lodge that was now her home.

Taking off his headdress, Wind Dancer put it in its place. He pulled off the bleached hide shirt and leggings, and neatly folding them, he put them away. His movements were unhurried as he tried to give Silver Dove a few minutes to grow accustomed to being in his lodge before he attempted to coax her closer to the fire.

It was just as he turned back to face her, and was wearing only his breehcloth, that their attention was drawn to a commotion outside the lodge. Several young braves had gathered, and as a joke on the groom, they called for Wind Dancer to come outside and settle a bet that had been made.

"As chief of our village, only you can decide this bet, Wind Dancer," Black Bull called loudly, knowing his friend would be loath to leave his beautiful bride. Wind Dancer knew, however, that the braves would not go away until he complied.

As he turned to Silver Dove, a small grin was on his lips. "We will not be left alone until I go with them to settle whatever bet they are speaking of." He had joined groups of young braves when they had bothered other young couples on their joining nights, so he was not angered by the innocent fun of his friends. "Go over to the fire and warm yourself, Silver Dove. I will return as soon as I am able." He hoped that a few minutes with him out of the lodge would help calm her nervousness. Leaving the lodge, he was soon encircled by the group of braves, who laughed and jostled him toward the riverbank, where Little Otter and Short Bow were to have a swimming race. Because it was his joining night, he was to be the judge of this race. He hoped that he would be the judge of only one such contest, and not be parted from his bride any longer than necessary.

Alone in her husband's lodge, Danielle slowly made her way to the warm fire. For a few minutes, she stood in indecision; her thoughts were a jumble. She wondered what had brought her to this moment, to be alone in a warrior's lodge. She knew that it was far too late for any doubts she might still have. She had joined herself to this man as his wife. Though it had been an Indian ceremony, she had understood much of what Medicine Wolf had said. He had asked blessings from the Great Spirit over their union, which she knew was the same as asking her own God to bless their marriage. Everyone in Wind Dancer's village, as well as Wind Dancer himself, considered her to be his wife.

Stepping away from the center fire, with a nervous glance thrown in the direction of Wind Dancer's sleeping couch, she went to the side of the lodge, where earlier, Autumn Woman and another woman had brought her belongings and left them in leather bags. Lifting one, she felt around until she found the comb, brush, and mirror set that Wind Dancer had given her.

She returned to the fire and silently sat down on the furs that had been spread out in a lush display. Her hands rose and she was lost in thought as she unbraided her hair and took the headband from her brow. Combing out the pale silver curls, she wondered if she would please Wind Dancer. Would their life together as man and wife give him the happiness he had been looking for—the happiness he deserved? A small noise drew her attention toward the entrance flap of the lodge, and with a start, Danielle saw a lovely young Indian maiden boldly step into the interior of the tepee.

No words were said for a full moment as the two young women stared at each other over the fire. Danielle saw the coldness of true hatred in the dark gaze that she now recognized as Spring Lilly's, and involuntarily a small thread of fear laced its way up her spine.

"I see that Wind Dancer has already left you on your joining night, *wasicun winyan!*" Spring Lilly spat out with all the venom she felt for this white thief with the silver hair.

Danielle rose slowly to her feet. With what she saw in the woman's features and heard in her tone, Danielle knew there would be no swaying Spring Lilly's feelings of animosity. Trying to appear brave in the face of the other woman's hatred, however, she stated, "Wind Dancer will return soon if you wish to speak with him." She felt an instant spark of jealousy and annoyance at this woman's appearance in Wind Dancer's lodge on their joining night.

"Oh, I can speak to Wind Dancer anytime I please, *wasicun winyan!* It is you I have come to speak with this night.

"What is it you wish to say to me?" Danielle had seen her by the river that evening with the other women, and wondered why she had not approached her then.

"You do not belong here among my people! You do not deserve to be Wind Dancer's wife! He belongs to me!"

Anger stirred to life within Danielle's heart after the other's proclamation. "I'm afraid if you have come here to make such statements, you are a bit too late. I am Wind Dancer's wife!"

Spring Lilly threw back her head, her shimmering hair cascading darkly down her back. "It will never be too late for Wind Dancer and myself! He will tire of your pale body soon enough, and when that happens, he will seek me out!"

"He will never do that, Spring Lilly. He is joined to me!" If nothing else, Danielle knew that Wind Dancer was a man who took vows seriously. He would never seek out another woman to commit adultery.

An evil smile pulled back the young woman's lips and revealed her shiny teeth. "Stupid *wasicun winyan!* A warrior such as Wind Dancer will have many wives! And on the day when we are joined, you will wish you had never come to this village!"

What was this woman talking about? Danielle had never even considered that Wind Dancer would wish to take another wife. She had been taught that a man had only one wife; could Wind Dancer possibly think that she would stand by and allow him to have more? Some small inner voice told her to remain calm. Spring Lilly was only trying to provoke her anger. Raising her chin, she looked the woman directly in the face. "If Wind Dancer had wanted you, he would have asked you long ago to be his wife. He will need no other woman now!"

Spring Lilly's cheeks blushed hotly with the white woman's taunting words. "You have bewitched him with your pale looks and silver hair! You have taken what is mine!" The words, spat out in the Indian language, were laced with hatred.

Slowly, Spring Lilly lifted up her hand, which had been hanging down at her side, and she revealed a long, wicked-looking knife held tightly in her fist.

Danielle gasped aloud and intentionally took a step backward. The threat of the sharp blade was a real one, and Danielle could read the intent in the other woman's eyes. "Surely you know that Wind Dancer does as he pleases! I could never have bewitched him! I could not have kept him from you if he had wanted you!"

For a flashing moment, the ugliness of revenge and hatred was swept from the girl's features, and Danielle caught a glimpse of true beauty as Spring Lilly remembered a time when Wind Dancer had desired her. "He did desire me before Red Fox brought you here to our village! We would have joined together this night if you had not come among us. He forgets Spring Lilly, for he is blinded by your pale looks!" Once again, her features contorted with fury and her need for vengeance. "After Wind Dancer mourns your loss, he will again turn to Spring Lilly! He will find me willing to give him warmth and comfort. He will find much pleasure in my arms!"

Feeling her own anger rising with the other woman's words, Danielle looked around for something to use as a weapon as she stated coldly, "You are insane, Spring Lilly, if you think for one minute that Wind Dancer will take the killer of his wife to his heart! He will shun you if he does not kill you himself!" She slowly bent and picked up one of the furs near the fire to use as a shield if the girl attacked her.

"Wind Dancer will never know that it was I who put the knife through your witch's heart! When he returns from the river, he will find you lying in a pool of your own blood, and I, Spring Lilly, will be there to comfort him!" Spring Lilly cautiously stepped around the fire, her eyes never leaving Silver Dove's as she drew back her hand.

With spellbound eyes, Danielle watched the shining blade coming toward her. She back away, holding up the fur as a shield while the other woman rushed forward.

Wind Dancer's fierce war cry broke the intense quiet of the lodge as he rushed in. Seeing Spring Lilly attack Silver Dove, he threw his large body on the slender Indian maiden, his huge fist slamming down on the arm that clutched the knife. His actions sent the young woman crashing to the floor.

With wide, staring eyes of disbelief, Danielle watched the scene before her, hardly able to breathe. She watched as Wind Dancer clutched the hand that held the cruel knife, his other hand wrapped around the young woman's slender throat. The vengeful look in his glittering black eyes was terrible to behold, intent as he was upon bringing the attacker under complete control. "No!" Danielle at last cried out as she witnessed the girl squirming beneath his body, her face turning blue from lack of oxygen. Fully regaining her senses, Danielle ran to Wind Dancer's side and grabbed hold of the hand around the other woman's throat. Slowly, her pleas for the Indian maiden's life penetrated the void of blackness that had overtaken the warrior's brain. The large hand relaxed and Wind Dancer's gaze turned toward Danielle.

"You are unhurt, Silver Dove? he questioned before turning the girl loose from his hands.

Nodding her head, Danielle watched Wind Dancer rise slowly to his feet, his dark gaze going over her form to make sure she was unharmed. His eyes then lowered to the woman at his feet.

"She intended to kill me," Danielle whispered in English, and for the first time, her tears began to fall.

"She will be punished for her actions, Silver Dove. Have no fear—she will never dare such a thing again." He wrapped his strong arms around her. "I will go to Brave-Bull myself and tell him of his daughter's treachery."

"No, Wind Dancer, please don't leave me." Danielle wiped away her tears with the back of her hand. "Spring Lilly loves you, and hoped that one day it would be she who married you. I have not the heart to see her punished for her feelings."

"I have given her no reason to think that I would ever join with her." Wind Dancer tightened his grip upon his bride, not certain if she had believed him capable of deceiving the maiden or not.

"She is indeed very foolish." Danielle felt a great weight being removed from her heart as Wind Dancer looked deeply into her eyes. She knew that he had spoken the truth. "You need not go to her father. Spring Lilly has already been given enough punishment."

Spring Lilly staggered to her feet. Hearing the two speaking in English, she lowered her dark eyes as they filled with tears. She had believed, in that moment beneath Wind Dancer's hands, that she would die. The white woman had saved her life, and this fact intensified her hatred.

"You will not come near Silver Dove again," Wind Dancer said harshly in the Sioux tongue. "Silver Dove is mine, given to me by Wakán Tanka, and no hand shall touch her in harm! If you dare such an act again, I will not release you from my grasp until your last breath has gone from your body."

Spring Lilly raised her tear-swollen face and looked upon the fierce visage of the man she had loved for so long. She knew that he was lost to her as long as the white woman lived. The spell Silver Dove had cast upon him was so strong that it left him blind to any other woman. He would even kill one of his own people for her. A shudder coursed through her body as she silently nodded her head. Then without another look upon the white witch, she turned and fled the lodge.

Chapter Thirteen

After Spring Lilly's departure from the lodge, the couple settled down on the furs at the edge of the fire. Neither spoke as they looked into the flames and gave their bodies time to calm down from the happenings of the evening. Wind Dancer kept envisioning the large knife that had threatened his beloved wife, and he shuddered to think of the sharp pain of loss he would have suffered if he had not entered his lodge when he had.

Sensing when Danielle was finally relaxing before the warmth of the fire, he ventured softly, "Do you fear me, Silver Dove?"

Danielle was not sure how she should respond to such a question. When she was around him, she could think only of being held in his arms. *Did she fear him?* He had never harmed or threatened her, and she knew that he would protect her with his life. Why should she fear him? Perhaps she feared his way of life, or perhaps she feared the strange, alluring power he had over her. But when asking herself if she feared that he would ever harm her, she had to answer honestly. Silently she shook her head.

A soft sigh escaped his chest. "I know you are

nervous about this thing that is between us and the feelings that come over your body when you are near me, Silver Dove. I wish you to know that I will not push you. I have waited a lifetime for you, and I am willing to wait longer, until you are sure of what lies within your heart."

He spoke tenderly and wisely to her, and Danielle could not calm the wild fluttering of her heart at his nearness. So much had happened this evening—their joining, then Spring Lilly's appearance in the lodge. She felt a fierce attraction for him, but was helpless to know how she should handle her feelings. She would have thanked him for not rushing her, but she was unable to get the words out of her dry throat.

"You did not ask me what the braves wished for me to judge, or the reason that my hair is wet." The best course of action might be for them to talk about other things, and give her time to adjust to his nearness.

Danielle looked at him with questioning eyes. She had totally forgotten to ask him what happened when he left the lodge, and in truth, she had barely noticed that his hair was wet. "What did the braves want?" she softly responded.

Relaxing against the furs and the willow backrest, he smiled tenderly upon her, his hand reaching out and lightly caressing the length of her arm. "I was made to judge a swimming race between Little Otter and Short Bow."

"At this time of night, they had a swimming race?" Danielle was surprised, and turned her full attention upon him.

"Han, my heart. It was a diversion the braves thought up to keep us apart for a short time this night." Thank Wakán Tanka that he had remained

no longer with the other men than he had. His hand tightened on the fur beneath his palm. Silver Dove would have been taken from this life if he had been delayed for only a few more minutes.

"And who won the race?" Danielle could think of nothing else to say, and with his nearness, and the warmth of the fire, she was beginning to feel very comfortable indeed.

Wind Dancer's husky laughter filled the lodge. "Little Otter, of course. When he was very young, he could outswim all the other boys in the village. That is why his father, Standing Elk, named him Little Otter."

Danielle smiled at his response. "And your hair? Why is it wet?"

"After the race between Little Otter and Short Bow, I had to race the winner in order to be able to return to my lodge." His husky laughter filled her ears, and made her feel more at ease. "Why do you not hand me your brush, Silver Dove, and I will tend to your hair?" He saw the brush lying on the furs, and having desired to do this since the first day he had laid eyes upon her, he waited for her to hand it to him. Her silver tresses were an invitation he could not resist.

Danielle handed him the brush, then moved between his muscular thighs as he patted the furs before him. "Come, Silver Dove," he invited her. "Relax before the warmth of the fire, and I will brush your hair."

She could only comply, and within seconds, her long hair was covering his lap, her back brushing lightly against his chest as her slender thighs were surrounded by his powerful ones. Her eyes closed tightly, her breathing shallow, she felt his strong fingers roaming through her hair.

Drawing the brush through the silver softness, Wind Dancer could not remember a time in his life when he had felt so at peace. Here in his arms was the woman of his heart, and with a warm fire burning and shedding its light, he could ask for little more from the Great Spirit. "Why do you not tell me about your life before you were brought here to my village?" Perhaps the one called Samuel still plagued her thoughts. With the speaking of him, she could chase his image from the lodge, and she would be able to enjoy the attentions of her husband, Wind Dancer thought to himself.

Danielle was unsure where she should start. "What do you wish to know, Wind Dancer?"

"Whatever you wish to share with me." Wind Dancer gently ran the brush through her hair, and as he looked down and glimpsed the tresses lying over his bronzed thigh, he marveled at the beauty and texture of such hair.

For a moment Danielle hesitated, but as the quiet of the lodge relaxed her, she began to tell him about her parents, and their death.

Hearing the sorrow and pain of loss in her voice, he said, "I was fourteen summers when this happened. It was when I sought out my vision and saw you for the first time. The Great Spirit knew of your loss and your need. He also knew what my need would be as a man."

Danielle gave no reply to his softly spoken words, but told him about her aunt and uncle and how they had all started out for Oregon.

"Did you wish to go to this place called Oregon, Silver Dove?"

Truthfully, Danielle had not cared about going to Oregon. She would have preferred to stay on her father's farm. At first, the wagon train had seemed like a grand adventure, but life on the trail, and Samuel Taylor, had been tiresome. "It doesn't matter now, Wind Dancer," she responded.

She had grown comfortable in his arms while talking about her life, and as she leaned against the sturdy bulwark of his chest, Wind Dancer questioned her softly, "What does matter now, Silver Dove?"

For a single, crazy moment, she was almost tempted to blurt out, *You are the only thing that matters to me, Wind Dancer,* but she caught herself in time. Such a confession would surely give this man too much power over her. Instead she responded, "I am not sure."

"Does your Samuel still matter in your heart?" Wind Dancer's breath caught in his chest as he waited for her reply.

"Samuel never mattered that much to me. I only agreed to marry him because it seemed like the right thing to do. My aunt and uncle were very happy at the prospect." But she would never have been able to go through with the wedding. She knew this now, especially after knowing Wind Dancer.

His breathing became normal after her confession, and his hand rose up to press against his chest. "Then your heart has waited for me, Silver Dove." The words were softly breathed against her hair as he inhaled the fragrant scent of sweet flowers, and chills raced down her length.

This man had a potent way of seducing her senses, but Danielle fought to keep some control. Turning her head to better view his features, she looked into his sable eyes and asked, "And what of your heart, Wind Dancer? Has it also waited for me?"

"I have told you that, from the day of my vision, I have waited for you to come into my life circle." Wind Dancer spoke honestly, but still he read in her gaze an unasked question.

"What of Spring Lilly, Wind Dancer?" She had not meant to bring up the other woman's name after what had happened that evening, but the Indian maiden's taunts about becoming Wind Dancer's second wife would not flee her mind.

"What is it you wish to know of Spring Lilly, Silver Dove?" He desired no lies between them. Whatever she asked of him, he would answer honestly.

"Did you intend to make her your second wife?" She blurted the question out at last. "I know that after what happened here this evening, you would never do so, but did you have such thoughts of taking another wife after me?"

Turning her body on his lap, he forced her face to turn to him. He could well imagine what Spring Lilly had said to her to bring about such questions. With his finger beneath her chin, he looked into her eyes and answered truthfully. "You alone hold my heart, Silver Dove. There is no room for another woman in my heart, or my lodge. I will never wish another wife; you are everything to me."

A smile came instantly over her lips. She believed him totally. "I'm glad, Wind Dancer," she admitted.

Without restraint, Wind Dancer's arms tightened around her. His head lowered, and tenderly his lips slanted over the inviting smile. There was no pressure or hurry in the kiss. Wind Dancer was content that he held the woman of his heart and that, from this night forth, she would share his life. As their lips parted, he leaned against the backrest, but his arms did not slacken their hold upon her. He drew her against him so that her soft cheek rested upon his broad chest. "I have often dreamt of this moment, Silver Dove. I am content to hold you in my arms."

Danielle was amazed at his patience. Any other man would not be content on their wedding night until he had claimed all that he believed due him from his bride. "Do you think that the ceremony Medicine Wolf performed was real?"

Her words barely reached Wind Dancer's ears, but their meaning instantly struck a nerve. Turning her back to look at his face, he calmly stated, "The joining ceremony of my people is real, Silver Dove. You and I are as one until we are parted from this life, and even then, we shall be reclaimed together with the sky people."

"I didn't mean to ask if the ceremony was real for your people, Wind Dancer," she tried to explain. "I mean, well, you lived with the white man. Do you think that our ceremony would be considered a real wedding by everyone?" She needed to hear his thoughts on this subject, for her own thoughts were so jumbled and clouded, she was not sure. If she wasn't sure about the ceremony, how could she truly consider herself a wife, and this man her husband?

"What is real to some people is but smoke to others. My people believe that their blessings come from Wakán Tanka. There is but one Great Spirit, Silver Dove. The white man calls Him God, we call Him by another name. Medicine Wolf prayed for Wakán Tanka to bless our joining and for Him to teach us His will for our lives. You felt the power in the sacred pipe as the prayers were being said. Would the God of your own people not honor our joining?"

Danielle was struck by how wise this man was. In his few words, he had summed up her fears and put them in their place. She had felt the strange current of power race up her arm as she had touched the pipe with Wind Dancer, when Medicine Wolf had prayed over them. Would her own God not consider such a ceremony binding? Was it truly necessary for a couple to wed in a church? She had heard of ships' captains wedding couples, and if a ship's captain could marry others, surely an Indian shaman could do the same. As Wind Dancer had said, there was only one true God.

Wind Dancer studied her features and glimpsed understanding coming to her. "Wakán Tanka whispered to me of you long ago, and filled my heart with your image. This night, He joined our paths throughout this life and all eternity. No one will ever change this." Looking deeply into the turquoise eyes rimmed with gold, he whispered softly, "You are the beating of my heart, the reason for my walk on Mother Earth."

Danielle felt her inner being melting from the heartfelt tenderness of his words. Truly, nothing else mattered except Wind Dancer and the feelings he evoked deep within her soul. He alone had the power to chip away at the defenses she had built up around her heart. His words promised that she would never again be alone. At last, someone loved her totally and completely!

Her woman's heart clung to the promise as she lost herself within the warm, ebony depths of his gaze. "Wind Dancer . . . I . . ."

"*Shhhh,* my heart. You do not need to say anything. What is between us is something deeper than words can say." His finger lightly traced the pouting outline of her lower lip. "We have this lifetime to learn of each other, and to let our feelings for one another grow." Slowly, his head lowered and followed the trail of his finger. He drew her lips apart, savoring the honeyed taste of sweet ambrosia.

Danielle's senses were totally ensnared by the power of this kiss. Within seconds, the gentle touch of his lips turned to seeking hunger, and she lay against his chest with her arms around his shoulders, fingers twined within the silken strands of his midnight hair.

Without the usual caution she felt in his presence, Danielle pressed herself closer into him, her mouth accepting and fully responding to the sensual assault over her lips. As he drew back, her breasts pressed tighter on his chest, and her mouth covered his own. Her small tongue roamed lightly over his lips and slipped into his mouth, brushing his strong, white teeth. Her actions made his body tremble as she leaned over him and, with a soft sigh, placed her small weight fully upon him. Wind Dancer could not hold himself still. His strong arms reached out and encircled her as his own tongue stroked and explored hers, delving deeply within the sweet cavern of her mouth and delighting in the warm, sweet taste of her.

Time seemed to stand still as lips and tongues endlessly discovered the pleasurable contact of one another. When his lips left hers, Danielle thought their heated experimenting was at a finish. She was pleasantly surprised when his lips and tongue resumed their roaming, drawing a path over her chin and down her slender neck. His fingers unfastened the beaded collar and the top lacings of her dress, then his moist lips roamed lower.

Gasping softly, Danielle delighted in the wanton feelings his branding mouth was igniting in her body. Wondrously, his tongue laved her breasts. From one darkly tipped mound of flesh to the other, he kissed and suckled. As his mouth left one breast untended, fingers gently caressed and stroked it as his lips captured and teased the other. Danielle's breath came in tiny gasps of sensual delight.

Deep within her secret depths, Danielle felt a growing ember beginning to flame. She leaned her head back, giving Wind Dancer complete access to her throat and breasts. The feelings he stirred left her trembling with an inner need. She felt as though she were but a piece of clay being molded by a master's hands as Wind Dancer seared her very being with the touch of his hands and the fire of his lips. Her entire body quivered beneath his experienced touch.

Wind Dancer knew that he could easily put an end to the wild torment that raged out of control throughout their bodies. From the first moment he had set eyes on this woman, he had craved her as no other. His body throbbed with a longing that was beyond anything he had ever known. As he gently nibbled at the soft underflesh of her breast, he breathed against her pale skin, "Let us go over to my sleeping couch. We will be much more comfortable." Still he wished not to rush or frighten her.

She was powerless to resist, or say the words that would keep him from gathering her into his arms and carrying her to the soft fur sleeping couch. Seconds later, Danielle lay upon the lush mound of furs. With the tenderest care, as Wind Dancer's onyx gaze looked deeply into hers, his hands eased her dress and leggings from her body. For a breathless moment, as he stood next to the sleeping couch, he stared down at the luscious perfection of her curves. The heat in his eyes seared every inch of her flesh as he gazed upon the fullness of the twin globes with dusty-rose-colored buds, down the length of her trim rib cage, to the tiny indent of her navel. His eyes took in the womanly flare of her hips and the long, slender, shapely legs. His gaze caressed the delicate ankles and slim feet, and roaming halfway up, his eyes filled with burning desire as he boldly looked upon the junction of her womanhood with its feathering of pale curls.

As his gaze returned to her face, Danielle's lips parted as if she would say something. But she was far too enthralled with the game of love play to force any words that would put a halt to this desire that was consuming her. As his heated gaze locked with her own and she glimpsed the unbridled lust in his eyes, she felt the escalating rampage of her heartbeat. She knew that Wind Dancer desired her above anything else in his life, and with that knowledge, she felt the full power of her woman's body. This was the raw essence of power, and her passion-laced wits welcomed the assault of his heady seduction!

With but a single pull of the leather tie at his waist, Wind Dancer allowed his breechcloth to fall from his body, his tall, broad frame standing for a full moment next to the sleeping couch as he watched his wife's azure gaze roam over his length.

Pure, primeval, muscular strength stood for her

viewing! Her flashing turquoise eyes moved slowly over the shimmering strands of midnight hair that lay against his back and caressed his tanned, muscle-rippled shoulders. His forearms and chest exuded power as they bulged with unleashed strength. Hard slabs of muscle-corded flesh covered his ribs and tapered down to a narrow waist and hips. The tight contours of his buttocks and powerful thighs were only glanced at as her attention was taken over by the giant, throbbing lance which protruded from his lower body. The sight left Danielle gasping, and as his gaze rose swiftly up to his, she saw there in his features a storm of desire that totally possessed her.

With their gazes still tightly locked, Wind Dancer lowered his body down upon the sleeping mat next to his wife's, his hard body brushing against her soft woman's curves. With the contact of naked flesh touching naked flesh, their passions ignited, and as the irresistible pull of pleasure's sweet promise sang throughout their bodies, Wind Dancer's head bent to her, his mouth descending as large hands reached out in exploration. "You touch this warrior's soul deeply, Silver Dove. Throughout my life, I have seen nothing that compares to your beauty. Your skin is softer than a floating snowflake sent from Grandfather Winter to Mother Earth." His hands, ever so tenderly, caressed her arms, his thumbs lightly brushing the fullness of her breasts as they traveled over her ribs and down her slender waist, to roam over her hips and upper thighs. "Your lips taste as sweet as a wild summer berry." His mouth covered those tempting petals, and for a time, he sampled the lushness.

As his mouth left hers, he feathered kisses along

her cheek and down her jawline to the tempting swell of her breasts. Locking and nibbling the tender flesh, he lavished his attention upon her breasts, his straight, white teeth caressing the underflesh and driving Danielle mad with desire as a moan escaped from deep within her throat. At the same time, his dark head lowered to the line of her rib cage and the tempting space of her waist and hips.

Long, tanned fingers slowly wound their way down over her belly, causing a shudder to course over her whole body. They lowered to the nest of her womanhood, and with the touch, she gasped as his fingers sought out her sheath of warmth, the very fountain of her being.

Moaning aloud, Danielle was totally consumed by the sensations that Wind Dancer erupted within her, his mouth upon her body, his fingers gently probing and tantalizing until she felt the heat of her body's passions flooding her entire being. Her slender form rose up from the bed to meet the movement of his hand.

Not wishing to hurry these first moments of love's awakening for his wife, Wind Dancer did not heed her moans for fulfillment. He desired her to be on fire for him, totally and completely consumed with the need for his body and their joining. With gentle movements, he pressed her back down upon the sleeping couch. The taste of her sweet young flesh and the feel of her satin-smooth body combined and seduced Wind Dancer into a physical wanting that knew no bounds! His hands splayed over the firmness of her belly, then gathered her lightly under the hips as he drew her closer. His tongue sent scalding sparks throughout the lower portion of her body as he laved the in-

PHOEBE
CONN

sides of her thighs. As the searing touch of his mouth followed the path made by his hands and touched upon her woman's jewel, Danielle's body bucked in surprise. Sweet, forbidden pleasure was snaking its way through her womb and down her limbs!

Riding high upon this newfound tide of pleasure, Danielle clutched Wind Dancer's hair, her fingers twining in the thick strands as his mouth opened her luscious pink woman's petal to reveal the priceless treasure within. His tongue plunged inside, tasting the bounty of her sweet essence, while this caress cast her headlong into the boundless pits of storming rapture. Her body arched forward with the first assault of his heated tongue, his strong hands upon her hips keeping her positioned as again and again he filled her with his stroking heat!

With her mind whirling out of control upon the outer edges of a swirling vortex of unbelievable feelings, Danielle was subject to an igniting deep within the lower depths of her belly, which slowly began to gush hot, molten sparks of insatiable desire coursing over her body and pulsing throughout her womanhood. She was consumed by a blazing inferno! The burning flamed higher and erupted! Her hands clutched his hair, raked his back; her head and shoulders rose off the furs as a cry of trembling pleasure burst from her mouth, and her entire form shook with a convulsing of satisfaction that she had never known before!

Wind Dancer continued his love play for a time longer, his tongue plunging into her moist, sweet depths, lingering over the nub at the center of her woman's peak as she quaked with shudder after passionate shudder. The sound of her cries filled his ears, furthering his desire to pleasure her to the very fullest.

With the relaxing of her fingers in his hair and the calming of her trembling, Wind Dancer rose from his position between her thighs. His lips seared branding kisses over her body as he pressed his full length against her. Witnessing the sated passion on her features, he bent his head to cover her lips.

Could this be that secret thing that goes on between a man and a woman? Danielle fleetingly considered as his lips plundered hers with a hunger that was even more demanding. Never had she experienced such passionate feelings! Never had she believed such feelings ever existed! The things Wind Dancer had done to her had swept away all reason, and taken her to a place where her body had responded with a hunger she had never known existed! But still, some portion of her innocent brain told her that there was more to experience as he pressed his length fully against her. The hot, thickened length of his throbbing rod sprang between them and sought out that place where, only short moments previously, his mouth had left her breathless.

There was no recourse for Danielle but to open to him; nor did she think otherwise, for she was too swept up in the rapture of the moment. As his searching tongue filled her mouth, the sculpted-marble head of his manhood made contact with the opening of her moist, shivering cleft.

His buttocks drew upward, and as an inch of his shaft entered her, he felt the tightness of her warm, pulsing sheath of love. Another inch and the velvet trembling of her inner sanctum drew forth a rumbling from deep in his chest, which filled the space of the lodge with an animal-like groan.

With the breaching of her virgin's body, Wind Dancer's body stilled atop her. His dark eyes glimpsed the small pain which crossed her delicate features, and he allowed her time to adjust to his presence within her. His mouth kept a steady assault upon her own, gently lulling her toward that passionate burning of moments before. As his tongue plunged again into her mouth, she felt her body beginning to respond. Slowly at first, she moved, and feeling little of the stinging pain gained from his first entry, she moved again, more fully against him, as though seeking out that elusive delight that she knew was within reach.

Wind Dancer felt her movement, but still he lingered, wishing her to accept him fully, not wanting to cause her any more pain but desiring to express and to share with her all the love he was feeling.

He did not hold back long, for Danielle's passion was as great as his own, and her movements coaxed him toward the full expression of his love. As Wind Dancer looked down into her delicate features, he softly whispered her name, "Mázaska Wakinyela," and in that moment, he wanted to share all with her. Even her pain, he took to his heart. His lips slowly descended in a kiss that caught her within the blooming of a tender budding, and slowly it grew to a tempting hunger. HIs body moved in a slow rhythm, not allowing the full thrust of his massive size to claim her, but remembering always to be considerate of her virgin's body. Slowly, he probed deeper into her velvet depths, then withdrew to the lips of her moist opening. Over and over, he plied her with his skillful seduction until, at last, she gave over completely to his masterful touch. She clutched his back, her head thrown back in mindless ecstasy as the fullness in her loins drove her toward a frenzy of swirling desire. Each time the brand of his lance drove into her hidden regions and stirred her, her body of its own will moved toward total fullness. Her legs slowly rose as she sought to capture the entire length of him.

Even as he felt the first stirrings of a shudder convulsing in her depths and traveling the length of his manhood, even as her sheath suddenly trembled and tightened, Wind Dancer forced himself to draw in deep gulps of air, willing himself not to let go of the true fury of his raging passions!

Danielle's entire body centered upon the branding flame of his probing shaft. Ecstasy coursed over her as her movements stroked and tightened around the swollen length of him. She slipped beyond control as her body thrashed wildly about, her hips jerking convulsively as she was swept into the realm of true and utter satisfaction.

Wind Dancer knew the power of her climax, and for a moment, he fought the heated need that raced through his loins to join her. His hungry gaze looked down into her features, and he witnessed the passion that filled her, heard the climatic moans escaping her lips. Each thrust was now torture-laced as he fought off the aching need for his own fulfillment. It was only when he knew she was descending from the dazzling heights of satisfaction that he allowed himself to give vent to his own steaming desires. His mouth covered her lips, and as he plunged just a fraction deeper into her soft velvety depths, scalding pleasure burst from the center of his being and showered upward, racing through his powerful shaft and erupting in a shimmering burst of pearl essence. "*Mázaska Wakinyela, mitá wicánte;* Silver Dove, my heart!" The words were torn from his lips, then his mouth covered hers in a kiss that joined them forever as one.

Chapter Fourteen

"Does it always feel like this? I mean, is it always so . . . so . . ." Danielle couldn't finish, and at the moment, she was glad that her face was pressed closely against his chest, so Wind Dancer couldn't view her blushing features. She knew for a fact that Penny had been lying to her about what took place between a man and a woman. These feelings, the love that she and Wind Dancer had shared, had been far more glorious than anything she had known in the past!

"Between you and me, it shall always be like this, Silver Dove." Wind Dancer delighted in the innocence of his young bride, and freely admitted that what he had shared with this woman, he had shared with no other. Never had he felt such overwhelming passion in another's arms. For all of her innocent ways, his wife had proven to be more woman than he had ever known.

"Then why have we waited so long to do this act of joining?" She remembered the times she had gone to him at night when he had been playing the courting flute, and how she had lost herself within the swirling ardor of his embrace. It would have been an easy thing for her to have given herself to him then, and she wondered why, when joining with him felt so heavenly, he had forced them both to wait until after the ceremony that Medicine Wolf had performed.

Wind Dancer had asked this same question of himself, but even now, with her soft curves closely drawn up against his own, he knew the answer. He had wanted their first time coming together to be right; not only for her, but in the eyes of his people and the Great Spirit. "The feelings that I have for you could not be expressed until after we were joined by the pipe, Silver Dove. I want you to know the full meaning of what is in my heart. What we shared this night with our bodies is unlike anything I have ever known in my past, but there is so much more than these feelings of the body. What burns in my heart tells me that I want to give you all that a man has to offer a woman. I freely give unto you all that I possess—I give you my lodge, my horses, the promise of protection, and provisions, from this day until my journey upon this life path ends and I go to join the sky people."

Danielle drew somewhat away from his tight embrace, to better view his face. "You need not say these things to me, Wind Dancer." She felt uncomfortable that he would offer her so much.

"To my people, a woman is the center of all things strong and good. She maintains the peace within the lodge, and her children are her own. I would willingly give you all that I own, knowing that if you found disfavor with me, you could turn me away from my lodge and my belongings. But I promise I shall never turn away from the promises I made to you this night. When I am an old man, you can set me from you, but I will still make sure that you have all that you are in need of."

"I would never turn you away, Wind Dancer." She was surprised at his words, and though her feelings for him were confused and she had not had the time to put them in order, she knew that what they shared could not be easily set aside.

"I tell you this only to express my feelings. Deep within my soul, I burn with a desire to take care of you, Silver Dove. I will be your shield against all the worries and problems of this life. I would desire never to view the crease of concern on your brow, or a frown upon your lips. When we have children, it is I who will teach them the way of Wakán Tanka, and lead them to be strong and brave of heart. I will never allow you to know disappointment. I want to take care of you!" His dark eyes touched her face and quickened the tempo of her heartbeat.

A soft cry expelled her lips as she clutched his neck and drew his head toward her. Before their lips joined, she responded as she felt tears filling her eyes, "No one has ever given me so much." She knew, as their mouths touched, that she alone held this brave warrior's heart, and with that knowledge, her head spun and her body reacted with fierce desire to give herself over to him without reserve. Her silken-smooth arms drew him even closer, and as a fiery kiss consumed them, her tongue tentatively entered his mouth and hesitantly swirled around his own.

With a groan of pure lust, Wind Dancer crushed her length to his own. The warm glow of passion was now rekindled to a full blaze once again, and with a quick movement, he pulled her on top of him, settling her legs astride his hips. Slowly, he drew her downward and filled her with the length of his manhood. His hands rested upon her hips and guided their motion as her head bent and her mouth heatedly caressed every part of his face.

Her lips then trailed a fiery path along his broad neck and over the rippling strength of his chest. Her silver hair enclosed them in a fine, delicately webbed curtain of silken threads as her body was caught up in the movements of his passionate strokes. Her entire body moved with his to a primal, lust-filled beat that was generated somewhere deep within their inner beings. Moving and seeking, her body rocked up and down as her breathing came in short, ragged gasps.

As his turgid manhood moved in and out of her honeyed depths, his heartbeat reached a racing tempo of searing desire. Her sweet mouth and moist lips roamed a seductive path over his muscular torso, as his hands guided her hips, and roamed freely over the tender flesh of her belly and buttocks. His head rose up from the fur coverings of the pallet, and his mouth closed over one rose-tipped nipple. His tongue swirled around the ripe bud in a teasing fashion, his teeth gently tugging as he suckled. He heard a cry of ecstasy leave her lips, and was driven to chart a dampened path from one straining breast to the other as she rocked, back and forth, upon the searing heat of his branding lance.

Scalding, rapturous ecstasy soared higher and higher until Danielle felt a flaming surge of passion igniting in her depths, growing out of control. She felt herself spinning into the heart of a whirling rush of euphoria, and she pulled Wind Dancer into its glowing center with her. For a time, they spun together upon the spiraling brink of a magnificent vortex.

Held within the raging throes of a towering climax, as Danielle cried aloud spasms swept her entire length. Only then did Wind Dancer seek out his own release. His manhood surged with one, last, mighty thrust, and with a hot gush of release, his seed erupted and showered into her womb.

Danielle lay spent upon Wind Dancer's chest. His breathing slowly grew even, and with some disbelief, he marveled that their second coming together could prove so wondrous. His fingers gently roamed over the soft curves of her slender back, and twined within the silver strands of hair. With a movement of his hand, he drew her chin upward and covered her lips with his own. "You are so much more than I ever thought to have in a wife; I am truly blessed," he breathed with the parting of their mouths.

Danielle was content to lie upon his chest forever. Never had she felt so deliciously exhausted, or so warmly protected. Each time he spoke to her, a small portion of her heart ached from the tenderness he extended. What type of man was he that he could pull such heartfelt feelings from her soul?

Without further words, Wind Dancer turned his large body and settled her down against the furs. Rising from the sleeping couch, he strode naked across the space of the lodge, and bending to the fire, he stoked the dim embers back to life. Drawing out a leather water pouch that rested near the fire, he retrieved a few heated rocks from the pit fire with a deer antler, and placing them in the pouch, he allowed the water a moment to heat.

Danielle watched his movements with a hungry feasting of her eyes. His powerful, bronzed body was beautiful to behold, and as the firelight caught the reflection of his handsome features, she felt her heartbeat fluttering in her chest with the thought that this man was her husband!

Wind Dancer picked up a cloth and took it and the water pouch, back to the sleeping pallet. Tenderly, he drew the dampened cloth over Danielle's breasts and across her belly. Then with the gentlest of touches, he bathed the flecks of blood that stained her inner thighs. "Tomorrow we leave the village, Silver Dove," he said as he bathed away the evidence of their passion.

"Where are we going?" Danielle questioned as she delighted in his tender ministrations.

"For the passing of a few suns, we will go to a place in the mountains that few of my people know about. We will go there and learn of each other, away from the villagers and prying eyes."

"A honeymoon?" Danielle sat up upon the bed of furs, her turquoise eyes glistening with the prospect of being all alone with her husband.

"I do not know this *wasichu* word that you speak." Wind Dancer set aside the cloth and water pouch. His dark eyes touched her face as he wondered about this word she had spoken: *honeymoon.*

"A honeymoon is a thing that my people do after they marry. They go away together, and like you said, they learn about each other." Danielle was excited at the prospect of being away from the village. It would be heaven to be alone with Wind Dancer!

"We, too, shall do this thing. I admit that you taste as sweet as the honey from a comb. I will enjoy this *honeymoon!*"

* * *

Shortly before daybreak the following morning, Wind Dancer kissed his sleeping bride. "Come, Silver Dove, it is time to waken."

Danielle snuggled closer against his body, responding without a second thought to the hard curves of his naked form. "*Hmm,*" she responded, her arms rising up and circling his neck.

Wind Dancer smiled softly, admitting to himself that he enjoyed wakening to the lush form of his wife. "I wish to leave early for this thing that you call *honeymoon,*" he whispered against the side of her throat as his lips planted tantalizing kisses against the swell of her bosom. "I thought we would avoid Autumn Woman and the other women of the village that will arrive at our lodge, after Wi has broken the sky, to inquire about your health and happiness."

Danielle stretched next to him, wishing to linger abed but knowing from his tone that he would have his way. "I'm so tired," she confessed next to his mouth before he covered her lips.

"I have already readied our things. You have but to come with me to the horse. Then you can sleep in my arms." Wind Dancer nuzzled her, not allowing her to fall back to sleep.

Within short moments, Wind Dancer was helping her to dress, not bothering to put on her moccasins. Then he carried her to his horse, which was tied outside the lodge with the Spotted One. Another mare had already been packed with the provisions the couple would need for their time away from the village.

"When did you ready all of this?" Danielle questioned after he lifted her onto the back of his pony.

"While you slept, I brought the horse to the lodge. Yesterday, I packed what we would need."

"Are you sure you got everything?" Danielle thought about all the things they might require—clothes, food, furs to sleep on, and even a lodge for shelter.

Wind Dancer saw the concern on her face, and quickly assured her, "Do not worry yourself, my heart. You will have everything you need. And what more could you ask for besides a strong husband to take care for you?"

What more indeed, Danielle wondered to herself, but before she could voice her worries, Wind Dancer jumped on his pony's back behind her, and taking hold of the lead rope to the mares, he set the horses into motion. "Trust your husband, Silver Dove." He gently eased her head against his chest, and cuddling her in a comfortable position in his arms, she found herself being lulled back to sleep by the motion of the pony and the trusting heartbeat sounding in her ear.

Danielle was unsure how long she slept, but when she awoke again, the sun was well into the sky. The route Wind Dancer took led through a forest; the trees overhead blocked the penetrating rays of the sun and enshrouded them in a cool canopy. Instead of speaking, Danielle kissed the hard, muscular flesh above her husband's breast.

"I wondered if you would sleep the day away," he softly said, and lightly kissed the top of her head.

"I'm sorry." She quickly tried to right herself, thinking that perhaps she had been an uncomfortable weight in his arms.

Wind Dancer's low, husky laughter filled her ears and his pony snorted at the noise from his master, which disturbed the quiet of the forest. Drawing her back against his chest, he assured her, "I have enjoyed every moment of holding you next to my heart, Silver Dove. I would spend the rest of my days in this fashion, if possible."

Danielle smiled softly to herself, knowing that he could view only the top of her head with her cheek pressed against his chest. "And I would love nothing more than to stay right here in your arms."

Her words were so softly spoken, he had to strain to make them out, but with the slim confession of her feelings, he felt his spirit soar. Thus far, she had been very quiet about her feelings for him, and with each tiny confession he gained, his heart sang in triumph.

"How much farther do we have to go before we get to the place you have chosen for our honeymoon?" Danielle tilted her head up to look at him, and was struck again by how handsome he was.

"It is not much longer." He bent his head and allowed his pony to continue down the forest trail on his own as he kissed the petal-soft lips that appeared to be waiting for his sampling.

Danielle eagerly kissed him in return, her slender arms wrapping around his neck as she delighted in the feel of his naked flesh beneath her hands. She liked the kissing and touching that went along with being married to this man!

"Are you hungry, Silver Dove?" Wind Dancer asked as his kisses feathered against the side of her mouth.

"*Hmmm,*" was the only response Danielle could make, as her own lips caressed his sculpted cheek, and seductively, her tongue roamed over his sensual lips.

Once again, his rumbling laughter started in his

chest and, escaping, filled her ears. "My hunger has no concern for food either, my heart."

"Such hunger will have to wait to be appeased," Danielle replied, with some regret in her tone. She had not thought herself capable of desiring a man's touch, but last night, Wind Dancer had taught her how much a woman could want a man. As she felt an inner heat beginning to grow within her depths, he caressed and kissed her, and she knew the full force of her longing to be taken completely by him.

"And why would we have to wait to claim what we both desire?" Wind Dancer said, his dark eyes burning into hers and leaving her staring at him in breathless anticipation. Without waiting for her to answer, he turned her body in his arms. His Indian saddle was large and comfortable, and he held her facing him, drawing her shapely legs up to slip easily around his waist. Right before his mouth slanted over hers, he murmured softly, "Did I not promise to take care of all your needs?"

And indeed, Wind Dancer was as good as his promise! As his pony slowly made his way down the forest trail, the lead rope to the two mares tied to the saddle, Wind Dancer drew Danielle's dress over her hips. With an easy movement of his hand, he freed the ties of his breechcloth, his manhood boldly displayed as he reached out and gently gathered her buttocks in his hands.

Danielle's indrawn breath caught in her chest as her turquoise eyes were captured and held within the power of his sable depths. As he drew her closer, she felt the heat of his shaft as it slipped into her moist opening. Slowly, he lowered her tight passage down upon the distended length of his powerful erection. Danielle gasped at the feeling of fullness, and her hands tightened around his shoulders, her hips beginning to move as sensual delirium swept over her.

With her movement, Wind Dancer's hands upon her hips stilled her. "Do not move, my heart. Let your body feast upon what I would feed it, as Little Brave Pony takes us to our destination." Wind Dancer's lips feasted of their own accord over the sweet flesh of her throat and breasts, and she was powerless to resist his erotic assault on her body and senses.

With each step the pony took, she felt the blood thickened length of him moving deeper, brushing against her womb, and then with the next step, withdrawing an inch. Another step and he moved back into her velvet-soft depths, then again back out. Every fiber of her being was attuned to his movements, his every caress, every kiss. She felt the swelling of his maleness, the pulse beat of his heart seeming to center within the throbbing tightness of her sheath. How much of this rapturous assault was she supposed to take before her body turned into a feverish caldron of unquenchable need?

Wind Dancer's feelings were much the same. Each time the horse moved, he felt the exquisite stirring of his manhood moving in and out of her tight, moist depths, and with a strong will, he mastered his desperate desire for a quick release. "You are so beautiful, Silver Dove," he murmured as the ties of her dress fell about her shoulders, and her breasts were bared for his gaze. "I love you with a passion that is so consuming, I fear that all of my heart, mind, and soul are caught within your spell."

The sound of his voice, whispering husky words

of adoration, the feel of his mouth and hands, his scent, his strength, his very taste, spurred Danielle's body on as she trembled upon the turgid heat of his lance. Her body was a mass of quivering sensations, her breasts aching with delightful yearning which was wrought by his lips, tongue, and hands. Unable to remain still a moment longer, she writhed against him, driven by a blinding need as her senses took complete control and led her into undreamed-of bliss, turning her silken limbs into instruments of pleasure that enfolded her husband and urged him onward.

As her body moved against him, Wind Dancer no longer had the will to resist the silken pleasure as she moved up and down upon his shaft. His mouth caught hers, his hands spanning the fullness of her buttocks as they helped her find fulfillment, and as a surge of pulsating rapture caught and pent-up cinders exploded, his own passions ran rampant within his body.

Danielle was drawn into a fiery, consuming need, lost to his touch, his feel. Rapturous explosions shattered deeply within her until she was certain her body and soul had joined as one. With a hoarse cry, she clutched tighter to his shoulders, her legs rising higher about his waist, accepting all that he had to offer her and delighting in matching his rapid, pulsating rhythm.

Husband and wife, male and female, their bodies became as one, their senses intermingling. Danielle felt deeply within a surging tide beginning to erupt. Her body trembled and strained, shuddered and pushed toward him, as she spiraled upward, seeming to fly above the earth and soar upon the fleecy down of heaven's clouds. She was entirely lost to everything but this man she was joined with, this fierce and bold warrior who had shown her the sweet, searing flame of passion's bliss!

With a deep growl, Wind Dancer also crossed the sweet abyss of pleasure's satisfaction. As he lost himself in a sparkling cascade of brilliant rapture, his lower body arched and he expelled his release.

Clasping tightly together, slowly, ever so slowly, their world came back into focus as bird calls filled their ears, and Little Brave Pony threw his head back in wonder at the strange creatures on his back.

"Will we always feel this powerful need for each other?" Danielle's soft words touched his ears in a breathless question. Her dampened forehead lay against his chest as his heartbeat filled her ears and seemed to be a part of her own quickening heartbeat. She had so many unanswered questions about these feelings she harbored for this man, and knew no other way to put them in order besides asking him his thoughts on the subject of what was between them.

"It shall never be any other way, Silver Dove. When I am an old man sitting before my fire, telling my grandchildren about my deeds as a young brave, I will look across our lodge and view you with longing in my blood. I will never grow tired of feeling you against my body, of touching your soft skin and hearing the sounds escape your throat when you are deep in passion."

Could ever a man love so completely, so fully, that he could make such a statement? She wondered at this love as she looked up and viewed the truth on his features. He seemed so sure of himself and his feelings. She wondered if the feelings that she harbored in her own chest for him could possibly be love? Could it be true that she loved this warrior chief?

Chapter Fifteen

The word *honeymoon* took on new meaning for Danielle over the next few days as she and Wind Dancer spent every waking moment learning more of each other, and every sleeping moment, wrapped in each other's arms. The spot where he took her was the most beautiful place she had ever seen, and upon first glance she knew it would be imprinted upon her memory throughout her life.

Little Brave Pony had followed the forest trail, and as the rushing sound of water filled their ears, Danielle gazed around in awe at the panorama of spectacular beauty.

For a few minutes, neither spoke as they looked upon the cascading waterfall which, like shimmering, rushing silk, showered down from the side of the mountain in a wondrous display of swirling, glittering diamond droplets. The afternoon sunlight sparkled full upon the falls in a dazzling cast of brilliant, multicolored gems as the rushing water was captured within an appealing crystalline pond.

"It is wonderful," Danielle whispered, her gaze transfixed upon the sight.

Wind Dancer did not speak, but squeezed her waist slightly, now viewing the sight before him with different eyes because Silver Dove was there with him. The beauty and serenity he had experienced in the past were intensified because he was sharing the scene with the woman who completed his life circle.

"This is the perfect spot for a honeymoon!" Danielle smiled, her turquoise eyes spying the tepee that had been erected not far from the pond. "When did you set up the lodge? Whenever did you have the time?"

"Black Bull helped me." He pulled her off the pony, and dropping the reins, he allowed the animals to graze on the tall, sweet grass, knowing they wouldn't wander far. "Black Bull told me some time ago that he and Pretty Quill had sought privacy for a few days after they joined, and without question, I knew that this spot was where I would bring you. I am pleased that you like it, and that you are here to share this beauty with me." He took her hand into his own, and led her toward the lodge.

The tepee near the pond's edge was much smaller than Wind Dancer's lodge in the Sioux village, but inside, he had built a small, center fire pit, and in one corner of the space was a pile of lush furs. It was cozy and inviting, and turning toward her husband, Danielle smiled. "And I was worried that you wouldn't remember everything we might need."

"I will take care of all your needs, Silver Dove." He turned her in his arms and for a moment they silently shared the bounty of passion that sparked heatedly between them when they were close. "I will unpack the horses, then let us go for a swim."

Danielle remembered the last time they had swum together, and anticipation raced through her veins. The day they had swum in the stream during the buffalo hunt had been one of the best days of her life.

As promised, as soon as Wind Dancer finished unpacking and putting away their provisions, he and Danielle took a swim in the cool, sparkling clear pond. Danielle felt somewhat self-conscious about shedding her clothes at the side of the pond in broad daylight, but with Wind Dancer at her side, teasing and playfully putting her at ease, she soon forgot that she and her husband were totally naked. Within these isolated surroundings, the couple spent the rest of the day frolicking and swimming in and around the falls. It seemed the most natural thing to feel Wind Dancer's large hands circling her waist and lifting her, only to plunge her down into the cool, swirling depths once again.

The afternoon was warmed by the heat of the sun, but the water in the pond, being fed by the waterfall created by the mountain's runoff of icy water, was chilly indeed. Wind Dancer watched Danielle's lips turn blue and her teeth begin to chatter. Hugging her tightly, he said, "I will warm your blood, *mitá wicánte.*"

With a push against him, Danielle won her freedom, and hurriedly swimming toward the opposite bank, she shouted, "I think you had intentions of freezing me to death when you set up camp near this pond!" Hearing him not far behind her, she pushed her limbs harder to outrace him.

Wind Dancer grinned heartily, pleased by the afternoon play they had shared. He allowed her to go some distance from him as he watched her sure strokes, and the pleasant picture of her silken curves rising above the water's surface filling his heated gaze.

As she neared the bank, he swam with swifter strokes to gain distance. Diving beneath the water, he grabbed her ankle and pulled her down into the cool depths, and into his waiting arms. "I will never allow you to flee me, *mitá wicánte.* There shall never be any escaping these arms that now possess you!" He laughed aloud as they rose up together, the pond's glistening water droplets shimmering over their naked torsos.

"I have no wish ever to flee your arms, Wind Dancer." Danielle's tone turned serious, though her words were softly spoken. She knew herself to be stating the truth.

"Nor will I ever allow you to, Silver Dove. I will do all in my power to keep you happy here at my side." He rose to his full height with her still cradled in his arms, her arms wrapped around his neck. Carrying her to the pond's edge, with water still clinging to their bodies, he lowered her upon the soft grass and whispered words of love into her ears. They touched and caressed until their ravenous hunger for each other had to be quickly quenched.

Instantly responding to his gentle, searching hands and the Indian love words he whispered next to her ear, Danielle succumbed to the desire burning through her. His fingers elicited a rapturous trail of fire over her flesh as he caressed her full, firm breasts. When his tongue followed the same path, scorching her body with endless kisses, she knew within her heart that this man was totally hers, for this moment and forever. Whether time stood still or was borne on wings, there would be no changing this warrior's heart. He loved her with a depth that left her breathless. At the moment, nothing else in her life mattered but the words of adoration he whispered in her ear.

Her senses pulled her deeper and deeper into realms of feeling that only he had the power to awaken, and soon she was responding just as hungrily to each touch, each kiss.

The gentle arch of her body, the simplest touch of her slender fingers against his back, were heady inducements, which caused every cell in Wind Dancer's body to be attuned to her wants and desires. Lips meeting and hearts beating wildly, for timeless minutes they soared where no other had dared, before their senses softly floated back to reality.

Against the backdrop of soft green grass, with a cool canopy of trees overhead, their coloring was in vibrant contrast; her skin like a translucent pearl, his like polished copper. Lifting one of the pale, damp curls from her shoulder, Wind Dancer kissed the silken flesh beneath, his ebony eyes looking deeply into Danielle's face as he leaned over her upon an elbow. "The time we share here together will remain deeply etched in my heart, Silver Dove," he whispered softly.

Danielle knew that his words mirrored her own thoughts, but still she could not bring herself to say those things that he had stirred in her heart. These feelings were too new still, and she unsure of herself.

Wind Dancer read some of her feelings in the depths of her sparkling eyes, but he was determined that he could wait for her to express what was in her heart, without rushing the admission from her lips.

* * *

The next few days passed far too quickly as they loved and learned of each other. There was not a moment they did not share together. They swam, played, hunted, and slept side by side. Their souls seemed to have joined, as had their hearts and minds.

Oftentimes throughout these days, they sat together along the pond's edge, neither feeling the need to speak. The life-giving sun was warm upon their backs, for Danielle, the second day at the falls, had been convinced by her husband to wear only a small breechcloth that tied at the waist. In their seclusion, only his eyes could view her naked beauty. Silently, they would sit and watch the smooth glitter of the swirling pond's water, and the gentle forest breezes working magic among the many trees as dancing butterflies fluttered by and the sweet sounds of bird songs flittered through the treetops.

Wind Dancer's large hand would move gently over her back, and loving his touch, Danielle would lean her head back, accepting the caress of his hand which traveled over her cheek and along the outline of her slender throat. The soft, loving looks he gave her bespoke his inner feelings, and bending toward her, he would kiss her every so often. There was nothing to be said during these times, nothing else to do or be; only this place, this time of oneness together mattered.

Hand in hand, they walked through the surrounding forest. Wind Dancer took time to teach his bride how to make a snare to capture a rabbit and how to use his bow and arrow. Danielle had no desire to learn to hunt, but she could not resist the temptation of feeling Wind Dancer's strong arms around her, as he helped her steady the arrow and draw back the bow. With new eyes, Danielle took in the sights of the forest. Before coming to the Sioux village, she had been alone, but now with Wind Dancer at her side, she saw much through his eyes. Together they would spy a pair of cardinals building a nest for their young on a low-hanging branch, a raccoon sitting alone beside the river and washing his breakfast, or a deer and her fawn feeding in the lush summer grass. She saw and felt as he did. A mysterious inner unity that had bound their flesh as one had settled over their minds, claiming them as one being. Perhaps since the very beginning of time, this joining of their bodies and minds had been awaiting discovery.

Not a night passed when they did not explore the delights of the flesh. As Wind Dancer looked upon Danielle's naked body on the softness of his thick bed of fur, his breathing deepened in passion, and slowly he would lean over her and claim her lips with his own. His kiss was always gentle at first, then more demanding, all-consuming; without a second thought, Danielle would loop her arms around his neck, pressing her full length against him. Her small tongue darted forward to meet his, the searing contact sensual and inviting.

His mouth would slant over hers and continue to conquer her skillfully again and again. Lovingly his kisses would rain along her chin and down her slender throat, capturing a taut breast, his tongue circling with a warm wetness that drove Danielle mindless with desire. His hands roamed over her body, sliding gently over her upper limbs, down her firm belly and ribs, and across shapely hips, lingering seductively at the crest of her woman's passion. His fondling continued until he brought her to such heights of rapture that she, with a deep-throated moan, would arch her hips against his probing finger, her body undulating and writhing with an unquenchable need for fulfillment. When she thought she could take no more of this searing torture, Wind Dancer would slide down the bed, part her legs, and move between them, his large manhood filling her completely.

Their joining was all-encompassing, leaving no room for thought as he moved atop her, and she responded fully to every pulsating, rhythmic stirring deep within. Wrapping her legs around his hips, she matched him movement for movement. They glided upon the wings of creation's bliss, sweeping toward the starry, velvet heavens in the arms of wonder. They were one, their heated murmurings of love sealing their union. As Wind Dancer plunged deeply, Danielle began to tremble in the center of her body. She called out her lover's name as she shook from head to foot, her body spinning into a vortex of shattering fulfillment.

Wind Dancer looked down into the passion-laced wonder in her face, and he, too, rushed over the brink of rapture, his large body quaking as his life-giving seed spilled within the womb of the woman he had claimed for his heart.

No words were spoken, for none were needed to express their feelings as they were wrapped tightly in each other's arms. As sleep lulled Danielle's senses and her eyelids fluttered closed Wind Dancer gently tugged the fur coverings up beneath her chin, as though she were an innocent child. For a time, he looked upon her loveliness by the dim light of the pit fire, and words resounded in his head: *Throughout this life I have known that I love you, Silver Dove. But never did I imagine it could be anything like this. The Great Spirit looked upon me with favor and surely blessed this warrior with his most priceless treasure when he sent you to me.* Only his own heart heard these words, but they were engraved within his soul forever.

Chapter Sixteen

Gazing upon the red dawn of early morning, Wind Dancer held out his pipe and greeted Wi at Mother Earth's edge. Gratefully he murmured prayers of thanksgiving for this gift of a new day. As he did each morning, he beseeched Wi to lead him toward wisdom and understanding of all things around him.

He turned toward the south, his pipe outstretched, he intoned prayers of thanks for the shelter, plant food, and medicinal herbs that the south powers imparted.

Facing the west, his prayers of thanksgiving were called aloud to the west winds that brought forth the life-giving rains that fed Mother Earth. All great power came from the west.

Facing the north, he looked high into the mountains and viewed the blanket of white snow upon the mountain tops. He thanked the north power for the gift of this cleansing coolness, which melts in the springtime and leaves Mother Earth refreshed and pure.

Bending, he touched his pipe to Mother Earth and acknowledged the power of life that she held. Even the deer, pierced by his arrow, was created to feed the people by the power of Mother Earth. In his pain, he would lie upon the earth seeking comfort, and pushing the arrow farther into his body, he would give up his life to feed those in need.

Lastly, Wind Dancer held his pipe upward toward Skan, toward the mighty power of Wakán Tanka, and thanked Him for the bounty that filled his life. He was blessed, and never tired of speaking the feelings from his heart that he had for the Great Spirit. His life path was in oneness with all things, now that Silver Dove was his wife, but this morning, as on each since Silver Dove had been brought to his village, he prayed that she would accept her heart and joyfully accept him as that part of her life that was meant to bring her a wholeness of mind and body.

Stretching lazily upon her pallet of furs, Danielle reached out in search of her husband's warm body. Finding the opposite side of the bed empty, she rose up on an elbow and searched the dim interior of the lodge. Not finding any sign of Wind Dancer, she rose naked from the sleeping couch, a small yawn escaping her lips, and made her way to the entrance flap. Wind Dancer had secured the flap on the outside of the lodge in order for a morning breeze to stir within, and without stepping outside, Danielle caught sight of her husband standing on the pond's edge. He was entirely naked, the morning sun glistening from his bronzed skin. His powerful and male beauty stood there for her complete viewing. Seeing his lips move as he held the pipe over his head, she knew him to be in prayer.

As she studied him, she gained more insight into this man's character. His size and strength commanded respect, his wisdom having earned him the high honor of leading his people, but looking at him now, she saw more into the man himself. He was secure in his place in this world. Unlike any other man she had ever known, he was confident in all things around him and in the god of his people.

Silently leaving the lodge, she approached him. His back was turned to her as he faced the pond, but she could still hear his words of prayer over the rushing sound of the falls. She stood directly behind him, and wanting not to interrupt him yet somehow to participate in this moment, she pressed herself against the muscular contours of his back.

She heard the slight noise of his indrawn breath, but his prayers did not cease, and for a few minutes, she listened to his request that the Great Spirit bless his home and his family. When at last he turned to face her, he saw the tears that dampened her eyes. "I awoke and you were gone from the lodge," she tried to explain, even though her heart trembled from hearing the heartfelt words he had called out to his god.

"Even away from our village, I must greet Wi with a morning prayer. It is a wise man who knows his own limitations, and knows his need to depend upon that One who is above all others." He explained no further. Instead, he said, "Today will be our last day in this place. We return to the village tomorrow morning."

"I know," Danielle replied, feeling sad that they would once more have to share their lives with others. The past few days had been wonderful, and if in her power, she would have remained there with Wind Dancer forever.

He read her thoughts in her face, and they were

not far from his own. "I will show you a special place today. We will spend our last day there."

Danielle couldn't imagine what place he was referring to. They had wandered the forest for miles around the camp, but he had made no mention of another special place.

"Let us go and eat, and then I will show you the treasure I have kept for this day."

Danielle heard the excitement in his tone, and eagerly followed him back to the lodge, where they shared a hasty breakfast.

"But Wind Dancer, we have swum everyday in the pond. There is no special pace near camp." Danielle's disappointment could be heard in her tone as Wind Dancer led her back to the pond after their breakfast. She didn't know what she had expected, but it certainly was not taking another swim in the pond.

Ignoring her words, he dove into the sparkling cool depths of the pond. "Follow me, my heart," he called to her.

For a single second, she was tempted to call in return, *Wherever you lead, my husband,* but she caught herself just in time. Could she allow him to have this much power over her? Her strength was waning by slow degrees as far as he was concerned, though she still resisted dashing headlong into the ensnaring web of his sensual courting of her. She was his wife, yet she still acknowledged her need to retain that part of herself that made her who she was—Danielle Hansen. Instead of saying anything, she dove in after him and followed as he swam toward the falls.

Glancing over his shoulder only once to ensure

that she was following, he did not halt when he reached the falls but, instead, climbed upon the large rocks where the chilled water rushed down and slid into the pond.

Maintaining a path to the right of the falls where the water did not rain down so harshly, Danielle also climbed the rocks, her curiosity high.

As the morning sun directed its rays upon the falls, Danielle blinked her eyes twice as one moment she saw Wind Dancer standing beneath the falls, and in the next he disappeared. She called aloud his name, but the sound of the falls covered her words.

She stood beneath the falls, the water pouring down in a shimmering cascade over her head and shoulders, when she felt a hand grab her arm and pull her. With a gasp, she found herself within the dry shelter of a cavern behind the falls, the glittering droplets of water shielding the entrance of a cave. "Wind Dancer," she gasped, surprised and excited at the discovery. "This is wonderful!" She peered around the interior of the cave and found to her surprise that it was large.

Wind Dancer grinned with pleasure as he viewed the joy on her face. "I found this place long ago. No other knows of it." He took her by the hand and began to lead her toward the back of the cavern. Noticing steam rising from a pool of water, she looked at him with questioning eyes.

"There is a hot spring that feeds the pool, Silver Dove. At first the water feels warm to the touch, but the effect upon the body is relaxing and invigorating at the same time."

Danielle couldn't believe her eyes. A hot spring! And near the back side of the pool was a cool, sandstone ledge that jutted out and over the water for several feet.

It was to this ledge that Wind Dancer led her, and sitting down, the couple dangled their feet in the heated water. The interior of the cavern was dim and cool, the showering droplets from the falls raining in the entrance, and casting a light spray almost to the spring.

"I am pleased that you find happiness with this place, Silver Dove. In all things I wish to please you." The sparkle in her azure eyes testified to her excitement, and Wind Dancer felt his pulses flying with his own joy. The coolness of the rock ledge beneath their buttocks, and the warm water at their feet, lured their senses. With an easy movement, Wind Dancer drew his bride off the ledge and into the heated pool.

Danielle's body felt instantly relaxed as Wind Dancer pulled her alongside him to a place where the spring was not too deep. The warm water surrounded and lulled her, the rising steam bringing drops of perspiration on her forehead.

"This place is much like a sweat lodge; you will be much refreshed afterward." Wind Dancer gently brushed back her long, thick curls, and wiped away the sheen of water on her forehead.

"Hmmmmm," was all Danielle could reply. Already her body was feeling light, as if melting from within. The combination of the warm water and her husband's body so closely drawn up to her own made her a bit senseless.

The warm, circling water encased them and parted with velvet smoothness as she pressed her belly against his, her slender arms feeling weightless as they automatically wrapped around his neck. At the same time, his large hands cupped the fullness of her rounded buttocks.

A timeless moment passed as Wind Dancer stared into her gleaming turquoise eyes, the raging passion flickering like quicksilver in his own as his head slowly lowered and his mouth slanted over hers.

Danielle clung to him as though he were her only lifeline. With gentle movements, Wind Dancer brought her legs up and wrapped them around his hips, his legs braced apart to carry the full burden of their passion as he drew her downward, her womanhood opening to the brush of his manhood. As he slowly slipped into her tight opening, he felt her body shudder and a tiny gasp filled his ears.

The water intensified Danielle's sensitivity. She felt each curve and muscle of Wind Dancer's large body, her breasts pressing against the muscular contours of his chest, and with the contact, the dusty-rose buds turned to hard nubs.

The contact of Wind Dancer's hands caressing her buttocks, then gathering her legs and settling them against his hips, drew her breath away. As she felt the velvet smoothness of his lance touch the heart of her passion, her breath clutched in her chest. She could feel the warm water circling her and filling her, a small amount of the heat traveling before the brand of Wind Dancer's powerful shaft, and showering within the depths of her womb. The feeling was so erotic, it set off a trembling that left Danielle rocking back and forth upon the hardness of his manhood.

Wind Dancer was lost upon the raging tide of their passion. He felt every caress, every pulse of her body, as she moved against him. The flaming cauldron of white-hot passion stirring within the depths of his loins raced upward, and the moment he heard Danielle cry aloud his name, her body coursing with trembling shudders, head thrown back and eyes tightly closed, Wind Dancer met her release with his own storming climax.

"I love you, Wind Dancer." The words escaped her parted lips as shining tears filled Danielle's eyes with the realization that the feelings that burned so fiercely in her chest were, indeed, those of love. It had been so long since she had trusted anyone enough to admit that she loved them. When her parents had died so long ago, she had thought herself incapable of ever expressing feelings of love to anyone. She feared that if she loved too hard, or too fully, the one she loved would be taken away from her. But she was unable to withstand the feelings that raged within her heart for her husband. She had to share these feelings, or she would be driven mad with her need to express them.

"What did you say?" Wind Dancer feared that he had not heard her right over the noise of the falls. He thought he had heard her admit that she loved him. His heart almost thundered out of his chest as his ebony eyes stared down into her face, and for a long, breathless moment, he awaited her reply.

Chapter Seventeen

"I know you probably think me foolish, for you are always so sure of yourself." Danielle felt her face blushing with the confession. "But I was not sure what these feelings were that I had for you."

"And you know what they are now?" Still he dared not release his pent-up breath, not until he heard her repeat the words.

Looking into his loving regard, she knew that she now was sure of her feelings. Slowly she nodded her head. "I know what they are now, Wind Dancer."

He waited for her to speak the words. He would not push her where her feelings for him were concerned.

"You were right. I had but to open my heart and look within, to know that I love you. You are everything that I could ever desire in a man, in a husband."

His heart took flight, his blood singing in his veins as he looked down at her. Placing his hands at her waist, he lifted her to sit upon the ledge, his body still in the water as he studied her face. "I have waited a long time to hear these words, *mitá wicánte*. It seems as though I have waited forever, but the sound of these words from your lips is worth any wait I might have endured."

Saying these words to her husband and meaning them was one thing, but the reality of them was quite another thing. She was a white woman and he an Indian; their worlds were far apart. Slender, trembling fingers of fear lightly caressed her spine, and she would have voiced her thoughts except that Wind Dancer pulled himself up on the ledge and drew her tightly against the side of his body.

Seeming to read her thoughts, he lightly drew her head against his shoulder. "I know that these steps we travel upon Mother Earth can easily twist and turn. Some people will not understand the love that we share, but they are of little importance. What matters on this life path is that we are together, for this was meant from the beginning. We will face together what comes against us, and in doing so, we will find that our feelings have grown. Our love for one another can only bind us closer."

How could such a love not succeed, when Wind Dancer was so determined? Danielle asked herself. While he was at her side, she felt no fear; she could trust in his strength. "I believe you, Taté Wicípi."

Her simple trust furthered his desire to see her protected from all harm in this life, but wisely, he knew that with the passage of time, many things would come before them that would threaten to destroy the love they felt for one another. For now, though, it was good to feel her soft flesh next to his own, and to hear the tender words of love that freely left her lips.

The couple rested upon the cool, sandstone ledge. Their bodies were sated from the heat of the spring and their bout of lovemaking, and their hearts were content with the knowledge that what was between them was fully shared.

Returning to the Sioux village brought reality back into Wind Dancer and Danielle's everyday life. As chief of his village, Wind Dancer spent much of his day attending to the troubles and cares of his people, and Danielle soon found herself seeking out the company of Autumn Woman and the other women of the tribe. Throughout the day, Wind Dancer's lodge was a natural meeting place for the elders of the tribe, or for the young men eagerly planning a raiding party against a small band of Crow, who had stolen three of Tall Wolf's buffalo ponies.

"Is my daughter happy to have a husband of her own?" Autumn Woman asked this same question of Danielle almost daily, and now she asked it once again as they sat outside Pretty Quill's lodge.

"*Han, Iná.* I only wish I saw more of my husband."

Several heads nodded in agreement. "The men will leave early tomorrow morning on the raiding party," Standing Fawn offered. "Each time Gray Hawk goes on such a raid, I worry that he won't return."

"There is no need for such worry, Standing Fawn. Your son is a brave warrior; the Great Spirit will see that he is not harmed." It was Pretty Quill who offered this assurance.

"Sometimes it is the bravest of the warriors who cross the other side with the sky people." Whirling Moon Woman looked up from her sewing as she spoke. Her first husband, Blue Cloud, had stepped upon the star path years ago. He had been well known for his bravery in battle.

Danielle paid close attention to the conversation as she beaded the front of the hide shirt that Autumn Woman was helping her to make for Wind Dancer. This was the first time she had heard that the raiding party would be leaving in the morning, and as she listened to the other women, the first small traces of fear touched her heart. Why had Wind Dancer not told her that the raiding party would be leaving the village so soon? He had said nothing about going along with the other braves; in fact, he had said very little about the entire affair. "Will Black Bull go with this raiding party?" She turned her attention to Pretty Quill. Even as she asked the question, she didn't know what she hoped for. If Black Bull was going along, then perhaps her husband would not, but then because his friend was going, he would probably want to accompany him.

Nodding her head, Pretty Quill kept her attention focused on the piece of hide she was painstakingly tanning with a fleshing knife. "Black Bull will go. Tall Wolf is his friend, and would do the same for him if it had been Black Bull's ponies stolen by the Crow."

"Don't you fear for his safety?" Danielle asked in low tones, her own work lying forgotten in her lap, as she looked at Pretty Quill for an answer.

Pretty Quill's dark eyes fixed upon the white woman as she replied, "Black Bull will not be defeated by a Crow! They are all cowards, who sneak about under the cover of night. Our warriors will find this Crow band of thieves and they will pay for venturing so close to our village!"

Pretty Quill, like most of the men and women of

her tribe, had a hatred for their enemies that had been instilled from a young age. The threat of such an enemy coming close enough into their valley to be able to steal horses was something they all knew had to be dealt with. To the young woman, it would be an honor for her husband to take part in the raiding party, but to Danielle, the thought of Wind Dancer leaving her in order to exact vengeance from his enemy for stealing a few horses was totally insane!

She soon set her sewing aside completely, too worried about Wind Dancer to concentrate any longer. She made excuses to the women, and hearing Autumn Woman laughing that her daughter still had much to learn, and that in time she would appreciate the moments she could steal away from her husband, she hurried her steps toward her own lodge.

When she entered the lodge, Black Bull was sitting near the fire with Wind Dancer, and as both men turned their attention upon her entrance, their conversation halted. "I will take care of those things you have suggested." Black Bull rose to his feet and, without another word, left the lodge.

Wind Dancer sat near the center fire, his hands busily working on an arrow; once feathered and tipped, it would be put into the quiver that rested near his thigh. "I am pleased that you have returned, Silver Dove. Whenever you come into our tepee, it is as though you bring the sunlight with you."

"What are you doing, Wind Dancer?" She had never seen him making weapons, and his actions increased her worry.

"Come and sit by my side and I will show you the color and design of my arrow." Each warrior fashioned his own arrows, so that it was easy to see who had brought down the enemy or the game that was being hunted.

Danielle was too anxious at the moment to sit and watch him making arrows. Trying to take her mind from her troubling thoughts, she set about making a stew for their dinner.

"What is bothering you, *mitá wicánte?*" Wind Dancer paid little attention to the arrow in his hand. His gaze watched his young wife's movements as she cut off chunks of deer meat for the stew.

Her turquoise eyes lifted from her work and rested upon her husband. "Are you planning to go on this raid with the other warriors of the village, Wind Dancer?" Her heart stilled as she awaited his answer.

Wind Dancer had put off saying anything to his bride about the raiding party until the last minute. He had planned to speak to her on the subject that evening, after they had retired to their sleeping couch. At that time he would calm her worries about his leaving her so quickly after their joining.

As the silence in the lodge stretched out, Danielle set the knife down. "You do plan to go, don't you?"

He recognized the look of betrayal in her features, and quickly tried to ease her worries. "It is my duty to go with the other warriors, Silver Dove. It could have easily been some of my own horses that were stolen."

"I've already heard all this from Pretty Quill and the other women, Wind Dancer." Her eyes filled with unshed tears. "We have only been back to the village for a few days. Why can't Black Bull or Running Elk or any other brave in this village take your place?"

"Do you think I would allow another to take my place against the enemy?" His dark eyes stared at her a though he were trying to read more into her words.

Danielle knew her husband would never ask another to take his place, but still it didn't seem fair that he would leave her so soon after they'd wed. How could he take the chance that something might happen and she would never see him again? Her fear mounted and her tears could no longer be held back. "You said you love me, Wind Dancer. If you do, you will not go with the other braves and risk your life over some stupid horses!"

Wind Dancer stepped away from the fire, and reaching her side, he looked upon her with a mixture of sadness and the first traces of anger. "My love for you is real, as is the threat the Crow pose to my people."

"But you are chief here. You don't have to go!"

Wind Dancer did not reach out and draw her to his chest as he longed to, in order to soothe away her fears, but instead, he was determined to make her realize the importance of the situation at hand. "Perhaps Tall Wolf's horses are stupid creatures in your mind, Silver Dove, but five winters past, it was not 'stupid horses' that a raiding band of Crow came after in our valley. Late one night, they stole into our village, and while all slept, they took the daughter of one of our people. Before leaving, they cut the throats of her mother and younger brother."

Danielle gasped aloud at the horrible images he had placed in her mind.

"None of my warriors tried to turn away from

his duty. We followed the band's sign through the forest. When we found them, the maiden was already dead, after being savagely abused. None of the Crow from this raiding band lived to tell the tale of their foul deeds."

"I can understand why you had to go, Wind Dancer." She relented, not able to even imagine what the young girl and her family had been put through. "But they only stole horses this time."

"This time, they stole Tall Wolf's horses. The next time they raid our valley, they could steal you, or our daughter, or our son!" He would not argue anymore with her on the subject. She would have to realize that the very survival of his people depended upon their strength, and as their leader, he had a duty to strike out against their enemies as swiftly as possible. "I will go now and make sure that all the braves going against the Crow will be ready. We leave at the breaking of Wi in the morning." With this, he left the lodge, knowing that they both needed time to calm their anger. He hoped she would think upon his words, and realize that there was no way he could stay behind in his lodge while the other braves of his tribe were attacking the Crow. He hoped with all his heart that this would be the way of things, for he did not wish to leave his lodge in the morning with the knowledge that she was upset. How could he go against the enemy and fight bravely with the image of Silver Dove left behind, weeping in their lodge?

Danielle watched his retreating back. As she brushed away the falling tears, she realized there was nothing she could say that would sway his mind. How could he be so cruel and uncaring, she fumed, as she picked up the knife and finished cutting the meat for their dinner.

Setting the trade kettle full of water upon the glowing coals of the pit fire, she sat down upon the furs, which earlier Wind Dancer himself had been relaxing upon. This had been their first argument, and Danielle felt not only heartsick but numb throughout. The thought of his leaving her and not returning so terrified her that she could do little more than sit there and silently weep. What would she do if something happened to Wind Dancer? It was not the fear of remaining in the Sioux village without protection that frightened her, but instead, the fear of living without her husband that kept her frantically searching her mind for something to say or do to keep him at her side.

It was not until after dark, and Danielle had retired to the fur pallet, that Wind Dancer returned to the lodge. Silently, he ate the food she had left for him near the fire, his dark eyes resting on her shapely form beneath the fur coverings. He knew she was not asleep; he could feel the touch of her eyes, even though the area around their sleeping couch was cloaked in darkness. At the finish of his meal, he placed a few small branches on the fire, for the nights were starting to grow cold. Turning back to his bride, he approached the bed, discarding his breechcloth. Before climbing beneath the furs with her, he stood silent for a lingering moment. "What is it you fear most, Silver Dove?"

The tenderness in his tone went straight to her heart, and unable to withhold the fear and upset that had taken hold of her, she sat up as she cried, "Oh, Wind Dancer, I only fear losing you! I didn't think I would ever feel this way about anyone, but I love you so much, I can't stand the thought of your leaving in the morning and never returning to me!" Tears rushed from her eyes and rolled down her cheeks.

"This is not what love is supposed to do."

"I know, and I'm sorry. And I'm sorry for calling Tall Wolf's horses stupid. I didn't mean it, I mean . . . I don't mean it."

Bending down, he pulled her into his embrace as he settled upon the pallet. "Perhaps our love is still too new."

"I don't think I will ever get used to the idea of losing you," Danielle wept upon his chest.

Pulling her face up and glimpsing the ravishment there from her weeping, he placed a tender kiss upon her brow. He was reminded of his vision, and the features of the girl-woman who had been represented through the silver dove. That day so long ago, he had viewed these same tears, the same look of bereavement. He had also heard her cry of loss. "Silver Dove, our love is strong. I will not leave you. You are the very beating in my heart. How can I leave that which my body needs so desperately?"

Danielle gulped back a sob, his words not calming her fear but magnifying the terror of her imagined loss. "I want to go along on this raid with you, Wind Dancer." She had come up with this plan while she had been waiting for the stew to cook this afternoon. If something were to happen to Wind Dancer, she wanted to be right at his side! "I can shoot a rifle as well as most men, and I can ride a horse. I won't be in the way, I promise." Her tears had stilled as she looked up into his face and awaited his reaction to her words.

"That won't be possible, Silver Dove," he replied.

"Why? Because I'm a woman?" She tried to draw away from his embrace.

"There have been warrior women among our people in the past, Silver Dove. I would not keep you from going against our enemies, if that is truly what you desired. But this fear you have is something that must be dealt with from the heart, not by facing a Crow warrior." Danielle would have argued then, but he stilled her words with his own. "I know well this fear that you hold in your heart, Silver Dove. I have the same fear when I think of losing you. Before we joined our life paths, I possessed a great fear that you would be lost to me, and I would be forced to live my life forever in loneliness."

"But it is not the same, Wind Dancer. You are leaving me with the knowledge that something horrible could happen and you won't return." Though her tears had subsided, she would not release her fear.

"Do you not love this man for who he is, Silver Dove?" Wind Dancer's eyes burned into her as he waited for her to answer the question.

Silently, she nodded her head.

"Then would you not love him less if he did not follow what he knows is right, if he did not protect his people?"

He watched her, not releasing her gaze but demanding an answer. She knew she could not turn away; she had to answer truthfully. Her gaze lowered as she admitted, "I love you for who you are, Wind Dancer. I would not want you to change." She took a deep breath before quickly adding,

"But I still don't want to lose you to the arrow of a Crow warrior."

"Do you not yet know that there was a reason for our coming together, Silver Dove? Do you not believe that the Great Spirit will watch over each of us for the other? From my youth, I have loved you, and I know within my heart that this love will grow, and when I am an old man, I will still feel the quickening of my blood flow while in your presence. Do not fear that you will lose me, Silver Dove, for I am a part of you that cannot be taken away. As you are my heart, I am now yours."

"I just wish it were that easy to believe."

Wind Dancer's clasp upon her tightened. "It is hard to believe those things that we cannot see before us. It is much easier to trust."

"Trust?"

"Trust in our love, Silver Dove. Trust in this, when I say to you that I would move Skan and Mother Earth to stay at your side. My strength is great; my enemy will not find me lacking when I have your image in my mind, and know that you await me, here in our lodge."

"Oh, Wind Dancer, I don't mean to be a nagging wife, or to keep you back from the things you feel you have to do. It is only that I never want to lose you." She knew as she looked into his eyes that she had no choice but to do as he said and trust in their love.

"You could never be a nagging wife, Silver Dove. You are far too beautiful." His head lowered as he greedily pressed his mouth over hers. Drawing back, he murmured, "I will be gone no more than four suns, but during every hour that passes, I will long to be here in your arms."

Danielle was lost to the tender words and tantalizing taste of him, the touch of his hands upon her flesh, the heat of his large body pressed tightly against her. Four long days and lonely nights without him! The thought stoked her inner passions with a hunger to taste and feel all he had to offer. Each moment that passed throughout this night, she would savor over the course of the next few days.

Strong, probing, plundering fingers roamed freely over Danielle's body, and at the same time Wind Dancer's lips seared a path from her lips down to her breasts. He worshipped the twin globes of pale flesh, taking each rosy-hued nipple into his mouth to suckle.

Danielle could not get enough of the feel of his large, bronzed body as her hands reached out and caressed any part of him that she could reach, her body writhing beneath the onslaught of his wild seduction. As he leaned over her and feasted upon her breasts, her mouth met his muscular shoulder and her lips made a bold pattern of tiny kisses down toward the upper portion of his broad chest. Her slender hands glided over the strong planes of his muscled body, outlining the broadness of his sculpted back, down to narrow hips, and over firm buttocks. Her breath caught as she brushed against the pulsing length of his turgid shaft.

With the slight touch of her hand across his manhood, the size of him enlarged, swelling and throbbing to mighty proportions as the blood rushed throughout his loins, and a deep groan started in the depths of his chest and rumbled upward with release.

Swept up in the throes of rapture, Danielle delighted in the knowledge of her woman's power as she felt Wind Dancer's response to her touch.

Wrapping her slim fingers around his thickened member, she slowly drew them up the length until she touched the heart-shaped head, then slowly, tantalizingly, she traveled back down the swollen, pulsing measure of him, inch by inch.

"Ah, my heart . . . your touch is enough to drive a warrior beyond all measure of control." His hand reached out and stilled the attention she was giving to his manhood. The husky words were whispered against her ear, and from there, the flame of his tongue scorched a trail over the delicate contours of her cheek, down her slender throat, across the fullness of her swollen breasts, gliding over her ribs and scorching a path over a rounded hip. His hand boldly touched the crest of her woman's jewel, and spiraling sensations swirled throughout her body and centered upon his caress. The feeling was so intense as he touched her that Danielle had to clamp her teeth tightly together to keep from crying aloud.

With the heated contact of his mouth upon her, she could not help the cry which was torn from her lips as she rose up and clutched Wind Dancer's dark hair. She was consumed with searing desire as she rode out this incredible journey of raw ecstasy. Her mind was void of all but the rippling waves of hot, trembling passion that filled her body and erupted into scalding pleasure in the center of her womanhood. As shudder after shudder left her trembling and writhing, release came . . . and with it, Danielle's cries filled the lodge.

As he rose above her, spreading her creamy thighs gently, his vein-ridged, throbbing manhood pressed into the entrance of her heated sheath. Her turquoise eyes were passion laced as they locked with his of searing jet. As Wind Dancer felt the quivering velvet warmth settle around him and welcome him, he was pulled farther into the tight, quaking folds of her womanhood. An animal-like groan of pure pleasure filled his being and slowly escaped his throat.

With her satin feel and softly molded curves, Wind Dancer's body slowly developed a sensuous, luring rhythm. Danielle willingly wound her sleek arms around his neck, her body moving against his with a silken grace as her soft, petal-pink lips parted and small shivers of sweet rapture set her entire body to trembling in his arms.

Wind Dancer wrapped Danielle's satin smooth legs about his waist, probing deeper and deeper into her nether regions, and in doing so, he made her body one burning unquenchable force, striving for the earth-shattering pleasure she knew was so near.

And when that moment came, Danielle was saturated in the delight of rapture as it flamed through her body, wrapping her senses in sheer, pulsating pleasure. "Wind Dancer, I love you, I love you." Her cries filled his ears, and with her confession, he also felt sheer, brilliant delight start at the center of his being and expand in a mighty, plunging storm of searing rapture.

"Tell me you will hurry back to me. Tell me that you will not stay away a moment longer than necessary," Danielle begged as her heart trembled beneath his own.

"Not a minute longer than I have to," he promised as he pressed his lips over hers once again.

Chapter Eighteen

Wind Dancer did not wake his bride before he left with his band of warriors the following morning. The goodbyes said between them had been whispered long into the night. Awakening, Danielle found herself alone, and as her sigh of regret filled the lodge, she pulled a piece of fur up beneath her chin and inhaled her husband's masculine scent. Silently she willed him to hurry back to her.

The first day without Wind Dancer would be the worst for Danielle. After dressing, she went to the river to gather wood and water, then take a swim. Returning to the quiet of the lodge, she felt little like cooking for herself, so she went to visit Pretty Quill and her children. In the afternoon, she went to see Autumn Woman, and the second night she stayed with her adopted mother.

It was during the second afternoon, when she was sitting outside Autumn Woman's lodge with several women, that Spring Lilly approached her. "May I speak to you, Silver Dove?" The young woman asked kindly after smiling warmly at the small group of women.

"Why, of course," Danielle responded, wondering what the Indian maiden could have to say. After their last meeting, on her wedding night, she had thought that Spring Lilly would keep her distance. But not being one to hold a grudge, if the young woman wished to make amends, Danielle followed her a few feet away, out of earshot of the other women. "What do you wish to say, Spring Lilly?" She maintained a small space between them, not forgetting the wicked-looking knife the other woman had wielded in the past.

"I wish to apologize for my behavior on the night I came to Wind Dancer's lodge. I am sorry for my actions, and know now that Wind Dancer was never meant to belong to me."

Danielle felt some pity for the other young woman. In her heart, she knew what an attractive man her husband was, and she could well understand why Spring Lilly loved him. "You don't need to apologize, Spring Lilly. I wish we could all just forget what took place that night in the lodge."

"You are very kind, Silver Dove. Not many women would be so forgiving." She certainly would not be if she were the one joined to Wind Dancer, she thought to herself. But instead of stating these true feelings, a wide grin split her lovely features.

Danielle waited a moment longer, feeling there was something more the young woman wished to say. When Spring Lilly hesitated, Danielle smiled in return, though a bit more warily. "I guess I should return to the women, and my sewing."

"I . . . I have brought you a gift, Silver Dove." Spring Lilly held out her hand and in the palm was a beautiful tortoiseshell comb, which was a brilliant red in color and had been carefully beaded on the edges.

Danielle was at first hesitant about accepting a gift from the Indian maiden. "There is no need for you to give me anything, Spring Lilly. You should keep your comb."

"But I want you to have it, Silver Dove. I will find no peace until I know that you are not angry with me."

"I'm not angry with you. I have accepted your apology; that is enough."

Reaching out, Spring Lilly forced the comb into Danielle's hand. "I wish to be your friend, Silver Dove."

What could she do? Danielle asked herself. Slowly she nodded her head. "Thank you for the gift, Spring Lilly. It is very beautiful."

Spring Lilly's grin widened with the white woman's words. "I saw you at the river this morning and would have spoken to you, but I was unsure if you wished to be friends."

"Oh, I didn't see you at the river." But Danielle knew that her thoughts had been on Wind Dancer and what had taken place between the two of them last night. She had seen several women at the river, but had paid little attention.

"Perhaps tomorrow morning, I will join you in your swim and we can talk together?" Spring Lilly appeared anxious as she awaited Silver Dove's reply.

"Well, I guess we can," Danielle stated, rather perplexed at this new turn of events.

The wide grin never left Spring Lilly's face as she watched Danielle return to the group of other women. Turning away, she had her own destination in mind as she made her way through the village.

"That one gives Indian maidens a bad name," Autumn Woman spat as she watched Spring Lilly walking away. "My daughter would be wise to stay away from such a spiteful woman."

"I think she is truly sorry, and wishes to be friends." Danielle had not told anyone about what had taken place in Wind Dancer's lodge between Spring Lilly and herself, but it had been obvious to the women of the village that the Indian maiden was jealous of Danielle and Wind Dancer.

"My daughter has a soft heart. But it is better to keep your distance from one such as Spring Lilly." Autumn Woman was never shy on giving her opinion, and several heads nodded in agreement as the other women listened to the mother and daughter converse.

It was rather odd that Spring Lilly had approached her when Wind Dancer was gone from the village, Danielle thought to herself later that night when she tried to fall asleep on her old sleeping pallet in Autumn Woman's lodge. The older woman's snores seemed to have grown much louder since Danielle had been away from her lodge, and Danielle was finding sleep difficult to come by.

Perhaps Spring Lilly had been so embarrassed by her actions, she could not force herself to approach while Wind Dancer was nearby. That had to be why she had waited until now. It might be nice if she and Spring Lilly could develop some sort of friendship. Danielle missed having a woman her own age to share things with. On the wagon train, she had had Penny, and even though they were very different in nature, Penny had been a lively companion—lively enough to be, in part, the reason why they had been captured by Indians! If not for Penny and her nightly invitations to the river for a swim, she and the other woman would still be with their families. But of course, if she were still with her aunt and uncle, she would never have met Wind Dancer.

Before falling asleep, Danielle wondered what had happened to Penny, and as she had so many times in the past, she offered up a prayer for the young woman. Then, putting thoughts of Penny and Spring Lilly from her mind, she dwelt upon the image of her husband. Two days had gone by; there were but two more left before he would return.

Throughout the night, Danielle awakened, searching for Wind Dancer's warmth. When she arose in the morning, she silently left Autumn Woman's lodge while the old woman slept on. Going to the river, she thought to refresh herself with a swim before going to her own lodge, then trying to find something to do that would help pass the time.

It was with some surprise that she found Spring Lilly sitting alone upon the river's bank. Seeing her, the other young woman smiled with pleasure as she greeted Danielle. "I have been waiting for you, Silver Dove. I know that you come to the river early and hoped that you would do the same this day."

Danielle did not know what was expected of her. Last night she had hoped they might become friends, but she had to admit that there was something in the way the other woman looked at her that kept her somewhat on guard. "Have you bathed already, Spring Lilly?"

"I waited until you came to the river. Perhaps you would like to bathe downriver?" Spring Lilly noticed that several other Indian women were making their way down the path from the village, gathering wood as they headed for the river.

Danielle was used to bathing each morning with the women who ventured to the river in the early morning hours. "This is fine for me." She sat down and began to unlace her moccasins and calf-high leggings. "Sometimes Pretty Quill brings her children to the river with her, and I help her bathe them." She had no desire to go down the river with this woman. The image of Spring Lilly's fist tightly wrapped around her knife was one that would not easily be shed.

Spring Lilly did not seem to mind Danielle's preference to remain at the river where the other women were bathing and filling their pouches with water. She eagerly began to pull off her moccasins and dress, and diving into the river's cool depths, she called out for Silver Dove to hurry in after her.

For the next hour, the two women swam and bathed in the river, their conversation guarded. Spring Lilly appeared to be going out of her way to make friends. It was not long before Danielle forgot to keep up her defenses and was laughing loudly as she dunked Spring Lilly below the surface and raced for the other side of the river.

Like Danielle, Spring Lilly seemed to be enjoying herself, and when Danielle stated that she had to dress and return to her lodge, the young woman appeared genuinely disappointed.

"Perhaps we can meet again tomorrow morning," Danielle offered as she glimpsed the frown marring the Indian maiden's delicate brow.

Spring Lilly welcomed the invitation, agreeing to be at the river early the next morning.

Danielle remained in her lodge during the day, spending much of her time working on the shirt she was making for Wind Dancer. Her thoughts often strayed to the last night she had shared with her husband as she wondered how he and his band of warriors were faring. *They should return to the village tomorrow,* she told herself. But as the loneliness of the lodge surrounded her, she knew that tomorrow would take forever to come.

It was late in the afternoon when Spring Lilly called from outside the lodge. Going to the entrance flap, Danielle peered out to find the young woman standing alone, holding a bowl of wild berries.

"I picked these this afternoon while I was walking in the forest. I thought you might like them."

Danielle did not invite the other woman inside, but stood before the lodge. Reaching out for the berries, she thanked Spring Lilly warmly for her kindness. "They look delicious, Spring Lilly. I will eat them with my supper."

The Indian maiden smiled widely, appearing pleased that the white woman had found pleasure with her gift. "Do not forget, I will meet you at the river in the morning."

"I won't forget. I had a wonderful time this morning." She was about to admit that she had missed the companionship of other young women, but something held her back. She would first learn how far this new relationship would go before she confided her feelings to the other young woman.

Spring Lilly did not linger outside Danielle's

lodge, and with her departure, Danielle was left alone to think about her husband. After a meal of pemmican and the berries Spring Lilly had brought her, she readied herself for bed. Lying awake for some time, she watched the colorful flames in the pit fire. Anxiously she awaited the passing of this last day before her husband's arrival. That night her dreams were of Wind Dancer. His handsome visage drifted in and out of her consciousness, leaving her restless, and upon occasion she was jerked awake as though she could feel his presence.

Wind Dancer had found himself staring up at the stars, unable to find rest this last night on the trail. The raiding party had gone well against the Crows. They had retrieved Tall Wolf's horses, and many of the Sioux braves had counted coup against the enemy. They had struck hard, letting their enemy know that the mighty Sioux would not put up with thievery so near their village. None of Wind Dancer's warriors had been injured, but four Crow had been killed and more had been wounded.

As leader of his small war party, Wind Dancer had not demanded total vengeance against their enemy. He had allowed several of the Crow and their wounded to flee into the forest after the first attack. Now he was glad that the warring was over and they were returning to the village. He missed Silver Dove much more than he had anticipated, and even now, as he tried to sleep, her image filled his mind. He could see her pale form lying soft and inviting upon their bed of furs, and he ached to be at her side.

Black Bull had joked with him that evening as Wind Dancer sat silently next to their campfire. His friend knew where Wind Dancer's thoughts were, and had laughed that he was like a love-struck youth. Wind Dancer had joined in the laughter, not defending himself from the joking remark, for he knew that his friend spoke the truth.

Finding sleep impossible, he arose from his pallet. It was no use—he could not sleep another night without being able to reach out and feel Silver Dove next to him. Rolling up his blanket, he made his way to the horses and placed his belonging on his pony's back.

Before leaving the darkened camp, he awoke Black Bull and told him that he was going on to the village. He would see him and the other braves when they returned late the next afternoon.

His friend laughed sleepily. "Go on, Wind Dancer, and return to your young bride. The night will be past, though, so you will have to be content to moon over her like the love-sick warrior that you are."

"You are right, Black Bill. I will not arrive at the village until morning, but at least I can gaze upon Silver Dove's beauty and not be forced to look at your ugly face," Wind Dancer rejoined good-naturedly.

"Pretty Quill is pleased with my looks. That is all that matters," Black Bull grunted before rolling over and going back to sleep.

Without another word, Wind Dancer mounted his pony and headed back in the direction that would bring him to the Sioux valley with the breaking of Wi.

* * *

Danielle was awake long before dawn's arrival, and stoking up her fire, she craved some activity that would keep her busy until Wind Dancer and his band of warriors arrived in the village. It was just at first light that she picked up her water pouch and stepped out of the lodge. To her surprise, she found Spring Lilly outside, waiting for her.

"I thought we could walk down to the river together, Silver Dove," the Indian maiden hastily explained, to account for her being there so early in the morning.

"I'm surprised you are going to the river at this hour, Spring Lilly." Indeed, it was early even for Danielle. She usually went an hour or so after daybreak.

"I know that you go early, and thought we could swim again together, as we did yesterday."

There was something odd about the other woman's manner this morning, Danielle thought. She appeared edgy, her dark eyes often looking over her shoulder as they made their way down the path that led to the river. But the prospect of swimming for a while held off Danielle's feelings of uneasiness. "I will not be able to stay at the river too long this morning. Wind Dancer and the braves should be coming back to the village sometime today."

Spring Lilly heard the excitement in the white woman's voice, and she had to force herself to keep walking down the path instead of turning on her and lashing out as she desired. "Perhaps they will not arrive today, but tomorrow instead. It is hard to say when a party of braves will return to the village." Spring Lilly laughed inwardly as she saw the smile on Silver Dove's face turn into a frown.

Reaching the river and finding themselves alone, Danielle set her water pouch down and began to unlace the leather binding at the shoulder of her dress.

"There is a much better place to swim, a short way down along the river, Silver Dove. The water is deeper and the current is not as swift." Spring Lilly's dark eyes looked at the other woman innocently.

Danielle's first impulse was not to go with the other woman, but she could not find the words of refusal. What harm could there be in going down the river to a better swimming spot? Silently she followed the other woman down the riverbank until they were out of sight of the path, and anyone who might be going to the river to bathe or get water.

"This is a good place," Spring Lilly at last announced, halting her steps near a thicket of trees that grew along the bank.

Danielle could see little difference between this spot and the usual swimming area, but the girl seemed pleased so Danielle didn't say anything. Sitting down, she began to pull off her moccasins and leggings. As she looked back up in Spring Lilly's direction, her face clearly showed surprise as she saw Red Fox standing at Spring Lilly's side. The couple stood silently watching her.

"What is going on? I thought we were going for a swim." Danielle knew that her words sounded foolish to the ears, but she couldn't help them. She was caught totally by surprise, and the looks that both directed at her held no warmth or friendship.

"If all the *wasichu* were as stupid as you, Silver

Dove, it would be easy for our warriors to wipe them from the face of Mother Earth!" Spring Lilly spat out with venom.

"But I thought you wanted to be friends." Danielle clutched her moccasins to her breast as she rose to her feet and faced the pair. "Why have you brought me here?" She had her first true taste of fear as she realized that this young woman had only been lulling her into a sense of friendship so she could lure her down the riverbank.

"Do you really think I would ever desire a *wasicun winyan* as my friend?" The dark eyes glittered threateningly as the Indian maiden took a step in Danielle's direction. "You stole Wind Dancer from me, and now it is time that you pay for your thievery!"

Danielle could not believe that she had been so foolish as to come to this secluded spot with Spring Lilly. She thought of turning and running, but just as her glance turned somewhat away from the couple, Spring Lilly made a lunge and grabbed her by both arms.

Perhaps Danielle could have had a chance if she had had only to fight off the young woman, but with Red Fox there, she knew she would have to use not only her strength but her cunning. Shoving the girl away, her own eyes flashing with the heat of her anger, she cried, "Don't touch me, Spring Lilly! My husband has already warned you what would happen if you tried to harm me again!" Turning her glance upon the warrior, she added, "He will not take kindly to you either, Red Fox, if you help this woman do harm to me."

The smile that came over the brave's lips was not a pretty sight to behold. It was more of a threatening sneer, the pale scar standing starkly against his bronzed skin as he stepped before Danielle. "I do not fear Wind Dancer, Dove. When he returns to his lodge, he will find it empty. He will never know more. Perhaps he will search for you, but he will not find any sign of his silver bird."

The threat was too real! Turning quickly, Danielle started to run, and her piercing scream filled the air right before Red Fox grabbed her from behind.

"Cover her mouth, and take her farther down the river!" Spring Lilly commanded as her dark stare glared upon the pale woman in Red Fox's tight grip.

As he quickly covered her mouth and held his knife up to her throat, Danielle could only glare disbelief and anger at the woman who had tricked her so horribly.

"She's yours now, Red Fox. Do with her as you wish, but don't let her escape. I will return to the village in case someone heard her scream. I will claim that I was the one who made the noise; I was swimming and saw a snake."

Not lingering, Red Fox began to drag Danielle toward the copse of trees, which he had been hiding in as he waited for the two women to come down the riverbank. "If you scream again, Dove, I will cut your throat now!" His harsh words touched her ears as he lowered his hand from her mouth. Farther into the trees, he turned her around to face him.

Danielle was too terror-stricken to do anything but obey him. She saw the gleam of madness in the black eyes that stared at her, and as the sharp knife pressed against the hollow of her throat, she knew that he would carry out his threat without a second thought. Silently she nodded her head, hoping that he might listen to reason and let her go back to the village. Perhaps Spring Lilly had talked him into this venture, and she could convince him to release her.

Without warning, the knife flashed, swiftly severing one shoulder lacing of her dress and then the other. Danielle gasped aloud, her hands automatically reaching up and holding the hide dress over her bosom.

The point of the blade pressed into one hand and drew a pinprick of bright red blood. "Move your hands, Dove. I have waited a long time to view your naked beauty, and I will not be deprived!"

"No!" Danielle gasped, even as she felt the knife cutting deeper into her flesh. There was no doubt that he was insane, and she knew, in that instant, that she was going to die. It didn't matter if she obeyed him or not—he was going to kill her. He had to, for if he didn't, Wind Dancer would kill him. If she was going to die anyway, she had to make a brave attempt to keep him from touching her body. With that thought, she broke away from his grasp. She would rather die than have any man other than Wind Dancer touch her!

A low growl escaped Red Fox's lips. His insane lust for this woman and his hatred for Wind Dancer caused him to throw all caution to the wind as he charged toward her, the knife outstretched, not caring if he cut her or not, because eventually he would slit her throat and leave her dead near the river. He would take great pleasure in watching Wind Dancer's pain and sorrow when the Dove's lifeless body was brought back to the village.

Turning, Danielle tried to run, branches and bushes hindering her progress. Within short seconds, Red Fox was on top of her, shoving her to the ground as he straddled her waist.

"You *wasichu* bitch! You think you are too good for Red Fox! I will teach you like I taught your friend that a warrior can take what he pleases from the *wasichu!*" The knife slashed against the hand that was still held up to protect her breasts from his viewing.

The instant sharp pain brought a scream from Danielle's lips. Another slash of searing pain, and her screams filled the air without ceasing.

"Scream, Dove. It gives me great pleasure! I only wish we were in my lodge and I could tie you up to stakes." Red Fox's deranged appetite for blood and pleasure would be satisfied only by hearing the screams of the woman he had inflicted pain upon, and as he heard the woman beneath his knife crying out, his manhood swelled with a violent reaction. He would have her before he halted her cries, he told himself, and cutting away the rest of her dress, he fought off her feeble defenses as he released his distended organ.

Chapter Nineteen

"Ayyeeeeayyeeee!" The fierce, bloodcurdling battle cry pierced the brittle morning air and blended with the screams that were coming from the copse of trees along the riverbank. Wind Dancer's muscular legs sprinted down the bank, his heart dashing violently against his breastbone as his ears were filled with the sounds of his wife's terror. His cry escaped his lips and mingled with hers even as he pulled his hunting knife free from its sheath and charged headlong into the trees.

Red Fox did not hear Wind Dancer's war cry because he was too intent on trying to penetrate Danielle's abused body. His attention was caught by the sounds behind him only when he heard the noise of the underbrush crashing. Looking over his shoulder, he viewed the cold fury on Wind Dancer's features, and in that same moment, he raised his hand, the sharp knife glinting beneath a ray of morning sunlight as it plunged downward and struck Danielle's chest. His own features were crazed with hatred as he jumped to his feet and faced Wind Dancer. "The Dove is dead!" he sneered. "It is your turn now, Wind Dancer. Come and join your *wasichu* bitch!" In his madness, Red

Fox truly believed himself invincible, and welcomed this confrontation between himself and the warrior he had hated with a burning jealousy for years.

For one single moment, Wind Dancer feared that his own heart had stopped beating. Standing still he gazed upon the woman lying pale and bleeding on the ground at Red Fox's feet. It was only as he glimpsed some small, weak movement of her chest that his senses began to return, and when they did, he faced Red Fox with a savage thirst for vengeance that he had never known before. With his knife clutched tightly, he charged the other brave, the full weight of his body clashing against Red Fox's, pushing him back into the trees.

Red Fox's strength was minimal compared to Wind Dancer's, and within short seconds he was well aware of this fact. As Wind Dancer's muscular arms pinned him down, and though his arms flayed out as he tried to strike him with his knife, all his efforts were ineffectual. Wind Dancer's powerful fist came down and struck him again and again in the face.

There was no mercy given. Wind Dancer's only thought was to finish with Red Fox and get to his wife. As though purely by instinct, he placed his large hand around his opponent's throat, and lifting him from the ground, he tightened the pressure, not releasing until Red Fox's knife dropped to the ground, his eyes staring out at a dark world as his breathing came in small, strangled gasps, then finally halted completely.

As though it were a worthless substance that no longer had the form of a human being, Wind Dancer flung the lifeless body to the ground, and without another glance in that direction, he raced back to Danielle's side.

"Silver Dove." The name escaped his parted lips as his dark eyes took in the damage that had been done her. Only pieces of her dress were left to cover her naked body; her hands and chest were covered with blood. The ground beneath her was a puddle of blood made from her wounds, and her pale curls were now a reddish hue. Great tears fell from his dark eyes as he lifted her tenderly in his arms. For a moment he did not move, but placed his ear next to her heart and the large hole made by Red Fox's knife.

Every fiber of his being concentrated upon hearing some small sound of her heartbeat. A minute passed . . . his soul, his heart, his very life was centered upon one single movement in her chest . . .

There was a slight flutter of movement, but barely, and he feared he had imagined it. Again, he held his breath as he listened, and at last the faintest flutter could be heard from deep within her chest.

He wanted to cry out to the heavens that she lived, but he did not waste the time this would take. Instead, he turned, and with his bride in his arms, he raced toward the village.

Many of the villagers stood before their lodges, watching their chief striding quickly through the village with the silver-haired woman's pale form cradled in his arms. Wind Dancer's features were immobile as he looked straight ahead, the only sign of his grief the great drops of tears that fell from his eyes and rolled down his sculpted cheeks.

It was to Medicine Wolf's lodge that Wind Dancer took his wife. The old shaman drew back the entrance flap even before Wind Dancer had a chance to call from outside, then the chief quickly entered the dim interior of the herb-scented tepee.

"Place her upon the pallet near the fire," the medicine man instructed as though he had already prepared himself for this tragedy.

With the tenderest care, Wind Dancer bent and laid Danielle's still form down upon the blanket-covered furs. There was no movement from her, and he was not even sure if she still breathed. With a tormented glance, he looked up at Medicine Wolf. "Can you save her?" The question was a plea torn from the depths of his soul.

"If it be the will of Wakán Tanka," Medicine Wolf answered, and before going to his patient, he broke pieces of sage grass and cedar and put them in the fire. As he began his work, he pulled from his hide shirt an eagle bone whistle that was held by a strip of leather around his neck. To him, this whistle was sacred and would call forth the powers that would be needed this day in his lodge.

As Wind Dancer silently watched, the aged medicine man used an eagle feather to spread smoke above Danielle's body and the area of the pallet. Once this was completed, he laid his leathery finger against the weak pulse beat at her throat and blew an ancient melody through the slender bone whistle.

After a few minutes, he appeared satisfied that he had felt some small sign of life within the pale woman's body. Not casting the slightest glance in Wind Dancer's direction, he turned to the herbs that were laid out on the floor against one side of the lodge. Mixing a small amount of sacred gopher dust and puffball fungus in the hollow of a deer antler, he placed the concoction over the wound on her chest and the deep gashes on her hands in order to stop the bleeding.

Next, he fixed a tea of burr root, forced her lips apart, and poured a small bit of the tea down her throat, with the hope of halting any internal bleeding. With this completed, the eagle bone whistle fell back to his chest. "The bleeding will stop. The rest is now up to Wakán Tanka."

"Is there nothing more you can do?" Wind Dancer had watched everything that Medicine Wolf had done, but still he could not see any change in his wife. She lay still and pale as death upon the pallet; not even the soft sounds of her breathing could be heard in the quiet of the lodge.

"You can go to the river and get water to bathe her and make her comfortable. There is nothing else." Medicine Wolf turned away from the young man, and pulling out his medicine drum, he sat down next to the pale woman and began to tap his hand lightly upon the tight hide cover. He could now feel her heartbeat as if it were a part of her inner being, and as he closed his eyes and sang a prayer of healing, his hand moved upon the drum to the faint beating of her heart.

Feeling helpless as he looked on, Wind Dancer slowly arose. As though taking each step in a trance, he went to his lodge and retrieved a pouch for water and cloths for Silver Dove. The sound of the medicine drum echoed throughout the village—thump . . . thump . . . thump. The sounding of Danielle's heartbeat filled Wind Dancer's body, and he clung to the sound as if it were his own pulse. Thump . . . thump . . . thump. Then the drumbeat stopped, and his own movements halted as he gasped for breath, willing Silver Dove to breathe, her heart to keep beating.

A long moment passed, and finally the drumbeat resumed. Slowly Wind Dancer made his way to the river, not seeing those standing around him or hearing their respectful wishes for his wife's recovery. He heard only the sound of the drum.

"Wind Dancer, I have prayed to the spirit of Matóhota to give Silver Dove strength and let her live."

Wind Dancer looked up from where he was bent down filling the water pouch, and saw Spring Lilly standing along the riverbank. "Why would you pray to the mighty grizzly on behalf of my wife, Spring Lilly?" As he spoke, his mind was attuned to the sound of Medicine Wolf hitting his medicine drum.

"While you were away, Silver Dove and I became friends."

For a moment, he looked at the Indian maiden with a touch of disbelief. Remembering that this woman had threatened Silver Dove with a knife, and that she and Red Fox had become friendly lately, his glance displayed more interest as he asked, "Did you know that Red Fox was at the river this morning?"

"How would I know this? I am sorry that I did not come to the river this morning and swim with Silver Dove as I did yesterday morning, but I confess I was tired and stayed in my father's lodge longer than usual." She hoped he would not question her father about this statement. When she had left her father's lodge that morning, everyone had been asleep, but when she had hurried back after being assured that Red Fox had Silver Dove in his possession, her father was awake and had watched her as she lay back down upon her pallet. "If I had come to the river, perhaps I could have done something to help Silver Dove." She hoped her voice sounded convincing. By all accounts throughout the village, the pale woman had not long to live on Mother Earth. Wind Dancer would need someone to comfort him when she was gone, and Spring Lilly had every intention of being that someone!

Wind Dancer paid the woman little further attention as the drumbeat stilled again. He stood facing the direction of Medicine Wolf's lodge, his entire body tense as he clutched the water pouch in his hand. He waited a moment . . . then another . . . but still no sound of the drum. He felt as though he had been punched in the stomach. He couldn't breathe. His face turned pale as his mind cried over and over, *Beat . . . beat!*

The slightest sound of a drumbeat at last touched his ears, and in his relief, tears fell unashamedly from his eyes. He had to strain to hear it but the drumbeat was there. *Thump . . . thump . . . thump . . .*, a small pause, but it picked up more quickly this time, *thump . . . thump . . . thump.* Without another word to Spring Lilly, he started back to Medicine Wolf's lodge, his mind and body as one with the drumbeat of his wife's faintly pounding heart.

For two days and nights, the sound of the medicine drum echoed over the valley, sometimes faintly heard, at other times seeming to still for a breathless minute. But with the passing of the second day, the sound became stronger as each breath Danielle took was more peaceful, no longer the struggling breaths for life that they had been.

"Why does she not awaken?" Wind Dancer

asked the shaman as Medicine Wolf spooned some horsemint and yarrow root tea between Danielle's lips. The day before, she had developed a fever, and Medicine Wolf had made the mixture to combat the fever and the infection in her wound.

"While she sleeps, she heals in mind as well as body," the shaman replied as he prepared himself and Wind Dancer bowls of stew. Before taking the stew to his chief, he set a small bowl aside, near his fire, for the spirits to eat from. "Silver Dove has much healing to do. The spirits will help while she is in that place where she has gone from this world. She is as all women put here on Mother Earth—frail of body but strong of mind and will. That is why she still lives. A man with such a wound near the heart would not have lived. We do not have that pact with the spirit world to be allowed to remain here on Mother Earth because of those we love. A warrior would rather pass over and join the ancestors who are hunting great herds of buffalo and smoking their pipes without worry of hunger and thirst."

Whatever her reason for such a strong will to live, Wind Dancer was thankful for it. Not a moment passed when his eyes did not go to her chest, to check for the movement that would prove she was still breathing. "I should not have left her to go against the Crow. She wanted me to stay with her, here in the village." Wind Dancer took the bowl offered him but set it aside. His worry over his wife was so great that he was still unable to eat.

"Perhaps she sensed what was to come." Medicine Wolf had no lack of appetite and eagerly gnawed a rabbit bone. "I have not heard of the *wasichu* having this power of knowing what the future holds, but Silver Dove is not like any other wearing pale skin. Wakán Tanka brought her among our people; his hand is placed upon her."

Danielle did not wake up until two more days had passed, and when she opened her eyes, she was greeted by the sight of Wind Dancer leaning against a beaded backrest and sleeping in an upright position. She tried to move, her hand stretched upon the furs, but a moan of pain caused by this simple effort escaped her lips.

Instantly, Wind Dancer's dark eyes were staring down at her. "Mázaska Wakínyela," he breathed softly as he saw the beautiful turquoise and gold-flecked eyes staring back at him. The opening of her eyes was the most beautiful event he had seen in days, even as he viewed the pain that crossed her features, his heart rejoiced. She would be all right. She would need to heal, but there would be time for that. The main thing was she was awake, and she would live!

"I hurt," she sighed. The pain in her chest burned unbearably with her slightest movement.

"Lie still, *mitá wicánte.* Medicine Wolf will give you something for the pain when he returns to the lodge."

"Are we in his lodge?" She looked around at the strangeness of her surroundings.

"*Han,* Silver Dove. I brought you here to Medicine Wolf's lodge in order for him to heal you." Wind Dancer glimpsed the strain that talking was having on her, and as her features grew paler, he tried to quiet her. "You should try to rest. Do not worry about anything. I am here at your side and will tend all your needs."

"Red Fox?" The name escaped her in a frightened whisper.

"You have no need to worry about him. He is no longer on Mother Earth." He hoped that this information would reassure her. In time her body would heal, and he desired her mind also to heal, without fear that such a brutal assault could happen again.

"And Spring Lilly?" Her eyes closed, and she fell back to sleep before hearing her husband's reply.

"Spring Lilly?" Wind Dancer softly repeated the maiden's name, but seeing that his wife had fallen back to sleep, he was left alone to wonder why Silver Dove had mentioned that name. Did she fear that Red Fox had also harmed Spring Lilly? Wind Dancer was perplexed. Spring Lilly had told him that she had been in her father's lodge the morning that Silver Dove had been attacked—why would Silver Dove even think about the other young woman?

Ever since Silver Dove had been lying unconscious in Medicine Wolf's lodge, Spring Lilly had portrayed herself as very concerned and consoling. She had even offered several times to come and sit with Silver Dove while Medicine Wolf was away from the lodge, and in so doing, she could allow Wind Dancer a small amount of time to himself. Strangely, as Wind Dancer looked down upon his wife's fair features, he felt a sense of relief that he had not taken the other woman's offer into consideration. Something still troubled him about the manner in which Silver Dove had spoken the maiden's name directly after asking about Red Fox.

* * *

It was not until the following evening that Danielle felt strong enough to talk for any length of time. When she told her husband the part that Spring Lilly had played in her attack, Wind Dancer's features did not reveal the cold fury that coursed through his body. As he helped his wife to bathe, and lovingly brushed out her silver curls, he swore to himself that the first chance he had, he would ensure that Spring Lilly never caused him or his family any more harm.

The following day, before the high council of the village, and with Brave Bull in attendance, Spring Lilly was exposed for her part in the attack on Silver Dove.

Standing next to her father, the young Indian maiden wept openly, pouring out her sorrow and regret. She stated to all that it had been her love for Wind Dancer that had driven her to entrap the *wasicun winyan.*

The council had little sympathy for the young woman. They had already been advised of the treachery she had shown the night of Wind Dancer's joining with the silver-haired woman, and this second occurrence could not be tolerated.

Spring Lilly was banished from the Oglala tribe. She was allowed only a few possessions, those needed for her survival in the wilderness. As those she had known all her life turned their backs upon her, she fled the valley, knowing she would never be welcomed among her people again.

Chapter Twenty

"What kind of man was Red Fox that he could do this to me?" Danielle asked Medicine Wolf after he had replaced the bandage on her chest with a fresh one. Her wounds were healing nicely, but there would obviously be a scar above her left breast. Each time Medicine Wolf tended her wounds, she felt heartsick at the sight. Twice Wind Dancer had offered to do this job for the medicine man, but Danielle had refused him. Now reclining upon the old shaman's backrest, she looked to him for some kind of explanation for the horror she had suffered at Red Fox's hands.

"Red Fox was much like Iktome. My people also call Iktome the wicked spider man, and at times the mean trickster or prankster. If Red Fox had not attacked you, he would have done some other evil to touch Wind Dancer's spirit. He was jealous and vengeful."

"And this Iktome was like Red Fox?" Since being in Medicine Wolf's lodge, Danielle never tired of the old man's storytelling. He had a story to tell for each occasion, and it seemed that the subject of Red Fox was no different.

Medicine Wolf settled down next to his fire, and

picking up his pipe, he drew slowly on the mouthpiece. He had enjoyed the past two weeks with this woman in his lodge. He would miss her and Wind Dancer's company when she returned to her husband's tepee. Many of the younger people of the village did not have the time to listen to an old man's stories, but this Silver Dove was always ready for one of his tales. Expelling the smoke from his lungs, he began, "Upon this turtle's back that we live on, the place called Mother Earth, all things move in a never-ending circle, and all living things are related in one way or another to each other. The buffalo on the plains and the wolf who lives high in the mountains are our brothers, the birds flying overhead, our cousins. No matter the size of the creature, small or large, or the tree or bloom, we are all related."

"Long ago when the first men and the first women lived upon Mother Earth, the people could understand and talk to the animals. The animals could change themselves into people, and the people into animals. There was a better understanding of living things than there is today; it was a time before man decided to take charge."

"It was during those long-ago days that my story occurred. In a small forest, hidden from the people, there once lived a very friendly, good-natured rabbit. One day the rabbit was walking through the forest when he came across a small clot of blood. As most rabbits, this rabbit was playful and curious, so he lightly hit the clot, and when it rolled upon Mother Earth, he hit it again and again, as though it were a small red ball.

"There is much power in motion. The people call this mysterious power of motion Tákuśkanśkan, and its spirit is in anything that moves. At times, such motion can cause things to come to life. This day the rabbit caused the power of Tákuśkanśkan to enter the clot of blood. As the rabbit hit and rolled the clot, it slowly took form and shape until it became a small boy. The rabbit named him Rabbit Boy.

"The rabbit took Rabbit Boy home to his mate, and both of them fell in love with him, as though he were truly their own son. The mother rabbit made the boy a fine buckskin shirt, which was beaded and painted, and the three of them lived together happily for a long time. Then one day, the father rabbit took Rabbit Boy aside and told him that he was not truly a rabbit but a human. The pair of rabbits loved their son, but they were wise and knew he needed to live among his own people.

"Rabbit Boy left the rabbits that afternoon and began to walk until he came to a village. The villagers were surprised to see a handsome young man in such fine clothes coming among them. They asked him where he was from, and he told them from another village, but that was a lie. There were no other villages; this village was the first upon Mother Earth.

"In this village, there was a beautiful maiden who fell in love with Rabbit Boy. The villagers also wanted Rabbit Boy to marry into their village, because they knew that he was a man with great mystery power. He had visions of himself wrestling, racing, and playing games with the sun, and he was always the winner in these visions."

"In this time, Iktome also lived in the village, and he desired the beautiful maiden as his own. He began to speak badly of Rabbit Boy. He told the braves of the village that he had a magic hoop to throw over Rabbit Boy, so that they could set upon him.

"Several other braves in the village were also jealous of Rabbit Boy's handsome looks and kind ways, and they agreed with Iktome and began to fight Rabbit Boy. The Spider Man threw his magic hoop over Rabbit Boy, rendering him helpless. But Rabbit Boy was not truly as helpless as they believed; he only pretended to be, in order to amuse himself.

"The village men overcame Rabbit Boy and tied him up, then Iktome encouraged them to take out their knives and cut Rabbit Boy up.

"Rabbit Boy asked only that he be allowed to chant his death song, after which the villagers killed him and cut him up. But Rabbit Boy was not hurt easily. The sun hid its face from Mother Earth, and all things were covered with darkness.

"When the sun returned, the villagers found that Rabbit Boy's body had disappeared. Those who had been watching closely said that they had seen Rabbit Boy's body taking back form, and going up into the heavens on a beam of light. One old medicine man told the villagers that the Rabbit Boy had powerful medicine. He had gone up to visit the sun. He would return to them, stronger than before, because he would gain the power of the sun. The villagers decided to hurry and marry Rabbit Boy to their maiden.

"Iktome was very jealous, and cried, 'Why do you bother with a foolish Rabbit Boy? Look at me! I am much more powerful! Tie me up, and cut my body into pieces! Be quick!' " Before they did as he wished, he began to sing the same death chant that Rabbit Boy had sung earlier. Only

Iktome did not sing the death chant right, since he could not remember the words.

"The villagers did as he bid them, but Iktome never came back to life again. The evil prankster had finally outsmarted himself." Medicine Wolf set his pipe down upon the flat piece of stone near his fire, which he often used as a resting place for his pipe. "Those like Iktome and Red Fox usually outsmart themselves, Silver Dove. They are the ones who are made to pay in the end."

Though she saw the similarities between this Iktome and Red Fox, Danielle felt small comfort in Medicine Wolf's story. She, too, had been made to pay for Red Fox's jealousy against Wind Dancer. She would have not only the scars in her mind because of his attack against her, but also the scars on her body from his knife.

Medicine Wolf's searching gaze wisely discerned her thoughts. "It is time that you return to your husband's lodge, Silver Dove. There is nothing more I can do for you here."

Danielle reacted strongly against this announcement. "But my wounds." She had not been alone with Wind Dancer since the evening before he had left the village to attack the party of Crow. So much had happened to her since that night, she felt as though she were an entirely different person.

"Your wounds have healed well, Silver Dove. Those things that we can see heal quickly; it is the wounds that are not seen that take time."

"Do some wounds never heal, Medicine Wolf?" She felt tears stinging the backs of her eyes as she looked at the ancient wise man.

"All wounds heal with time. You have been touched by the hand of Wakán Tanka, Silver Dove. The knife wound inflicted upon you was close to your heart. Another might have passed over, but the Great Spirit wanted you to remain here on Mother Earth. I am an old man and have seen much with these eyes. I tell you that all wounds heal, but you have to allow yourself to step into that place where you can be free from the evil spirits that wish to bring you down."

The following day, with tears in her eyes, Danielle left Medicine Wolf's lodge with her husband. She had grown fond of the old medicine man and would miss him now that she was returning to her own home. But more than that, she had become dependent upon him as a buffer between herself and Wind Dancer. Once they were in their lodge, she would no longer be able to hide her body and her thoughts from her husband.

Arriving back at their lodge, Wind Dancer was attentive to Danielle's every need. He insisted that she rest throughout most of the day near their pit fire, and in the evening, he anxiously watched her settle upon their comfortable pallet. He did not join her on their sleeping couch, but instead sat near the fire. As the hours passed, his dark eyes kept returning to her sleeping form.

He was wise enough to know that something troubled her greatly, but he was sensitive enough to realize that some things had to be worked out within one's self. This was such a time, he knew instinctively, and contented himself with the knowledge that Silver Dove was safe under his protection, and once again in his lodge.

Over the next few days, however, a silent rift developed between the couple. Danielle avoided the slightest intimacy. If Wind Dancer brushed against her while she lay upon their sleeping couch, she would hurriedly move aside, allowing him plenty of room. If he glanced at her with desire, she would make excuses to leave the lodge, going to visit either Autumn Woman or Medicine Wolf or Pretty Quill and her children.

Wind Dancer was at a loss as he watched her behavior in their lodge. It seemed that all her joy had been taken from her with Red Fox's attack. She shied away from his every attempt to bring their marriage back to the way it had been before he had left with the war party. Though he told himself to be patient with her moods, his patience was wearing thin.

The haunting sounds of Wind Dancer's flute filled the lodge and filtered through the parted entrance flap. The melody was lost by the sound of the rain as it traveled beyond the lodge. It was late afternoon as Wind Dancer rested against his beaded willow backrest, his thoughts reflected in the mood of the music he was playing.

Danielle lay upon their fur pallet with her back turned toward her husband. As she listened to the sounds of the flute, the loneliness that she had created around herself brought tears to her eyes. Turning to face the lodge, her gaze rested upon her husband. He appeared intent as he played the instrument, the parted entrance flap allowing the fresh smell of an early fall rain to fill the interior of the tepee. As the music mingled with the sounds of the rain, Danielle stated softly, "I am already on your sleeping couch, husband." Her words were barely louder than a whisper, and the most personal she had dared since leaving Medicine Wolf's lodge.

Wind Dancer played on, appearing as though he

had not heard her words. With the finish of the tune, his dark gaze looked directly at her, and as softly as she had spoken, he returned, "But where is your heart, wife?"

Danielle felt as though she were drowning within the hold of his eyes. Her heart tripped dangerously as her fingers clutched the pallet of fur. His question was easy for her to answer. Her heart was where it had been from the first moment Wind Dancer had kissed her. Her heart belonged only to him! But so much had changed since Red Fox's attack. She felt different inside. Her body was no longer the same as it was when Wind Dancer had whispered loving words about it the evening before he had left with the war party. "Things are not the same," she said at last.

"It is the way of all creation that everything changes, nothing stands still. Change can be good if we learn from it, Silver Dove. We are lost when we wallow in self-pity. Like the tree that has been standing in the forest for many years, when a great storm arises and tears down one of her shapely limbs, does she cry out her outrage and loss to the gods, or does she grow even lovelier branches, which add to her beauty?"

"And do you think this is what I am doing? Wallowing in my own self-pity?" She felt a stirring of old anger. Why couldn't she wallow in self-pity if she wanted to? Who had more right? Everything had been taken from her; she wasn't the same as before the attack.

Setting the flute aside, Wind Dancer left the willow backrest and silently approached the bed. His dark eyes locked with hers of turquoise, and he easily read her fear in their depths. "Why do you fear your husband?"

"I don't fear you," she whispered in return, turning her gaze away to break the penetrating depths as he stared down at her.

Sitting down on the pallet, he took one of her hands and turned it so that he could glimpse where her wounds had been. He lightly kissed the healed cut on the backside, where Red Fox had pushed in the point of the knife. "If I could take this mark, and these others on your other arm, away from you, Silver Dove, I would not." Lifting the other hand, he placed another kiss on the arm above the wrist where Red Fox had slashed her.

Danielle had not expected these words, and her gaze turned back to him.

"The second day, while you lay in Medicine Wolf's lodge, a fever took hold of you, and you spoke of what happened at the river. You wept in your delirium and told how you tried to conceal your nakedness from Red Fox, using your hands."

Danielle turned away again. "I don't wish to speak about this, Wind Dancer. I am tired. We should go to bed."

"And what then, wife? Should we turn our backs on each other? Should we let this thing between us fester and grow until what is left is but a shell of what once was?"

"How can you say these things to me? What do you want from me?" Large drops of tears filled her eyes and rolled down her cheeks, dampening the furs beneath her head.

"I say these things because I love you. I want you to trust me, trust the love that I have for you." His long, bronzed finger reached out and brushed the tears from her soft cheeks.

"I want to, Wind Dancer."

Her voice sounded innocent and childlike, and it

touched Wind Dancer deeply in his soul. "What do you fear?" he gently questioned. He was not about to let this thing go, now that he had brought it out in the open. If he left her alone as she desired, things would only worsen between them.

"I don't fear . . ." As she looked into his eyes, she knew that she could not lie to him. "I fear that if you look upon me, you will turn away at the sight of my ugliness."

Wind Dancer thought he had mistaken her words, but as he looked into her gaze, he knew that she had spoken from her heart. She spoke about the scar on her chest. A soft sigh escaped his lungs; his thoughts were now confirmed. He had suspected the scar was her reason for turning away from him when she dressed and shying away whenever he looked upon her with desire. "Trust me, *mitá wicánte*. There is no part of your body that I would look upon without seeing beauty."

Slowly Danielle pulled away the piece of fur covering her breasts, and as tears fell from her eyes, she asked, "Even when you look at this?"

Wind Dancer had not seen the wound upon her chest since the day he had carried her to Medicine Wolf's lodge. Looking down at her beautiful breasts now, he easily saw the scar that marred the upper portion of her left breast. The wound had healed nicely, though—the scar was but a red line that would fade and perhaps eventually disappear altogether.

For a moment, he appeared to study the scar before speaking. There was no sympathy, nor was there surprise or horror on his face when he looked back up into Danielle's eyes. "When you look upon my body, Silver Dove, do you wish to turn your face away?"

At times, Wind Dancer totally confused her, and this was one of those times. Her tears still in her eyes as she answered, "Of course not. You have a beautiful body."

"Do you not think the scars upon my chest ugly?"

Her eyes lowered to his broad chest, and she looked upon the scars that appeared faintly white over the bronzed skin above his nipples. He had told her proudly, shortly after they had been joined, that the scars had been gained during the sun dance ceremony, which he had performed four times. He had also explained the ceremony and it significance to his people. "But your scars were earned bravely, Wind Dancer. Mine are not the same."

"No, they were not gained in the same manner. Each time I participated in the sun dance ceremony, I did so for my own reasons. I knew what was expected of me, and the pain that I would endure as I was held in midair by the leather thongs tied to the sun dance pole, and to the eagle claws piercing my chest. Your scars came from an enemy. You could have given in to Red Fox's desires that morning, and none could have blamed you, but you did not. You fought him even as he cut you with his knife. Tell me who earned their scars bravely?"

She gulped back a sob, but before she could speak, he added, "I care not about such scars, nor would I care if your entire body had such scars. I care only that my heart is allowed to beat because yours does the same." His own eyes filled with tears as he revealed these inner feelings, and bending downward, he placed a tender kiss upon the scar above her breast.

His words spoken out of love, and the proof being the light kiss upon her breast, went straight to Danielle's heart. With a cry, she threw her arms around his neck. "Oh, Wind Dancer, how did I ever deserve you and your love?"

"Our love was destined from the beginning. There is no right or wrong, no yes or no. You are mine, and I am yours." His lips sealed the promise with a kiss that chased away her fear that anything could ever come between them again.

That afternoon, a detail of soldiers were attempting to set up tents for shelter from the threatening storm that loomed off in the distance. A scout returned with the information that a small band of Indians were on the move, not far up ahead.

Lieutenant Hampton Cole did not appear interested in the information, but when the scout added that he thought he had glimpsed a white woman in their midst, his attention was quickly sparked.

"Have Sergeant Langford ready the men to mount at once. Instruct him to leave a few men to set up camp, and we will go and take a look at these Indians."

Within minutes, the detachment of soldiers that had been sent out from Fort Laramie on patrol were mounted and riding north, toward the band of traveling Indians.

The young lieutenant rode at the head of the patrol, and as the scout had indicated, over a small rise there was a small, ragged band of Arapaho. Most of the braves were old and weary, the women and children lean and ill kempt. As the detail advanced, the cry was sounded from the Indians, but none attempted to brandish weapons. It was plain that this band had had ill luck, and they were not willing to tempt it further by fighting with the blue coats.

The soldiers surrounded the small group, the lieutenant's steady gaze silently going over each woman. Had the scout made a mistake? Surely there was no white woman living among these savages! But then something in one of the women's features betrayed the fact that beneath all her filth, she was different from the rest of the women sitting on the ground near her. "You." He pointed a finger at the filthy woman wearing hide clothing with her hair braided down her back. "Come here, and let me take a look at you."

The woman hesitated, her eyes enlarging. The other women hurriedly moved a small distance away from the one who was being singled out.

"Don't you understand English? I said come over here." The lieutenant's command was harsh, but as he saw tears rolling down the woman's cheeks, his tone softened somewhat. "Do you understand English, mistress? You don't have to be afraid. You can answer my questions."

The woman's eyes quickly looked around at the men and women who made up the small band of Arapaho, and seeing that they were not going to try and stop her, she rose to her feet. Nodding her head, she tried to get words out of her dried throat. "I . . . I . . . do . . . do under—understand English."

"God's teeth, Lieutenant! I told ya she were a white woman!" The scout stared from the woman to the lieutenant.

"What is your name, mistress?" Lieutenant Cole ignored the man at his side as he put all of his attention upon the woman.

"Penny . . . Penny Smith." Her voice seemed to be growing stronger.

"Penny Smith?" he questioned softly. The name sounded familiar to him. "Why are you here with these Arapaho?"

The tears began to flow in earnest now. "I . . . I was traded to them by the Sioux."

Lieutenant Cole needed to hear nothing else. "Sergeant Langford, have one of your men give this woman his horse. He can ride double with another man back to camp."

One of the braves, who appeared younger than the rest, made a slim attempt to hinder Penny's rescue as he stepped up to her and took hold of her arm.

"Sergeant Langford, point your rifle at that savage! If he does not step away from the woman, shoot him!" Lieutenant Cole commanded.

Penny jerked her arm out of the Indian's grip. Lame Deer had not been as vicious and unfeeling toward her as Red Fox had been, so she made this small attempt to save his life. If he grabbed her arm again, however, the soldier could shoot him and she wouldn't shed a tear. He was a savage Injun, like all the rest!

The brave seemed to understand as he stared at the end of the rifle barrel that was pointed at his chest. Silently, he watched as the woman mounted the horse the blue coats had given her, and the soldiers rode off in the opposite direction.

Lieutenant Cole did not question the young woman until they were back at camp. Soon enough she told him who she was and which wagon train she had been stolen from.

"How soon will we be heading back to the fort?" she asked as she tried to scrub off the months of grime from her arms and face with the soap and rag a young soldier had provided.

"We will head out as soon as the storm passes," Lieutenant Cole assured her. He couldn't wait to see his commander's face when they returned to Fort Laramie with Penny Smith. He now remembered who she was. There had been a search for her and the other young woman who had been stolen with her, but nothing had come of it. The two women had been written off as dead.

"I have to get word to my husband, and also to Danielle Hansen's family. They will be interested in knowing how their niece is living inside the Sioux camp." The hard look on Penny's features told much of her feelings.

Chapter Twenty-one

Secure within the total embrace of tranquil love, Danielle and Wind Dancer passed the slow winter months together. They eased into the routines of husband and wife, learning more about each other with every passing day and loving all that they discovered.

For the most part, Wind Dancer stayed near his lodge. The interior was often filled with braves, asking advice or making suggestions for the benefit of the tribe. The elders of the village paid visits as well, telling stories of days long past and coups won in battle, or just passing time as they circulated the pipe around the central fire pit. When Wind Dancer was not in his lodge, he found himself watching for the slender figure of the pale-haired beauty who was his bride. He could not get enough of her, in his vision or in his arms.

Danielle's feelings were little different from those of her husband. During the long days of snow and cold, she spent much time in the warm lodge. Sewing or tending to a meal, she never tired of looking up and finding Wind Dancer's warm, dark eyes upon her. Whenever the weather permitted, she spent time with Autumn Woman. The older woman had taken a cold at the start of winter, and depended upon Danielle to help her tend her lodge and prepare her meals. Danielle's life was happy, her world, for the most part, content. Only her thoughts of her aunt and uncle disturbed the perfect life that she and Wind Dancer were living.

When she spoke to Wind Dancer about the worry she had caused her relatives, he suggested that she write a letter, and as soon as the snows melted, he would take it to the trading post and have Josh Kingsman send it to Oregon for her. The idea appealed to Danielle. She only wanted her aunt and uncle to know that she was happy and doing well with her husband. She knew that her life was here in this Sioux village with Wind Dancer. She did not miss the world she had grown up in; rather, she was blossoming in the quiet, easy life of her husband's people.

With the onset of spring, Danielle wrote out her letter to her aunt and uncle, with Autumn Woman's help. There was no parchment or ink, so she had to improvise with a fine piece of bleached hide and an eagle feather and paint. The letter was a simple one, telling her aunt and uncle that she loved them and would never forget them. She stated that she was happily married, and God willing, perhaps in the future they would see each other again.

After she had completed her letter, Wind Dancer made plans to take it to the trading post. "I also have furs that I will trade for goods for our lodge," he told Danielle. "And I will enjoy seeing my old friend Josh Kingsman once again."

"I'll go with you," Danielle announced without hesitation.

Wind Dancer looked at her in the fashion that a tolerant father does his beloved child. "I am afraid that will be impossible, Silver Dove."

Instantly Danielle's chin lifted, determined that if her husband was going to travel to the trading post, she would go along with him.

Wind Dancer smiled at her show of stubbornness. "You have grown bored through the winter, I know, but it would be far too dangerous for me to take you along." He was just as determined that he would not risk her.

"How can such a trip be dangerous for me, and not for you?"

"I am a warrior, and you . . . you are a beautiful *wasicun winyan.* Though you are my woman and I will protect you with my life, Silver Dove, your silver hair would be a temptation to any man, Indian or *wasichu.* You are safer here in our village."

There was little Danielle could say to sway her husband's mind, but she resolved that, when he left the village for the trading post, she would be at his side.

The following day, she visited Medicine Wolf's lodge and told him that she wished to go along with Wind Dancer, but because of her light hair and complexion, her husband was adamant about her staying behind in the valley.

After some careful thought, Medicine Wolf went to his herbs and plants, and mixing some ingredients, he handed Danielle a pouch, which held a dark, strong-smelling substance.

"What is this?" She made a sour face as the odor hit her nostrils.

"This will darken your hair and your skin for a

short period." The old man smiled widely at her reaction.

"I bet no one will come close enough for any kind of inspection as long as I am wearing this goop!" She wasn't even sure if she would be able to stand the dark substance on her skin, or if Wind Dancer would allow her to use it.

"If you wish to travel with Wind Dancer as one of the people, and not as a *wasicun winyan,* this is the only way I know." The medicine man's dark eyes twinkled merrily.

"Thank you," Danielle murmured as she left the lodge with the pouch in her hand. If she wanted to go with Wind Dancer, she knew now that there would be a price to pay. Instead of going to the lodge she shared with her husband, she went to Autumn Woman and had the older woman help her put the contents of the pouch in her hair and over her skin.

"Wind Dancer will not know his own wife when he looks at her," Autumn Woman chuckled after she stood back and looked at her handiwork. "No one will know that you are not one of the people from birth, as long as they do not look into those eyes that are a mixture of sun and sky."

Danielle grinned at her adopted mother. "Do you think I smell bad, *Iná?"* She had actually grown accustomed to the odor, and could not smell it as strongly now that she was wearing the dark stain mixture.

"The odor flees with time, daughter. It is not as strong as when we first put it on your body. Perhaps by the time Wind Dancer sees you, it will have fled completely."

Danielle could only hope this would be the way of things. Leaving Autumn Woman's lodge, she slowly made her way to her own. As she went, several of the villagers stared at her.

Danielle sighed with relief when she found the lodge empty. Going to the place where she stored her hand mirror and brush, she looked at her reflection in the glass. Peering closely at the strange woman staring back at her, she had to agree with Autumn Woman. The only way someone would be able to tell that she was a white woman was if they looked into her eyes.

Some soft noises at the entrance of the lodge drew her attention away from the looking glass. Wind Dancer stood still, his dark eyes going over his bride from head to foot. "What have you done, Silver Dove? Where is the silver woman?"

Trying to appear brave and assured, Danielle laughed at the serious look on his features. "Don't be silly, Wind Dancer. I am here, only I have colored my hair and my skin so that I can go with you to the trading post."

Wind Dancer eyed her suspiciously with this pronouncement. "Where did you get this . . . color that turned your pale hair dark?"

She could not tell by his tone if he was pleased or not, and thus far he had said nothing about any odor. "Medicine Wolf mixed it up for me. I think it conceals that I am a white woman completely—what do you think?" She swallowed hard as she waited for his wrath or approval.

"I liked your silver hair much better." His dark eyes could not look away. It was amazing—she did look like an Indian maiden!

"It will wash out, don't worry," Danielle hurriedly supplied. "As soon as we return from the trading post, I will wash it out and it will be as before."

Looking into her turquoise eyes, Wind Dancer could not deny her. Slowly he nodded his head. "We leave in the morning. You should pack what we will need for the trail. It will take us two days to get to the trading post."

In truth, Danielle had not expected him to give in this easily. Rushing to his side, she threw her arms around his neck and hugged him tightly. "Thank you, Wind Dancer." Standing on tiptoe, she pressed a kiss to his lips, her eyes sparkling with the prospect of the adventure ahead.

Wind Dancer sniffed the air and wrinkled his nose. "What is this I smell, Silver Dove?"

A nervous laugh escaped her lips. "I am afraid that is the only ill effect of Medicine Wolf's concoction. It also will wear off in time."

"I hope you are right," he replied.

"You'll see. By tomorrow there won't be any trace of the odor."

"That is fine for tomorrow, but what about tonight?"

The couple set out early the next morning, with Wind Dancer's furs and their supplies strapped to the back of a pack horse. Danielle's spirits were high with excitement and expectation as they left the village. She and Wind Dancer had not been totally alone since they had gone to the falls after their joining ceremony. Though she had grown accustomed to the traffic going in and out of their lodge throughout the day, she desired time alone with her husband, without the frequent intrusions.

It took two days' travel to reach the Kingsman trading post, and the couple shared each of these days to the fullest. When they hunted small game along the way, Danielle helped her husband set up a rabbit snare, or sat along a stream bank and laughed uproariously as Wind Dancer lost his footing in his attempt to spear a fish. Their nights were spent side by side next to their fire, wrapped tightly in each other's arms and delighting in the star-bright sky.

The third morning they rode through the open gates that surrounded Josh Kingsman's trading post. It was a small post built in the wilderness by the Kingsman family. Josh and his brother, Emeroy, dealt fairly with Indian or white man alike, and because of this policy, the trading post had survived. The wooden walls around the post would have done little good during an attack.

Danielle's eyes looked busily at everything inside the trading post's walls. She noticed two women washing and hanging out their laundry at the side of the largest building, which was obviously the trading post itself. It was a two-story log structure, with the upper portion used for housing the owners and their families. Several other outbuildings were probably used for storage.

The Kingsman trading post was a busy place. Several horses were tied outside to the hitching rail, a few having the trappings of their Indian owners. There was a heavyset Indian woman sitting on the front step, and a white man, holding a whiskey bottle in one hand, said something to the woman that caused her to blush and grin widely, revealing several missing front teeth.

As Wind Dancer tied their horses to the rail then gathered his furs, he led his wife up the steps, ignoring both the couple and the curious glances they cast in their direction.

"I be happy to warm up that warrior's blankets."

The fat woman spoke in English, her eyes looking directly at Wind Dancer.

"You'd be happy to warm up any man's blanket, Buffalo-Woman." The unkempt man laughed at the Indian woman's remark. "Have a drink of this whiskey, and then you can show me what you would like to show that buck." He handed her the bottle as the couple entered the front door of the trading post.

The interior of the building was as neat in appearance as the outside. The wood floors were scrubbed often, and the rows of shelves containing goods were dusted weekly. There were barrels of food stuffs, such as flour, sugar, salt, and coffee, against one wall; along the opposite were bolts of materials, beads, and blankets. There were knives, hatchets, picks, and shovels, as well as all manner of farming implements. Behind the long counter, at the far end of the building, several rifles hung against the wall, and below them on a shelf was ammunition.

It was toward the back counter that Wind Dancer made his way, with his wife at his side. Much of the noise inside quieted as a pair of men playing cards and others sitting or standing around stopped what they were doing to eye the brave and his woman.

Before they reached the counter, the tall, thin-featured, gray-haired man behind it thumped his fist down hard upon the wood surface and good-naturedly shouted, "Why, damn these old eyes, if'n it ain't Wind Dancer himself!"

Setting his bundle of furs upon the counter top, Wind Dancer smiled warmly at this old friend. He stretched out his hand and it was taken in a firm grip.

"Emeroy, get yourself out here and see who just come through the front door!" Josh Kingsman called through the open door behind him, which led to the storeroom. "It's been some time since you were last here, Wind Dancer. Let me see—it must have been two years now. I saw Black Bull a while back, and he told me you were well."

"I am well, Josh Kingsman." Wind Dancer had learned much in his youth from this white man, and considered him a true friend. "I have brought furs to trade."

Josh Kingsman eagerly nodded his head as he glimpsed the pile of lush furs. "Who you got there with you? Black Bull didn't say anything about you having a woman of your own." His eyes settled on the top of Danielle's head while she kept her eyes lowered.

"This is my wife, Silver Dove," Wind Dancer said with pride, and when Emeroy entered the front room a few minutes later, he made the introduction between his wife and the owner's brother.

In the Sioux tongue, Wind Dancer instructed Silver Dove to pick out the supplies she desired for their lodge, and as she eagerly left his side to wander through the building, he kept a protective eye on her while he visited with his old friends.

Taking her time, Danielle gathered supplies, choosing a colorful blanket for Medicine Wolf and a length of bright red cloth for Autumn Woman. While she was looking over some kettles, she felt a presence at her side. Looking up, she was met by the piercing, dark eyes of an Indian brave.

Her first reaction to the man's closeness was to return to Wind Dancer's side, but thinking such an action would appear foolish, she picked up a pot and examined it. Before she could walk away, the brave said, "Why do you not come with me and my friends over there?" He nodded his dark head toward two other braves standing near the open front door. "We trap furs high in the mountains. The nights are long and cold without a woman in our camp."

Danielle could make out much of what he said, and an instant gasp escaped her lips at the proposal. "My husband would not be happy to let me go," she at last got out, and turning away, she started back to Wind Dancer.

She had gone only a step or two when the warrior grabbed her forearm. "He is but one man. My braves and I can take care of him!"

"No!" Danielle gasped aloud. "I don't want to go with you!" She tried to jerk her arm free, but his hold was too powerful.

Immediately, Wind Dancer sprang into action, his sharp hunting knife bared as he advanced upon the brave. "Take your hand away from my wife!" He gave this warning, only because of his surroundings. If this had happened anywhere else besides the Kingsman trading post, he would have taken the man's hand away from his wife by cutting it off.

"The woman wishes to go with me and my friends!" The Indian was almost Wind Dancer's size, and as he spoke, he showed little fear of the Sioux brave.

Not taking the warrior lightly, Wind Dancer reacted at once. With a movement of his hand, he pressed the sharp knife against the brave's wrist. A line of blood appeared instantly. "Remove your hand from my wife, or I shall do it for you!"

There was no mistaking the threat. The brave knew that if he attempted to pull out his own knife, the warrior would sever his hand, then plunge the blade into his heart. Slowly, as though loath to release the tender flesh beneath his grip, the brave turned Danielle loose. His dark eyes glared at Wind Dancer with a savage promise of revenge.

"That'll be enough of such goings-on in my post!" Josh Kingsman rounded the counter with a rifle held in his arms. "Now, you braves are finished with your business here. Get your supplies and be gone with you all! This ain't a place for you to be harassing someone's woman!"

The three braves knew well what the trading post owner was saying, and as they eyed the rifle pointed in their direction, they sullenly picked up their supplies and started out the front door. The brave who had grabbed Danielle's arm turned and looked one last time at her before glaring again at Wind Dancer.

Danielle released her pent-up breath with their leaving, and noticing it, Josh Kingsman attempted to soothe her. "Some people just ain't got no manners, Silver Dove. Don't be letting them frighten you. They'll be gone soon, and forget all about what happened here—as soon as they pull out that whiskey bottle in their supplies."

Wind Dancer seemed to agree, but Danielle could not forget that parting look from the warrior. His eyes had held a threat, or a promise! An hour later, Wind Dancer led her out of the post, and after strapping their supplies to the back of the pack horse, they departed from the main gates.

As they were leaving, a small detail of soldiers passed them. Keeping her head lowered, Danielle followed behind Wind Dancer's mount, but she glanced up just as the last soldier went by. She gasped as she recognized one of the men. He was not dressed in a blue uniform, but instead wore a plaid shirt rolled up at the sleeves and a pair of jeans. Traces of his blondish brown hair could be seen beneath his wide-brimmed hat. *Samuel Taylor.* The name sounded within her brain, and even though she told herself that it could not be him, she turned around in her saddle and tried to get a better look. Unfortunately, the young man was swallowed up in the press of soldiers around him as they tied their horses outside the building and started up the front steps.

Wind Dancer did not notice his wife's look, nor did he see her glancing back toward the trading post. As Danielle followed behind his lead, she told herself that the young man could not have been Samuel Taylor. What on earth would he be doing here in the wilderness? He was in Oregon with his family!

That evening, shortly after dusk, a fire was started in the front portion of the Kingsman trading post. As Josh and Emeroy Kingsman and their wives attempted to retrieve buckets of water from the well, which was several feet away from the building, one by one, they were murdered. As the building was caught up in flames and the bodies lay sprawled in the dust, three braves silently rode away from the sight of the Kingsman trading post.

Chapter Twenty-two

"Why do you not bathe and wash the darkness from your skin and hair?" Wind Dancer suggested after they had made camp for the night. He had purposely camped near a riverbank for this reason. Now that they were on the trail once again and heading back to their village, he felt little fear of having her reveal her natural beauty. These last few days he had missed seeing her silver hair and pale body.

Danielle eagerly agreed to the invitation. "I would love a swim, as long as you go with me." The anticipation of feeling Wind Dancer's strong body against her own in the water left her heady with mounting desire.

"Is it help with washing the darkness from your hair or something else that you desire, wife?" Wind Dancer smiled warmly in her direction as he tended the fire he had just built.

Danielle felt a blush heat up her cheeks.

Wind Dancer did not press her for an answer, but instead he went to their packs and pulled out a small box. Going to her side, he opened the box to reveal an assortment of bars of soap.

"Oh, Wind Dancer, I didn't see these at the trading post." She picked up one and sniffed, the delicate scent of jasmine filling her nostrils. The soap she used in the village, made by Autumn Woman, had no such fragrance.

Wind Dancer had watched his wife carefully as she selected their supplies, and he had noticed that she selected gifts for both Medicine Wolf and Autumn Woman but chose nothing for herself. While she had picked out foods and blankets, he had made some choices of his own. All of them, like the soap, were for her.

Danielle hurriedly removed her clothes, as anxious as Wind Dancer to be rid of the dark stain in her hair and on her body. Wading out into the water, she shivered from the cold until finally she dove into the swirling depths, her hand still clenched around the soap.

Wind Dancer knew how cold the water was, and knew also that after their long day on the trail, their bodies would be much revived after a swim. Without hesitation, he dove in after her.

They swam and played, and then Wind Dancer insisted that he wash her hair and body. As they stood not far from shore, he lathered the long curling tresses with the tenderest care. Moonlight shone down on the area and held the couple in a golden sphere as his fingers roamed from the crown of her head, over her delicate shoulders, and down her slender back to the full curves of her hips. "Perhaps you have grown accustomed to the smell of Medicine Wolf's stain, and will not enjoy the flower scent of this soap," Wind Dancer teased as his fingers toyed along the indent above her collarbone.

"Have no fear on that account," Danielle said,

sniffing. "I believe I smell heaven all around me," she laughed softly.

Wind Dancer's voice stole over her in a husky whisper. "Hmmmm, and this place called heaven is what you feel like beneath my hands."

Leaning her head back, Danielle willingly submitted to his ministrations, delighting in the touch of his hands over her body.

After washing the darkness from her hair, he cupped both hands together and carried the water to the crown of her head. Allowing it to fall freely, he washed away the soap and stain. Beneath the brilliant moonlight, Danielle's hair curled in silver splendor. His fingers strayed over her body, his palms cupping the full weight of her breasts as she stood still before him. Holding her eyes captive with his own, he whispered, "Your beauty is breathtaking, Silver Dove."

Danielle felt light-headed. Her eyes darkened to a deep azure as they were lost within his ebony hold.

As they stood in waist-deep water, his head lowered to her breasts and gently he pulled one of the dusty-rose nipples into his mouth. Tenderly he suckled, his tongue lightly circling and toying with the hardened bud. "Your flesh is sweet, Silver Dove." His husky voice touched her ears, and as she would have reached out to draw herself closer to him, he stilled her movement by placing his hands along her lower arms. As he lowered his dark head beneath the surface, he feathered light kisses over her abdomen and across the junction of her womanhood.

Danielle felt her senses swirling in a heated rush. His hard, masculine body was fully aroused, his erect shaft rising proudly from the dark nest at his groin and pressing heatedly against her belly. With one long, smoldering look, he clasped her tightly against his chest and kissed her deeply with a hunger that knew no bounds. He showered desire-filled kisses over her face, her ivory throat, and fleetingly over her full, straining breasts, his free hand slipping between her thighs.

Her response to his stroking fingers was instant and powerful. Arching her body backward, she cried out her husband's name to the velvet heavens. Her fingers clamped over his bronzed shoulders as the flaming ardor coursing throughout her body mounted, fueled by the stroking rhythm of his fingers as he plundered her secret depths and the heat of his branding lips kissed and suckled at her breasts.

Swirling, cool water . . . storming desire . . . fervently heated caresses—the combination was irresistibly erotic. Caught up within a searing need for fulfillment, she cried out with longing, pleading for him to enter her, to be quick with his joining of her before she perished from desire.

With his strong arms tenderly cradling her, Wind Dancer waded back to the riverbank. Her arms were clutched tightly around his shoulders, her head tucked comfortably into the angle of his neck and shoulder.

At the edge of the riverbank, with the cool water lapping gently against their naked bodies, he lowered her, pressed against her thighs until she opened to him, and took her, riding her lush body with a virile mastery that left her moaning with delight. His body surged and pulsed with the rushing lapping of the river's water. His thrusts entered her as the cool liquid settled about her, until she knew not where one ended and the other began. Her husband and the water caressed her, filled her, and tempted her with a spinning rapture that was unbearable to withstand without crying aloud her need for release.

"Soon, my heart, soon, we will ride the slender threads of passion's promise together." Wind Dancer's dark eyes were steeped in desire as he looked down into her features, his body rocking against her, moving deeper . . . and deeper. His strong hand raised her hips, and he thrusted, lifting her up to meet his body, to greet the startling rapture that awaited them as together they claimed the sweet promise of fulfillment.

With the calming of their racing hearts, Wind Dancer carried her to the pile of furs that made up their bed next to the fire. Laying her down, he tenderly caressed the silver curls spread over the dark fur. "Each time we join, it is better than the first. My heart knows only joy with you as my wife."

Danielle drew his head down to her and lovingly kissed his lips. "I love you, Wind Dancer." She spoke from her heart, but with these words, some small, nagging reminder of Samuel Taylor intruded upon her thoughts. If it had been Samuel whom she had seen at the trading post, what was he doing there? Could he still be looking for her? Tightening her grip on her husband, she knew that her future was with Wind Dancer. She could never return to her old life. For a moment, she thought to tell Wind Dancer that she may have seen Samuel, but she knew that, with the announcement, the contentment they shared that evening would be shattered, and they would be reminded of the outside world. No, it was better to wait and tell him after they returned to the village.

Settling his body next to hers upon the bedding,

Wind Dancer wrapped his arms around her, and it was not long before he heard the easy sounds of her breathing. Soon his own eyes shut as he found sleep.

Sometime during the late hours of the night, Danielle was awakened by the slight pressure of Wind Dancer's hand against her mouth. "Keep quiet, and remain here upon the furs. Someone is approaching our camp." He whispered this in her ear, and she felt him pressing something cold into her hand; intuitively she knew it was a knife.

The fire had dimmed down to light glowing embers. The area around camp was shrouded in darkness as the horses stirred restlessly where they were tied against a lead rope. Danielle lay still, hardly daring to breathe as she felt Wind Dancer ease his body off the furs and slip away from the fire. She felt entirely alone at that moment, her heart pounding wildly in her chest as her hand tightly clutched the knife.

When the attack against them came, it was sudden and savage. A terrible war cry split the quiet of the night sky as three warriors rushed toward the mound of furs, their weapons brandished overhead. They had one goal in mind—to kill the warrior who stood in the way of their taking the woman for themselves.

Danielle could no longer remain still. She jerked upright in time to see one of the warriors, the one closest to her, fall to his knees, his hand going to the arrow that had penetrated deep into his throat. With a cry escaping her lips, the second Indian rushed her. Wind Dancer leaped out of the shadows, but before he could rescue her, the third brave charged him.

Danielle screamed as the Indian grabbed hold of

her, and with the feel of his savage touch, she struck out at him with the knife held tightly in her fist.

Surprise . . . amazement . . . or perhaps shock filled the warrior's face as his hold upon her slowly fell away, his face reflecting horror as he looked down and saw the knife handle sticking out of his chest. His eyes rose up to her face before he fell backward into the fire, causing sparks to shower the night sky.

Turning frantically toward her husband, Danielle watched as the largest man of the three faced Wind Dancer with a war club and a hatchet. The look upon his face was deadly as he swung the club viciously in an arc over Wind Dancer's head, missing him by mere inches. Next, he swung the hatchet, and Wind Dancer had to jump back to miss taking the deadly blade in his stomach. When he attempted to raise the hatchet overhead and swing again, Wind Dancer charged and caught the man's arms by the wrists. Then Wind Dancer applied viselike pressure until the brave dropped his weapons to the ground.

Wind Dancer's war cry was carried by the night breeze as he released the brave. In the flash of an instant, the brave grabbed for his hatchet. But Wind Dancer was faster, and he scouped up the war axe then, without hesitation, threw it straight at the brave. The hatchet flew straight into his chest; the brave fell with a dull noise to the ground.

Not sparing a second on his attacker, Wind Dancer hurried to Danielle's side. As she clung to his chest, his hands roamed over her freely and comfortingly. "Are you hurt, Silver Dove?" His breath caught in his throat until he heard her reply.

"It was the Indians from the trading post!" she gasped out when she was at last able to speak.

Wind Dancer nodded his head slowly. "They were foolish to attack our camp."

"But I killed him, Wind Dancer!" She looked down next to the fire. The man's final, stunned look was still on his face.

Wind Dancer tightened his embrace, enfolding her tenderly as he brushed back pale strands from her cheeks. "You did what had to be done. He would have done worse to you if the three of them had succeeded in their attack. Thank the Great Spirit, and His wisdom, that I am a light sleeper and heard their approach while they were still a distance from the camp."

His words echoed all the horrible images that had run through her mind when the brave had rushed toward her and grabbed her arms. She had known that she had no choice but to defend herself from him and his friends.

They cleaned up the camp area, then for the rest of the night, Wind Dancer held her, there next to the fire.

Shortly after Penny Smith's rescue from the Arapaho by Lieutenant Hampton Cole and his detail of soldiers, word was sent to Willamette Valley in Oregon. Penny herself was in no condition to make the trip herself, the commander at Fort Laramie decreed after one glance at the filthy, underfed woman who had been brought to his office after her arrival at the fort.

A dispatch was sent posthaste to Penny's husband, William Smith, and also to the guardians of Danielle Hansen. It was not until winter had passed that the reply came, in the form of a young man known as Samuel Taylor.

"Where is William?" Penny questioned Samuel breathlessly. She had run all the way to the commander's office from Mrs. Borden's house, where she had been boarding until her husband came for her.

Samuel's blue eyes went over the young woman, taking in her flushed cheeks and the bobbing curls that dangled around her shoulders. No one would ever know, by looking at her, the terrible ordeal she had endured, he thought to himself. Commander Boxlier had earlier informed him about the young woman's circumstances, and what she had been put through by the Indians. "I'm sorry about the baby, Penny. Commander Boxlier told me what happened."

The sparkling gleam that had been in her eyes dimmed with his words. "Thank you, Samuel," she responded politely, but in the next breath, she again asked, "Where is William? He did come with you, didn't he?"

Feeling uncomfortable about being the one to tell her, Samuel shook his head. "I'm afraid that a lot has happened since last I saw you, Penny."

"Where is he, Samuel?" Penny had endured more than most people, and no one needed to hedge words with her.

"I'm afraid that William left Willamette Valley shortly after we arrived. I'm not sure where he was heading."

"He didn't leave word, in case I was rescued?" Penny's large eyes filled with tears.

Samuel shook his head again, and swallowing hard, he knew he had to tell her everything. "You see, Penny, I guess that William didn't think you and Danielle would ever be found. Before we reached Oregon, he was seeing Dorothy Johnson."

"He ran off with her?"

Again Samuel was forced to be the bearer of bad news. "She ran away from her family in Willamette, and the two of them disappeared one Sunday afternoon."

Penny's body sagged in one of the straight-back chairs in the commander's office, feeling as though all the air had been knocked out of her. After a few minutes of silence, she spoke. "I reckon I deserve it after the way I treated poor William. I didn't really realize how bad I treated him until after those savages stole me. Soon enough, I was wishing I had poor William at my side. I even swore that if I did see him again, I would be the best wife a man could ever have." She looked at Samuel with the eyes of a much older woman.

"Where is Danielle, Penny?" Samuel could wait no longer to ask the one question that had been in his mind, night and day, since Tad Hansen had received the letter from Fort Laramie.

Penny felt much of her old strength returning. She couldn't blame William for running off like that, and she hoped he would be happy with Dorothy Johnson. But with the mention of Danielle's name and the concern she glimpsed in Samuel's features, she directed her anger upon the young woman who had been kidnapped along with her. "She's still with the Sioux. I was traded off to the Arapaho, but she stayed on in the village, in the Sioux valley."

"How was she when you last saw her?" Samuel had been tormented these many months with horrible thoughts of Danielle being abused at the hands of those red devils. "Did she seem all right?" He had to know that she could at least survive until he rescued her.

"Oh, she seemed well enough, Samuel. In fact, the last time I saw her, she was dancing and laughing right along with those savages!" Penny remembered the beautiful dress Danielle had worn the night of the buffalo dance, and how her pale curls had been swept back by a beautifully beaded headband. She had appeared healthy and happy, giving no indication that she had suffered the abuse that Penny had.

"How can you say these things?" Samuel felt instant anger at the woman. Danielle could not have been laughing and dancing with her captors! In his mind, he saw her suffering from the degradation of being forced to live among savages!

"From what I could make out, Samuel, she was given to the Sioux chief, and then some old hag adopted her." Penny didn't mince words. Danielle had never appreciated this young man, and she hated to see him still believing that she was so innocent. It had been months since she had seen the other woman. She was sure by now that Danielle Hansen could lay no claim to innocence.

"I don't believe you. If Danielle is still alive, it is because she endured, only to wait for the day of her rescue!" Penny had not changed in the least, Samuel told himself. While they had been on the wagon train, more than once she had told him that Danielle didn't wish to wed him, and that he would be wise to look for a woman more like herself. Now that she knew her own husband had deserted her, he could only reason that she was making up these lies with the hope that he would forget Danielle and look toward her.

"Suit yourself. I've been through too much to

worry if you believe me or not. If you intend on chasing after Danielle, you'll see for yourself what's going on between her and those savages!" Penny allowed her glance to roam over Samuel's length for the first time. He was still one fine hunk of a man. Perhaps this would be her chance to get away from the fort and go on to Oregon. Once he found Danielle, he would see her for what she was, and when that day came, Penny would be standing in the background with wide-open arms.

Samuel put her remarks down to jealousy. "Lieutenant Cole and a small detail of his men will accompany me to this valley, to rescue Danielle."

"Then I warn you to go easy. These Sioux are not like any Indians you have ever met. They'd as soon kill a white man as look at him." She thought of Red Fox and a shudder coursed over her body.

Samuel had already been advised about the Sioux Indians, but he had no choice. He had to rescue Danielle! "We leave in the morning. Our first stop will be a trading post that is reported to be two days' ride from the Sioux valley."

"Why don't you come on over to Mrs. Borden's house this evening? I'll fix you up a good dinner before you head out on the trail." She would say no more about Danielle Hansen. If Samuel found her, he would see the truth with his own eyes. Until then, she would do everything she could to make him see her as the lady she wanted him to see!

Chapter Twenty-three

Returning to the village, Danielle spent the next few days in relative calm. With each passing day, she grew more accustomed to her husband's lifestyle, and often she helped Medicine Wolf in his work as healer of the Sioux village. It was not unusual for her to sit with him as he tended an ailing grandmother, or to hold a sick child in her lap as Medicine Wolf poured a healing potion down his throat. She had a lot of faith in the ancient shaman since her healing time in his lodge. If not for him, she would not have survived Red Fox's attack.

Medicine Wolf seemed pleased to have the silver-haired woman as his student. There was much he could teach her, and he was willing to take the time to patiently explain the ceremonies and medicines of his people. Silver Dove had a sound mind and did not ask too many questions; he admired these qualities in a woman.

About a week after her return to the village, Danielle arose early one morning to gather wood and water for her lodge. Wind Dancer had gone with Black Bull for a day of hunting in the mountains, and she was planning to gather herbs for Medicine Wolf along the edge of the forest. He had already shown her the plant he wished her to pick, and with a willow basket tucked under her arm and a special digging stick tucked into her waistband, she mounted the Spotted One and started off in the direction of the forest. She had brought along pemmican so she would not have to hurry back to the village in case she got hungry.

She enjoyed these times alone in the woods. As her hands and stick dug in the earth, she could lose herself in her thoughts, and the hours passed quickly by.

For a short time, she stayed near the edge of the forest that overlooked the valley; finding patches of the herb, she chose only the best to go in her basket. The Spotted One grazed on the sweet, tender spring grass growing along the edge of the forest, and as Danielle slowly made her way deeper into the cool haven of the woods, the horse silently followed.

The forest contained a vast variety of different plants and herbs. As Danielle bent over, digging with her little stick, she thought once again about the day she and Wind Dancer had left the trading post. Had she really seen Samuel Taylor? She had not said anything to her husband, and as time passed, she saw little reason to do so. Even now she was less sure that the young man with the soldiers had been Samuel. It must have been someone who resembled Samuel. She wondered how her aunt and uncle were doing in Oregon. Wind Dancer had given his friend Josh Kingsman her letter, and he had promised to send it on. She hoped that they would understand her reasons for not wishing to come to Oregon, and her desire to stay with her husband and his people.

Some slight noise pulled Danielle from her inner thoughts. As she glanced over her shoulder, her stick fell to the earth. "Samuel!" she gasped, not believing her eyes but fearing she had conjured Samuel Taylor up from her earlier thoughts.

For a full moment, Samuel could not speak. He stared at her as though she were a creature from another world. She barely looked like the young woman he planned to wed. She wore a beaded Indian dress of hide, hide leggings over her calves, and moccasins on her feet. Her beautiful hair lay in a long, thick braid down her back, and as her turquoise eyes turned on him, he thought he saw confusion and fear. There was no joy, nor was there the expected relief on her face. Even his name leaving her lips was filled with accusation. "I have come to take you home, Danielle," he said as he broke free of his emotions and took a step or two closer.

"What are you talking about? How did you find me?" Danielle's head whirled in confusion as she looked at him. Appearing behind him were several army soldiers.

Perhaps she was suffering from some kind of shock, Samuel told himself, and took the steps that brought him standing before her. Reaching out, he took her by the arm and pulled her to her feet. "I have come to take you back to your aunt and uncle; to Oregon, where you will become my wife."

Danielle tried to break free of the grip he had on her arm, and looking up into his face, she told herself to remain calm. "How did you find me, Samuel?" She relaxed beneath his hand, believing that everything would be all right once she explained to him that she had no desire to go to Oregon, or to wed him. She was already married, and very happily so!

"Penny told us where you were."

"Penny?" Her eyes brightened. "Is Penny all right? I was so afraid for her when I found out that Red Fox had traded her. Where is she? Is William with her?"

"She's at Fort Laramie, and no, William did not come with me. Why don't you mount your horse, and during the ride to Fort Laramie, I'll tell you everything that has happened while you've been away."

"I can't go with you!" Again, Danielle tried to pull away.

"What do you mean, you can't? You must! You can't stay here among savages, for God's sake!" What on earth had these vile Indians done to her, that she believed she wanted to stay with them?

"Now, miss, there'll be no arguing about it. You're a white woman, and we have come to take you back to your family!" Lieutenant Cole stepped to Samuel's side. Without any hesitation, he would aid the young man to overcome the woman, if the need arose. He had come to Fort Laramie with the express purpose of helping to subdue and conquer the red vermin that plagued this country. It was not only his duty but, he believed, his moral right to take this white woman back to her family, whether she resisted or not!

Danielle's eyes went from Samuel to the lieutenant, the gold flecks sparkling brilliantly with her mounting anger. "And where is the law written that I must go with you if I don't wish to?" Danielle knew she couldn't get away from Samuel, and this fact forced her to try and use some reason. Once he released her, she would mount the Spotted One as quickly as possible and race down to the valley, to the safety of the village.

"The only law is one that every decent woman should abide!" Lieutenant Cole was beginning to lose his temper. Mrs. Smith had hinted that this Miss Hansen might well be happy among the Sioux, but on his honor, he would not stand for her having the choice!

"And what law is that?" Danielle defiantly shot back at him.

"A decent woman would not have to ask, but since you have, I will explain. No white woman would wish to stay among heathens! It's not right!"

Danielle turned her gaze away from the lieutenant and focused her attention fully upon Samuel. "And is this your belief also, Samuel?"

Without hesitation, he nodded his head. "You don't know what you are saying, Danielle. Once you are back at the fort—"

"I won't go to any fort with you! I am going to remain here with my husband and his people, and there is nothing you can do about it!" She hated to break the news of her marriage in this way, but Samuel had left her no choice.

"Danielle, you don't know what you're saying!" Samuel's grip tightened.

"I know very well what I am saying, Samuel. I am married to Wind Dancer, the chief of the Oglala Sioux, and I won't be going back with you to Fort Laramie, or Oregon." She saw the devastation in his eyes but knew there was no help for it. Their mission had been for nothing. Now all he and the soldiers needed to do was turn around and return to the fort. "I am sorry, Samuel, but the truth is, I would never have married you anyway. We were never right for each other."

Her words were more than Samuel could take.

"You lie!" He began to shake her. "Those savages have done something to you to make you act like this! You loved me! We were going to be married, and still will, as soon as we reach Oregon!"

Lieutenant Hampton Cole had heard enough of this foolishness. He had his orders. They were to bring this woman back to Fort Laramie, and that was exactly what he was going to do. Placing his hand upon Samuel's shoulder, he called for Sergeant Langford. "Fetch the woman's horse, and see that she mounts up. We have little time to waste here in the forest. Any minute, someone might come looking for her." He had heard much about this Wind Dancer, whom she claimed to be her husband, and he did not want to face the wrath of the war chief of the Oglala Sioux with only a small detail of soldiers.

Without question, Sergeant Langford did as ordered. The horse resisted, but assigning the task of its capture to two of his men, the Spotted One was soon in hand and waiting for the woman to mount.

Danielle protested loudly about the treatment given to her horse, but no one paid her any attention. When the sergeant turned to her and ordered her to mount, she adamantly shook her head. "I will not! I am not going anywhere with you!"

"I'm right sorry, ma'am, but I got my orders." Sergeant Langford stepped in between Samuel and Danielle, and saying nothing further, he picked her up and started toward her horse.

"Put me down! You can't treat me like this!" Danielle was furious, and she pushed against the large brute's chest.

"Gag her, Sergeant Langford. We can't have the Sioux riding down on us," Lieutenant Cole ordered, as he, Samuel, and the rest of his men mounted up.

"I'm sorry again, ma'am." Sergeant Langford took out his handkerchief, and pulling it over her mouth, he knotted it at the back of her head.

The minute Danielle felt herself being placed in the saddle, her hands automatically reached out for the reins, her one thought being to escape, to race down to the village to safety.

The sergeant's reaction was quicker than she had expected. His hands found the reins first, and without a word, he pulled them together and led the Spotted One over to his horse.

Danielle would have cursed each one of them soundly and cried out her fury to the heavens above, except that her mouth was covered and only muffled sounds escaped. As her hands went to the handkerchief, the sergeant's sharp eyes watched.

"If you remove it, ma'am, I'm afraid I'll be forced to tie your hands too."

Danielle's glare told him that she thought him a miserable wretch, but as he wished, her hands lowered back to the saddle horn.

"Let's head out, Sergeant." Lieutenant Cole held his hand up in signal to the detail to move out of the forest the same way they had come.

Samuel's blue eyes never left Danielle's straight back as they traveled through the forest, staying clear of the Sioux valley.

The day's ride was grueling as the soldiers pushed their mounts to clear as much distance as possible between themselves and the Sioux. It was during a fifteen-minute midday break that Samuel approached Danielle. "I'm sorry it has to be this way, Danielle." His glance brushed over the delicate features of her face, and determined that the tan she now had was very becoming with the pale curls framing her face.

Her gag had been removed sometime ago, and as she looked at Samuel, all of her anger was revealed on her features. "You're not sorry, Samuel. You never really cared about my feelings."

As though he did not hear what she was saying, he reached out a hand and lightly pushed back the fine wisps of curls that lay against her cheek. He ignored the quick movement of her head to resist his touch. "You will forget this nonsense. This whole affair will seem like a bad dream once we reach Fort Laramie, then head on to Oregon."

"Do you really think so, Samuel?" The question was sharp. "Do you think I can so easily forget the man I love?"

He visibly flinched at her words. His tone was harder as he replied. "You'll forget, I promise you. It wasn't that long ago that you loved me. You'll do so again."

"I never loved you, Samuel," she confessed with a soft sigh. She had never wanted even to agree to wed Samuel; she had felt pressure not only from him but from her aunt and uncle. She was stronger now, and no one would ever again push her into agreeing to things she didn't want to do. She would love Wind Dancer until the day she died! And as though the thought of her love bolstered her courage, she looked Samuel full in the face and said, "My husband will not be pleased when he returns to the village and finds me gone. He will come for me."

Samuel took a step back as though the venom in her tone had singed him. "Let this Wind Dancer come. The army will take care of him, and anyone who comes with him!"

Danielle's gaze did not falter at Samuel's words, even though pain shot through her heart with the thought of Wind Dancer being harmed. She would not show Samuel or anyone else that she feared they could hurt her husband. "He will come." This time her words were softer, but they conveyed no doubt.

"Mount up!" The command was given, and as those around Samuel and Danielle began to obey, for a lingering minute the young man looked upon the woman he believed himself to be in love with. She had grown hard over these past months; there was little trace of the Danielle he had desired so much. With a sigh, he turned away from her and started toward his horse. The old Danielle would return; he refused to believe otherwise. Once they reached the fort, she would forget about this heathen called Wind Dancer, and everything would return to normal.

Wind Dancer and Black Bull did not return to the village until shortly after dark. Going directly to his lodge, with the buck elk he had killed secured across the rump of his pony, Wind Dancer was anxious to see his bride and show off his kill. He never tired of seeing the pride in Silver Dove's eyes when she looked upon some feat he had accomplished. In everything he did, he rejoiced in her approval. After he had pushed aside the door flap, the grin on his lips slowly disappeared as he viewed the dark interior. This was strange, he thought, as he entered and began to build up the fire. But perhaps it was not that strange. Silver

Dove more than likely had gathered her herbs, then spent the afternoon with Medicine Wolf. The pair were probably in the shaman's lodge, turning the plants into healing medicine. Or perhaps someone in the village had taken sick, and she had gone with the medicine man to offer her help. This would no be unusual for his wife.

Allowing his initial worry to vanish, he finished building up the fire then went outside and tended his kill. He was sure that Silver Dove would return to the lodge by the time he had butchered the elk.

But he soon finished his work, and still Silver Dove had not returned to their lodge. Wind Dancer then went in search of her, to Medicine Wolf's lodge. He was surprised when the shaman stated that he had not seen Silver Dove at all that day. He had expected her to bring the herbs they had spoken about yesterday, but when she did not come to his lodge, he had assumed that she had decided to wait for another day to go to the forest for the plants.

Wind Dancer's first assault of panic struck while he stood outside the old man's lodge and listened to his words. Silver Dove had spoken of little else last night besides going to the forest to gather the required herbs. What reason could there be that she did not do this? Trying to remain calm, he told himself that perhaps she had gone to Autumn Woman's lodge and found the old woman sick. She had suffered greatly throughout the past winter, and perhaps before going to the forest, Silver Dove had found that the old woman had had a relapse.

That had to be it. After assuring Medicine Wolf that all would be well, he went directly to Autumn Woman's lodge. Here, too, he found only disappointment. Autumn Woman had spent most of the day with Little Brave Woman, and had not seen Silver Dove. There was only one other place his wife could be, but even as he walked toward Black Bull and Pretty Quill's lodge, he knew that she would not be there. She went often to visit Pretty Quill and play with her children, but Wind Dancer knew deep down that Silver Dove would have returned to their lodge long ago if she had been with his best friend's wife.

Still he hoped that he might be mistaken, but found he was not when he arrived at Black Bull's lodge and found only his friend's family within. "Has her horse returned to the village?" Black Bull questioned as he heard Wind Dancer worriedly explain that he was searching for Silver Dove. "If she went into the forest, perhaps there was trouble. The Spotted One would have returned to the village."

Wind Dancer admitted that his concern had been for his wife. He had not thought to see if the Spotted One was with his other horses. Black Bull went with him to check for the animal, and not finding Silver Dove's horse, they both set out to get their horses, and torches as well, to attempt to find a sign of the missing woman.

Wind Dancer's heart raced with fear as he mounted his pony and met Black Bull on the outskirts of the village. As they rode toward the forest, each man held a burning branch which had been smeared at one end with buffalo fat, to keep the fire burning brightly.

It took the men some time before they found a spot on the edge of the forest where it looked as if someone had dug up plants. They silently directed their ponies into the forest, where they could see that the earth had been pushed down sometime during the day. Wind Dancer dismounted, his torch held overhead as his dark eyes studied the ground around him.

Black Bull also dismounted and he was the first to voice the obvious. "These are marks made by Silver Dove's horse." As his gaze shifted from the ground to his friend, he added, "There are also marks made by other horses. It must have been the *wasichu.* The prints made here are of animals wearing iron shoes."

"Maybe the blue coats." Wind Dancer's worst fears were coming true. Whoever was here in the forest must have taken Silver Dove. The anger in his heart mounted when he found the area where Danielle had been standing on the ground, and he saw the boot prints of three different men. He saw that her moccasin signs disappeared, and knew that one of the men must have picked her up. He wanted to lash out at the fates for daring again to pull Silver Dove from his arms. Instead, he drew in great breaths of air, forcing himself to remain calm. He had to decide what to do next. "I have to go after them."

"I will go with you," Black Bull offered.

"No, you are needed here in the village. I will take Blue Hawk with me."

Black Bull nodded his head, knowing that Wind Dancer would feel secure with him in the village if a problem arose. Blue Hawk was brave and not as reckless as most of the younger braves of the village. "It will be hard to follow their sign while it is dark. Perhaps you should wait until morning."

Wind Dancer shook his head. "I will leave as soon as I return to the village and get Blue Hawk and a few supplies." He had no time to lose. He had no idea how his wife was being treated, or in fact, who it was that had taken her. If he remained in the village, he would not be able to get a moment's sleep, so he would follow the sign as best he could.

Within the hour, Wind Dancer, with Blue Hawk at his side, returned to the forest and picked up the sign of the horses' prints once again. It would be a long night and the travel would be slow, but inside his chest, Wind Dancer's heart burned with vengeance toward those who had dared to steal his wife. They would be made to pay for such actions, he silently promised. He would have Silver Dove back. Nothing on Mother Earth would stand in his way!

Chapter Twenty-four

That first day, the soldiers pushed hard until long after dark. When Lieutenant Cole finally called for a halt, in order for them to get a few hours sleep, both Danielle and her mount were exhausted. However, as she lay on the blanket the lieutenant had spread out for her near the fire, sleep did not come. By now, Wind Dancer had surely discovered her missing. She imagined his reaction, and knew that he would come after her as soon as he found the soldiers' sign in the forest. She prayed that he would find her before they reached Fort Laramie. The sting of tears filled her eyes and silently rolled down her cheeks. "Wind Dancer." The name escaped her lips on a soft breath that carried all of her feelings.

Samuel sat not far from where Danielle was lying, with his back propped up against a tree. His hand rested on the butt of his rifle. Lieutenant Cole had posted three guards around the camp to ensure they were not attacked by surprise, but Samuel had no intention of leaving his safety up to others. His eyes studied the shapely form of the woman who, by all rights, should be his. He remembered how devastated he had felt when she was taken from the wagon train, and how he had sworn that there would never be another woman for him. When her family had received the message from the commander at Fort Laramie, informing them that they had rescued Penny Smith and believed they knew the whereabouts of Danielle, Samuel had been elated; at last his dreams were to come true! He put from his mind any thoughts of her having been forced upon by those red savages, knowing that Danielle was a lady of high standards. Each time he had held her in his arms, she had resisted him. He had envisioned her fighting off any heathen to the bitter end! Now he felt his hurt that much deeper as he recalled everything she had said to him since they had found her that morning in the forest.

She had shown none of the happiness he had anticipated. She had not asked about her aunt and uncle, and remembering the look on her face when she spoke about the savage she called her husband, Samuel felt anger course over him like a heated flush. As his temper slowly cooled, he thought that perhaps the savages had used some means to control her mind. He had never heard of such a thing, but surely it was possible. She was no longer the sweet, innocent young woman she had been before her abduction. Hopefully with time, the Danielle he had loved and wished to wed would return. As his blue eyes gazed upon her, he finally nodded off to sleep, his body resting for the long day ahead of them.

Before daylight, Lieutenant Cole roused his men. The company, with Samuel Taylor and the woman they had rescued, were once more on the trail. Danielle did not complain, but remained silent as she mounted the Spotted One. Samuel had approached her and asked if she had rested well, but she refused to acknowledge him.

Sleep for her had been fitful. Each time she closed her eyes, she had seen Wind Dancer. The look upon his handsome face was one of worry and concern for her. As the sun rose, she thought of each morning when she awoke, to find Wind Dancer standing before the entrace flap of their lodge, with his hands upraised in prayer. Again, she shed tears of pain and anguish at the cruelty of being torn away from the man she loved.

They had been riding for a little over an hour when they passed the Kingsman trading post. It was a silent procession that passed the charred remains of the post, which only a few short days ago had stood ready for business. "Sergeant Langford, make a note that once we return to the fort, a company is to be sent back here to investigate, and to bury the dead." Lieutenant Cole's glance surveyed the burned-down main building that had housed the Kingsmans, then glimpsed the outline of a woman's body not far from the well.

"They should have known better than to try and live out here in the wilderness with these red devils!" one soldier declared, and to emphasize this statement, he spat a dark stream of tobacco juice on the ground at his horse's feet.

"The only good Injun is a dead one!" another soldier intoned.

Danielle brushed tears from her cheeks as she saw what had happened to the Kingsmans. She was furious that the soldiers now had an excuse for their unreasoning hatred of the Indians. And she could feel the pain her husband would experience when he came this way and viewed the trading post. Josh Kingsman had been his friend from his youth. Wind Dancer would grieve over his loss, and Danielle hated the thought of his learning of this tragedy on top of her being taken by Samuel and the soldiers. She wished she could be with her husband and offer him comfort when he learned of this tragedy. By following their sign, he would likely pass this same scene of death and destruction, but she, alas, would not be near.

Wasting no time, with the ever-present threat of being attacked by Indians themselves, Lieutenant Cole pushed onward, leaving behind the trading post and the eerie silence that hung over it.

For the rest of that day, the detail remained more silent than the day before, perhaps more aware of what could befall them after viewing the Kingsmans trading post. There were few stops; Lieutenant Cole pushed hard and did not give the call to make camp until well after dark, when it was too hard for the animals to travel any farther. "We'll only take a few hours' rest, men. We'll sleep soundly when we reach the fort. Our main objective is to get ourselves and the woman back to Fort Laramie, alive and in one piece!"

For the next two days, Lieutenant Cole kept driving them hard toward Fort Laramie, determined to reach their goal before they were under attack from the Sioux. The young lieutenant did not breath a sigh of relief until the thick walls surrounding Fort Laramie came into sight. He, as well as his men, gave elated shouts for the sentries to open the gates wide and allow them entrance.

After they had entered the fort, the lieutenant called for the gates to be closed again and for extra sentries to be posted upon the ramparts, to keep a keen eye out for any sign of Indians.

The minute Danielle dismounted, the lieutenant

stepped to her side, and taking her by the elbow, he stated in a cool tone, "You are to come along, ma'am, to the commander's office."

Danielle tested the hand that held her by her elbow and found the lieutenant's grip unrelenting. Feeling many pairs of eyes upon her, she silently went along with him. Soldiers and their wives stepped out of buildings to see the white woman who'd been living among the Sioux and to gawk at her Indian dress. She could not resist the temptation to stare back hard at everyone.

Samuel silently followed behind Danielle, anxious to see the outcome of her face-to-face encounter with Commander Boxlier. Thomas Boxlier was a seasoned campaigner whose goal was to see the red man quelled and the West taken over by white men. Perhaps the commander would be able to bring Danielle back to her senses and make her realize that the Indians were their enemies!

Thomas Boxlier sat silently behind his desk when the small group entered his office. An aide had brought him the news that Lieutenant Cole and his detail had entered the fort gates, and yes, there was a white woman with them. For a few seconds, the commander's watery, red-veined eyes swept over his officer, the woman, and the young man who followed behind them. Then he put his full attention upon the young lady he believed to be Danielle Hansen. As he looked her over, a frown creased his already wrinkled brow and his forefinger reached up to toy with the edges of his gray mustache. She was a beauty, but for God's sake, couldn't the lieutenant have found her something different to wear? Even a soldier's shirt and breeches would have been preferable to the hide dress that covered her body. Why on earth had someone not offered her a hat, or even a scarf, so she could take off that damn Indian headband? His gaze returned to the lieutenant, as though expecting an explanation without having to voice the question.

Hampton Cole quickly saw the revulsion in the commander's face as he studied the woman's appearance. "We have been riding hard, sir. There wasn't time to clean up."

"I daresay you must have pushed yourselves hard indeed, not to be able to take the time to relieve the young lady of these savage trappings!"

"Exactly, sir."

"Was there a need to push this hard? I thought the plan was to find the village, wait for an appropriate time to catch Miss Hansen alone, then after her rescue, return to the fort. Was there trouble?" One shaggy, gray brow arched upward.

"All went as planned, sir. We found the Sioux valley, as Mrs. Smith had told us we would, and the detail waited in the forest for two days before Miss Hansen appeared to gather some plants."

The commander's gaze shifted back to the woman. So, the savages had allowed her freedom in the village, he thought.

"The day we rescued"—or *captured,* Lieutenant Cole thought to himself—"Miss Hansen, she informed us that the Sioux war chief, Wind Dancer, would be sure to follow us."

"And why would this Wind Dancer chase after you?" Again his glance roamed over the woman. He knew the answer. Anyone would, by just looking at Danielle Hansen. With her white hair, and those turquoise eyes with bits of golden flecks, it was obvious that this chief of the Sioux would not be willing to let such a captive go!

"She claims, sir, that he is her husband." Lieutenant Cole's face was unreadable; not with the slightest hint did he allow his feelings to show.

Commander Boxlier almost jumped to his feet, his action tumbling a stack of papers to the floor. He totally ignored the papers as he focused his full attention upon the woman standing between the lieutenant and Samuel Taylor. "Is this true, Miss Hansen?"

Danielle's chin rose preceptively before the commander's sharp regard. "It is true. Wind Dancer is my husband, and you have no right to hold me here against my will. I told your man here"—she looked at Lieutenant Cole—"that I did not wish to return to the fort with him. I was perfectly happy to remain with my husband and his people."

Samuel was about to interject that Danielle did not know what she was saying or, in fact, what was good for her, but the commander did now allow him time to speak.

"Young woman, are you aware of what you are saying?" For a few seconds, he thought about his own wife and his daughter, who would soon be nineteen years old. They had not followed him on this western campaign, but had remained in Norfolk, Virginia, with his wife's family. He felt assured that if either woman from his family had been in the same situation, they would have fought off any Indian to the death before willingly lying down in front of the vile heathens!

"I do, sir. I wish to be released to return to my husband." Danielle prayed that this Commander Boxlier would be a sensible man and abide by her wishes.

Thomas Boxlier, however, considered it his

Christian duty to set this young woman straight. "Miss Hansen, perhaps you are unaware of the fact that no decent white woman would willing spread her thighs for a red savage, and no decent white man would want her if she did!" His face flushed, with as much anger as embarrassment over the words that had just left his mouth.

Looking him straight in the eye, without being intimidated in the least by his rude comment, Danielle declared, "There is not a white man I would want, nor one that is equal to my husband in character. I don't care what you or anyone else thinks of me! I love Wind Dancer, and if you do not release me from this fort, I will leave of my own accord, the first chance I get!"

Commander Boxlier slammed his fist down hard upon his desk. "By God, woman! I'll hear no more such talk from the likes of you! The matter is out of your hands. If you attempt to leave the fort before Mr. Taylor takes you to Oregon to be reunited with your family, you will be placed in the guardhouse! Lieutenant Cole, see that she has shelter and is properly clothed. Also, make sure that an extra guard is placed along the walls of the fort. If this Wind Dancer does come after her, I want no surprise attacks from the Sioux!"

"Yes, sir. I will take Miss Hansen to the Bordens'. She can room with Mrs. Smith until other arrangements can be made."

"How soon can I take her back to her aunt and uncle?" Samuel still felt deeply hurt, and this interview between the commander and Danielle had not helped matters. He resented the commander's suggestion that he was no decent white man because he still wanted Danielle. That wasn't fair! He admitted, though, that his own patience was growing thin. Once he got her to Oregon, Tad Hansen would know how to deal with her. Her uncle would not put up with this nonsense about her loving a savage!

"You'd better wait around and see if there is anything to her claim that this Wind Dancer will be coming for her. I wouldn't want to be you if you leave the fort and those savages come upon you with the woman. No, you'd best wait here, for at least a week or so, just to see what happens. A wagon train should be arriving soon, and perhaps you and the two women can join up with it." Commander Boxlier sat back down behind his desk, satisfied that he had settled the matter concerning Miss Hansen. She would remain at Fort Laramie until it was safe for her to go to Oregon with Mr. Taylor, and then he would be well rid of her!

Chapter Twenty-five

While Lieutenant Cole spoke to the Bordens about Danielle staying on with them until she left the fort, she found herself alone with Samuel in Lucy Borden's small, front parlor. "You haven't told me a thing about Aunt Beth and Uncle Tad, Samuel." Her voice was soft, as though she was inviting conversation between the two of them.

"I guess that's because you haven't asked about them." Samuel's retort was sharp, but as he looked at her sitting nervously on the edge of a chair, he relented. "They're fine, Danielle. Everyone's fine. Tad, as well as my own father, are trying to get in an early spring crop. That's why I came for you. Tad was going to come, but I would have come anyway, so he decided to stay on in Willamette Valley. He was in the middle of plowing when the letter came from Commander Boxlier."

"And Aunt Beth? Is she happy in her new home?" Danielle could remember how often her aunt and uncle had spoken about the Valley as though it were the land of milk and honey, waiting for them to come and settle.

"This past winter was hard, but with the help of their neighbors, your aunt and uncle now have a fine little house. Overall, everything is much as we expected. Costs are a little higher than we anticipated, but with a good crop, this time next spring, our families should be doing fairly well."

"I'm happy for them, Samuel. And did you get your land, like you wanted?" Sitting in Mrs. Borden's parlor, Danielle felt uncomfortable. It had been some time since she'd been surrounded by crocheted table covers and lacy dollies.

For the first time since finding Danielle, Samuel felt some hope. "I did get my property, Danielle. The logs have already been cut for our house." His eyes spoke the words he dared not voice aloud.

Instantly, Danielle knew she had made a mistake by asking anything personal of him. "I'm sorry, Samuel," was all she could offer.

Before he could say any more, Lucy Borden and Lieutenant Cole stepped into the parlor. "Why, dear, of course we have room for you here in our little house." Lucy Borden was a short, rather plump woman, who could not abide seeing the slightest creature suffering. As soon as Lieutenant Cole told her that the young woman sitting in her parlor had been the same young woman who had been captured by the Indians with Penny Smith, she gave her consent for Danielle to stay in her house. It would be a little crowded, but the two women could share a room until it was safe for them to leave Fort Laramie and head on west to Oregon. Jacob Borden was the army blacksmith, and Lucy was certain that her big, teddy bear of a husband would be more than happy to share his home.

After Lucy showed the lieutenant and Samuel out, she turned her full attention toward Danielle. "Why, dear me, the first thing we must do is find you something to wear. I'm certain Penny would be more than willing to share one of the dresses that the ladies of the fort gave her when she arrived here."

At first, Danielle thought to turn away the offer of clothes, but wisely she kept her mouth shut. She vividly remembered the commander's threat to place her in the guardhouse, and she didn't want to cause any unnecessary problems for herself. As soon as the moment was right, however, she would escape! Once she got outside the walls of the fort, she would be able to find her way back to Wind Dancer. For all she knew, right this minute he might be out there watching the fort and planning her rescue.

Penny had spent the morning visiting with one of the army wives, and having heard that Samuel had returned and had brought Danielle with him, she had deliberately prolonged her visit with Pamela Jefferies to delay seeing either one of them. It was with some surprise that she found Danielle sitting in Lucy Borden's parlor; both women were apparently waiting for her arrival.

"Why, Penny dear, can you believe how fortune has blessed us? Danielle, like you, has been rescued out of the hands of the heathens, and will be staying with us until you all go to Oregon!" Lucy Borden's plump cheeks were rosy-red with excitement.

Penny looked Danielle over from head to toe. "I see that you have changed little since the last time I saw you, Danielle." She still appeared well fed and clothed. As she had told Samuel, his little Danielle was the darling of the Injun village!

"Well, you certainly have changed," Danielle countered as she looked at the young woman. The night of the buffalo dance she had been mere skin and bones, and wearing filthy rags. Today, her brown hair curled charmingly about her shoulders, and wearing a peach, flower-sprigged dress, she looked very becoming. One would never know by looking at her what Red Fox and his braves had put her through. "I'm glad you were rescued, Penny. I heard about it."

"As though you really cared what happened to me," Penny lashed out, not able to hold back her feelings of jealousy and bitterness.

Lucy Borden looked from one young woman to the other, for the first time seeing this ugly side of Penny Smith.

"What are you talking about? Of course I cared what happened to you. When I returned from the buffalo hunt, I searched for you and found that Red Fox had traded you to another band of Indians. I had gotten a horse, and hoped that we could plan our escape."

"And who gave you a horse? That old hag who adopted you?" Penny spat out, not believing a word of what Danielle said. While she had been tormented and abused, Danielle had been petted and pampered. Why would Danielle have given a second thought to what happened to her?

"No, Wind Dancer. The Spotted One is here at Fort Laramie with me." Danielle had seen this nasty side to Penny in the past, but she had ignored it, for the most part. She did not have to ignore it any longer. "I would like to correct you, Penny. Autumn Woman is not an old hag. She is a kindhearted woman who helped me through a very hard time. You will not belittle her again."

Penny ignored her remarks about the old woman, but focused on the part about the Indian chief and the horse. "If this Injun gave you a horse, after you found that I was gone from the village, why didn't you try to escape by yourself? I certainly would have!"

Even Lucy Borden looked at Danielle and listened for her answer. Like most white women at the fort, she thought that the red man was something vile and unchristian—to be avoided at all costs!

"I would have . . . only . . . only a lot happened after I returned from the buffalo hunt." Danielle tried to defend herself, feeling both women staring at her.

"Like what, Danielle? You fell in love with one of those beastly savages, didn't you? It was that chief you were given to after we first arrived at the village, wasn't it?" Penny accused. While on the wagon train, Danielle had been engaged to the best-looking young man around, and then when they arrived at the Indian Village, she had been chosen by the chief. Now again she was to gain all the attention and praise. Samuel Taylor had risked his life to rescue her and would be taking her back to Oregon to be his bride, even after Danielle had welcomed the advances of that savage Sioux chief!

She drew in a deep breath before replying. "You're right, Penny," she said softly. "I did fall in love with Wind Dancer."

Both women looked at her with disbelief—Penny, not believing she would admit such a thing, not now after being rescued, and Lucy Borden, wondering if Danielle's soul had been entirely lost during the time she had spent among the heathens.

"Did you tell Samuel?" Penny asked.

"He knows how I feel, and also knows that I wanted to remain with Wind Dancer and his people." She had shocked Lucy Borden enough without revealing that she had wed the Sioux chief.

"What did he say? Does he still want to take you to Oregon with us?"

"What does it matter what he said? I am not going to Oregon. There is nothing there for me."

Strangely enough, her answer seemed to satisfy Penny. "I guess, then, that you are going to stay here until you decide what to do?"

Mrs. Borden seemed to come to her senses. The first thing to do, to help this poor, fallen woman come back to the ways of God, was for them to get her out of her heathenish clothes. "Oh, Penny dear, Danielle is in need of clothes. I had hoped that you would be willing to lend her something. You have so many beautiful things now." She was not sure if the young woman would be willing to do such a charitable deed. Her tone, while talking to Danielle, had not been very friendly; in fact, it had been hostile.

"Of course, Mrs. Borden. I will be happy to find a dress for Danielle." Her tone seemed to sweeten as a smile settled over her lips. "Come upstairs, Danielle. I'll find you something."

Penny's attitude had made a complete reversal, and Danielle was taken totally off-guard. Silently, she followed Penny up the staircase and into a small bedchamber, which contained twin beds with lacy, cream-colored canopies and had sheer net draperies on the windows.

"You can take that bed." Penny nodded her head toward the one near the window. "This one is mine." She went to the cedar wardrobe, and for a few minutes rummaged through the gowns hanging within. "I guess you'll be needing shoes too?"

Now that they were alone in the chamber,

Danielle could detect a little of the bitterness returning to Penny's tone. She watched her pull out a dark brown dress of heavy material, which had seen far better days, and a pair of brown leather shoes. Danielle's first thought was to turn down the offer of clothes and keep her comfortable hide dress on, but knowing that such an action would be seen as traitorous by those at the fort, she told herself to go along with their wish for her to conform. As soon as she had won their trust and was free to move about the fort, she would make her escape.

"These will have to do. I simply don't have anything else." Penny slammed the wardrobe doors shut, thinking the other woman had not viewed the contents. "Brown will suit that god-awful complexion you have anyway!"

Danielle didn't argue. She wouldn't be wearing the dress for long. Taking the dress, she laid it over her bed. First she unbraided her hair, then took off her hide dress, leggings, and moccasins.

Penny's jealous gaze took in the slender contours of Danielle's back. Danielle had no tan lines, and Penny could imagine her swimming naked each day in the river in the Sioux valley. The sooner Danielle made her way back to her Indian lover, the happier Penny would be! Her chances of catching Samuel's eye were slim to none with Danielle around. If the other young woman were to leave Fort Laramie to rejoin Chief Wind Dancer, she and Samuel would be alone on the long trail to Oregon. She felt the tingle of goose-flesh forming on her arms at the thought.

When Danielle turned and faced her, Penny could not help but grudgingly admire the other woman's shapely curves. It was not until her eyes went to her full, high breasts that a gasp escaped her lips. "What on earth happened to you, Danielle?" Penny drew closer to take a better look at the red scar over her breast.

As Danielle began to pull on the underclothing Penny had given her, she explained, "You were not the only one that Red Fox abused."

Penny's eyes enlarged. "He did that to you?" Now up closer, she could see that the scar was not that old. "When did he do it? And why?" In some strange way, Penny thought she had understood Red Fox's treatment of her. She was a white woman, he an Indian, and he had taken out his hatred upon her body. But she did not understand why he would do this to Danielle, when she had been adopted into the tribe and had the protection of the chief.

Pulling the dress on, Danielle responded, "One of the Indian women resented me because she was in love with Wind Dancer. She pretended to be my friend, and one day when I went to the river with her, she lured me away from where the women swim and gather wood and water. I went with her down the riverbanks where Red Fox was waiting."

It was obvious that the wound had been made by a knife, and was very near to her heart. Penny was astute enough to realize that Red Fox had almost killed Danielle. "I'm really sorry, Danielle. I had no idea, when I said those things to you in the parlor, that you had suffered so much in the Sioux valley." Penny had thought Danielle had had it easy, while she had had it so hard, but at least she had no telling marks on her body from what she had suffered at the hands of those savages.

Danielle smiled as though a far wiser woman than her years. "Don't feel sorry for me, Penny.

When I first saw the scar, I had enough self-pity in me to last a lifetime. Wind Dancer showed me that I have nothing to be sorry for. In time, they will disappear altogether."

"Are there more marks than that one?"

Danielle held out her hands so Penny could see the other marks, which had now almost faded away.

"And Red Fox?" Penny could barely get the question out. She had endured so much at his hands, she had trouble even saying his name.

"Wind Dancer killed him that day at the river before he took me to Medicine Wolf's lodge."

Penny let out a long sigh. "Good. I'm glad he killed him. Maybe this Wind Dancer isn't half bad." Anyone who would stand up to Red Fox's brutality was all right in her book.

"No, he's not half bad, Penny." Danielle laughed for the first time since Samuel and the soldiers had brought her to the fort.

"So what do you plan to do about it?" Penny asked.

"I don't know yet. Wind Dancer will come to Fort Laramie. I hope I can get out of here before any harm comes to him." Danielle wasn't sure she should tell Penny this much, but for the first time, the two young women had something in common to build their friendship on—their hatred for Red Fox.

"You're right about that. If your Injun chief comes here, he will surely be set upon, and there's no telling how he will be treated! He'll be thrown into the guardhouse at the least."

Danielle sat down on the bed as though she had just heard her worst fears voiced aloud. She felt weak of limb. "Commander Boxlier ordered an extra guard posted around the fort. Maybe tonight I will be able to find a way out." As she made this statement, she doubted its substance. Fort Laramie's walls were thick and too tall for her to scale. Her only chance was to somehow slip outside the double gates. But this feat would be next to impossible for her to accomplish.

"I don't think you should try it tonight," Penny said, drawing Danielle's full attention. "You're right about an extra guard being posted." Pamela Jefferies's husband, Paul, was one of those guards. Though he had seemed mild mannered enough when Penny had met him in his home and though his eyes had grazed over her with more than friendly regard, Pamela had told her that he took his job of soldiering very seriously. "Tomorrow night would be better. We'll see who is posted at the gate."

"You'll help me escape?" Danielle's excitement was reflected in her eyes as the gold flecks glittered brightly. If Penny helped her, perhaps she would have a chance.

Penny nodded her head eagerly, her soft brown curls bouncing on her shoulders. She would help Danielle return to her Indian chief and, in the process, help herself to win Samuel Taylor. "It's a pact, Danielle. Tomorrow night you'll sneak through the fort's gates, and once outside you can find your Wind Dancer!"

Chapter Twenty-six

Fort Laramie was awash in excitement the day Lieutenant Cole returned with the young woman he had rescued from the Sioux. There were rumors that the woman had resisted her rescue and had even claimed to be in love with the chief of the Oglala tribe. Extra guards were posted throughout the night, and more than once, a shot was fired out as a young soldier thought he saw a shadow moving close to the outside wall surrounding the fort.

By the next morning, tempers were short; the tension hanging in the air was thick enough to cut with a knife. The Sioux were the deadliest Indians the soldiers at Fort Laramie had to deal with, and knowing that the wife of a Sioux chief was held behind their walls made the men feel edgy. Even Samuel appeared a bit nervous when he paid a visit to the Bordens house at midmorning.

"I hope you ladies slept well last night," Samuel said as Lucy Borden showed him into her front parlor. He had not been able to sleep a wink, and hence had spent most of the night along the ramparts of the fort, in the company of Lieutenant

Cole. It had been eerie out there, waiting for some sign of Indians, and with the morning light, his uneasiness had increased, as had the fear of most of the soldiers he had spoken to.

"Quite well, indeed Samuel. It is so kind of you to inquire." Penny was more than willing to chat with Samuel. As Danielle sat near the parlor window, appearing distracted, Penny took charge. She directed Samuel to a chair and offered him refreshment.

"Perhaps a cup of coffee," Samuel responded, hoping Penny would leave the room so he could speak to Danielle.

Penny was more than happy to run to the kitchen to heat Samuel a cup of coffee. If things worked out as planned, she would be doing this every day when they were on the trail, heading for Oregon.

Turning his full attention toward Danielle after Penny had left the parlor, Samuel stood up and approached her. "I trust you've had some time to think clearly, Danielle. And that you've come to your senses concerning our future."

Danielle did not respond, but only stared at the young man. She did feel some sympathy for him, but she would not allow this feeling to rule her emotions as she had in the past.

"They say that a wagon train should be arriving at Fort Laramie most any day. Lieutenant Cole is sure that the wagon master will be willing to give you, Penny, and me free passage to Oregon. He thinks that the families on the wagon train will share their space, because of the hardship we have suffered." Samuel leaned over her chair and covered her hand with one of his own.

At that moment, Penny returned with the cup of coffee.

Penny immediately saw the hand that was covering Danielle's, and also noticed how the other young woman hastily withdrew her own. "Here's your coffee, Samuel."

He would have requested sugar, in order to have an added moment alone with Danielle, but noticed that the cup sat on a small tray with a bowl of sugar resting next to it. "Thank you," he responded politely and returned to the chair he had vacated a few minutes earlier. "I was telling Danielle that Lieutenant Cole said a wagon train should be arriving at the fort soon; he thinks we will be able to go on to Oregon with it."

"Well, that will be wonderful, Samuel." With a ladylike grace, Penny spread her full skirts over the chair opposite his, her eyes looking toward Danielle to see the other young woman's reaction to his words. Noticing the way her features remained impassive as she returned her gaze back to the window, Penny's smile brightened. She turned back to Samuel. "I, for one, can't wait to go to Oregon. It has always been my dream to live in Willamette Valley." He would have her words to think about while he remembered Danielle's coolness!

"Yes, Willamette Valley is lovely at this time of the year." Samuel relaxed back in the chair, content for the moment to sip his coffee and talk about Oregon.

Danielle paid little attention to the conversation going on around her. Her thoughts were miles away, in the Sioux valley. She missed the easy life of the village people. She missed leaving her lodge and going to the river to bathe with the other women of the village. She missed the feel of her soft bed of furs, missed looking across her lodge to gaze into the warmth of her husband's eyes. She felt the pressure of tears, but forced them not to fall. She would be strong until she saw Wind Dancer again. *Tonight . . . tonight.* Her heart sang the word. Penny had promised to help her escape the fort . . . *tonight!*

Unable to get a moment alone with Danielle again, Samuel did not linger at the Borden house, and after his leavetaking, the two young women continued making their plans for the evening ahead.

According to the best plan they could come up with, they would wait a short time after dark and Penny would approach the guard posted at the gate. While Danielle stayed out of sight, Penny would flirt with the soldier and convince him to open the gate, in order to take a quiet stroll beneath the moonlight.

Danielle wasn't sure if such a plan would work. It sounded very risky to her, but Penny seemed to think it was the only way for her to get outside the fort. She wanted to take the Spotted One with her, but saw no way to get the horse out of the stables and keep her silent until she made her escape.

Wind Dancer and Blue Hawk silently spent the day in the woods not far from Fort Laramie. The soldiers' tracks had brought them to the fort, and wisely, they had kept out of sight as they watched the activity along the ramparts. It was obvious that the soldiers standing with rifles over their arms were waiting for any type of attack.

"Silver Dove is in the soldier fort," said Wind Dancer. "When Wi sleeps and darkness covers Mother Earth, I will go over the wall and find her." He and Blue Hawk were lying on their bellies in the tall grass next to the woods. From there, Wind Dancer's dark eyes watched every movement that went on around the fort.

"We should return to the village and get Black Bull and some other braves. Then we can attack the blue coats." Blue Hawk did not like the idea that Wind Dancer would go alone into the *wasichu*'s tall fort.

"There is no time to go back to the village. I must find Silver Dove, and make sure that she is not harmed." His wife was so close, and yet she seemed miles away. He had to see her to make sure she was well. Perhaps she would not want to return with him to the Sioux valley; but quickly he pushed the thought aside. She was his wife, his heart. They had gone through too much for him to have any doubts about their love. "I will find Silver Dove and bring her out of the soldier fort."

Blue Hawk silently shook his head, knowing how dangerous it would be for Wind Dancer to go over the fort walls. But he also knew that nothing he said would convince his chief to wait any longer than this evening to find his wife.

Danielle and Penny dressed in dark clothes then paced nervously around their bedchamber after dinner, waiting for the hour when they would sneak away from the Borden house and approach the guard posted at the gate.

When they had finally left and were making

their way to the double gates, Danielle became apprehensive about the entire affair. Everything seemed to hang on Penny's ability to lure the guard away from his post.

Seeing the darkened figures of two guards at the gates, Danielle clutched the sleeve of Penny's gown. "There are two of them!" she whispered. Their plan had been made with only one guard in mind.

"Don't worry," Penny whispered back, and shoved Danielle toward a barrel next to a building. "Stay there until it is clear for you to get through the gates." Penny would do whatever she had to, to help Danielle return to her Indian chief. She didn't want her at the fort when the wagon train arrived and she and Samuel joined up with it to go to Oregon.

Danielle nervously stayed hidden next to the barrel, her turquoise eyes watching Penny as she swayed her hips in a provocative fashion and approached the two soldiers.

"I thought I would come out here and talk to you boys for a little while." Penny dazzled the young soldiers by brushing back her curls from her shoulders and flashing them a wide, inviting, friendly smile.

"Why, thank ye, ma'am. Me and Charlie here have been downright hankering fur some female company," the tallest and most talkative of the pair answered immediately.

Penny was in her element as she flirted outrageously with the pair of men. "Why, you two boys must be the most handsome of all at Fort Laramie. I guess that's why they put you out here alone at night! The officers must be fearing you'll court all the single women if they don't keep you on guard duty." Penny winked knowingly at the pair of them, and the one called Charlie eagerly nodded his head.

"Didn't I tell you, Eddy, that that's why old Sarge Hicks keeps giving us guard duty at night? He just wants to keep us out of the way!"

"I brought something with me to take off the chill of the night." Penny slipped a silver flask from her skirt pocket and handed it to Charlie.

Danielle watched the scene in disbelief. Penny had said nothing about getting the guard drunk!

Eddy was a little reluctant at first. "I'm afraid, ma'am, that we're not supposed to be drinking while we're on duty." He eyed the flask in Charlie's hand.

"And who's to tell?" Penny grinned. Placing her hands on her hips, she sidled up to Eddy and rubbed her breasts against his arm.

"Aw, come on, Eddy, she's right. Who's going to find out if we take a little nip? Ain't no one out here tonight. The Injun scare is about over with. The sarge said that if'n that Injun didn't come last night or today for the white woman, he more than likely smartened up, and knows better than to try and attack a fort this size."

Charlie's argument seemed to win his friend over, because Eddy reached out and took the flask. Tilting it to his lips, he took a long drink.

Penny watched with interest, and after Charlie had taken the next drink, she coaxed them, "You know, boys, if you think we might get caught here, we could just slip through the gate and take a little walk outside the fort, if you know what I'm talking about?"

Both men seemed to take her meaning quickly enough, but it was Eddy who tried to hold back.

"We could get court-martialed for leaving our post. And going outside the gates would more than likely get us shot!"

"What's wrong with living a little?" Penny openly began to unfasten the top buttons of her blouse. "Some chances are worth taking!"

"Come on, Eddy, what's the matter with you? Don't you know what she's offering the both of us?" Charlie was hot for the woman, and the prospect of sharing her with his buddy was even more inviting to his sexual appetite.

"Injuns!" The shout rang out from the back of the fort, and with it there was a volley of rifle fire.

Charlie and Eddy appeared not to be able to come to their senses for a moment. Then at last, grabbing their rifles, they looked at Penny with regret and longing. "I guess we best put this off till another night, ma'am." Charlie said sadly as he motioned Penny back in the direction she had come from.

Desperately she made a final appeal. "Why, they're fighting at the back of the fort. We can still slip out the gate and have a little fun."

Before either man addressed this ridiculous statement, another soldier walking along the ramparts near the gate shouted, "Tate Lewis took an arrow right through the heart. Keep yer eyes wide, boys. Them red devils might be all around us!"

Penny knew it was hopeless. Charlie and Eddy totally forgot about her as they climbed the ladder leading up to the ramparts. "Damn it all!" she swore as she reached Danielle's side.

"It must be Wind Dancer." Danielle's heart pounded against her chest with the thought that her husband was out there somewhere, or could already be inside the fort.

"Well, how the hell are we going to get you out of those gates now? Your Injun chief sure has lousy timing!"

"Maybe I could climb up that ladder to the ramparts and slip over the wall." Danielle felt desperate, knowing that Wind Dancer was close but having no way to reach him.

"What, and break your neck in the process?" Penny had always thought Danielle was a bit rash, and this proved it.

"If I had a gun, I would force them to open the gates!" Danielle felt her desperation growing as men ran about the fort and shots were being fired.

"We had better get back to the Bordens' before someone finds us out here and starts asking questions." Penny grabbed Danielle's elbow, not giving her the chance to do anything foolish.

It was just as the women turned to make their way back to Lucy Borden's that they glimpsed a figure running across the fort.

"There he is, men! Catch him!" the call was sounded, and there must have been fifty soldiers racing after the lone figure.

"Wind Dancer!" The cry was torn from Danielle's throat, and even as she would have started to run in his direction, Penny clasped her hand around Danielle's forearm.

"Are you insane? Do you want to get shot too?"

"But they'll kill him! I have to go to him! I have to help!"

"If they capture him, you'll help him better by not being involved. And then again, maybe they won't catch him." Penny clutched Danielle's arm and would not allow her to go anywhere as they waited to see what would happen next.

"He's over here, near the stables!" another man called, and the women could hear the sound of racing boots heading in the direction of the stables.

The sound of Wind Dancer's fierce war cry filled the night sky, and then the screams of several soldiers followed as they attacked the Indian then fell away wounded from Wind Dancer's knife or wickedly lashing tomahawk.

Danielle couldn't stand it any longer. Breaking free of Penny's grip, she ran in the direction of the fighting.

"Charge him, men. The commander wants him alive to hang, so don't kill him!" she heard a man shout.

Another cried, "We're doing our best, sir, but he's a savage one!"

"The only good Injun is a dead one!" a soldier shouted before rushing into the foray.

When Danielle came upon the scene, the area was illuminated by several soldiers holding torches high overhead. She heard the officer in charge shout, "Rush him now, men!" She did not see Wind Dancer at first. There were at least ten men scuffling around and on top of him. Several men went flying away from the group, as though they had been knocked backwards with a fist. Other men were cursing and screaming. In the end, the soldiers pinned the prisoner on the ground. It took all ten to subdue him, and when at last they dragged him to his feet, bound hand and foot, Danielle gasped aloud.

The noise drew his dark eyes, and seeing the

woman of his heart, her name escaped his lips. "Mázaska Wakínyela."

Danielle would have run to him, but Penny grabbed hold of her. "You can see him later. Now's not the time." Penny knew that the soldiers wouldn't look kindly upon a white woman trying to protect an Indian. More than likely, Danielle would only get shoved around for her efforts, and Wind Dancer would suffer more abuse trying to protect her.

Danielle was not able to break away from Penny's hands this time, and helplessly, she watched as the soldiers dragged Wind Dancer away to the guardhouse. "I have to help him!" she cried.

"You won't be helping anyone if you go after him now. Those men will see you as an Injun lover and will treat you with little respect. Wait until they lock up your Injun chief, then we'll try to get you into the guardhouse to see him."

"You'll help me, Penny?" Danielle brushed away the tears falling from her eyes as she looked at the other woman.

"Yeah, I'll do what I can." For Penny, it was still the only way for her to get Samuel Taylor. She would do whatever she could to help Danielle free her Indian and to see that both of them left Fort Laramie forever.

Waiting near the woods as he had been instructed by Wind Dancer, Blue Hawk heard the sounds of gunfire within the fort. As an hour and then another passed without a sign of his chief, the brave realized that Wind Dancer had been captured by the blue coats. He waited longer, allowing more time to pass before leaving the woods and heading in the direction of the Sioux valley. There would be no rest for him on this trek back to the village. His chief's life was at stake—every minute counted!

Chapter Twenty-seven

The plan for the soldier posted at the guardhouse was similar to the one Penny had used on the soldiers at the front gates. On the evening following Wind Dancer's capture, she and Danielle made their way to the guardhouse. Danielle stayed hidden next to the guardhouse walls while Penny slipped through the front door.

Only a short time passed before Penny was leading a young soldier outside, her seductive words touching Danielle's ears as she coaxed the young man to follow her—flask in her hand—to a darkened corner.

As soon as Danielle heard Penny croon, "Now isn't this better?" and then heard the young man murmur his reply, she cautiously slipped to the front door and eased it open.

There was a small desk with a low-burning lantern on its edge in the front room. Taking a look around to ensure that no one else was within, Danielle hurriedly made her way through the open doorway, which lead to the pair of cells housing the army's prisoners.

Wind Dancer was standing at the door of his cell. The moment she stood in the doorway, he recognized her scent. *"Mitá wicánte,"* he called aloud.

"Wind Dancer!" The cry escaped her lips as tears fell and she ran to the barred cell.

Clutching hands, Wind Dancer's husky voice washed over her as he whispered, "Mázaska Wakínyela. I had little to do today except dream of this moment when I would see you."

"Are you all right, Wind Dancer? The soldiers, they didn't hurt you, did they?"

"I am fine, *mitá wicánte.*" His fingers toyed with the wisps of hair lying against her soft cheek. It had all been worth this moment, he told himself. Everything—the hard ride to the fort and even his capture—had been worth seeing Silver Dove this one last time.

"You shouldn't have come to the fort. You shouldn't have risked yourself, Wind Dancer." Danielle could not halt the tears that fell down her cheeks.

"There was no choice, Mázaska Wakínyela. I had to come for you. I am nothing without you, and would face all the blue coats to see you again, and to know that you are not harmed."

Danielle kissed the back of his hand. His words matched those in her own heart. "What are we going to do now? If Penny could get the cell keys, she was going to leave them in the front room. The guard must not have been persuaded to give them up." Everyone at Fort Laramie was aware that Commander Boxlier had decreed that a week from this day, Wind Dancer, chief of the Oglala Sioux, would be hanged. Danielle felt her desperation mounting, but was powerless to do anything that could save her husband's life.

So her friend, Penny, was here with her, Wind

Dancer thought to himself. It was good that his wife was not alone now. She would need the other *wasicun winyan* during the days ahead. "Do not weep, Mázaska Wakínyela. I cannot bear to see you sad." Wind Dancer felt as powerless as she did. His only hope lay with Blue Hawk outside the fort walls. His friend would not see him left in the *wasichu*'s prison for long. He would go and get help, or he would attempt to rescue him. He did not say this to Silver Dove, since he did not wish to give her any false hope.

"Perhaps I can get a gun, and I can force the keys away from the guard," Danielle thought aloud.

"You will not do this, Mázaska Wakínyela! You will not take such a risk!" Wind Dancer's hands tightened over hers. "I could not bear being locked behind these bars and unable to help you if you were to be caught trying to release me. It is risky enough that you have come to me this night. No, you will do nothing! If the Great Spirit wills, he will bring me help."

Danielle agreed, although reluctantly. But she knew in her heart that she would not allow anyone to hang her husband without putting up a fight.

Their parting was bittersweet as the couple clung to one another through the cell bars. At any moment, the guard might come back, and time was precious. "I love you, Taté Wacípi," she whispered.

He could taste the salty tang of her tears as his mouth covered hers in a kiss that had the power to sweep away danger and sorrow. For a single moment, they were one, as it was meant to be.

Then Wind Dancer broke away, and forced himself to stand at a distance from her. "You must go, *mitá wicánte,* before someone finds you here."

Danielle nodded her head, knowing that he was right but hating to be parted from him. "I will return if I can," she promised before going back to the front room and slipping away into the dark shadows around the guardhouse to wait for Penny.

"Damn, that soldier half mauled me to death!" Penny declared as the two women made their way back to the Borden house. "I don't know if we'll be able to do this again. He wasn't too pleased when I didn't give him everything he wanted." Penny made a vow to herself that she would not be used by any man again for any purpose other than her own. The next man she planned to bed was Samuel Taylor, and she would have none before him! Living among the savages, she had had her fill of being misused, and she would not be treated so again.

"I have to do something, Penny, to try and save him from being hanged!" Danielle's tears had intensified now that she was out of the guardhouse. "I can't just leave him there to wait for the week to be up!"

"I know, but I'm just not sure what we will be able to do. If we're caught helping him, they won't go easy on us. The commander dislikes you, and it wouldn't take much for him to throw both of us into the guardhouse, too."

Danielle couldn't argue with these words of truth. "Perhaps I could go to Commander Boxlier and ask him to spare Wind Dancer's life," Danielle blurted out in her desperation.

"You can try, but my advice is for you to save

your breath. He hates Indians, and won't take any pity on one who killed and wounded some of his men. He would have hanged Wind Dancer anyway because he came into the fort, but now he has a better reason."

Danielle could not find a moment's sleep as she lay abed and relived every second she had spent with Wind Dancer. Somehow, she had to help him get out of the guardhouse! There had to be a way to win his release!

Penny had been right about Danielle's wasting her breath by going to Commander Boxlier and begging for Wind Dancer's release. The commander of Fort Laramie laughed outright when Danielle made her plea. "Madam, you must be insane if you believe I would release that savage so he can murder more of my soldiers!"

From that point, her meeting with the commander turned worse. Danielle called him a cruel-hearted bigot, and he ordered her from his office.

The next day, having heard what had taken place in the commander's office, Samuel went to the Bordens' house. Finding Danielle alone, he demanded to know why she had gone to the commander's office and begged him to spare the Indian's life.

Danielle did not hold back her defense of her husband. "I had no one else to turn to, Samuel. I will not sit back and watch Wind Dancer hang!" Her eyes sparkled angrily. She had had enough of these pigheaded men telling her what she should, and should not, feel for her husband!

"Every soldier at the fort is talking about you,

and what they're saying isn't kind. You should have come to me first, Danielle."

"And what can you do, Samuel?" Danielle demanded.

"Perhaps I can help the Indian escape the guardhouse, and get out of the fort." Samuel's words were spoken softly, since he didn't want anyone else to hear.

Danielle felt instant excitement, but then suspicion filled her. "Why would you want to help Wind Dancer, Samuel?"

His blue eyes bore into her. "I don't want to help him. I want you, Danielle. Make no mistake about that fact."

"Then what do you mean?"

"Maybe I can help the Indian get out of the fort, if he agrees to go back to the Sioux valley and you promise to go to Oregon with me."

For a full moment, Danielle stared at him as though she had not understood his words. "You will help Wind Dancer if I agree to go to Oregon with you?"

"And once there, you agree to become my wife," Samuel added, believing that he held the upper hand.

"What? But I can't. I am married to Wind Dancer." Danielle had not expected this, but a portion of her mind told her to consider his offer. It might be the only way to save Wind Dancer's life!

"And who would honor some Indian ceremony between a white woman and an Indian as being legal?" Samuel was swallowing his own pride by talking with Danielle about this. What man would want a woman who had bedded an Indian? But looking at her, and seeing her exceptional beauty, his old longings surfaced. He would promise her anything if she agreed to become his wife. "When we leave Fort Laramie, we will forget this ever happened. Promise you will become my wife, and I will see the Indian freed before the day he is to be hanged."

What choice did she have? Her turquoise eyes filled with the desperation her heart was feeling. Was Wind Dancer's life worth her losing him forever? Was she strong enough to forget that she had ever known him and go to Oregon with Samuel? Deep in her heart, she knew she would never be able to forget what she and Wind Dancer had shared. But wouldn't it be better to know that he lived, although she would never see him again, than to know that he had been hanged because he had come to Fort Laramie to rescue her? A tear filled her eye as her pale head slowly nodded in agreement. "Help to free Wind Dancer, and I will do whatever you want, Samuel."

Her words were softly spoken; he had to strain to hear them. But as their meaning touched his ears, his heart soared. She would be his once again!

Each day, Danielle waited to hear word that Wind Dancer had escaped. She told no one, not even Penny, about her pact with Samuel. She feared that, by speaking of Samuel's plan, it might not happen. She clung to the hope that Wind Dancer would be freed, even if it meant that she would never see him again.

She no longer walked by the guardhouse during the day, hoping that she might catch a glimpse of him, nor did she speak to Penny about another nightly visit. She would only be tormenting herself by seeing Wind Dancer again, and she could not bear the hurt.

One day slowly passed another, and Wind Dancer was still locked up in the guardhouse. The day before Wind Dancer was to hang, Penny forced Danielle to reveal Samuel's plan.

"I can't believe you're taking this so calmly, Danielle. I thought you loved your Injun chief." Penny looked across the parlor at the other young woman, who was sitting before the window making fine stitches on a linen border cloth for Lucy Borden. "If that were my man in the guardhouse, you wouldn't see me calmly sewing!" She had almost said that if that were her *Samuel* in the guardhouse, the other woman wouldn't see her calmly sewing!

Danielle laid the sewing down in her lap and looked at Penny. "What can I do?" Her only hope lay in Samuel, and with each minute that passed, that hope was draining away. She had gone to Samuel twice and asked when he was going to do something. The last time, he had told her not to ask him again or he would leave her Indian lover to face the hangman. He promised that he was taking care of everything. She hoped he would act tonight.

"They're going to hang him tomorrow, Danielle," Penny reminded her. "We have to get him out of this fort."

"Don't you think I know that?" Danielle stood up and began pacing before her chair.

"Well, what are you going to do about it?" Penny pressured her.

"Nothing. I can't do anything but wait!"

"Wait for what? To see him hang? Did you know that the soldiers are taking wagers on how long it will take him to die once he's swinging on the rope? There's no time to wait!"

"Samuel promised me he would do something!" Danielle shouted, Penny's words filling her with horror.

"What did Samuel promise you?" Penny's tone calmed as her eyes settled on the other woman. Why would Samuel promise he would do something to save her Indian?

"You mustn't say a word, Penny. Promise me you won't. It could be Wind Dancer's only chance for freedom." Danielle would not say another word until she had Penny's promise.

"Oh, of course I won't say anything. Who would I tell anyway?" Penny had to know what was going on between Samuel and Danielle.

"Samuel promised he would help Wind Dancer get out of the guardhouse, and away from the fort."

Penny found this hard to believe. "Why would he promise you such a thing? What did you have to promise him in return, Danielle?"

"That I would go to Oregon with him, and that I would marry him."

"You didn't promise, did you?" Penny felt an instant flush of anger. She could see her dreams dissolving all around her.

"I had to do something to try and save him! I couldn't just sit by and watch the soldiers hang the man I love!"

"But you could promise to marry Samuel when you don't even love him?"

"What does it matter? He will have what he wants, and Wind Dancer will be free."

"It matters to me, Danielle! It matters because I love Samuel Taylor!"

Penny's outburst took Danielle completely by surprise. "I had no idea you felt that way about Samuel. I was trying to save Wind Dancer."

"So you thought to pay a martyr's price in order to do so?"

"What would you have done, Penny? When Samuel came to me with the plan, I couldn't send him away without agreeing."

"Your Injun chief is still in the guardhouse. If Samuel doesn't fulfill his end of the bargain, he will still expect you to fulfill your end. In the meantime, Wind Dancer will be swinging on the bad end of a rope!" Penny forced herself not to fall to weeping. There might still be a chance that she could talk some sense into this woman.

"Samuel wouldn't back out of our deal!" Danielle had not even considered that Samuel would not help Wind Dancer. She had trusted, even at this late hour, that he would see him released from the guardhouse.

Drawing in deep breaths of air, Penny tried to think clearly. "When did Samuel come to you with this plan, Danielle?" When she learned it had been the day after Danielle had visited Commander Boxlier, she had all the information she needed. "Don't you see, he could have come up with this plan to keep you quiet until it was too late. What alternative will you have if your Injun is killed? You will have to go to Oregon to be with your family, and Samuel knows this!"

"It can't be true! Samuel wouldn't do this! I would never marry him if he didn't try to help Wind Dancer!"

"For God's sake, Danielle, it's time to wake up! Samuel would be a fool to try and help an Indian escape the guardhouse. He could well be the one swinging tomorrow!"

Danielle had not considered any of the things that Penny was saying. Knowing she had no other hope but that which Samuel had offered, she would not let herself dwell on the other woman's words. "Samuel has to help him tonight, Penny, he just has to! There is no other way for Wind Dancer to live."

Penny saw hope mixed with fear upon Danielle's face, and with a soft sigh, she stated, "I hope, for your sake, that you're right."

She had to be right, Danielle told herself. All her hopes depended on Samuel getting Wind Dancer out of the guardhouse before morning!

Chapter Twenty-eight

The front room of the guardhouse was silent. The guard had settled back in the chair behind his desk, his eyes shutting drowsily. His soft snores could be heard through the open doorway to the cells beyond.

Wind Dancer sat on the floor of his cell. He did not feel the way one would expect a man to feel when he was facing death. Instead, he was filled with expectation, his energy level high as each noise around the guardhouse drew his attention. Throughout the day, he had prayed to Wakinyan, the thunderbird, for strength and wisdom. Forgoing all meals that day, Wind Dancer relived the vision of his youth. As he had that day in the mountains, he felt a closeness with Wakinyan. That day, Wakinyan had promised to aid him in his time of need, and he clung to that promise.

He waited for a vision, and he received the image of Silver Dove. She had not come again to the guardhouse, and though Wind Dancer knew that it was safer for her to stay away from him while he was imprisoned, he could not still his desire to look upon her beauty. He hungered for the sight of her as though he were a starving man.

Jealousy settled over him when he thought about the *wasichu* who had come to the guard-house yesterday afternoon. This *wasichu* did not know that Wind Dancer could speak the language of the white man, and when the man had spoken the things from his heart, Wind Dancer had silently regarded him. The young man, named Samuel Taylor, had shown little self-control when he declared that Wind Dancer had stolen the woman he was supposed to marry. He had silently watched the young man vent his feelings upon one whom he believed could not understand him. He had wanted to face Wind Dancer before he was hanged, and while Wind Dancer's features had remained emotionless, Samuel had spoken aloud his desire for Silver Dove and also his belief that after Wind Dancer was out of the way, Silver Dove would turn to him. Wind Dancer's anger had been roused, but his trust in his wife never faltered. Samuel Taylor was a foolish young man. He now knew why Silver Dove had never loved him. He had told Silver Dove that he would help him escape the guardhouse, but after Wind Dancer was hanged, he planned to tell her that he had tried and failed. The young man was not being led by wisdom, but instead by foolish emotions. Silver Dove would never turn to him, even if the blue coats were to succeed in hanging her husband. She would see through his lies and realize the type of man he was.

His inner resolve weakened momentarily with thoughts of another man desiring to claim the woman of his heart. With a will, he calmed his emotions. Some small noise from the front room of the guardhouse pulled Wind Dancer away from his inner reflections. He heard the door shutting, a dull thud, then some scuffling on the floor.

Wind Dancer was standing at the cell door when Black Bull entered the back room. Wearing his war paint and carrying a sharp tomahawk, the warrior turned the key in the lock and set his chief free. The two braves clasped each other tightly for the briefest second before silently leaving the guardhouse.

Outside, in the dark, Wind Dancer looked around as though not sure what direction he should take. "The soldiers on the west side of the fort are sleeping. We can slip over the walls without notice," Black Bull whispered. This was the way he had come into the soldier fort without being noticed, and if all went well, this was the way they could get out.

"Silver Dove?" Wind Dancer would not leave the fort until he had his wife at his side once again.

"When the blue coats wake up in the morning and look outside the walls of their fort, they will willingly release Silver Dove," Black Bull stated with assurance. Wind Dancer said no more, but followed his friend to the west side of the fort, and within minutes, the warriors disappeared into the night.

"Indians! We're under attack! They're surrounding us!" At first light, the dozing night sentry awakened and stared in disbelief at the thousands of Sioux sitting on horseback all around Fort Laramie. In a few seconds, he regained his composure and shouted for all he was worth. He awakened the rest of the soldiers, as well as most of the fort.

Commander Boxlier was startled awake by the

pounding on his bedroom door. "What the hell is going on?" he demanded.

"It's Indians, sir." The voice of the young soldier behind the door quivered slightly. He had been one of the first to climb the ladder to the ramparts and look out at the sight of the mighty Sioux nation surrounding Fort Laramie.

"What do you mean, it's Indians? For God's sake, can't a man get any sleep? It isn't sunup yet. That Indian isn't to be hanged for another hour!" Thomas Boxlier rubbed at his eyes. He had stayed up late last night reading, and writing a letter to his wife. He needed another hour's sleep if he was going to be worth a damn today!

"I don't mean the Indian in the guardhouse, sir. I think you should come and see for yourself. There's Indians outside the fort."

Commander Boxlier still did not appreciate what was about to take place at Fort Laramie. "A few ragged, thieving Indians begging outside the gates, and you wake me up? Where is Lieutenant Cole?"

"He's outside, sir." The soldier had passed him not long ago, making his way to the ramparts.

"Well, go and get him, soldier!" Commander Boxlier made a mental note of replacing the soldier. He had been his personal aide for a few months, and it appeared he was too emotional for the duty. Indians indeed!

Lieutenant Cole was on his way to the commander's house and almost pushed the young soldier aside as he came through the front door without knocking. "Where is he?" Hampton Cole shouted, not lingering in the front room but marching straight up to the commander's bedchamber.

The soldier followed a few steps behind. "I tried to tell him, sir. He's still in bed."

Without a by-your-leave, Lieutenant Cole entered the bedroom.

"What is going on here? Is everyone mad?" Thomas Boxlier was still reclining on his bed, and had thought to catch a few more minutes' rest. What impertinence, just bursting into this room! Lieutenant Cole's features stilled the rest of the scolding Boxlier was about to shout out.

"I'm afraid, sir, that you are going to have to get out of bed." Lieutenant Cole looked at the aging, pot-bellied commander and wondered at Fort Laramie's fate, which rested entirely in this man's hands. There were more savages outside the walls of the fort than he had ever seen before!

"Well, I guess you're right, Lieutenant Cole. It appears that between you and my aide, I'm bound not to get any more rest this day!"

"There are Indians outside the fort, sir."

"I know, I know. They're probably here to watch one of their own hang. Give them some food, and send them on their way." Why was it that he had to deal with every little problem at Fort Laramie? Perhaps Saddie, his wife, was right—it was time for him to retire.

"I'm afraid you don't understand, sir. There are not just a few Indians outside the gates. There are more Indians out there than we probably have bullets to kill!"

"What? What do you mean, more Indians . . ." Commander Boxlier slid his feet off the bed and into his slippers. He had never known Lieutenant Cole to exaggerate. "Surely, man, you are overstating the situation?"

"I'm afraid not, sir."

"Well, what do they want?" He slipped his pudgy arms into the house robe that the aide held out, and patting his hair down with his hands, he left the bedroom with Lieutenant Cole and the aide following close behind.

"What do you mean, sir, what do they want?" Lieutenant Cole looked at the commander as though he had taken leave of his senses. "I guess they want their chief!"

"Oh, right. The Indian in the guardhouse." Looking around as though not sure what he should do first, the commander told the aide, "You had best fetch my jacket and breeches. I will have to take a look at these Indians before I can make any decision."

In Lieutenant Cole's mind, there was no decision to make. Those Indians outside the fort were there for only one thing, and that was to either get their chief or attack the fort. Their presence was not to be taken lightly, as the commander seemed to be doing. Hampton Cole seriously doubted they could hold out against so many Indians.

Another thirty minutes passed before Commander Boxlier was properly dressed and ready to take a look at the Indians surrounding the fort. Standing on the ramparts, the commander hissed through his teeth, then rubbed his eyes in disbelief. Looking back inside the fort at the men, women, and children staring up at him, the thought ran through his mind that before this day were over, they would all be dead! Swallowing hard, he tried to gather his wits. He had been trained to deal with situations like this. He was the commander of the fort, and everyone within its walls was looking to him to make the right decision.

"Lieutenant," he called to Hampton Cole, who

was standing with Samuel Taylor a few feet away. "Go and release the Indian from the guardhouse. Put him on a horse, open the gate, and let him go!"

Before the lieutenant could do as ordered, Samuel burst out, "You can't do that! He killed one of your soldiers! You can't just release him and let him go on his way!" Samuel wasn't thinking about the full potential of the disaster that awaited them outside the fort. All he knew was that the Indian chief stood in the way of his reclaiming the woman he wanted for his wife!

"I am the commander of this fort, Mr. Taylor," Boxlier reminded him. "Lieutenant, do as I told you. If this civilian gives you any trouble, have him put in the Indian's place in the guardhouse." Commander Boxlier had no time for the young man and his desire to get rid of the Indian so he could claim Miss Hansen. There was more at stake here than one white woman. By God, there must have been two thousand Sioux out there! There were only three hundred men stationed at Fort Laramie. They would not be able to hold out for long, and with no way to send for help, he could not risk the lives of everyone in the fort just to punish an Indian for killing one man!

A few minutes later, Lieutenant Cole returned, his features grim as he reported, "The Indian escaped, sir. The guard is dead. It looks as if he was rescued by one of his own. It must have happened during the night."

"Well, what the hell are they waiting around for, then?" Commander Boxlier demanded.

"I'm not sure, sir. I guess, we'll have to ask them what they want."

"Go find a white flag, Lieutenant. And be quick

about it. They seem to be waiting for something, but there is no telling how long that will last."

"Yes, sir." Lieutenant Cole hurried to do as ordered.

The silence within the fort hung ominously in the air. If a child cried, the mother only had to give a stern look for him to quiet. The tension mounted by the minute, as everyone waited for an attack.

Returning with the flag of truce, Lieutenant Cole held it high over the fort's walls. Within minutes, a lone warrior, on the back of a prancing war horse, advanced.

Wind Dancer had been waiting for a sign from the fort. He had not called for an attack, hoping that their show of power would force the blue coats to agree to his demand. Seeing the white flag, he told Black Bull to wait for his return. Kicking his pony's sides, he rode toward the fort's gates.

Commander Boxlier cautiously eyed the large Indian wearing the splendid war bonnet. He advanced upon the fort without fear that he would be shot. "Make sure none of the soldiers shoot, Lieutenant." As he watched the Indian, he wanted to ensue that there were no mistakes that would cause the Indians to surge forward in an attack.

Lieutenant Cole shouted out the order to Sergeant Hicks to keep the men under control. "That looks like the Indian that was in the guardhouse, sir." Hampton Cole studied the advancing rider carefully. "I'm sure it's him, sir."

Wind Dancer halted when he was about two hundred yards away from the fort. Sitting proudly upon his pony's back, he looked up at the commander.

"What is it you want?" Commander Boxlier

called down. The Indian should have been hanging that very minute instead of making demands!

"You hold my wife within your soldier fort. Send her out, and we will not kill all behind these walls!" Wind Dancer's features were serious, his words direct.

"He wants the woman, Lieutenant." Commander Boxlier repeated Wind Dancer's demand as though the men standing around him could not hear the words for themselves.

"You can't just give her over to him!" Samuel cried out.

"If you don't keep quiet, I will send you to the guardhouse!" The commander was finding Samuel's interruptions annoying. How was he supposed to think straight with this man constantly bothering him?

"I have a guard at the Borden house, sir. Should I send for the woman?" Lieutnant Cole was ready to do whatever he was ordered. Commander Boxlier only had to give the word.

"It's not like she doesn't wish to go with him," Commander Boxlier said aloud; and even as he made the statement, he knew that he had little choice in the matter. Perhaps, if the woman had spoken out against the Indians, or had claimed that she had been treated unfairly by them and would resist returning to them, he would not have considered sending her out of the fort. But from the moment she had been rescued, she had made it clear that she wanted to return to this Indian and his people. Why should he risk the lives of everyone in the fort when the woman didn't want his protection? "Go, and bring the woman here, Lieutenant. If she doesn't wish to go with him, we will have no choice but to fight. If she wants to go, we will free her."

"Yes, sir!" Lieutenant Cole called to Sergeant Hicks to send someone to bring Danielle Hansen to the commander.

Fingering the handle of his pistol, Samuel stared down at Wind Dancer with all the hatred he was feeling in his soul. He couldn't watch them hand Danielle over to this savage! He had to do something to save her from the red devil! Silently he slipped away from the lieutenant and the commander. Standing near the ladder, he waited for Danielle to appear.

A few minutes later, Danielle, with Penny at her side, came hurrying toward the gates. "Your Indian is out there, Miss Hansen, and he demands that you be released from the fort, in order to go with him."

"Wind Dancer is free?" Danielle's heart skipped a beat, her joy revealed on her flushed features.

"He escaped during the night. There is more to worry about than his escaping. He has much of the Sioux nation outside our walls and is demanding that you leave the fort. What do you say, Miss Hansen?"

Every eye in the fort was turned upon Danielle at this moment. "You mean I can leave with him?" Her blood rushed fiercely in her veins with the thought of being free to leave Fort Laramie with Wind Dancer.

"If that is your desire." Commander Boxlier was too much of a gentleman to demand that she leave the fort. If she indicated that she didn't wish to go, they would be forced to fight the Sioux to the death.

Penny's hand slipped into Danielle's and

squeezed tightly in friendship and encouragement. "Yes . . . yes, I wish to go with my husband!" Danielle declared for all to hear.

"You can return to your men," Commander Boxlier shouted back to Wind Dancer. "The woman will be out as soon as she is given a horse." He wouldn't call for the gates to be opened until the Indian rode back from where he had come.

Lieutenant Cole and Commander Boxlier watched as Wind Dancer turned his pony around and joined the encircling warriors. "Sergeant Hicks, ready the lady's horse," Lieutenant Cole shouted.

Before mounting the Spotted One, Danielle hugged Penny tightly. "When you get to Oregon, tell my aunt and uncle that I love them dearly, and that I am very happy with Wind Dancer."

"I will, Danielle. And don't worry about Samuel. I'll take care of him." Penny grinned widely as she watched the other woman mount up and wait for the fort's gates to be opened.

Everyone standing within the fort was amazed at how fast Samuel acted the moment the gates were opened and Danielle started through. Before she could pass the gates, Samuel leaped out of the shadows and grabbed hold of the horse's reins. His pistol was out of its holster and pointed at Danielle, so she had no choice but to halt the animal. "Samuel, what are you doing?" she cried as he leaped upon the Spotted One's back behind her.

"Samuel, *nooo,*" Penny cried as he shouted and the horse shot through the gates.

Chapter Twenty-nine

"I'll report it a suicide, sir," Lieutenant Cole remarked to Commander Boxlier as both men watched from the ramparts. Samuel Taylor held his gun pointed at Danielle as he directed the horse straight at the line of Sioux warriors.

"If I can't have you, Danielle, that stinking savage won't either!" Samuel declared next to Danielle's ear as he kicked the horse to push her harder.

"Samuel, you must stop this! You know I don't love you. Wind Dancer is my husband!" Danielle cried, trying to make him listen to reason as they advanced upon the Indians. She could see Wind Dancer sitting on his war pony next to Black Bull, his features enraged as he witnessed Samuel on the back of her horse with a gun in his hand. "You still have a chance, Samuel. Turn the horse back around. I will tell Wind Dancer that you made a mistake. Please, don't do this!"

But Samuel wasn't listening. His features were hard as he looked at the line of Indians ahead of them. They would move out of his way, he told himself. They would not chance him shooting Danielle! He counted on this, in order for him and

Danielle to make good their escape. Commander Boxlier might be afraid of these savages, but he wasn't! Once he made it through their lines, he and Danielle would head for Oregon, where they would be safe and happy. He kicked the horse's sides, forcing the mare to a faster pace, and as he had thought, the Indians parted to let them pass.

Wind Dancer's fury was overpowering as he watched the man holding the gun next to Silver Dove's forehead. With a shout to the warriors around him, he instructed them not to shoot the *wasichu,* but to let him pass with his wife. He could not risk that Samuel Taylor would shoot Silver Dove. The *wasichu* had to be insane to chance such a daring flight, straight through the lines of the enemy! "I will go after them alone," he told Black Bull as he turned his pony around. After Samuel and Silver Dove disappeared into the woods near the fort, he began to follow.

Danielle will be only mine, Danielle will be only mine! The words replayed themselves over and over in Samuel's mind as he plunged headlong through the line of Indians, not slowing his pace as he directed the horse into the woods. Once within the cover of trees, he and Danielle would be able to lose themselves. The savages would eventually give up searching for them.

Danielle frantically clutched to the saddle horn, in order to keep her seat. Samuel's gun lowered from her head as they entered the woods, but he was still tense, and she knew that the gun could return to threaten her with the slightest provocation. Wind Dancer would not be far behind, and she prayed that he would be careful. In Samuel's state of mind, she was not certain what he was capable of. She had never seen him like this, and feared that he might shoot anyone if taken by surprise.

Wind Dancer stayed well out of sight of those he was pursuing. He easily followed the trail made by their horse, biding his time until Samuel was forced to rest for the night.

During the day, Samuel would not halt even for a few minutes' rest, despite the exhausting, never-ending ride through the forest. "We will rest this evening," he repeated after each one of Danielle's complaints of weariness. "By this evening, the Indians will have given up looking for us. We will rest, and I will find us something to eat." By late afternoon, he felt assured that they were no longer being followed, and at dusk, he halted the horse and helped Danielle to dismount.

"I'll build a fire, and you can lie down and rest." His gaze kept circling the area where he had decided to halt.

"I'm hungry and thirsty, Samuel. You promised that you would find something for us to eat." Danielle tried to keep her tone calm, but she desperately wanted him to leave this chosen campsite in order for her to try and flee. She knew that Wind Dancer would be out there in the trees searching for her.

"No. I've decided that we'll rest tonight, and tomorrow we'll find water and food."

"But Samuel, I'm hungry and . . ." Danielle pleaded, her words coming to a halt as he once again brandished the pistol.

Pulling a blanket off the back of the horse's saddle, he threw it to the ground. "You can stay there until I've made the fire." He pointed at the blanket with the barrel of his pistol, his eyes hard as flint as they rested upon her.

Wisely, Danielle nodded her head and complied to his demands. Sitting on the blanket, she watched as he made the fire, then took the saddle off the horse and tied him to a bush.

"You get some sleep, Danielle. I'll sit here against this tree, and make sure that no one bothers you." This was Samuel's plan. He would protect Danielle from everything evil, even from herself if the need arose.

Danielle lay down on the blanket. Maybe he would fall asleep, she thought, as she watched him sit down against the trunk of a tree and place the pistol in his lap.

"This is how it will be when we reach Oregon, Danielle. I will protect you. I will build us a cozy cabin, and one day we will have children, just like I planned from the start."

As he talked about the future he had made up in his mind, Danielle was reminded of the days when the thought of children was the one positive aspect of being married to him. Now, the thought had no appeal to her whatsoever. Wind Dancer was her husband, the man she loved, and the only man she wanted to father her children.

"Did you hear me, Danielle?" Samuel looked at her, not sure if she had already fallen asleep.

"What did you say, Samuel?"

"I was telling you about the church that is in Willamette Valley. It is a little white building sitting on the edge of town. It will be the perfect place for our wedding. Your aunt and uncle will be happy, and my parents, well, you know how they have always wanted us to wed."

"Is that why you're doing this, Samuel?" Danielle asked softly.

"You know why I did the things I've done, Danielle; I love you."

"How can you, Samuel, when you know I don't love you?" Danielle pulled herself up on an elbow to look at him.

"You will love me again when we reach Oregon." His tone was confident.

"Samuel, you know I never loved you."

For a long, drawn-out minute, he remained silent. "You loved me, Danielle. You were too innocent to know your feelings for what they were." That savage had taken her innocence away from her, and with the thought, Samuel's anger flamed anew.

"I never loved you, Samuel. Penny is the one who loves you."

"Penny?" He said the name as though it were foreign to his tongue.

"She loves you, Samuel, and would be happy to go to Oregon with you. She told me so."

The *wasichu* never failed to prove to Wind Dancer how inept they were. Perhaps, if Samuel Taylor had not built a fire, he would have passed by their small camp without notice. But smelling the smoke from a far distance, he tethered his horse and, on foot, silently approached the camp.

He saw Silver Dove lying on a blanket near the fire and Samuel Taylor sitting with his back against a tree, with a gun in his lap. For the time being, he dared not make his presence known. It could be dangerous for his wife if he did not catch the *wasichu* by surprise and overtake the weapon. Staying well hidden among the trees, he waited for time to pass and for the voices to quiet. Samuel Taylor would eventually fall asleep, and when that moment came, he would pounce on him.

Wind Dancer did not have long to wait. Though Samuel tried to stay awake, the long day's hard travel and the stress he had been under at Fort Laramie had wearied him. An hour passed, then another, and slowly Samuel's eyes closed, his chin falling against his chest.

Wind Dancer's movements were quick and precise. With his sharp hunting knife clutched in his fist, he slowly advanced into the camp. As he neared Samuel Taylor, his lithe body sprang into action and he leaped the distance that was between them. His body hit Samuel with a hurtling speed that sent the pistol spinning into the air. It landed a few feet away.

Taken by surprise, Samuel needed a few seconds to recover. But then he jumped to his feet, his blue eyes looking for the gun. Seeing it on the ground, he instantly sized up his opponent and the wicked blade in his hand. "You'll not take her away from me again!" he cried as he lunged at Wind Dancer, grabbing the wrist of the hand that was holding the knife.

Wind Dancer was surprised at the *wasichu*'s strength, but Samuel Taylor was no real match for him. The men struggled for the weapon, but Wind Dancer, with a supple movement of his body, bent and threw Samuel over his back. Within seconds, he was straddling his chest, his knife pressed tightly to the white man's throat.

"No, Wind Dancer, don't kill him!" Danielle screamed from where she stood near the fire. She had awakened shortly after the initial attack on Samuel, and with a pounding heart, she had watched the two men fighting. Running to their side, she cried again, "Don't kill him, Wind Dancer. Send him back to Fort Laramie. Penny will take care of him. She loves him!"

"If I do not finish him now, he will always be a threat to us, Silver Dove." Wind Dancer did not remove his knife but pressed a little harder, and a thin line of blood appeared.

Samuel stared at the Indian sitting over him, realizing that his life was about to end. When he heard Danielle crying for the warrior to spare his life, his gaze shifted to her.

"He will no longer be a threat, Wind Dancer. He knows that I never loved him. Tell him, Samuel. Tell him that you know I don't love you. I never loved you!"

Looking at her, standing there begging for his life, Samuel did realize for the first time that she did not love him. He was not even sure if he had ever truly loved her. She was beautiful and had been something he wanted to possess, but had that ever been love? Silently, he nodded his head at the Indian, indicating that she spoke the truth.

"I told him this evening that Penny is the woman who loves him. He can return to Fort Laramie, and the two of them can go to Oregon." Danielle placed her slender hand upon the one that held the knife, and with her touch, her husband slowly released his hold on Samuel.

"Come, Wind Dancer, it is over. We can return home to the valley, where we will know peace." Tears filled her eyes as her husband rose up and left Samuel lying in the dirt.

As the couple walked out of the camp, to the spot where Wind Dancer had tied his horse, his arms reached out and cradled her in his embrace. Forgotten for the time being were Samuel Taylor, Penny, and Fort Laramie. At last, they were together again; that was all that mattered. As her slender arms encircled his neck, Danielle whispered against his throat, "I love you with all my heart, Wind Dancer."

His arms tightened. "You are *mitá wicánte,* Silver Dove."

Epilogue

Sitting near his lodge fire, Wind Dancer looked upon his wife sitting on their bed of furs. Her body was swollen with their first child, her hide dress stretched across her abdomen. His ebony eyes lingered over the silver threads of her silken hair, and he felt his heart skip a beat. As he admired the perfection of her face, a tender smile settled over his lips. His life, his world, was complete.

"I have finished my letter to my aunt and uncle, Wind Dancer." Danielle looked across the space at her husband as she rolled the piece of hide that she had used as parchment and tied it with a leather binding.

"I will have Blue Hawk take it to the trading post tomorrow." He, Black Bull, and a few other braves had gone to the Kingsman trading post, and had given his old friend and his family an Indian burial ceremony the day after he had brought Danielle back to the village. Another family had built the post back up, and Wind Dancer's people found Nate Hollings a pleasant man to trade with. Silver Dove wrote regularly to her family in Oregon, and received letters from her aunt.

"Can you believe that Penny and Samuel had twins?" She had received the news from her aunt in her last letter, and Danielle laughed at her image of Penny tending to two small infants at once.

"It is good that the *wasichu* has found happiness with a woman of his own," Wind Dancer replied, and glancing at her belly, he wondered what their child would be like. He prayed each morning to the Great Spirit that his wife be delivered without trouble and that the child would be healthy. In the back of his mind, he hoped this first child would be a girl and have the turquoise, gold-enriched eyes of her mother.

"What are you thinking about, Wind Dancer?" Danielle saw his distracted look and wondered at his mood.

"I was thinking of our child, Silver Dove."

Danielle smiled warmly, "Why don't you come over here, upon our furs, and share your thoughts with me, husband?" She began to untie the leather thongs at the shoulders of her dress, anxious as always for her husband's large body to press against her own.

As Wind Dancer gathered her against his chest, his lips tenderly settled over hers. "Your taste is as that first kiss, long ago, the night of the buffalo dance." His fingers entwined with the silver strands of hair lying across her breasts.

As always, Danielle felt her body tremble at the sound of his husky voice and the feel of his skillful touch. "Love me, Wind Dancer," she murmured softly against the side of his mouth.

"*Han,* throughout this life, and that beyond, I will love you, Silver Dove."

Sioux Glossary

Han yes.
Hanbelachia vision hill.
Hoka hey charge.
Iná mother.
Inyan rock.
Íyotaka to sit.
Maka earth.
Matóhota grizzly bear.
Mázaska Wakínyela Silver Dove.
Mitá Wicánte my heart.
Pilamaya thank you.
Ptanyétu Winúhcala Autumn Woman.
Pte buffalo cow.
Siyotanka flute.
Skan the sky.
Tatanka buffalo bull.
Taté Wacípi Wind Dancer.
Wakán Tanka god.
Wakinyan thunderbird or thunderbirds.
Wasichu white man.
Wasicun Winyan white woman.
Wi the sun.

Wicasa Wakán holy man.
Wicoti Mitawa my village.
Yúta to eat.